33581000001303

B<small>IRDIE</small>

DATE DUE

			PRINTED IN U.S.A

1400

2018

Amazon

BIRDIE

Candace Simar

First Edition, May 2011
Second Edition, July 2015
Printed in the United States of America

Originally published by North Star Press of St. Cloud, Inc.

To Mom
With Love
Olive M. Jensen
1925 to 2010

ACKNOWLEDGEMENTS

I owe a debt of gratitude to Angela Foster, Claudia Lund, Faith Kimbler, Becky Eagleton, and Keith Simar for editing assistance. Many writer friends provided emotional support and much needed encouragement along the journey. A Five Wings Art Grant through the McKnight Foundation allowed me to attend a Split Rock Writer's Conference with Sheila O'Connor. Special thanks to Diana Ossana and Larry McMurtry for helpful suggestions and critique.

Mange takk!

Part of the Abercrombie Trail Series by Candace Simar

Abercrombie Trail, 2009

Pomme de Terre, 2010

Birdie, 2011

Blooming Prairie, 2012

Other titles by Candace Simar

Farm Girls, co-authored with Angela F. Foster, 2013

Shelterbelts, 2015

BIRDIE

Minnesota

Dakota Territory

Wisconsin

Fort
Abercrombie

Tordenskjold
Township

Crow Wing River

Foxhome

Clitherall

Millerville

Pomme
de Terre

Alexandria

Pomme de Terre River

Mississippi River

*Sauk
Centre*

St. Cloud

Hutchinson

Fort Snelling

Minnesota River

New Ulm

Mankato

Rick

PROLOGUE

1865

A NOVEMBER WIND PIERCED THE cabin chinking and caused Ragna's kneeling body to shiver in spite of her flannel nightgown. Her words hung as puffs of vapor before her lips. "God bless Mor and Far and Baby Brother in heaven." Ragna tugged her nightcap down over her ears and squeezed her eyes tighter. "And God bless Uncle Evan and Auntie Inga and the boys." She peeked out of one eye and saw Auntie Inga's chapped hands folded around the candleholder.

"And please bring my little sister, Birdie, home again. Amen."

Ragna leapt to her feet and jumped into the little bed, the one she shared with an already sleeping Gunnar. Her cold toes found Gunnar's warm legs, and he stirred but did not awaken. Auntie Inga pulled the heavy quilts up under Ragna's chin and kissed her goodnight as Ragna clutched the button hanging on a string around her neck. It was her most precious possession, a button from Birdie's dress. She never removed it, always kept it close.

Auntie Inga's eyes spoke before her lips moved, and Ragna tried to close her ears to the words she knew were coming. "Birdie has been in heaven with your parents and brother for three years." Auntie's long hair hung down her back and the candle's single flame framed her face in light. "It's not right to ask God to send her back. She's happy with the angels."

Tears welled in Ragna's eyes. They had been through this before. "But Birdie has no grave marker—she's alive."

Auntie Inga sighed and leaned over Ragna to kiss three-year-old Gunnar on the forehead. The scent of fresh bread and homemade soap touched Ragna's nose, and she reached out to finger the waves of brown hair that cascaded across the bed.

"We'll talk about it another day."

Panic choked her throat as the only light left the room. "Auntie Inga!" Ragna was nine years old and too big to be afraid of the dark, but she couldn't help it. "Please . . . leave the door open!"

"*Ja*, the door is open. You'd freeze otherwise on such a night."

A trickle of light filtered through the open door, and Ragna's eyes adjusted to the gloom. Ragna was glad their little room had no window. She heard Auntie throw another log in the stove, the whoosh of flame up the chimney when the metal door opened, the clang when it slammed shut. The sweet smell of burning oak.

"Good night, Auntie."

"It's time for sleep, *Lille Kjaeresten*, Little Sweetheart."

"When does Uncle Evan come home?" The sound of a human voice comforted her in the darkness, and she didn't want it to stop.

"Tomorrow."

It was scary without Uncle Evan to protect them. He drove the stagecoach from St. Cloud, Minnesota, to Fort Abercrombie, Dakota Territory, and then back again. The stage stopped during the winter, and tomorrow he would be home for good. Ragna cuddled closer to Gunnar.

Tomorrow was *Winter Day*. Auntie promised to make *rommegrot* to celebrate. It was always a celebration when Uncle Evan came home, feast day or not.

Ragna listened as Auntie slammed the shutters and dropped the bar across the door. Fisk, the gray cat from Uncle's friends in Foxhome, jumped into bed, purred a friendly song, and climbed under the scratchy blankets between Ragna and Gunnar.

It was even darker in the cabin with the window shuttered but Ragna did not mind. She did not want to see the face in the window, that face painted half-black and half-green that haunted her dreams.

The face of the Indian who had stolen Birdie away.

1

Weed "Family Favorite" Sewing Machine: For Simplicity,
Durability, Easy Movement, Capacity for Work, and Beauty of
Stitch. The St. Paul Dispatch, *June 6, 1873*

EVAN JACOBSON PUSHED OUT THROUGH the barn door but stopped midstride. Fear clutched his chest and stole his breath. Above him, eleven-year-old Gunnar wobbled on the ridgepole of the storehouse situated next to the barn, his silhouette weaving and dipping against the blue morning sky as he sought to maintain balance. The *stabbuhr* stood tallest of the farm buildings and boasted slippery cedar shingles.

The boy tipped hard to one side and then righted himself with both outstretched arms.

Evan stifled a cry. A warning might cause his son to lose balance altogether. Time stopped as Gunnar inched bare feet across the roof peak and halted midway, tottering against the skyline.

Barn swallows nesting under the eaves of the *stabbuhr* fluttered wings against marauding cowbirds. Evan willed Gunnar to focus on the ridgepole and ignore the circling birds.

He could not imagine what Inga would do if the only child from her first marriage fell to his death. It always seemed to him that Gunnar was her favorite.

Gunnar steadied himself, balanced for a long moment and then inched across the remaining distance. At the far end of the long ridgepole, Gunnar grabbed hold of the rusty weather vane and squatted on the edge of the roof, hanging on for all he was worth. Even from where he stood, Evan could see Gunnar's scared face below his thatch of dark curly hair.

Evan's terror stormed into rage. It was the old demon, the rage of the *berserkers* from his Viking ancestry. The fury that took hold of a man and made him indestructible in battle.

"Get down from there!"

Gunnar scrambled down the ladder on the far side of the *stabbuhr*.

Evan stretched lanky legs while fury danced white spots before his eyes. He grabbed the boy by the scruff of his neck, jerked him off the last rung of the ladder and shook him until his teeth rattled.

"*Ei ska trosk Hauan dokker!*" Evan pushed back the ferocity that roared through his veins. "I'll thrash your head!"

"I'm sorry, Far." Gunnar sprouted fat tears and confessed that he had been imitating Hjalmer Peterson, a neighbor boy with a reputation as a trou-blemaker. "I won't do it again!"

Once last winter, Hjalmer had convinced Gunnar to smoke a cigar. The little boys found Gunnar passed out in the snow. When he came to, Gunnar promised his parents that he would neither smoke again nor imitate Hjalmer's behavior.

Now, foolishness with the high beam. My God, the twins might have seen him. Lord help them if the little ones tried such a stunt.

"Get back to your chores and be quick about it." Evan's breathing came in great gasps as he pushed the boy toward the potato patch.

Evan's thoughts swirled back eleven years to the Indian massacre. Curling smoke and screeching wheels. Horses straining and groaning with the weight of the stagecoach while his whip goaded for more effort to escape the Red Men. Finding the dead along the stage route. Finding his friends mutilated and killed. Crooked Lightning, his Sioux friend, turned killer and hanged in Mankato.

He leaned against the ladder and willed his thoughts back to the present. Inga and the baby in the kitchen. The twins chasing blackbirds in the garden. The older boys at work in the potato patch. Ragna hanging out the wash.

Evan forced himself to breathe and sucked in the fresh June air. Slowly, the trembling left his hands and the rhythm of his heart returned to normal. Fisk, their gray cat, rubbed against his legs and meowed for a saucer of milk.

It seemed any fear stirred up the old terror.

Almost without thinking, Evan walked to the pen where Old Doll dozed in the sun. He whistled, and she nickered in response as she nuzzled for sugar. Evan searched his pockets and came up with only a few dried tobacco leaves. She licked them from his hand, showing yellow teeth.

"Good girl." Evan hugged her around her neck and laid his head against her mane. Since the epizootic horse disease had swept through the country, horses were in short supply. If he had any sense, he would trade Old Doll for a team of oxen while the prices were high. She was getting too old for the plow anyway.

Selling Old Doll would be like selling a member of the family. He reached in his pocket and bit off a chew of tobacco from the plug he always carried.

"Evan," Inga called from the open cabin door, propped to vent heat from the stove. "Your breakfast is getting cold." She spoke in Norwegian, their mother tongue, the language always used at home.

To the east of the house, Ragna, their foster daughter, draped wet clothes on a line stretched between the privy and the woodshed. The cloths drooped over the line, not enough breeze to stir them. Crows squawked and a warbling plover called, "Widder, widder, widder." Barn swallows continued their war against the cowbirds. Brown cows plodded toward the north pasture. The lake beyond the pasture lay still as a looking glass next to a patch of pink wild roses.

A rooster crowed and Evan moved a clucking hen out of his path with the side of his foot amidst a flutter of wings. Fisk raced after a snake slithering in the grass. The garden plot lay west of the house and beyond the garden, the growing wheat and corn fields. South of the log cabin, the long trail snaked toward Alexandria.

Evan took several deep breaths, scraped mud off his shoes on the wooden scraper next to the door and slumped into his chair at the rough kitchen table. The stove, stoked for laundry and baking, turned the cabin hot as a foundry. Sigurd's soakers boiled on a back burner as Inga arranged ten bread pans in the hot oven.

The baby whined and pulled at Inga's skirt until she picked him up, sat in the chair opposite Evan, and opened her bodice. His whining and impatient wails soon changed to greedy sucking. Inga's hair frizzed into tight curls around her red face. She pushed it back behind her coronet of braids as she fed the baby in the midst of her morning work. Dirty dishes sprawled across the table with drops of spilled milk and jam.

Evan pushed eggs into his mouth and wiped the plate with a heel of bread. Thoughts of the massacre were never far from his mind and the emotions stirred by Gunnar's antics on the ridgepole triggered another stream of memories: the horses that saved his life, the overturned stage with the mail blowing across the prairie like a flock of hens, and the folly of counting Crooked Lightning as a friend.

"You're not listening!"

"I am." He shook himself back to the present. "Heard every word." He laid his fork aside his egg-stained plate and picked up his cup. Inga's words irked him and set him on edge—or maybe it was the memories she had interrupted. He debated whether to bring up Gunnar's escapade with the ridgepole and decided against it.

"When we sell the wheat," Inga said, transferring Sigurd to her other breast. He wailed momentarily in protest before resuming nursing. "We should buy a sewing machine."

Evan stared in disbelief with his cup half way to his mouth. Blackbirds had ruined their early crops. Two years ago, they'd lost a heifer to milk fever. Steel Gray, their best horse, had died in the horse plague. Their savings had vanished when the bank failed in the 1871 Panic. They barely kept the wolf from the door as it was.

"Mr. Van Dyke says they're most practical." Her brown eyes held a hopeful look. "Sews a seam in minutes with the simple pumping of a foot." She smoothed Sigurd's hair with her rough hand as her voice rose to a higher pitch. "He's buying one for his wife as soon as he finds freight."

Surely it was bad luck to count profits before the wheat was headed, much less sold. The grain rustled in the back forty as only a green wave of promise.

"Not this year." Evan set his coffee cup down on the table so hard that brown splashes sloshed over the sides. It tasted bitter anyway—and lukewarm. He wiped his mustache with the back of his hand. "There's the bank note due and a hundred other places to put the money." He tried to lighten the mood with a weak laugh. "Besides, en *svale gjor ingen sommer*, one swallow does not make a summer."

"I'm worn down stitching for this family." Inga's brown eyes flashed.

"We need a mule before newfangled inventions," Evan said, "or an ox team." The fragrance of fresh bread wafted from the oven, and he wiped a bead of sweat off his forehead. "Another heifer would mean more cheese to sell to Van Dyke's Store." Sweat dripped down the back of his neck, and Inga's request for a summer kitchen rankled through his mind. Something else to do. "Besides, you have Ragna."

"Ragna's seventeen, confirmed and old enough to marry," Inga said. "I face another twenty years of sewing to keep these boys in britches." Tears welled, and she wiped them away with a bent wrist. "Ragna's a dreamer. I have to keep after her or she forgets what she's doing."

The tilt of her chin told him she would not back down. "And, I've enough to do without making more cheese."

Inga swiped her eyes with a corner of her apron and set the baby on the floor before rebuttoning her bodice. She stacked dirty dishes with quick, angry motions, grabbed the dishrag and scrubbed spilled jam off the table.

Sigurd looked up at Evan with milky lips, a toothy grin, and a loud burp.

"We might as well buy one," she said. "If we're going to live as *cotters*, renters without a place of our own, I may as well have the benefit of a sewing machine."

So there it was. It was not really about the sewing machine at all.

"Brush the crumbs out of your beard."

He hated when she treated him like one of the children.

Evan pushed the bench away from the table and left the cabin without speaking, brushed out his scraggly red beard with his fingers and reached for his tobacco plug.

Good Lord, times were hard. Of course, he had planned to own a farm by now. When he had the money, he'd foolishly banked it instead of buying land.

Something his Sioux friend, Crooked Lightning, had told him before the 1862 uprising made him hesitate to buy a place. "The white men will not stop until they own the whole world," Crooked Lightning had said. He had a point, even if he joined the hostiles during the Indian War.

Evan had thought he had plenty of time. He had not dreamed the bank would fail.

The cooler outside air was filled with the fragrance of blooming lilacs. Evan jammed his hat down on his head, grabbed a hoe and joined the older boys in the garden. Lady bawled from the pasture, soon to deliver her calf. Blackbirds and bluebirds sang from the grove. The roughness of the handle calmed him, the sun on his back as comforting as the tobacco chaw in his mouth.

Gunnar lacked enthusiasm for work of any kind, and Evan kept an eye on him lest he try to escape and join the twins playing in the pasture. Nine-year-old Knut was quieter, more obedient, and resembled Evan with his reddish-blond hair and freckled complexion. Evan noticed with satisfaction how Knut first grubbed around the potato plants and then tapped black dirt around them with the back of the hoe blade.

"Gunnar," Evan said. "Watch how your brother does it."

He tried to ignore the scowl on Gunnar's face, his flashing dark eyes so much like his mother's, and the way the boy sulked at his job. Inga was not the only one with work to do. It was not as if he had luxuries to make life easier. Sure, he had the boys for help, but sometimes it was easier to do it himself. There was no end to their mischief.

His anger seeped away with the sweat wetting his shirt. The potato plants grew lush and verdant around his feet, certainly a bumper crop beneath the black soil. He knelt down and dug beneath a hill, searching under the plant until he fingered marble-sized potatoes, then withdrew his hand and patted the soil over them again.

They would feast on new potatoes by the Fourth of July.

What his father would have given for such a rich field. Evan remembered the rocky soil of Norway and breathed a sigh of thanks he lived in America. He attacked another hill with vengeance.

Far had said a man needed a row of potatoes for each member of the family. With each new baby, Evan added another one. Eight rows lined this year's garden plot on the low ground beside the house. The weather had been perfect. First bountiful spring rains and then sun. Luck was not always bad. He would sell extra vegetables to Van Dyke's Store in the village.

Maybe this was the year they could finally get ahead and buy their own place.

Evan came to America to be a landowner and though he had been here almost fifteen years, he had yet to have his name on a deed of any kind. While he was driving the stage and earning regular money, he had lacked the time needed to homestead. Instead, he had thought to save and buy a farm outright. But then the panic.

"Far!" Knut shielded his eyes against the sun, squinting towards the west. "What is it?"

Evan spied a curious pearly mass swirling in the sky. "Just a cloud," he said, though he kept looking at it, mesmerized by its shifting colors. Cyclones were darker in color, at least the ones he had known. "Let's get back to work."

The cloud moved quickly toward them. Odd how it carried a strange sound. Like a chattering squirrel, only much louder. Fear clutched his throat.

"Run and tell your mor!" It was coming straight toward the house. "Get to the cellar!"

He threw down the hoe and raced towards the pasture, calling the twins. "Sverre! Lewis!"

Their faces turned toward his voice, blond hair reflecting the light of the sun like burning match heads. "Boys! A storm!" They hesitated only a minute, glanced at the whirling cloud, and ran toward their father as fast as their five-year-old legs could move.

Evan cast an anxious glance at the cloud, closer and noisier than before. It was lighter in color than other cyclones he had glimpsed during his time in America. Fear gripped like a vise. Lewis tripped over a hummock and Sverre pulled him back to his feet. Evan's heart pounded as he raced over the uneven ground. Where could they hide? He heard the cloud directly above him, felt it block the sun, throwing his world into shadow.

It was as if he ran in a dream, pushing forward as fast as he could but not getting anywhere. *Good God, help us!*

The roar was upon them now. It would strike before he could drag them to the safety of the cellar.

Just as Evan scooped the twins up into his arms, the first grasshopper slammed against his face. Sharp wings cut into the fleshy part around his eyes and in spite of himself, he cried out.

"Far!" Lewis' voice almost drowned out in the roar. "What is it?"

Evan hunched forward, pushed their faces toward his chest, and pulled his hat over his eyes. He tried to shield the howling boys as millions of grasshoppers rained out of the sky, covering every inch of ground around them. He reached up and brushed them off his face but they kept coming. They crawled down his neck and chewed a quick hole in his shirtsleeve. He tried to look up, to see if there was an end to the cloud of insects but could not see a thing.

It was as black as *morketid*, the Norwegian days in mid-winter, but without the comforting beauty of northern lights. It was as dark as a Minnesota storm in summer, but instead of thunder, only the clash of whirling wings and the roar of grinding jaws.

He lost his sense of direction. Where was the house? *Dear Lord, help us.* He glimpsed a light in the distance. *God bless you, Inga, for lighting the lamp.* Then he heard the sound of a banging metal pan and Inga's voice calling his name.

He dragged the boys toward the sounds and finally collapsed inside the door in a jumble of legs and arms and whirring grasshoppers.

2

Stearns County: Potato Bugs Busy But Cannot Get ahead of the Growing Vines

The St. Paul Dispatch, *June 15, 1873*

RAGNA SCRAMBLED UP ON A ROCK next to the birch clump overlooking the lake, glanced back toward the house, hoping her absence went unnoticed.

A letter from her Norwegian grandmother burned in her apron pocket.

Bestemor's letter came usually at *Jul,* Christmas, and a summer letter promised nothing good. She had to read it in privacy.

She tucked her feet under her skirt to keep grasshoppers off her legs. How she hated the dirty creatures that whirred in her face and spat brown tobacco juice on her stockings and skirts, leaving stains impossible to launder away.

It looked more like gray November than summer. Since the grasshoppers, rotten smells saturated the air instead of sweet smelling flowers. Layers of grasshoppers, living and dead, crunched and slimed beneath her feet. Sharp wings cut into her flesh, forcing her to wear shoes—even in summer. The sun baked the dead hoppers to a crisp. Birds ate their fill.

The birch stood high above the water, surrounded by oak trees and boulders. A small lake, she had to admit, but beautiful though the stench of drowned grasshoppers wafted towards the house if the wind was right. Foam rubbed against the shoreline, marking the sand with curious hieroglyphics— like the ones they had learned about in school.

To the right stood a dense hardwood grove and on the left a sloping pasture led to the cattle shed and chicken house. Behind her, nestled in the crest of the hill, sat the little log cabin and the *stabbuhr*, a storehouse built on pillars.

The farm belonged to her, inherited from her parents. Of course, even a boy could not own land until he reached majority. Someday Uncle would turn the farm over to her husband. She tried to imagine how a husband might look. Maybe yellow curly hair and blue eyes like her sister, Birdie. Or dark and handsome like her almost-brother, Gunnar.

Maybe she would never marry. Who would want to marry a skinny girl with mousy hair and plain brown eyes, an orphan without a real family? Birdie would not have had any trouble finding a husband. Birdie had been so beautiful with her curly hair and flashing blue eyes.

Ragna gathered her courage to open the letter. She glanced back toward the house to make sure Auntie was not looking for her. Cows pastured on a small patch of slough in the far field somehow missed by the horrid insects, wallowed in the wet spot, ate reeds and water lilies. It was past time to gather them home for milking, but a few minutes more would not matter.

The rock perch was Ragna's second favorite place on the farm. Her most favorite was the small fenced cemetery across the pasture where her parents and baby brother lay sleeping.

When she visited their graves, she could almost hear the laughter of her parents, the coos of her little brother, and the voice of Birdie calling her name. It was a comforting place, the place of her real family.

She often climbed the oak tree and sat in its sloping branch where long ago a sack-swing had dangled. Frayed ends of rope still wrapped around the branch. Her *far* had tied it, had touched that very rope. She and Birdie had played on the swing while their parents visited on the stoop. Nighthawks had swooped through the evening while she and Birdie screamed with delight and tried to catch fireflies in their hands.

The graveyard also stirred bad memories, horrible memories. Memories of the Indian's face in the window. Memories of smoke and screams, her mother's voice crying out to the Blessed Virgin, and she and Birdie dragged away by a *skraeling*, an ugly Red Man. Although she was seventeen and confirmed, Ragna still feared the nightmares that sometimes reoccurred after her visits to the little plot of ground.

It was her holy place, the place of her greatest joy and worst fears. She loved it and dreaded it at the same time.

Ragna drew a deep breath and pulled the envelope from her apron pocket. She examined the blue image of King Oscar's stamp, and then struggled to break the hardened blob of white wax. She pulled out the onionskin paper covered with spidery script that tilted up at the end of each line like the tail of a cat.

Bestemor urged her to leave such a violent place where Red Men lurked to do good Christians harm. She sent word that Uncle Ivar advised Mr. Jacobson to sell the farm and use the money for Ragna's ticket home.

Ivar Gunnaldson, her eldest male relative, had Ragna's best interest in mind. Since Ragna's confirmation, her Norwegian relatives agreed she was old enough to make the long journey home. Once back in Norway, they would find her a suitable husband.

Ragna crumpled the single sheet of paper and stuffed it into her apron pocket. She would never marry a man picked out by someone else! Anyone they might choose was sure to be old and bald with warts on his face. She shuddered.

A shadowy memory of sitting in *Bestemor's* lap flitted through her mind, the smell of *lefse* and the warmth of her kind arms. However, the memory stopped short of her face.

No Indians lived in Norway. If she returned to Tolga, she need never fear Indians again. She tried to imagine climbing aboard the ship, perhaps wearing a new hat, tossing her head in the sea breeze under the admiring gaze of sailors and fellow travelers. She pleated her worn apron with brown fingers, the nails chewed to the quick.

She could not leave.

An expensive boat ticket was out of the question. She could hardly chase Uncle and Auntie off the place, even if it did belong to her. They were godparents, not her real aunt and uncle, although Evan and Inga Jacobson had cared for her since her parents' death. They had been her family since the Indian war.

Besides, since the grasshoppers, no one would want the farm.

Conflicting thoughts churned her brain. Maybe Uncle and Auntie were tired of taking care of her. Lately Auntie Inga had been crabby and short tempered. Ragna tried to be helpful, to be more of a blessing than a burden. In spite of herself, a hot tear dripped down Ragna's face and splotched her apron.

Birdie would know how to please Auntie and Uncle if she were the one living with them. Everyone had loved Birdie. Ragna reached for the button around her neck and rubbed her fingers across the carved bone and slipped into a perfect dream

> *I look up and see a canoe gliding over the water. A handsome Indian brave paddles from the back of the paper-birch craft. He is a good Indian, not like the Indian with the painted face. Birdie rides in the stern, grown up now with yellow curls draped over her shoulders, the blue of the water matching her eyes. With every dip of the paddle, water foams around the canoe's pointy nose.*
>
> *"Ragna!" She tosses her paddle into the canoe and waves with both hands. "It's me . . . Birdie! I've come back!"*
>
> *I stumble down the hill and step across the etchings in the sand, wade into the water still wearing my shoes, feel the soft foam rub bare legs beneath my skirt, sniff the dead odor of grasshoppers in the water.*
>
> *"What took you so long?"*
>
> *Birdie's hair glows gold in the sunlight, a single black feather woven through the yellow curls.*
>
> *"You knew I'd come home," she says. "I couldn't stay away from my only sister."*

Ragna sighed and looked toward Gunnar who called her name from the cow yard. "Far says to fetch the cows."

"Coming!" She waved a hand as he turned back toward the barn.

Even if she had money for a ticket home, she would not go. She could not abandon Birdie. She would not leave the farm that was her father's dream.

Ragna had a clear memory of her father saying that Minnesota's good black dirt called to him across the wide ocean, urging him to America where dreams were possible. Her roots sank as deep as the graves where her parents and brother rested.

She would never leave.

Uncle Evan could not see the letter. He might feel obliged to follow Uncle Ivar's advice. Ragna plucked a grasshopper tangling her hair and threw it as far from her as she could. *Damn it!* The forbidden word drained her anger.

Ragna retrieved the letter from her pocket along with a stubby lead pencil. She turned the envelope and absently sketched Birdie's curly hair and feather. Then, almost without thinking, she lined a window in a cabin wall and drew a picture of the Indian with the painted face. The face seared on her memory, the terrifying face that had started all her sorrows. She shuddered, stuffed the paper back into her pocket, and climbed down from the rock.

She would never desert Birdie.

She shook a grasshopper from her skirt and strode quickly towards the pasture, grasshoppers flaring from her feet at each step. One flurried around her face, and she slapped at it in exasperation. The original horde had eaten their fill before lifting off as one giant whirlwind, flying east to destroy someone else's life. Their eggs meant the nightmare would continue another season. Ragna thought she could not endure more of their grinding jaws and whirling wings.

"Come, Boss!" Ragna picked up a naked branch and shooed cows out of the slough.

The hay was gone, the oats, and the wheat. She flicked her stick but there was no hurrying the skinny herd. What would they do without winter fodder?

Uncle Evan's face always seemed tight and drawn. Even Auntie Inga, usually so positive, drooped morose and silent. Auntie fixed salads out of pigweed and pie from sheep sorrel. There was little else to be had other than a few potatoes left in the garden.

Uncle Evan declared it was time to quit chewing tobacco. Hoppers had nibbled the clothes on the line and gnawed the hoe handle lying in the potato patch. Only the hens were fat and satisfied.

Ragna cast an anxious glance over her shoulder. Of course, there were no Sioux left in Minnesota. Exiled years ago, surely none hid along the pathway, waiting to reach out and grab her. She reached for the button around her neck and rubbed her fingers across the hard surface.

> *I turn the corner by the fence and find an Indian sitting in the grass. It is the skraeling with the painted face, the one who stole us. He looks up. His face is kind though I shirk away and struggle to hold back a scream.*
>
> *"I've brought your sister home to you," he says. He speaks American but I understand every word.*
>
> *Suddenly, Birdie stands tall and grown up before me, dressed in a leather Indian dress decorated with colored beads and painted porcupine quills. Blond braids frame her beautiful face and bluest of eyes.*
>
> *"Ragna!" Birdie hugs me tight. She smells like smoky Indian campfires. The quills on her dress prickle against my arms. I kiss her cheek and she tastes of salty sweat. Her voice has the sweet sound of memory . . . Birdie's voice and no other.*
>
> *"What took you so long?" I ask.*
>
> *My mind swirls with questions, accusations . . . but it no longer matters. We are together at last. Real sisters, flesh and blood, united forever.*

A lumbering brown cow strayed off the trail, and Ragna snapped it on the hindquarters with her switch, guiding it back to the worn path.

Before the uprising, she and Birdie slept together in the trundle bed. Two years apart, they played hide-the-thimble on wintry days and draped the baby's clean soakers over hazel nut bushes to dry. Life had been all her parents had dreamed it would be in America.

Until the Indians ruined everything.

Afterwards Uncle Evan found her at Camp Release. How relieved Ragna was to look up and see his thin face and bushy red beard in the crowd. She remembered little else of her captivity, but she would never forget how Uncle found her. A miracle.

Somewhere, Birdie still lived with the Indians.

Once Ragna had gone with Uncle Evan and Auntie Inga to visit Bror Brorson and his family by Cold Spring. The Brorson's were fish-eaters, Catholics who bowed to the pope and worshipped plaster idols. Uncle Evan bought Old Doll, their faithful horse, from Mr. Brorson.

While the men went to the barn, Mrs. Brorson pulled Ragna aside to teach her a novena to pray to the Blessed Mother for Birdie's safe return. Auntie Inga jerked Ragna away and changed the subject. Later Auntie said it was a terrible sin to pray to a statue, that Birdie was in heaven and that was that.

Ragna never forgot Mrs. Brorson's advice and wished she knew the novena. Besides, she had a vivid memory of her mother praying to St. Olaf before her brother's birth. Mor said she knew to call on the saint's help on such an occasion—the first American citizen in their family born on St. Olaf's special day, July 20.

But Auntie Inga said that Lutherans should not call on the saints as they did in pagan times.

It seemed to Ragna that Lutherans had little to help them through a crisis, even if they were the Holy Christian Church as stated in the Apostle's Creed. In fact, she had another dim memory of her mother's voice screaming, "Holy Mary, Mother of God . . ."

But maybe it was only a dream. Surely, no Lutheran would call on the Virgin Mary.

"St. Olaf," Ragna said aloud as she swatted the cow in front of her to hurry it homeward. The cow's bag hung heavy, swinging from side to side, dripping milk on the hard ground. "Have mercy on us poor sinners suffering from this plague of grasshoppers." There was no sound except the heavy plodding of the cows and the whirring hopper wings around her head. No Indians lurked along the well-worn path.

She dropped her voice almost to a whisper. "Holy Mary, Mother of God, please bring my sister home again."

3

Storms and Floods. The Air Lively with Horses, Cattle, Small Houses and Trees.

The St. Paul Dispatch, June 21, 1873

THE NEXT MORNING, RAGNA and Uncle Evan were up before daybreak when Lady had her calf. Ragna boosted the slippery newborn to its feet. His stiff legs braced and tottered. Ragna stretched out a steadying hand and nudged him toward his mother. Lady turned bright eyes toward her calf and licked his wet body hard with her long, rough tongue until it almost lost his footing.

"He's a strong one." Ragna watched him latch onto his mother's teat as a wave of fatigue washed over her. She liked the excitement and thrill of birthing. Most of all, Ragna liked helping Uncle Evan. At such times, she could imagine he was her real father.

"Wish it were a heifer." Uncle Evan's voice sounded tired. She watched him pour a careful measure of ground corn into the trough. Lady tossed curled horns and stomped her hind leg.

He reached for a gunnysack of dried corn hanging from a peg on the wall. With a start, Ragna realized it was next year's seed corn. Of course, hatching grasshopper eggs would destroy everything next year. It would be useless to plant the seeds.

The smells of fresh blood and pungent manure engulfed them. Lady chewed her cud. The new calf suckled. The barn hummed with the sounds of clucking hens chasing grasshoppers in the straw pile, grinding grasshopper jaws, and the harsh whirring of many wings. Ragna's pulse quickened. Maybe she would have a chance to talk to Uncle Evan before the boys swarmed into the barn to see the new calf.

Uncle Evan's scraggly beard never looked tended, and reddish hair capped his high, square forehead. His eyes were so blue they almost looked white. Usually he kept his thoughts to himself, especially about the past. Ragna wanted to ask questions about her family, find out all she could.

But it was a topic Uncle avoided.

He selected an ear of dried corn and sat on an old stump propped in the corner of the barn. He first shucked back the dead outer leaves and then stripped the dried kernels off the cob with his right thumb. The kernels dropped with a clunk into the wooden pail at his feet. Ragna pulled a cob from the bag and stripped kernels, too, kneeling by the wooden bucket. It was tedious work, only one row at a time, and brought a blister to her thumb.

"You shuck the husks," he said. "I'll do the shelling."

His kindness brought an unexpected lump to her throat. Auntie said that Ragna's father, Lars Larson, had been Uncle's best friend. That was long ago, before the uprising, before Evan and Inga had married. Surely, he knew many things about her family. Maybe he knew where Birdie might be found. Words formed in her mind. She gathered courage to speak them aloud.

"Uncle Evan," she said and willed her voice to be grown up, calm and even. "Can I ask about my family?"

A look of distress creased his face and it took all her courage to continue.

"I know you don't like to talk about it." She reached out a hand still stained with Lady's blood and touched his sleeve. "But I need to know." She waited a long time for his nod.

"How did you meet my parents?" Ragna started with easy questions in the hope of leading to more difficult ones.

"I drove the stage." Uncle Evan's voice sounded funny—like he was speaking from far away. "Your parents lived in this place on the route and I'd spend a night with them every time I went to and came back from Fort Abercrombie."

"What were they like?" She dropped another cob onto the pile of ears ready for shelling. She had a vague memory of the stage, nothing more, just a shadowy memory of the sound of the horses stopping in front of their cabin and Mor hurrying to put the coffee kettle on the fire.

Uncle Evan said they were from the same part of Norway and became friends here in America. Uncle Evan's voice trailed off, and he cleared his throat. "When your little brother was born, they asked me to stand as godfather."

"Baby Evan, named for you."

"*JA*, they named him Evan." He slipped into his own thoughts, and Ragna worried their conversation might be over. He reached for another ear and shelled furiously into the bucket, the kernels like hail pounding on a roof.

She fumbled for the words that might unlock Uncle's memories. "Far said he might grow up to be president." It felt strange to speak of her father after so many years had passed.

"*JA*, the first citizen, born in this country."

"I remember looking at the baby's shoulders, checking for stork bites." Ragna laughed and hot tears filled her eyes. She blinked and pulled the husk off another ear of corn.

"Mor said Birdie's birthmark was a bite from the stork." Words gushed from her mouth. "That's why I called her Birdie, because of the stork bite." She choked back the sobs but her voice broke. "I couldn't say Borghilde. It was too hard."

She knew from experience that Uncle Evan would not talk if she cried.

"On St. Lavran's Day, when your brother was baptized," his voice quavered, and the sounds of dry kernels dropping into the pail almost drowned him out. "He wet all over my good shirt. Lars said that wet clothes were the least of a *far's* worries."

Ragna held her breath to catch every word. She wished she had paper and pencil to write it down so nothing would escape her memory.

"It was at the baptism I made the promise." Uncle Evan brushed a grasshopper out of his beard and flicked it against the wall. "Promised to care for Lars's family if something happened to him."

"You found me at Camp Release?"

"St. Cloud." Uncle Evan's voice took on a flat edge, and he grabbed another ear of corn. "Soldiers brought you from Camp Release."

"I barely remember." Ragna's mind went to the swirling memories, the rocking of a wagon on a rough trail, the stinging slap of a hand across her cheek. She recalled the flood of relief when she first saw his face in the crowd, clinging to his leg and refusing to let go.

"You were little." Uncle Evan's voice took on a strained, nasal tone. "Not much older than the twins."

"And my sister?"

"Many were taken." Uncle Evan turned his face away and he looked off into the distance. "The survivors returned to Camp Release. That's all I know."

She knew there was more. She could feel him holding back. Ragna hurried to speak, to draw him back into the conversation.

"I remember the Indian's face in the window and the smell of smoke." It was like looking into a swirling mist, nothing clear in her memory. "Maybe the sound of a scream." Ragna wiped her eyes on the back of her sleeve. "Maybe it was my own scream I heard."

Ragna was surprised to see tears in Uncle Evan's eyes. At least they looked like tears, but surely, a grown man would not cry. His knuckles gripped a corncob until it broke in two.

"It was eleven years ago, Ragna." Uncle Evan cleared his throat. "Let the dead rest in peace."

Ragna searched her memories for something that would be a clue to finding her sister. But there was nothing—only smoke wafting over her head and the face in the window. Maybe the memory of being half-dragged and half-carried through the woods by the *skraeling* with the painted face. Birdie had been with her. She seemed to recall holding her hand. She remembered kind hands giving her a gourd of water and the grateful feeling she swallowed with the drink.

And the slap. Somewhere there had been a hard slap across her face. After that, only blackness.

Ragna's heart bounced in her chest and that familiar heaviness settled in again. Uncle Evan's mouth pursed into a thin line, and she knew he would say nothing more, even if she pressed.

"You're a good girl." Uncle Evan was not one to give praise lightly. "Inga says she would never make it without your help, especially since the twins."

Ragna saw his face relax, but it was as white as the heifer's spots. He sighed and picked up another cob, leaning back against the calf pen.

"Call the boys. We'll name the calf."

Ragna recited their conversation as she ran to the little cabin. Her *far* had said that wet clothes were the least of a father's worries. Baby Evan baptized on St. Lavran's Day. Uncle Evan promised to care for Far's children if something bad happened. Uncle found her at St. Cloud after soldiers brought her from Camp Release.

It was something at least, not much, but something.

Best of all, it proved Birdie could be alive. She had to be. Her parents and baby brother were dead, proved by their stones at the family cemetery. Birdie did not need a gravestone because she was still alive.

Ragna realized with a start that she remembered something new. A woman with gentle hands had given them water, but a man had slapped her. Ragna hoped Birdie still lived with the woman with the kind hands who had given them water so long ago. Surely, the bad man who slapped her was one of those hanged at Mankato. Auntie Inga said the army hanged all the bad Indians.

Ragna loved Auntie Inga and Uncle Evan and the boys, but she still wished for someone of her own. Somewhere Birdie lived with good Indians. Surely, God would answer her prayer and bring her sister home.

4

Martin County: Dr. Moor Reports this County a Blackened Desert, Destitute of Vegetation, Because of the Grasshoppers.
                              The St. Paul Dispatch, *June 21, 1873*

EVAN STOMPED A GRASSHOPPER and kicked it toward a clucking hen at his feet. He always froze up when Ragna asked about her folks. They were good people and she deserved an answer. But even thinking about that horrible day made his throat so dry that words, either Norwegian or American, lodged in his throat until he almost choked. He picked up the pitchfork and attacked the manure pile.

It had been a hot August day. Smoke billowed over the grove of trees by their cabin. He might have warned them had he hurried faster or started earlier. He had thought a million times of how he jumped off the stage and ran towards the burning house like a crazy man. A lurking savage could have killed him, too. Evan had left his gun on the stage and ran towards the house in a panic, thinking he could help somehow. Too late.

Evan kicked at a clod of dried manure with the toe of his boot, lifted it enough to wedge the fork underneath. All dead. Lars and the missus—sweet Jesus, the missus. He choked back a sob. And the baby. Dear Jesus. Would he never rid his mind of that image? He had called for the girls until hoarse, but they had vanished.

Lars had everything to live for—surely, a wise God would have taken Evan instead. To this day, the mention of their names caused his heart to pound, sweat to drip from his face, brought dark blotches in front of his eyes and made his mind swirl until he thought he would faint. Weak, he was.

He leaned the fork against the stall, threw open the top half of the barn door and watched Ragna run towards the house. She was a good girl. The heifers responded to her soothing voice and gentle hand. Already Ragna accompanied Inga when she midwifed in the community. He had been hesitant to give up the old ways but surely it did not matter if Ragna, unmarried though she was, delivered human babies. Inga named her a natural-born midwife. Said it was a good trade for Ragna to learn.

Soon she would be grown up and leave them. A panicky feeling fluttered in his chest. He had promised Lars to care for his children. He wondered if he had done enough, if there was something he had missed.

He returned to his perch on the log and pulled another ear of corn from the sack, grimacing at how little remained. The farm belonged to Ragna. When she married, they would have to move somewhere else. He had planned to be on his own place by now, but the years had slipped away. Of course, he might forbid her to marry until she reached majority at twenty-one, as was his right, and ensure four more years at this place. But someday a lovesick suitor would ask for permission to marry. Evan would not be able to refuse. He had never been able to refuse her anything.

At least that is what Inga said.

He had worked hard to build up the farm. Inga was right. All their hard work was for nothing. Not exactly for nothing, he corrected himself. He figured his labor a fair exchange for rent and Ragna and her someday husband would have a better start. Until the grasshoppers, Evan and Inga had enjoyed a fair living—except for the bank panic and the horse plague. A farmer had to expect a few troubles now and again. But the grasshoppers.

More than a few troubles.

Evan picked up another cob of precious seed-corn and shelled the rock-hard kernels into the bucket. It pained him to use it, but there was no meal left in the house. The millions of eggs left by the hoppers meant a death sentence for their future. The hoppers would hatch and eat everything next year and then plant more eggs. It would repeat the following year and the one after that.

He shelled the corn as fast as he could until a fat blister blossomed alongside his calloused thumb.

Besides, only God knew if the land would recover. If not, it meant that Ragna had nothing either. He had failed, after all.

The grasshopper infestation was spotty in this country. This farm destroyed and yet his neighbor, Waldo Herman, harvested a bountiful crop. Surely, the Hand of Almighty God had singled him out for destruction. Evan had never been an enthusiastic churchgoer and rarely attended the home meetings when itinerant Lutheran preachers visited. He had donated a dollar to the church building fund and offered to bring in five logs when construction started. He had raised Ragna, an orphan from the uprising, as his own daughter. He tried to live a God-fearing life.

He cast an anxious glance toward the heifer. Only two years ago, he had lost an otherwise healthy cow to milk fever. Evan had noticed she was twitchy after the birth but had been too busy planting to check back on her. That night he had found her lying with her head flopped back upon her flank, a sure sign of milk fever. He tried giving her whiskey, a remedy that sometimes worked, but it was too late. She was down and there was no getting her back on her feet. It had been devastating. If he had watched closer, he might have been able to prevent her death—but one never knew.

Dear God, have mercy. Another loss would be their death knell. He would watch carefully this time and keep the whiskey bottle handy if she even started to twitch.

Lars's cow once came down with milk fever, too, but he had managed to nurse her back to health. Lars had been an expert hand with husbandry. He always saw the best of everything, kept an even temper in stressful situations, and did not indulge in the luxury of panic. Evan should have told Ragna those things. He made a mental note to remember it the next time she asked. Lars worked hard to make a new life for his family. He had built the *stabbuhr* and the log barn, had been honest and trusting.

He would have been better off had he not been so trusting of the Sioux. Evan picked up another cob. They all would have been better off.

Maybe it was his mother's prayers. Or luck. Evan had spotted Ragna, dirty and forlorn, standing in a cluster of children at St. Cloud. His heart lurched at the memory, how she had cried for her parents, and the wicked bruise on her cheek.

My God, he had walked by the children on a whim, never thinking he would find someone he knew. He could just as easily kept walking without bothering to look. The thought weakened his knees. The little girl had not known a word of English. She could have ended up in an orphanage—maybe even raised Catholic.

Evan pulled another cob from the sack.

There was no explaining what happened to her sister. His stomach wrenched, and he reached for his tobacco plug before he remembered he had quit.

Borghilde had been only four years old when she was taken. Evan remembered how she sat on her *far's* lap and sucked coffee from a sugar lump, her soft golden curls. Of course, that had been before the uprising. He pushed the memory from his mind, felt the sweat bead on the back of his neck, and tried to slow his pounding heart.

Now Borghilde was dead, and her curls decorated some brave's lance. Or else she lived as some buck's squaw out in the Dakotas. Either meant she was dead to them. He hoped to spare Ragna the harsh truth, but she asked too many questions. The memories of blood and smoke refused to translate into mere words.

He grabbed the wall of the barn for support and willed his heart rate to slow, his mind to calm. Nothing good came from dredging up the old misery. The nightmares were getting better. It had been months since the faces of the dead had awakened him. This time of year always brought them to mind. It would pass. It always did. He pulled another ear of corn from the sack and shelled the kernels as fast as he could.

Evan had tried to locate Borghilde. Once he traveled all the way to New Ulm when he heard there was a Norwegian girl rescued from a band of renegade Sioux. However, when he got there, he found brown eyes instead of blue. Sometimes newspaper articles told of orphan survivors. He and Inga investigated every lead, writing letters asking about a birthmark on her shoulder, curly hair, and blue eyes.

But it had been eleven years since the uprising. The world had moved on. They would never find her.

He shelled corn so furiously that kernels flew out of the bucket. He didn't pause until he saw Knut and the twins, Sverre and Lewis, running toward the barn to see the new calf. Gunnar followed with Sigurd riding on his shoulders. Inga and Ragna carried the empty bucket and egg basket.

"Not too close, boys. Lady needs her space," Evan said.

Thank God, he had composed himself before they came. They would think their father a lunatic to be so upset about something that happened so long ago.

The boys skidded in their tracks, bumping into one another, eyes glued on the little calf sucking from his mother.

"Where did it come from?" Lewis popped his thumb in his mouth. He was too old to suck his thumb, and Evan gave him a stern look. Lewis pulled out his thumb and tucked his right hand in his back pocket. Evan swallowed a smile.

"Lady dropped her calf while you slept." Evan stood and brushed a stray kernel into the bucket. Each one was crucial for survival. "If you sleep late, you miss out."

Knut reached a hand out to the calf, and Lady swung her head in his direction.

"Stay back!" Evan took Sigurd from Gunnar's arms and carried him to the front of Lady's stall for a better look. "Lady is nervous for her baby. She needs a little room."

"Too bad it's a bull." Inga's brown eyes showed disappointment, and Evan remembered how they had counted on a heifer to help repay the bank note. A sinking feeling filled him. A heifer might have kept them afloat for another year.

"But *mange bekker same gjor en stor ae*," she said. Many small rivulets make a big brook.

He could always count on Inga to make the best of every situation. A strong emotion welled in his chest, and his eyes filled with moisture. How lucky he was to have Inga for his wife. Evan blinked away the tears. He was the *far*, after all, and needed to be the strong one in the family. Especially now.

If worse came to worse, he could ask Ole, his older brother, for help. Evan would hate to do it, but at least he had someone to turn to if it came to that. Evan had lived in America two years longer than Ole and felt that he should be the one to help Ole, not the other way around.

"A heifer would have paid the note." Evan's voice was gruff as he handed Sigurd to Ragna. The boys argued back and forth about which name would be best. "But a sturdy ox trained to the yoke is nothing to sneeze at neither."

He avoided Inga's eyes. She always seemed to know whenever he thought about the Indian war. He looked away. It was bad enough the calf was a bull. He had done the best he could until the grasshoppers.

"Far," Lewis said in a small voice. "Can we name him Bobcat?"

"Bobcat!" Gunnar hooted and pointed a dirty finger at Lewis. "What kind of baby name is that? He needs a strong name—like Stein Eric or Admiral." He spat in the straw. "Bobcat! Only a baby would think of such a name."

Knut stuck his tongue out at his brother.

Evan's face flushed warm up his cheeks. Gunnar was sometimes a bully and Knut an eager follower. Evan swooped Lewis into his arms and cast a warning glance toward Gunnar.

"Bobcat it will be," he said. "We'll call him 'Bob' for short."

Lewis's smile lightened Evan's mood. Where did the little man come up with such a name? Bobcat, indeed.

"Boys," Inga said. "Gather eggs. See if there are enough for a pudding."

Reluctantly the boys pulled themselves away from the calf and dragged their feet to obey.

"Sverre, you carry the basket," she said.

Inga always equaled out the attention given the twins. Lewis named the calf, and Sverre carried the basket. Sverre puffed out his chest while his brothers pushed and shoved to find brown eggs hidden among the straw. The boys were a handful. What one did not think of, the other did.

"I'll take the first milk now," Inga said.

Evan held Bob away from the heifer while Inga squatted down with the bucket positioned to catch every drop. The calf bawled and struggled to return to his mother's teat. It took all Evan's strength to hold him back.

"You did a good job, little mother," crooned Inga softly as she stripped the golden colostrum into the bucket. "You have a healthy calf."

Lady tossed wild eyes toward her calf, and Evan watched Inga rest her cheek on Lady's flank as streams of colostrum pinged into the bucket, the rhythmic sounds soothing to their ears, the barn still smelling of fresh blood.

When they first married, Evan once woke up screaming from a nightmare. Inga had thought the Indians were attacking and had leapt from their bed, grabbed the axe and headed to the door to defend her babies. The noise woke the children and upset them all. Another time he had cried out for Borghilde, and when Inga woke him, he had sobbed for almost an hour before he could go back to sleep. He hated to think how she must see him. He was not the strong man her first husband had been, the one who died on the ship coming over. Maybe she still yearned for Gunnar, the father of her oldest son, named for him although the son was unaware that he had ever existed.

It seemed the uprising affected Evan more than it did Inga. Perhaps because she had lost two husbands before her nineteenth birthday and had known the loss of parents and sister as well. He watched her reposition herself by Lady's flank. They never talked about it.

They also avoided talking about Evan's reluctance to own land. Crooked Lightning's philosophy aggravated Inga to tears—but it was the hard truth. The white man's greed for land pushed the Sioux into war and everyone paid the price.

He had left the Old Country to become a landowner. Maybe something was wrong with him that he could let go of the dream so easily. Renters never prospered. He should be planning for the future of their children. At least that is what Inga was always telling him. If the stage lines were still in business, he would take up the reins again. However, the best lines were gone with the railroads.

Now, the grasshoppers.

Inga flicked one off her skirt as the colostrum filled the bottom of the bucket. Evan stomped on it with a sickening crunch of wings. It was unthinkable that after all they had been through, they might lose everything because of an insect—or rather millions of devilish insects.

This enemy was impossible to fight, even worse than the Sioux. The hoppers ate everything green, even the hazel nut bushes and the green leaves on Inga's geraniums planted by the front stoop. She had thrown a quilt over the tomatoes but they chewed the quilt. They flurried and spat tobacco on their clothes, flew into their faces, cut into shoe leather. On that terrible day when they fell from the sky, they came through the chinks in the logs as fast as they could sweep them out.

Inga had stuffed sheets around the door and windows like a woman possessed. She pounced on each grasshopper that found its way into the house and threw it into the stove where it sizzled and popped, burning into an acrid stench that filled the cabin.

"Damn them!" Inga had yelled to no one in particular. "Burn them all."

The boys had stared with wide eyes, lined up on the bed as if they were on a school bench.

"Far," Gunnar said with a shaky voice. "Are we in the *Book of Revelation*?"

"*Nei.*" Evan answered. "Locusts were in the Old Testament, I think."

"But John the Baptist ate them," Knut said. "How could you eat a grasshopper?"

"Where does it say that?" Gunnar said.

Knut reached for the Norwegian Bible and thumbed through the ancient book. A grasshopper landed on the page and spit a stream of tobacco juice across the paper.

"Knut!" Inga yanked it out of his hands and slammed it shut, carefully wrapping it in her apron and shoving it under the bedclothes. "They'll eat the pages."

Through the single pane of glass, they had watched the chomping swarm of grasshoppers block the sunlight. The house warmed from its strange fuel but Inga never stopped. The boys fell asleep, one by one, sweat dripping from their red faces.

As if on cue, the hoppers then rose as one beast and flew to the east.

"It's over," Ragna said. "Thank God it's over."

"They planted their eggs," Inga had said with a voice flat and hard. "I read about them in the paper. It will never end."

NOW YOU CAN GO BACK TO YOUR MOTHER," INGA SAID.

The bucket held enough for pudding, and the twins carried eggs in their basket. Inga stretched out the kink in her back and covered the bucket with cloth. Evan released the calf. Fisk mewed around the heifer, lapping dripping milk from the ground beneath her.

Colostrum pudding was good for women of childbearing age. Pudding was a rare treat, and he knew Inga would see to it that she and Ragna had the bigger portions. Inga was right—Ragna was close to marrying age. Already he had noticed the young men in the community taking interest in their goddaughter.

With a start, Evan thought about Inga. He had not noticed morning sickness, and Sigurd was still on the breast. He sent a prayer anyway that God would not send another baby at such a time. They needed all their strength and every cent to make it through the crisis at hand.

"Sverre and Lewis!" he said. "Get busy with your chores. Gunnar and Knut, finish up before breakfast."

Gunnar shoved Sverre, and Evan felt his cheeks flush. None of the children angered him like Gunnar. It was as if he pushed against Evan every step of the way.

Lately Inga had been asking about whether or not they should tell Gunnar about his real father. Long ago, they had decided not to discuss the past with Ragna or the other children. Some things were better unsaid.

The children were older now. At least Ragna and Gunnar were old enough to know what had happened. He would discuss it with Inga again. However, with the grasshoppers, the bull calf, and the tormenting dreams about 1862, it was not the time to bring it up.

5

*Death of Mrs. Sherflius of Winona Yesterday Morning. She had
Started a Fire in the Summer Kitchen and in Order to Hurry it
Poured Kerosene On it. An Explosion Followed.*

The St. Paul Dispatch, *June 25, 1873*

L OOK WHAT I FOUND IN RAGNA'S POCKET," INGA SAID.
"What is it?" Evan put down the axe he had been sharpening. The
grindstone sat beneath the oak tree in the barnyard, but there was
little shade with the leaves eaten away. Evan wiped his sweaty face with the
back of his sleeve and rubbed both hands on the front of his pant legs before
taking the crumpled paper from his wife.

"It's from Norway."

He smoothed the paper and adjusted it so that he could read the scrawl-
ing Norwegian words from Ragna's grandmother, read silently for a moment,
and then smoothed and folded the sheet. He did not want to look at Inga
and see the accusation in her eyes.

"What will we do?" Inga whispered.

"There's nothing to do but as the letter says." Evan handed the letter
back to Inga. "We'll sell the farm and Ragna will return to Norway. I should
have thought of it myself. She's old enough."

"But what about us?" Inga's eyes filled with tears that splashed across
the paper in her hand. "We'll lose both our daughter and our home." She
quickly rubbed the back of her hand across her eyes. Her up-tilted chin told
him she was angry.

"We should have kept the farm in Pomme de Terre." Inga threw the envelope down on the grass and stalked off towards the cabin.

Evan sighed and reached for his pocket until he remembered he had no tobacco. They had always known they would have to move when Ragna married. He had hoped to have enough money saved up by then to start over. No one in his right mind would buy a farm filled with grasshopper eggs. He would not be able to sell it if he tried.

When they sold the Pomme de Terre farm owned by Inga's second husband, they had used some of the money to rebuild the cabin on this farm and repay a loan owed to his brother.

What a mess he had made!

He had foolishly invested his strength and money in Ragna's property. He would have been better off if they had purchased a place of their own— or stayed in Pomme de Terre at Inga's farm. Back then, he had wanted nothing to do with her farm, even if it would have been safe to move so far west.

They had rebuilt the cabin, and it was only fair to get their investment back. If they did find someone foolish enough to buy the place, there might be money for Ragna's passage back to Norway and a little left over for Evan to start over. It pained him that Ragna must repay him, but he had no choice. He could not let his own children lack.

His brother's prediction was coming true. Evan would never amount to more than a *cotter*. It was hard to explain the dark thoughts that kept him from success.

Of course, the easiest solution would be to buy Ragna's farm. If the grasshoppers had only stayed away, he might have been able to negotiate a mortgage with the banker.

Nothing could be done about that now.

Evan bent to pick up the envelope. His eyes flitted across the sketch on its back and he held it closer to study the drawing. His hand shook until the envelope fluttered.

He had never asked Ragna to describe the Indian who stole them. Of course, she was young at the time of her capture. He never thought she would remember. She remembered so little from the ordeal. Except for the face in the window, he reminded himself. She had always remembered the face.

He studied the penciled form. The dark eyes, the tilt of his head. It was Crooked Lightning. No doubt about it. No other Indian wore his distinctive war paint, at least none that he had seen.

Crooked Lightning hanged at Mankato, but his death gave Evan no peace. Evan had once written home of Crooked Lightning, his best friend in America.

Images from the past flooded his mind, the smell of burned bodies, the shriveled faces beneath scalped heads, and the look on Crooked Lightning's face when they had come face to face along the trail. His heart bounced in his chest, and he leaned against the rough bark of the oak.

His breath escaped him, and he bent forward, drawing in gulps of air while forcing his racing pulse to slow. *I believe in God the Father, Maker of heaven and earth, and in Jesus Christ His Son, our Lord.* It was long over, nothing to think about now. *Born of the Virgin Mary, suffered under Pontius Pilate, was crucified dead and buried.* Things had worked out after all, thank God. He'd found Ragna. Not Birdie. *From thence He shall come to judge the quick and the dead.* Somehow, God had let him marry Inga, the only girl he had ever loved. It was too good to be true. And their boys.

He picked up the axe and rubbed the stone against the edge of the blade so hard that sparks flew.

Could it be that Crooked Lightning had targeted his friends? Crooked Lightning had had his chance to kill Evan. They had come face to face along the trail, but he'd backed down without a word. Nevertheless, the drawing proved that Crooked Lightning had stolen the girls. He may have been involved with the other murders as well.

Evan had to admit that Crooked Lightning's influence had been his downfall. Land was cheap after the uprising, but Evan could not stomach owning property knowing that land ownership had caused the death of hundreds of innocents. At the time, it was easier not to deal with it. If he had not been so reticent, he would be successful by now.

Instead, he was thirty-five years old, a married man with five children and a wife to support, and with hardly a pisspot of his own. By God, he would own land if it killed him. It no longer mattered. Crooked Lightning was dead. The Sioux were gone.

He pedaled the grindstone, turning the blade again. Mor always said that bad news came in threes. First the grasshoppers, then the farm, and then Ragna. However, Crooked Lightning's face made it four. That meant two more mishaps would follow. *Dear God, I can't take any more.* The axe head was sharp at last. He straightened his back and started towards the woodpile.

RAGNA ARGUED BUT EVAN WAS ADAMANT.

He posted a notice in the bank and general store, spreading word that the farm was for sale.

One day Milton Madsen, a Civil War veteran, knocked on the door dressed in a worn union jacket and a blue cap faded near white from the sun. He was shorter than Evan, and heavier through the shoulders. He looked like a man who knew how to box, with a ragged scar on his chin and another by his left eye. Though Milton was a Dane, Evan was able to converse with him in a mixture of Norwegian and Danish, the languages being similar.

"I'm looking for a place to settle down," Mr. Madsen said. "I sold my Soldier's Homestead in Illinois and came west."

"What made you leave?"

"Let's put it this way, it was getting squally with the Grangers."

Evan showed him the buildings and walked with him through a field behind the house, past the family cemetery, and up to the property line that separated them from the Spitsberg farm. He always felt queasy around the place of massacre, a little unstable, as if he might lose control.

"And smothering, so close to the Rebs." Mr. Madsen spat into a hazelnut bush denuded of every leaf. He passed the tobacco plug to Evan but he shook his head.

"I'm looking for peace and quiet," he said.

"You see how it is," Evan said.

Surely, no one in their right mind would buy a farm stripped to the bone by grasshoppers. Mr. Madsen would walk away and they could all forget about it.

"Hard times can't last forever. I've heard in Missouri they're grinding up the hoppers for cattle feed."

"What next?"

"Some people eat them, too."

They might do as cattle feed. The chickens thrive on them. However, he knew there was no way this side of heaven that Inga would allow locusts in her kitchen.

"It wouldn't be the worst I ever ate." Mr. Madsen spat a stream of tobacco juice into the dust, disrupting a pair of grasshoppers dueling over a tiny blade of grass. "At Andersonville we ate anything that moved."

The man's seamed face looked older than his years. Evan guessed the man was about his age, in his mid thirties. Thank God, Evan had heeded his *far's* advice and stayed out of the War of Rebellion.

"Indians eat them," Madsen said. "At least the Pokawatamies back in Illinois do."

Maybe he had eaten grasshoppers at Crooked Lightning's stew pot.

"There's no guarantee," Evan said. "Crops next year are out of the question."

The man picked up a handful of black dirt and tasted it with the tip of his tongue. "I've no plans to farm—just run a few cattle and some hens. I need a quiet spot away from the war."

The man stood within view of the very spot of the Larson family's massacre. This place of nightmare became another man's sanctuary. Evan cleared his throat. His voice came out in a near whisper.

"Don't say I didn't warn you, Mr. Madsen."

"I'll risk it."

Evan looked around before he spoke. A purple finch sang in the branch of an elm, singing as if his heart would burst. The birds feasted on grasshoppers and had reason to sing.

"Sold." They shook hands and Evan felt a pulling sensation inside his chest. It was the right thing to do. It was time for him to leave this place and fulfill his dream of becoming a landowner.

"*Mange takk*," Evan said. "I'll need some time to make arrangements."

"How about three weeks." The man cleared his throat. "And call me Milton, for God's sake. You make me feel like my father."

"Milton," Evan said. "I'll be packed up and ready to leave when you get here."

Madsen mounted his horse and rode away. Evan headed back to the barn to finish the chores before dinner. He hoped to avoid questions so picked up the pitchfork and mucked stalls. The boys knew better than to come around at barn cleaning time. Flies buzzed around the steamy piles of manure, and grasshoppers crunched under his feet with every step.

Long ago in Norway, his brother had loaned part of his wife's dowry to pay Evan's passage to America. It was a bitter memory, the money only given because of their mother's demand. Ole's words rang down through the years. "You'll be back, begging for more."

How low he had sunk to seek Ole's help now. He had repaid the forty-dollar loan. Thank God for that. Even so, he would do just as Ole predicted, come back begging for help until they could get situated. The thought brought a taste of bile to his mouth. Ole would help him, he had no doubt of that, but with a gloating look in his eyes, maybe unspoken—but always there.

He might turn to his old friends, the Estvolds at Pomme de Terre, the Rognaldson family at Foxhome, or Bror Brorson near Cold Spring. But they had troubles of their own. Besides, Brorson turned Catholic, and Inga would have nothing to do with popery.

His knees weakened at the realization of their vulnerability. His world spun out of control, beyond management. He brushed a grasshopper off his shirt just as it spat a stream of tobacco down the front.

Evan renewed his shoveling with vigor. He needed cash. Inga had a little egg money, and Evan had two gold eagles tucked away for emergencies. If only the stage was still running. It had been regular money and there were no sticky philosophical thoughts about the original owners of the land. The line to Fort Abercrombie had stopped in 1870. Shorter lines still ran further west, and there were a few mail contracts. If all else failed, he would have to relocate and take up the reins again. His family would not starve.

Evan hung the pitchfork on a nail and picked up the homemade broom. He swept dead grasshoppers into the manure pile, then squashed a moving hopper at his feet and swept it into the pile. Milton's price would be enough to give him a start. It was little to show for eleven years of labor, but it would do.

He knelt down and picked up a grasshopper. He pulled the body apart and looked at the fibrous body under the wings. He smelled it, wondering what it would taste like cooked in a pot.

Ragna called him in for dinner but Evan was not hungry He braced himself for the difficult task of telling the family about the sale of the farm, their move to Uncle Ole's, and Ragna's trip back to the Old Country.

Ragna would not like it. He thought to tell her in private before telling the rest of the family. He sighed. They would eat dinner in peace and then he would tell Ragna.

The rest of the family could wait until later.

6

Startling Exposure! The Fort Snelling Swindle. How Frank Steele
& Co. Got 63,000 Acres for Nothing.

The St. Paul Dispatch, June 25, 1873

After dinner, Uncle Evan invited Ragna to go out to the barn with him. Questions swirled through Ragna's mind and her ears roared. She could not have heard correctly.

All because she had left the letter in her apron pocket.

Bobcat bawled in the stall. Hens scratched in the pungent straw at Ragna's feet. Fisk rubbed against her legs, and she picked him up and held him close to her chest, feeling the rumble of his purring contentment.

"You must obey your *bestemor's* wishes." Uncle Evan's face was grim though his voice was steady.

"I'm not going." A grasshopper lit on her shoulder, and she brushed it off with a quick flick of her hand. It left a stream of dark tobacco juice on her dress.

"I know this isn't your idea." Uncle Evan said. "I promised your *far* I would look out for you, and this is what he would have wanted."

"Far would not have me abandon Birdie." Hot tears stung Ragna's eyes and she bit back angry words she knew she would regret. She swallowed hard and wiped her eyes with her sleeve. "Never!"

"Your sister is dead." Uncle Evan's voice cracked. He picked at his mustache with his fingers and reached toward his empty pocket.

"She's alive!" Ragna clenched her fists at her side, leaning toward him, anger making her body rigid and her words sharp.

"We've looked everywhere." Uncle Evan reached a hand toward her but Ragna stepped away. "She's nowhere to be found."

40

"You've looked for her?" Ragna felt the blood drain from her face.

"After the uprising," he said. "We wrote letters and followed every lead about recovered children."

"She's alive," Ragna said. "I can feel her."

Suddenly she was in Uncle Evan's arms, crying into the front of his shirt stained with tobacco juice from the terrible hoppers.

"It's all right, *stalkers liten.*" He patted her back and made the same shushing sounds he used with the little boys. "Poor little one."

"I can feel her."

"Sometimes I feel my sister, Christina, as well. Those we love never really leave us."

"I don't want to go back."

"We don't want it either, but you have to."

It was what she always had longed to hear, that Uncle Evan and Auntie Inga wanted her. She had always known but had craved the hearing of it just the same. She gulped back the sobs. She was too big to cry.

Ragna forced herself to focus on the horrible news. The farm sold, the family cemetery owned by strangers. She forced to return to Norway and marry a man of Uncle Ivar's choosing. Her father's dream killed.

"I can't go." She hiccoughed and wiped her nose on her apron. "Birdie might come back."

Uncle smoothed his scraggly beard, and for the first time Ragna noticed a few white strands entwined with the red. "Ragna." His voice was serious, without any teasing edge he could have, no hint of humor. "She won't be coming back"

She felt an urge to reach up and smooth the wildness from his beard. The little boys shouted in the distance, and Ragna hoped with all her might that they would stay in the far field, that nothing would interrupt Uncle Evan. At the same time, a dark feeling of dread threatened to drown her and her feet ached to run away from his words.

"Listen to me." His left eye twitched, and Evan rubbed it with a calloused hand. "I found your parents."

She examined her apron. It was her best one since her every-day apron was still in the wash. Her fingers straightened the hem, pressed it flat against her leg.

"I drove west from Cold Spring," he continued. "Tried to warn people. Mostly folks had already heard." He looked off in the distance and Ragna could tell his mind was far away. "I was scared. Every shadow was an Indian with a tomahawk. I never thought to make it to Fort Abercrombie alive."

He picked up a grasshopper and stretched its wings. "When I got this far, I saw the house afire and knew I was too late."

Uncle Evan worked his lips but no sound came out. Ragna saw his eyes squint and tear as if he looked into the flames. She imagined how the black smoke must have whorled above the oak trees by the old house place. Although she remembered the smell, the greasy-thick odor that had pressed against her, she did not remember how it looked. Maybe there was a memory of being half-dragged and half-carried away. Perhaps the Indian with the painted face had not allowed them to look back.

She remembered the *skraeling's* voice, a sudden memory that made her throat thicken and her eyes gush with tears. "Quiet!" He had urged them to run faster. Birdie had stumbled and fell to the ground. He hesitated, looked first at the girls and then back at the house where screams and wild yelling mingled with the smoke.

Ragna remembered how when he turned his face toward the house she could only see the black paint, and then when he looked back, she saw the green as well. His face mesmerizing in its terror. Finally the Indian bent and scooped them up, one in each arm, and ran into the trees. Branches caught at her hair and slapped her face. The Indian smelled of rancid grease and wood smoke.

"Your *far* lay dead in the yard." Uncle Evan cleared his throat and she watched him pluck the grasshopper's wings off its body. "Your *mor* was . . . killed." His words strangled and his thick fingers pulled off the grasshopper's legs. "And your baby brother . . .," he said. "He . . . they . . ." He gasped a jagged breath, the grasshopper pieces littered the ground around him. "The little one was . . ." Uncle finally looked at her after a long silence. "He was gone."

Ragna remembered a scream, gentle hands with water, and the slapping hand across her face. All shrouded in clouds, maybe billowing smoke. She hoped her parents were dead before the Sioux killed the baby. It was too cruel, too terrible. She did not realize she was crying until Uncle Evan spoke again.

"I called your names," Uncle Evan said.

Ragna's eyes glued to the fine tremor of his hands. He had just missed them. She wished she had heard him call her name, that she had answered him from the woods, called out for him to rescue them. If only he had come a few minutes earlier.

"Such violent men will never bring Birdie home again." He stepped back from her and took a deep breath. His boot ground the grasshopper to green slime. "It is a miracle I found you."

Ragna tried to make sense of the words. She dragged ragged breaths from her aching chest.

"I suspect that deep down you know the worst," he said. "That's why you don't remember."

Ragna wished with all her might that she could remember, even the worst. She would rather know her sister was dead than wonder about it all her life.

"It doesn't change anything." Ragna willed her voice strong and steady. "I won't leave America until I know for sure."

"She won't remember her name or where she lived." Uncle cleared his throat. "You were older and yet remember so little."

It was true. Birdie would not remember where she lived.

"And she spoke Norwegian." His voice had a nasal strain to it that Ragna had not noticed before. "Few know the language."

It was as if he pulled the ground from beneath her feet. She had imagined Birdie coming home in a million ways.

Birdie would never come home on her own.

Uncle Evan sounded tired, his eyes red-rimmed, and Ragna watched him tuck trembling hands into deep pockets. "Times are bad—it's a miracle someone wants the farm."

She felt her world slide and skid and reached out for the wall to support her. She could not leave the place where her *far* risked everything to make a better life for his children.

Uncle Evan rambled on about moving and the price of wheat. She lost focus on his words, still reeling from the realization that Birdie could not find her way home. Instead, Ragna must find Birdie. She did not know where to look, where to begin.

"I invested Inga's money to rebuild this place after we sold her farm." She forced herself to listen to Uncle Evan's words. "We'll need our money back but there should be enough to buy your ticket home."

"When did Auntie have a farm?"

"It's hard to explain," he said. "Inga's man died in the uprising." He seemed to choke on the words. "After we married, we sold the farm and invested money into this place."

"Where was her farm?" Ragna said.

"Pomme de Terre," Uncle Evan said. "Not far from the Estvolds."

She had lived as their daughter for all these years and never knew about Auntie Inga's first marriage or that Uncle had been the one who discovered her family. It made her wonder what else they were keeping from her.

"Don't mention it to the boys." Uncle's white knuckles gripped another grasshopper, and Ragna watched legs and wings flutter to the ground. "We'll tell them when they are older."

Ragna had a dim memory of Auntie Inga and Uncle Evan kissing after Uncle found her in St. Cloud. She remembered how they laughed. Auntie said that Ragna's hair was lousy. It seemed that Auntie's stomach pressed hard against Ragna during the bath that followed.

Auntie Inga had been with child before she married Uncle Evan.

Ragna quickly calculated years, months, and birthdays. Gunnar was not Uncle Evan's son. Gunnar did not know.

The heavy weight staggered Ragna with a sudden, aching burden.

7

12,000,000 Acres! Cheap Farms! Union Pacific Railroad Company
St. Paul Dispatch, *July 15, 1873*

THERE'S CONGRESS LAND IN Otter Tail County," Inga read aloud from an old newspaper that wrapped a pound of prunes from Van Dyke's Store. "And Norwegian explorers are out to discover the North Pole." She turned the page. "And another problem with the banks."

Evan tucked the three-legged iron griddle into a wooden barrel. He chuckled a dry and bitter laugh. Inga looked up from the smudged print. The 1871 Panic took what little savings they had tucked away. Back then, he sat holding the best crop of barley he had ever raised with nowhere to sell it. Rats made storage impossible and he ended up using it for the family, grinding it into poor-quality flour. He fed the remainder to the stock before the rodents could get it. The bank still carried a note from his loss. He jerked on the griddle, forced it down into the barrel, and picked up the hasp.

Now he had nothing to lose. It did not matter whether the bank broke or not. His crop was gone, his money was gone, and now the farm as well. For once, it did not affect him.

Maybe the St. Cloud Bank would go under, and he would get by without repaying the note. He did not know about such things, but in his experience, the rich always figured a way to wrench money from the poor. He picked up the andirons and positioned them to the side of the griddle along with the cast iron ladle and an iron dipper. He tucked straw around the items to stabilize them against the jolting trip ahead.

Most of the items belonged to Inga from her previous marriage: the black iron cook stove, the cooking pot, the bread pans and the wool cards. When they married, he had nothing to contribute except his good name, fine horse, and strong back. His sigh made Inga look up again. They had so little room yet they needed everything for their growing family. If he left the ladder-back chairs, it meant he must make more when they arrived at their destination. They needed the Betty Lamps, the feather ticks, and flax hackle. He could not farm without the wheat cradle, the scythe, the adz, and the grindstone.

Old Doll was barely a shadow of her former strength since the epizootic plague. When she was younger, she could pull all day without breaking a sweat. The horse plague had taken almost every horse in the state. He had treated Old Doll with blankets and warm water. Somehow, it was enough.

Evan secretly thought of Old Doll as his best friend. He confided in the mare, whispered secrets into her ear when he treated her to sugar lumps or carrot tops. She did not mind that he spoke Norwegian or repeated a story. *Nei*, he must spare Old Doll if he could. Inga urged him to trade her for a team of oxen. He could not do it. She was his oldest friend. The children must walk the forty miles to Tumuli Township.

"Where will we buy Ragna's boat ticket?" Inga explored the newspaper. Her voice sounded younger and more hopeful than it had since the grasshoppers had landed. "Can we purchase one in St. Cloud along with her train ticket?"

Train fare to New York would dip even deeper into the meager funds from selling the farm. His stomach roiled at the thought. He knew what dangers lurked for someone so naïve and comely. It could not be helped. There was no money for someone to accompany her. Maybe there was not enough money for her passage back to Norway. Anxiety gripped him until great drops of sweat rolled down his neck.

"Did I tell you that Milton says they're eating the hoppers in Missouri?"

Inga dropped the paper. "You lie!"

"*Nei*," he said. "They're frying them up for supper and grinding them for cattle feed as well. The hoppers aren't all gloom and doom, you know."

Inga began a tirade about the dangers of eating unclean food that went all the way back to the 1348 Black Plague that killed half of Norway. At least she stopped asking questions without answers.

The barrel filled. He would tie the milking buckets and separator pans to the outside of the wagon. Old Doll might make it if the trails were good. She was a beautiful animal, purchased from his old friend, Bror Brorson.

"When will you buy land?" Inga's voice took on the sharp edge. "They advertise acreage for $1.25 an acre besides the Congress Land."

A sudden weariness filled Evan. He turned to the stove and poured a cup of thick, lukewarm coffee that tasted like bitterness itself. That woman would not be content until he bought a farm.

"We'll have to see." He forced his words to sound smooth and controlled. The last thing they needed was another argument. "Ole will know how things stand. We'll stay with him until we figure something out."

"It's almost August." He watched her chew her lower lip, a sure sign she was worried. "Will we stay with Ole all winter? Do they have enough room for all of us?"

"We'll come up with something," Evan said. "Maybe build a dugout to get through the winter."

"And live like gophers?" She pursed her lips. "I couldn't stand it."

"Don't worry. It's harvest time farther east. Maybe I can find work."

Evan picked up the wooden rolling pin and dough bowl, horn spoons and wrought-iron hog scraper and pressed them into the barrel, forcing them in, willing them to fit. He tacked down the barrel lid, hammering his left thumb in the process. He popped it in his mouth to cut off the curse words that would only rile his wife.

"Won't he ever get here?" Inga pulled aside the faded curtain over their only window. "The boys will be hungry before we start." She looked again at the china teapot and knick-knack shelf to be left behind. "Maybe I'd have time to walk to town. I'd like to give my teapot to Mrs. Clare. She's always admired it."

"There's no time." It saddened him that Inga must leave her treasures. It was different for a man. Leaving the chairs only meant he would have to carve more next winter. The chairs themselves did not matter. They were just pieces of wood put to useful work, like the rope beds and the wooden benches.

But Inga's teapot. It was her favorite possession, found unharmed in her cabin after the uprising.

Evan pried open the barrel and carefully removed the hay knife and Betty lamps. He took the newspaper from Inga's hands and wrapped the blue teapot, smearing streaks of ink across its surface. By strapping the Betty lamps to the side of the wagon and wedging the hay knife behind the plow, he was able to wiggle the teapot into the top of the barrel.

"Oh, Evan." He watched her clasp chapped hands before her mouth and he looked away, avoiding the tears swimming in her brown eyes. "*Mange takk.*"

"You're welcome." It was too easy to forget about little things that made her happy. Even after all these years of marriage, he still melted when she looked at him that way. He had nothing else to offer her but what small kindnesses he could remember to do. He wanted to say as much to her, but someone cleared his throat in the doorway.

Milton Madsen stood holding his worn union cap.

"Good. You're here at last." Evan tapped the barrel lid once more. "We're almost packed."

"You can unpack." Milton gulped and his Adam's apple bobbed. "The bank . . ." His face wore a wild look and Evan feared he might collapse. "I've lost everything."

"My God." Evan pulled over a chair and Milton slumped into it. Inga brought a dipper of water. "The panic?"

"Blood money," Milton said. "Cash I took from Old Man Watters to keep his son from the draft."

Milton's Adam's apple bobbed again as he swallowed the water and then leaned over, resting his head on hands supported by his knees. "I killed Rebs for that money." His voice cracked and his face darkened. "And a year of hell in Andersonville."

"Good Lord," Evan said.

"Gone because of Jay Cooke's wheeling and dealing." Milton smashed his fist on the table. "I'd like to get my hands on that lying crook."

"What now?" Inga said.

Evan's mind whirled. They were all packed. The livestock sold except for Lady and Bobcat. No fodder prepared for the winter. No hope of a crop next year. They could still go to Ole's, but Evan would have nothing to offer him, and little to help with the expense of feeding his family through the winter. Ole would gloat over him the rest of his life. Ragna's ticket to Norway. A cold sweat broke out on his back and chest. He placed a shaking hand on the rough wall behind him.

"Your mail." Milton dug the envelope from his jacket pocket. "Van Dyke asked me to bring it."

Evan carefully broke the wax seal, read the words, and felt the kick in his stomach. His mind swirled. Familiar blotches darkened his eyes. Inga's voice came as if from across the ocean. The boys gathered at the door, and Fisk raced under the stove after a mouse. Ragna shushed fussy Sigurd by the window.

"Are we ready to go?" Gunnar said.

"Evan." Inga gripped his arm and spoke again. "What is it?"

"Smallpox." Evan's voice rasped and scraped over the words, as if he felt the cutting edge of grasshopper wings in his throat. "Ole lost his youngest and the girls are sick. Says not to come."

Sigurd howled and Ragna bounced him on her hip. Inga turned white, with eyes as dark as Bossy's.

"Not little Emil." Inga slumped down on a chair. "He was just a year old, a few months younger than Sigurd."

"They thought it the summer complaint," Evan said. "Until the pox."

Inga pulled her apron up over her face and rocked back and forth. Evan knew it was her biggest fear, that a sudden disease would steal one of their boys. It was his fear as well, next to watching his family do without, of failing them.

"Are you all right?" Gunnar placed a protective hand on Inga's hair and shot an acrid glance at Evan is if he were to blame.

Evan took the baby from Ragna and pressed him tightly against his chest. No older than Sigurd. Thank the Good Lord they had been spared sickness. He could not bear to lose one of his children. He looked around the little cabin, empty of its possessions. The seed corn used up, the fields riddled with grasshopper eggs. He fumbled in his empty pocket for tobacco.

Sweet Jesus, they would starve.

8

A Bold Forgery of New York Central Railroad Bonds And Unsuccessful Attempt to Dispose of Them in Wall Street
St. Paul Dispatch, *July 16, 1873*

RAGNA NEVER MEANT TO EAVESDROP but in their small cabin, it was impossible not to hear. She stood folding the baby's clean soakers in the corner, her last task before they would leave the farm.

When Mr. Madsen spoke of blood money, a shiver went right through her, even though the oven radiated heat needed for the extra baking. The emotion in his voice made her think of Birdie. Of course, there was no connection between the bank closing and Birdie, but the emotion behind his words winged her thoughts toward Birdie just the same. She reached up toward her throat.

Birdie holds out her tiny hand, and the sun glints off her hair. I reach toward her but she is just beyond reach. I stretch but she is farther and farther away.

"Ragna!" Her voice is like a song on the wind.

I struggle to answer. Tears drip down my cheeks, and I swallow gasping sobs until a heavy hand slaps my face.

Someone drags me away in the opposite direction.

It was the dream that plagued her nights and robbed her sleep. The nightmare had caused her to wet the bed until she was eleven years old. She both loved and hated it. Loved that she saw Birdie and heard her voice. Hated that it always ended with the slap.

Maybe Mr. Madsen dreamed about the war the same way.

THAT NIGHT, RAGNA HEARD MORE words not meant for her ears.

"You can't be serious," Auntie's voice zinged with anger. "Your family would starve while you buy a boat ticket to Norway."

"It's what her family wants." Uncle's voice sounded weary and worried.

"What about what we want?"

"The passage may cost more than our savings. I'm not certain it's even possible."

Their bed squeaked, and Ragna heard the shuffle of dried cornhusks in their mattress.

"I'm with child." Ragna's attention perked. Maybe a girl this time. She would love a little sister. Then she realized from the tone of Auntie's voice that it was not good news. Auntie had been crabby all summer. Now Ragna understood.

A long silence followed.

"You're right," Uncle said. "We can't buy her ticket."

Ragna heard muffled weeping and more squeaks from the old bed.

"We've never asked a penny all these years." Auntie's voice muffled with weeping. "It's the least they could do."

"Just what do you want me to do?" Uncle's voice was low and Ragna strained to hear. "Write a letter and beg for a ticket?"

"If they want her back," Auntie Inga said, "they can send the ticket. They can't expect us to come up with the money."

Ragna gasped at the thought. She would not. They could not make her leave.

"We'll sell the farm eventually and repay them." Uncle's voice sounded bone weary. "It's all we can do."

Another muffled sound and more rustling of the corn shuck mattress. She heard Uncle and Auntie talking about finding work to tide them over. Uncle told her it would all work out, his voice a quiet protection in the darkness. They talked about the possibility of moving in with friends or starting over in California or Oregon.

"We'll stay here a little longer until something works out," Uncle said.

"*Nei!*" Auntie Inga said. "It's a sign. Don't you see? There's no blessing left here. There never was."

When it was finally quiet, Ragna knelt by her cot and prayed a fervent prayer to the Blessed Virgin, that Auntie would love her new baby, that Uncle Evan would find work, and that she could stay in America in spite of her *bestemor's* wishes. She thanked Him that the farm sale had fallen through. Then reconsidered and prayed that He would sell it to someone with money to spend on a ruined farm. She prayed for those with smallpox at Uncle Ole's farm. She ended with her own novena, the prayer she had made up and said every day since the uprising. *Please bring my sister home.*

Ragna reconsidered her words. Uncle said that Birdie would never be able to find her way home. *Holy Mary, Mother of God, help me find my sister.*

"Ragna," Uncle Evan said the next morning after a hurried meal of mush and milk. "I've written your *bestemor* and told her about the grasshopper plague." Ragna knew he avoided the whole truth. "I want you to post it at Van Dyke's Store after you finish the dishes."

Uncle looked so sad, so anxious. Such a kind person deserved better than a field of grasshopper eggs and a panicked bank. She began the tedious process of building up the fire in the cook stove to heat water, pouring hot water into the tin basin along with a handful of soft soap from the gourd on the dry sink, and dipping each bowl and spoon into the hot water and scrubbing with a rag. She scalded the clean dishes with steamy water from the old teakettle on the stove. A basket of eggs waited washing after the dishes.

Ragna would run away before she would go back to Norway. She would earn money to put an ad in the newspaper to find Birdie and write a letter to the governor and tell him about her missing sister.

Auntie Inga fetched another bucket of water, and Sigurd played at Ragna's feet with a wooden spoon. For once, she had time to think. She reached up and fingered the button around her neck, thinking again about her sister. She was soon lost in a delicious daydream.

Fisk meowed and hissed when Sigurd pulled his tail.

Ragna sighed and forced herself back to the duties before her. Mr. Madsen wanted Uncle Evan to travel east with him to help with the harvest. He claimed it was their only chance to earn money. The grasshoppers were patchy, some places were hit while many were not; perhaps they need not travel far. Their discussion never ended and as Ragna left the porch, they still debated whether to head southeast to St. Peter or north to Otter Tail County.

She finished the eggs and hurried to post the letter at Van Dyke's Store. What a relief to get away from the farm and the never-ending discussions.

Grasshoppers crunched under Ragna's feet and she ignored the bleak landscape. August fields and meadows were usually lush and green. Now only brown. *Holy Mary, Mother of God, pray for us in this time of calamity. St. Olaf, rid us of this plague.*

As she walked, she gathered her courage. Maybe she should rip up the letter to *Bestemor* and pretend she had mailed it. There was always the chance Mr. Van Dyke would speak of it, although Ragna thought it unlikely that someone would discuss a missing letter, perhaps a posted letter, but not a missing one.

She knew she was being foolish and yet she felt eyes on her back. Maybe a lurking Indian waiting to avenge his people. She fingered the wax on the envelope and felt it move beneath her fingers. Though her heart pounded and she thought she might faint with pure terror, Ragna pulled the single page from the envelope and read Uncle's large script. It was most unimaginative to stand on the path reading *Bestemor's* letter but there was no comfortable place to hide. She refused to join lurking *skraelings* in the plum thickets surrounding the path.

The letter was brief and to the point:

> *We agree that it is best for Ragna to return home but because*
> *of a locust plague and a national financial crisis, we are unable*
> *to sell the farm as you request. If you would send a ticket for*

Ragna, we will make sure she returns home. We have no funds available to purchase one, although we will continue efforts to sell the farm and will forward the money from its sale whenever the situation turns around.

Her face burned red and she flicked an annoying hopper off the paper. It was as if they discussed a heifer.

Ragna gathered her wits and thought what she could do. If only she could substitute another letter in the envelope. She searched her apron pockets and found a piece of brown wrapping paper rescued from the coffee beans purchased for their journey to Otter Tail County. It would have to do.

She smoothed out the paper and with a stub of lead pencil, wrote a quick note telling that the farm sale had fallen through due to the financial crisis and locusts. Since the farm could not be sold, it was impossible for Ragna to return home. She made no mention of the request for a ticket. The words flowed effortlessly, easily onto the page and Ragna wondered at her new ability to lie to Uncle Evan. Of course, what she wrote was not a lie, just not the entire truth—just as Uncle had not told her the complete truth about the letter to her grandmother. She stuffed it into the envelope and reworked the wax with her thumb.

The hardened wax was impossible to mold. Ragna laid the letter on a huge rock in direct sunlight. While the late-morning sun softened the wax, she painstakingly tore Uncle Evan's letter into a hundred tiny pieces and buried it beneath a wet spot at the side of the road. Then she pressed the soft wax and resumed her trip to town, the letter like a living lie in her hand.

Van Dyke Store stood on the edge of the village. Hard candy of every color and size waited in glass jars for those lucky enough to have a penny. Bins of rolled oats, ground flour, cornmeal, rice, dried beans, sugar, coffee beans, prunes, and dried apples lined the counters. Jugs of molasses, honey, and vinegar perched on a shelf. Spices, salt, pepper, dried fish, tea, and plugs of dried tobacco stuffed every available nook and cranny. Men's boots and ladies' parasols grouped around the door. Bolts of calico and linsey-woolsey stood next to a shelf of books and tools. The store was dark and dusky, and smelled of cinnamon and saddle soap.

Ragna's eyes adjusted to the darkness and fixed on a bolt of the most beautiful blue calico she had ever seen. She would be beautiful like her sister if she had a dress the color of blooming flax. She would add a lace collar, or maybe flower-shaped buttons like the ones in a jar on the counter. Perhaps she could embroider the cuffs.

The scraps would make a beautiful dress for her new baby sister.

"Can I help you, Miss Larson?" Mr. Van Dyke was an old man with a shiny head and a smidge of tobacco in the corners of his mouth. He spat into a brass spittoon at Ragna's feet, and she jumped back a full step, bumping into a young man reading a book in the shadows.

"Excuse me," she said and felt her face flush red to the roots of her hair.

The young man looked up from his book and hurriedly tipped his cap. Ragna had never seen him before. His smooth face quickly grew as red as her own. He was tall, her eyes level with his mouth. She avoided his eyes but a tooth caught her attention. His smile showed a chipped tooth. Just one corner of his right front tooth. She wondered how it had happened, how he had broken such an otherwise perfect tooth in a perfect mouth and smile.

She backed away, placed the letter and penny for postage on the counter and left the store in a whirlwind of confusion.

"Miss Larson," Mr. Van Dyke called out behind her. "Don't you want your uncle's mail?"

She slowed to a stop and forced herself to re-enter the store and accept two letters addressed to Evan.

"*Mange takk,*" she said. "I mean, thank you."

She looked quickly towards the young man to see if he had noticed her slip into Norwegian. He looked quickly away, back at the book held in his hands. She read the title, *The Last of the Mohicans.* His hands were rough and scratched and he had lost the top of his ring finger. A chipped tooth and a missing finger tip. He must have been in an accident.

She left the store at a more sedate pace. She thought she caught a glimpse of a face in the store window but walked calmly over the hill. When she was beyond sight of the store, Ragna picked up her skirts and ran home. How careless of her to speak Norwegian. She was an American, after all.

Who could he be?

And what, in heaven's name, was a Mohican?

9

The Country is Flooded with Forged Railroad Bonds
$\qquad$ St. Paul Dispatch, *July 19, 1873*

HIS NAME WAS ANDERS VOLLEN. Uncle Evan brought him by the cabin before he and Milton left to find work.

"I found a hired man to stay with you until we get back," Uncle Evan said as he introduced Anders to the family. "He's agreed to work for room and board."

Anders nodded to Auntie Inga with hat in hand. He then greeted the boys, shaking Gunnar's hand as an equal until Gunnar's chest almost burst the buttons on his shirt. However, when he saw Ragna holding Sigurd by the stove, he flushed and looked down at his scuffed shoes.

"This is Ragna Larson," Uncle Evan said. "She's our goddaughter and lives with us."

The baby fussed and Ragna used the chance to slip out of the kitchen, unable to stop the words that reached her ears.

"She's a pretty girl—almost of marrying age, Anders!" Milton said.

Then explosive laughter.

Ragna busied herself with Sigurd, looking away from the men and pretending she had not heard.

Uncle kissed Auntie Inga and the baby and told the boys to mind their mother. He called out a good-bye to Ragna before grabbing a rucksack of food and supplies for his journey. Then he and Milton walked north from the farm.

It was ridiculous. They could get along without Anders's help.

Ragna looked at him from behind the woodpile as she draped clothes on the line. She carefully hung the rags out of sight, along with her drawers and camisole. Anders showed Gunnar and Knut how to tie a jib on the porch railing. His blond hair made him seem almost one of the family. The twins gathered closer to watch.

"I was a seaman," Anders said. "You need to tie a strong knot, one that will hold when a North Sea swell almost knocks you into the water."

"Did a swell almost knock you into the sea?" Sverre lisped in his most serious voice.

"See my finger?" Anders held up the finger without a tip. "I wrapped the rope around my hand for safety during a storm. When the rope snapped in the wind, it cut my finger right off."

"*Nei,*" said Knut. "You're fibbing."

"I fib not," Anders said. "And I chipped my tooth when it knocked me on deck." He grimaced, showing his teeth. "It was then I decided to leave the sea and head for firm ground and safe harbor."

"Did you catch a *lutefisk*?" Lewis asked.

"Dumb head!" Gunnar said. "*Lutesfisk* is cod."

"Don't call him names," Sverre said. "I'll tell Far and he'll whip you when he gets home."

"He might never come home," Gunnar said. "Maybe a storm will come up on the North Sea and wash him overboard."

"He's not on the sea." Sverre wailed. "Far isn't on the North Sea."

Lewis put a comforting arm around his twin's shoulder and cast an angry look at Gunnar. Ragna hung the last soaker over the clothesline and headed for the stoop.

"Shut up, Gunnar," Knut said. "Don't make the little boys cry."

"You're telling me to shut up?" Gunnar hooked Knut around the neck with an elbow and soon they locked in combat, rolling around the dusty ground.

"Boys!" Ragna scooped Sigurd into her arms to keep him away from the roughhousing. Auntie came out of the house with an angry look on her face.

"Do you want a *chiliwink*?" Auntie said while Anders pulled the boys apart. "I'll give you a knock on the side of your head!"

Gunnar boasted a split lip and Knut a bloody nose.

"Shame on you," Auntie said. "You're too big to fight. And with Far gone! Sit out on the stoop until you kiss and make up."

"I won't kiss him!" Gunnar said with a pouty look on his face.

"Then you'll sit there until you do." Auntie wore a tired look, maybe a worried look. In fact, she looked close to tears. It reminded Ragna of what she had overheard in the night, that Auntie would have another baby. Maybe that is why Uncle arranged for Anders to stay with them. Auntie picked up the egg basket. "Come, Sverre and Lewis. We'll gather the eggs."

"Mor." Sverre pulled at his mother's apron. "A rope bit off Anders's finger."

Auntie Inga looked down at Sverre's tear-stained face, put the basket on the ground and picked him up in her arms. She gasped and quickly set him down again. "You're getting too big for me, little man." She rubbed her back.

"Are you all right, Missus?" Anders dropped a load of kitchen wood in the box beside the door. He scooped up the twins, one in each arm, dancing around the yard until they giggled with delight. "Your *mor* would need to be a giant to handle such big boys." He plopped them down beside Auntie Inga.

Auntie took Anders's hand and looked at his missing finger. "It must have hurt terribly," she said.

"*Ja,*" Anders said. "Like the blazes. But it's over now, and I'm none the worse for wear."

The look on his face made Ragna wonder if he left a mother in Norway.

He turned pink around the ears when he noticed Ragna looking at them.

"We'll gather the eggs, Missus." He whistled as he picked up the egg basket. "Have you kissed yet?" He thumped Knut and Gunnar on their heads with a bent finger. "Hurry up so you can go with us. We'll race to find the most eggs."

"He's a nice boy," Auntie Inga said as she watched the boys kiss and run after Anders. She and Ragna returned to the house. Auntie headed right for the dry sink and began peeling potatoes for dinner. Ragna took the broom, swept up a few grasshoppers into the dustpan, and dropped them into the fire. They hissed as they burned and released their acrid odor into the room. "He needed a place to stay, and we needed a man around the house. Sometimes things just work out."

"Where's he from?"

"Tolga, not far away from where Evan was born," Auntie said. "He reminds me of my brother."

"Uncle Trygve?" Ragna loved Auntie's stories about her life in the Old Country.

"He talked of coming to America but I haven't heard from him since Winter Day. "

What would it be like to have a real brother? If Baby Evan were alive, he would be the same age as Gunnar, not grown up like Trygve or Anders. Still, he would be company. Ragna reached up and fingered the button.

Birdie and Baby Evan stand beside the lilac bushes.

He looks at me with round blue eyes and a curious smile, narrowing his eyelids for a better look. "It's me, your brother."

"I thought you were . . ." I feast on the look of them, my little brother old enough to talk, my little sister so grown up and pretty. "I'm glad you're not . . ."

"Dead." His eyes accuse me and his smile turns downward into a scowl. "You only think of me as dead."

"But your gravestone," I say in defense. "You're buried in the family plot."

"But I don't have a stone," Birdie says. "And you think I'm dead."

"Ragna," Auntie Inga said. "Don't just stand there. Finish up and check on the twins."

"Of course." Ragna shook her head back to the present. At the end of the stoop, she shaded her eyes and saw the boys returning from the barn, Anders carrying the basket.

It was after the noon meal when Auntie took sick. She wobbled on her feet as she carried the stew pot to the table. Ragna noticed the white around her mouth, how her hands trembled. Before she could even think to act, Anders leapt to his feet and took the iron pot from her hands.

"*Mange takk!*" Auntie grabbed the table edge for support.

"What's wrong?" Ragna said.

"I don't know." Auntie's voice came out in a whisper as she lowered herself to the wooden bench beside Knut and leaned her head on the table. "I'm sick."

Ragna felt Auntie Inga's forehead. It dripped cold sweat. "You need to be in bed."

Auntie tried to stand, but her legs bobbled. "I'm too weak!" Panic sounded in her voice.

"I'll help you." Anders gently lifted her in his arms and carried her to the bed in the corner of the room.

A dark stain covered the back of Auntie's dress, and a fresh trail of blood dripped from the hem of her skirt. *Dear God!* Auntie was having the baby.

"Prop her feet up." Ragna pulled the feather pillow from underneath Auntie's head and passed it to Anders. When Auntie's feet lay higher than her head, the cornstalks rustled with her shivers. Ragna covered her with a blanket. Her mind scrambled to think what to do. She reached for an extra quilt from the chest. "Knut, get the clean rags off the line."

"What's wrong?" Anders said. The boys stared in shocked silence and Sigurd pounded his tin cup on the table.

Ragna had forgotten Anders was even there and startled at the sound of his voice.

"She's having a baby," Ragna said. It was not the subject for polite company and one that she would rather not discuss with this handsome seaman, but it was the truth. "It's coming early." Ragna felt Inga's forehead again.

"Is there a doctor?" Anders said.

"*Nei,*" Ragna said. "But maybe Mr. Van Dyke knows of someone."

"Who is the midwife in the village?"

"Auntie Inga," Ragna said. "She's the only one. Sometimes I go with her but I'm still learning."

The boys lined up beside the bed, Knut fetched the clean rags. "I brought the towels, too."

"Is Mor all right?" Lewis said. Tears and snot covered his face. He wiped his nose on his shirtsleeve. "Will she die?"

"*Nei*," Anders said and picked up the baby from the floor. "Your *mor* sleeps. She needs us all to be very quiet. Gunnar, you must run to Van Dyke's Store and ask him to fetch a midwife."

Gunnar paled. "But I'll have to speak American. I'm not sure I can."

"You can do it," Anders said in English. "Tell him your *mor* is sick and your *far* is gone."

"Hurry." Ragna smiled encouragingly at Gunnar who looked at his mother with a worried frown about his mouth. "Get going!"

Gunnar ran out of the house. Ragna took a clean rag from the shelf and dipped it in the water bucket. She wrung it out and carefully laid it across Auntie's forehead. Her eyes fluttered when the cold rag touched her skin and she whispered something that Ragna could not hear.

Ragna leaned closer to Auntie. "More rags," she said. "I'm losing it." Her words thudded heavy with grief. Last night she had been unhappy about the new baby. Maybe she now regretted what she had said.

Anders gathered the boys and herded them to the barn, lugging Sigurd in the crook of his left elbow. Thank God, he was there to help.

Ragna searched the ragbag for every available piece of cloth. She poured water into the metal dishpan and set it carefully on the stove to heat. "What else should I do?"

Auntie Inga cried out sharply and pushed a pile of rags beneath her. When Auntie pulled the rags out from under her, a tiny form lay on the bloody cloth.

Ragna lifted the rags and laid them on the table. Then mustering all her courage, she picked up the little one, so small she fit in the palm of her hand. Holding her felt like carrying a mouse—except there was no movement.

None at all. Strands of dark curls lay against the little head and Ragna could see veins through transparent skin.

"It's a girl." She did not know she was crying until she wiped her eyes. "Do you want to see her?"

"Take it out." Auntie turned her face to the wall and threw her right arm over her eyes. "Don't let the boys see."

"But Auntie."

"Mind me." Auntie's voice sounded cold as well water in January.

Auntie Inga had always wanted a daughter, had laughed and teased every time one of the boys had been born. Now she would not look. Ragna pulled a clean dishtowel hanging behind the wood box and swaddled the little body, gently pulling the corner of the towel over her face. She listened, expecting to hear sobs from Auntie's bed—but only silence.

"Auntie, are you all right?" Ragna's voice echoed in the empty room.

"*Ja*," she said with a voice as dull and flat as an old knife. "Do as I say."

10

A.B. Wileus UNDERTAKER! Coffins, Caskets, Shrouds and Metallic Burial Cases, A Hearse and Carriage Furnished.

St. Paul Dispatch, July 20, 1873

RAGNA CARRIED THE TOWEL-WRAPPED bundle to the big rock behind the cabin, cradling it in her arms. The weight of it was as nothing, like carrying a lead pencil wrapped in a cloth, and she clutched it tightly lest it fall out and get lost. She had obeyed Auntie and taken the baby out of the cabin. She did not know what to do next.

Stalkers liten, the poor little one was not to blame. If only the grasshoppers had not ruined everything. Surely, Auntie Inga would have welcomed the daughter she had always wanted. Ragna wondered if not wanting a baby caused a woman to miscarry. Ragna had never heard of such a thing. If only, there was someone to ask.

Dried grass rustled behind her and she turned to see Anders. She avoided his eyes, looking instead at the chip in his tooth. This time there was no smile.

"Is the missus all right?" he said.

"*Ja.*" Deadness muffled her words.

"Is that the baby?"

She could only nod her head.

"I'll get a shovel," he said.

Mrs. Cary hurried up the path from town with Gunnar who carried a large woven basket. He had given the English message after all. Good boy. Ragna walked carefully toward them, carrying her precious burden. She told them what had happened.

"Gunnar," she said. "The boys are in the haymow. Watch them for a while."

"It's a terrible thing, terrible." Mrs. Cary fanned herself with a wrinkled white handkerchief as Gunnar returned the basket to Mrs. Cary and ran towards the haymow. "How is Inga?"

"All right," Ragna said.

"That's it?" Mrs. Carrie nodded her chin towards Ragna's bundle.

"*Ja.*" Ragna did not want nosy Mrs. Cary gossiping about this baby all over the community. She would offer no information unless asked directly.

Mrs. Cary nodded grimly when Anders brought the shovel. After squaring her shoulders and taking a deep breath, she opened the cabin door and went in. Ragna caught a faint odor of fresh blood before the door closed.

Ragna sighed with relief. In spite of her nosiness, Mrs. Cary was most capable. She was indeed a gossip, but a good friend of Auntie Inga's. No doubt, the basket held a loaf of bread or a pot of soup. Maybe even a jar of honey. The Carys were known for beekeeping. It was the way of the settlements to help a neighbor when they were sick or in trouble.

Ragna looked to Anders. Without a word, they walked away from the house to the cemetery plot at the far side of the farm. Hoppers crunched beneath their feet, almost slippery at times. Once, Ragna lurched to one side, off-balance from holding the little bundle in her arms. Anders reached out a steadying hand, and Ragna felt a hot flush flood color into her cheeks.

"*Mange takk.*" She righted herself and readjusted her weightless load. She must be more careful lest she totally humiliate herself in front of the young man.

"Do you want me to carry it?"

"*Nei.*" Ragna shook her head. She could not explain it but felt the need to hold on to this small one forever. She dreaded putting it into the earth.

"It's St. Olaf's Day," Anders said. "Did you remember?"

A wave of emotion swept over Ragna and she reached out to steady herself on Anders's arm, almost without thinking. She remembered the sound of her mother's voice crying out to St. Olaf during Baby Evan's birth so long ago, the taste of sweet soup brought by Mrs. Spitsberg to celebrate, and her *far's* face as he laughed and bragged that his son might grow up to be president some day. She probed each memory, hoping for more, but they dissipated. Like always.

Her legs shook and wobbled. When they arrived at the cemetery, Anders pulled a dead log beside the smoke-charred chimney still standing among the burned-out ruins of the old cabin. He motioned for Ragna to sit down. A scratchy branch poked her in the face and Anders broke it off, throwing it into the grove where a mourning dove sang its mournful dirge.

As Anders turned the first full shovel of dirt, the fragrant loam tickled her nose and made her wish for fresh flowers to place on the grave. Of course, there were no flowers since the grasshoppers. Anders's shovel clinked against a stone.

Did her parents and little brother see them here? Would they welcome such a small one into heaven? Then a sudden, horrible revelation; the baby was unbaptized. She could not go to heaven.

Sobs burst forth from the deepest place in her heart, the place that remembered her mother's screams and the face in the window. She cried so hard the dishtowel sogged with tears.

His touch was tentative. He sat beside her on the log. "Are you all right?" Anders took the weightless burden from her arms and placed it gently in his lap. "Don't cry, Ragna."

"She wouldn't even look at her." Sobs muffled her words, and she gasped a choking breath. "She didn't want another baby. I heard her tell Uncle Evan." She wiped her nose on her apron but the sobs continued. "Even God doesn't want her."

"What do you mean?"

"She's not baptized." The words choked from her, from the deepest place inside of her. "She can't go to heaven."

Anders returned the baby to Ragna's arms. "Wait here." He ran back towards the house, his boots heavy on the denuded ground, little puffs of dust stirred by each step. She thought to call out to him, to ask him not to leave her alone, that there might be *skraelings*. Her voice was silenced by the weightless burden in her lap.

Surely, the Indians were long gone. She tried not to imagine one jumping out to snatch her. She twisted her brain to think of something else. The graves of her parents and brother lay before her. She noticed the birth date carved into her brother's marker, July 20, 1862. St. Olaf's Day. Would someone carve a marker for this helpless child in her arms?

Anders hurried back, holding his catechism in one hand and a rusty tin can filled with water in the other.

"It's an emergency," he said. "We can baptize her."

He turned his catechism to the back page entitled, "A Short Form for Holy Baptism in Cases of Necessity." He held it in front of her eyes, forcing her to read the words.

"But it's too late."

"*Nei*," Anders said firmly. "God will grant the gift of heaven if we baptize her before we bury her."

Ragna eyed the can of water with skepticism. It was an emergency. The catechism plainly said that in the absence of the pastor, any Christian might administer Holy Baptism.

"What's her name?" Anders read over the pages. "She needs one for baptism."

A beautiful name leapt into Ragna's consciousness and onto her tongue. "Ann Elin." The unwanted little girl would bear the name of Ragna's mother, the name on the gravestone before her.

Anders tenderly pulled back the towel covering the perfectly formed head. Ragna thought how the baby looked like a china doll, every feature perfect, just smaller. His voice squeaked, and she saw his hand tremble, sloshing water over the sides of the old can.

"Ann Elin Jacobson, I baptize thee in the name of the Father and of the Son and of the Holy Ghost. Amen."

He put his fingers into the water and flicked them across the tiny head. Ragna felt a few drops splash on her arms and hoped they would somehow strengthen her as well, fill her with the Holy Ghost so that she could carry today's grief. She closed her eyes and prayed with all her might that it would be so, that Ann Elin would enter heaven's gates and that she would find the grace to go back and face Auntie Inga's stony face.

They stood awkwardly beside the open grave. Anders covered the baby's face once more and gently laid her in the grave. He quickly covered her with dirt.

"The catechism says to pray the Lord's Prayer."

The familiar words calmed and comforted. Ragna's arms felt lonely and lost, almost a physical sensation. Anders's voice startled her.

"These must be the graves of your parents."

Ragna looked up into the bluest eyes she had ever seen. They held hers and she found it difficult to answer.

"*Ja.*" There were a hundred words she could say but none came to mind.

"How did they die?"

"The Red Men."

He looked down at his shoes and tucked the catechism inside his shirt. She wished there was something she could say to thank him for the baptism. She was confirmed herself and never thought of it, although she should have. If she ever became a midwife, she would carry her catechism with her in case an emergency might arise.

Maybe she would choose another path. She did not care to face such sorrow again. And even though the little one was baptized . . . Ragna shook her head. She would not think on it any longer. It was in God's hands.

"I need to check on the boys," Anders said. "And do the chores."

As he turned away, she spoke. "*Mange tussen takk.*" An insistent blue jay chattered in the ironwood tree and a blow snake slithered behind the broken chimney.

"*Welkommen,*" he said.

Ann Elin. It was easier when the baby had a real name.

11

Bulls and Bears! Indications of Another Panic on Wall Street. Jay Gould Reported in a Tight Place.

St. Paul Dispatch, *July 26, 1873*

IT WAS ALMOST ST. BARTHOLOMEW'S DAY, and they'd had found no work. Milton and Evan straggled northward, tired and footsore. Farmers needed help but had no money to pay for it.

At Millerville, a German Catholic community, they picked rocks in exchange for a meal. They worked all morning in scorching heat that droned with cicadas and lazy bumblebees. Boulders thrown up by spring frosts littered the fields. Evan remembered how Cleng Peterson had written back to Norway saying there were no rocks to pick in America's fields. Obviously, Cleng had not visited Millerville.

The harvest looked promising. In the adjoining field, wheat rippled in the hazy sun, just starting to fill in the kernels. Probably another week or two before a man could take his cradle to it.

Evan's wheat would have been the same if only the grasshoppers had skipped over their farm. He could have both paid his note and provided Ragna a ticket home. Maybe he could have purchased the farm from Ragna on shares or secured a mortgage. He hefted another stone and tossed it onto a sledge pulled by an old nag of a mule with a half-torn ear on its gray head.

It did no good to think about it. All ruined now with the grasshoppers and bank panic.

An Urbank farmer suggested they head east toward Parkers Prairie, another said they should travel all the way to St. Paul. A traveler on the trail said they may as well go home—because of the panic, there was no money anywhere.

Eijnar Carlson, a Dane living south of Leaf Mountain, gave them cool water from his well. "Try the Mormons in Clitherall," he said. "They're the only ones with both money and standing grain."

'The Saints?" Milton said. "I didn't know they were in this country."

"First settlers in these parts," Carlson said. "Bought their land from the Ojibwa."

"I've heard they're clannish." Milton took the remaining water in the hollowed gourd and threw it over his head and down his back, drying his face with the back of his hands and combing through his hair with wet fingers. "Maybe they wouldn't give work to someone of a different religion."

"You've nothing to lose by trying," Carlson said. "Ask for Syl Wheeling. I've had dealings with him. He's an honest man."

After a quick nooning of stewed muskrat and with general directions to Clitherall, they traveled north. They climbed Leaf Mountain, speechless with the panorama before them.

"My God," Evan swallowed a quick stab of homesickness. "It reminds me of home."

The strong emotion surprised him. Leaf Mountain, far different from the snow-topped mountains of Norway, offered the best view of the area. Acres of hardwood forest spread out, interspersed with blue lakes and open prairies. August meant everything was green. Shade after shade of greens. All wedged against a blue sky bluer than the fjords back home. Bird song filled the air along with droning flies and leaves whispering in the wind.

He let the beauty soak into his troubled mind, felt his body relax. Surely if God cared enough to make such a beautiful world, He would also help him feed his family in such troubled times.

Evan dropped to the ground and removed his left boot to inspect a blister. How he wished his *far* were alive. He needed advice. Funny, as a boy he had resented every word his father spoke to him. Now he scraped his memories for words that might still guide him.

"Look." Milton pointed toward the east where a farmer burned brush and slash off newly cleared fields. "That's smoke from Parkers Prairie." Milton settled on a big rock. "And Clitherall is in that direction." He pointed to the north. "Maybe I can see buildings—but it might be my eyes fooling me."

"Have you known Mormons?" Evan reached down, plucked a cocklebur from his trousers, and struggled to put on his boot. He slapped at a pesky deer fly buzzing around his head.

"Lots of them in Illinois."

"I heard once that the Mormon men have horns on their heads like yearling calves." Evan felt foolish even repeating such gossip. He understood so little English that he may have met them and never known. "And that their women have noses like fish-hooks."

"They're hated." Milton chuckled and slapped at a trio of deer flies eager to draw his blood. "They go against the churches. But they're hard workers. Keep to themselves." Milton stood up and stretched. "And I saw some mighty pretty girls in their group. Neither horns nor fish-hook noses."

They headed down the mountain, going in the direction of Clitherall. Evan's left heel brought a limp with each step. It seemed they would never get there.

The land changed to rolling hills and potholes filled with geese and ducks. His stomach rumbled in protest at the cold creek water that was his supper. The August night had almost a hint of chill in the air, reminding him of the season. They needed to find work soon or the harvest would be over.

They saw the fields before they spotted the town. A field of wheat looked ready for the scythe. Oats and barley grew in a spot of low land near the footpath. Several stacks of hay perched strategically close to the barns.

"Hear it talking to us?" Milton said. "It's telling us to come and harvest it before the hoppers come."

Evan hoped there would be no grasshoppers in this beautiful place with its lakes and rolling hills. "There it is." Milton's voice sounded hopeful, younger. Ahead were log barns and grazing cattle in fenced pastures. A sign boasted, "The Hope of Zion Branch." Stout log cabins lined the city square where older boys and barefoot girls giggled and played by a rope swing. A young girl squealed as she sailed through the air on the swing with her skirts flaring around her feet. Dogs barked a cautious welcome and one of the older boys looked their way in greeting. The sunset streaked orange and pink to the west and with the setting sun, hordes of mosquitoes swarmed and tormented.

The settlement beside the lake purred with smug prosperity.

They approached the young people, all about the age of Ragna or older, and asked for Mr. Wheeling.

"Yes sir." A young man brushed a lock of auburn hair away from his eyes as he spoke, his face pimply alongside the freckles filling his cheeks. A wispy growth of red beard lined his upper lip and chin. "That's my pa. I'll take you to him."

They followed the young man to a small cabin built on the shores of Clitherall Lake.

"Welcome, Friends. You have traveled far." Mr. Wheeling leaned on a diamond-willow cane at the door. His red hair was peppered with streaks of gray although his beard was pure ginger. Evan guessed him to be about ten years older than they were. "Come in and rest yourselves."

Evan entered the cabin cautiously, half expecting a devil of some kind to leap out and try to convert him from Martin Luther's true faith. Milton seemed to have no such qualms. Evan held his hat in hand, trying not to limp from the blisters on his left heel.

"You're hurt," the missus said. Her nose was decidedly normal and the mound under her apron told of another Wheeling on the way. "What happened to your foot?"

Before long, Evan soaked his foot in a basin of salted water as they feasted on blackberry pie from tin plates and cups of cool buttermilk.

"This is mighty fine pie," Milton said.

The missus jumped to her feet and served them each another slice. She had soft brown eyes and a pleasant smile. "The young-uns picked the blackberries just today. There's a fair crop if we can get them before the bears."

She scraped a few remaining berries onto their plates, leaving an empty pie tin.

"They're sweet," Milton said.

Evan envied his fluent English. The words always caught in Evan's throat when he felt nervous or tried too hard. He sat awkward and tongue-tied.

"It's maple sugar," Mr. Wheeling said. "We have two sugar camps and gather enough sap to keep the whole settlement in sugar with a little leftover to trade."

"It's good." Evan felt happy to add even a sentence to the conversation.

"And where do you trade?" Milton said.

"Have you met Lying Jack?" Mr. Wheeling said. "He stops by regular and trades for skins and crops or whatever else we can grow or make."

"Lying Jack?" Milton said with a laugh. "A name to scare an honest man."

"Yes," Mr. Wheeling said with a chuckle. "We watch him close and trust the Good Lord to give us wisdom. Though others have had problems with his measure, Lying Jack has always been fair with us."

Evan thought how that was the way with all of them, Mormon or Lutheran. A man did the best he could and left it in the hands of Almighty God. It was what Evan's father might have said. Evan breathed a sigh of relief.

Mr. Wheeling rubbed his right knee while he spoke. "And what brings you to the Branch of Zion?"

His voice was kind and Evan forgot to stammer. "Grasshoppers." His voice broke and he swallowed hard. "They took my crop."

Mr. Wheeling leaned forward with his elbows on the table. "What do they look like?" His eyes glittered in the firelight. A small child cried out from the loft and the missus excused herself.

Evan described the insects and the terrible day they devoured his farm.

"Locusts!" Mr. Wheeling said his voice dropped to a whisper. "And the shape of the locusts was like horses prepared for battle; and on their heads were crowns of gold, and their faces were like the faces of men."

Evan's heart skipped a beat.

"Book of Revelation, chapter 9 and verse 7." Mr. Wheeling's voice trailed off and a child cried out again from the loft. "The first settlement in Utah was almost destroyed by them," Mr. Wheeling leaned even closer and his eyes took on a strange light. "But God sent a flock of seagulls to save their crops."

"It must have been quite a swarm of seagulls to eat them," Milton said. "Millions of hoppers hit Evan's farm."

"The people repented of their evil ways," Mr. Wheeling said. "The locusts were sent as judgment—they had grown proud in their accomplishments and forgotten God."

Evan had known it all along but had not put words to it. The grasshoppers were God's judgment upon him because of his blind, foolish trust. Prideful trust, believing he knew better than others did, that he could handle it. His friendship with Crooked Lightning caused the death of Ragna's family. The old familiar panic start to rise up in his chest and he gripped the edge of the table until his hands hurt.

"We're looking for work." Milton's voice was calm. "Do you need men?"

"My knee is bad and I've fields to harvest." Mr. Wheeling's voice was even. "My boys can help but only Elijah is grown enough to do a man's share."

"We won't be a bother to your missus," Evan said. He willed the fear to leave him. He drew a deep breath and tried to sound normal. "We'll sleep in your barn and keep to ourselves."

In the end, a handshake sealed it.

12

A MORMON SENSATION! Brigham Young's Seventeenth Wife Sues for a Divorce.

St. Paul Dispatch, *July 26, 1873*

THE MORMONS WERE A STRANGE LOT. During their month-long stay, Evan found them to be cheerful in all weather, industrious and clear thinking. They never shirked a task or spoke evil of anyone. On the contrary, they seemed to go out of their way to make the best of any situation and keep a positive outlook on life. Their optimism troubled Evan. They tried much harder than any Lutherans he had known.

The first day started with prayers and Bible reading along with an early breakfast of cornmeal mush slathered with maple syrup. Purple banded the pre-dawn horizon while robins sang their hearts out in the standing grove of oaks behind the house.

"Eat hearty, men," Mr. Wheeling said. "We'll cradle and bundle oats today."

"*Mange takk.*" Evan gladly accepted another serving. He was hungry. The long walk and hard labor along the way had depleted his stores. The maple syrup was almost like eating candy for breakfast. How his boys would love it.

The missus showed a rounded belly as she reached across the table with more food. She reminded him of Inga back home, sending a stab of worry through him. Thank God, Ragna and Anders were there to help Inga. It was too much—the worry of the farm, the grasshoppers, the baby.

Nine children sat around the wooden benches, Elijah the oldest and Marion the youngest. The family ran mostly to boys, Evan noticed. They would be a mighty work force in a few years, as his own would be. A boy worked for his father until the age of majority. At twenty-one, he was free to go out on his own. He wondered if it was the same for the Saints.

"We'll start with the southwest forty," Mr. Wheeling said. "It's a fair yield."

He pushed back from the table, pulled his cane toward him, and grimaced as he stood to his feet.

"Watch that knee," the missus said. "Don't overdo." Her face creased with concern.

Evan took comfort that their help was necessary. It was hard to get the work done even with both knees in good health. A bad one meant a poor showing, no matter how you looked at it.

Evan calculated twenty dollars would buy enough food to get them through the winter. He would buy shot for his old Danzig shotgun and let Gunnar hunt for deer and elk. They could salt a supply of fish for the winter. Bass hungered in the fall. They would get by somehow. As they trudged through the dewy grass on the way to the oat field, Evan was feeling good. He had made the right decision to come north.

However, when they reached the field, the truth smacked him in the face. Twelve other men and boys gathered at the field, picked up their scythes, and started cutting. Evan burned with humiliation. They had come begging for a handout and in kindness. Mr. Wheeling had obliged. Evan reddened, and not just from the morning sun peeping over the trees.

The hot August sun quickly burned away the dew clinging to the oats, the heads bent over from the weight of grain. The oats swayed in the breeze with bowed heads the color of straw. Evan shook away the memory of how the sun had danced off Lewis's hair before the hoppers struck.

"Break into pairs," Mr. Wheeling said.

Evan walked over beside Milton who cradled the scythe. Milton sliced through the oat stalks with practiced strength and Evan bundled the fallen grain into sheaves, an efficient operation that felled the grain almost effortlessly, leaving standing shocks in uneven rows like Indian teepees scattered through the field.

Evan kept working until mid-morning when three girls from the settlement carried pails of vinegar water and a dishpan of fresh doughnuts, still warm from the frying pan.

"No coffee," grumbled Milton in a voice just loud enough for Evan to hear. "Damn the religion that steals a man's coffee."

It was their only complaint of the Saints. The food was excellent, the conversation interesting, the folks exemplary in all areas. But no coffee. Not even tea. Joseph Smith had been strict about that.

"*Uff da.*" Evan hoisted a sweating iron dipper to his lips.

"Hot enough for you?" Mr. Wheeling plopped in the shade at the side of the field. "At this rate we'll have the heaviest part finished by noon."

"Mr. Wheeling." Evan's voice trembled and he felt he was treading on dangerous ground, that they might lose out altogether. "It looks like you have plenty of help already. Maybe you don't need us."

"Please, call my Syl." Chaff sprinkled over his face and beard. "And yes, we help each other in our community." He swatted at a deer fly buzzing around his sweaty head. "But it is my responsibility to contribute, and as you see," he pointed to his leg. "I'm not carrying my load."

"So you're paying us to help your neighbors?" Milton said.

"We own everything in common," Syl said. "Strictly speaking, I own nothing and yet at the same time I own everything."

"Like a family operation," Milton said.

"Something like that." Syl slapped his right cheek with the flat of his hand and flicked a deer fly to the side. "We have covenanted together in the Name of God to help each other in the wilderness." He rubbed his knee and struggled up to his feet. "We hope to create a village where all men are treated like brothers, where no one suffers want."

"But how did you file for your land if it is all owned in common?" Evan was too interested in the topic to be nervous, and the English words came without a hint of stutter.

"We bought our land from the Ojibwa," Syl said. "We've treated them as the Good Book says, and they've been honest in return."

Lars and his missus had said the same but were killed anyway. The dark feeling started in his chest, and Evan forced himself back to work. The other men were already heading for the field. Evan found himself working next to Syl Wheeling's son, Elijah.

"How's Bertha?" A younger boy jostled Elijah deliberately on his way to another part of the field. Elijah blushed and busied himself with his scythe, the falling grain golden and prickly.

"What's this?" Milton said as he gathered and tied a sheave. "A sweetheart?"

"Maybe," Elijah said and pointed to a clump of sugar maple trees across the field. He seemed anxious to change the subject. "There's one of our sugar camps. We tap the trees every spring."

The rest of the morning passed in a flurry of deer flies and falling grain.

"Elijah," Milton said. "What do you know of Congress land?"

"Danes settled about ten miles away in a place called Tordenskjold. There's still good land open."

They talked about the possibilities of the unclaimed land, the fertility, the hunting.

"Look for sugar maples if you stake a claim," Elijah said. "Lying Jack takes all the sugar we make and begs for more."

The field soon lay naked before them except for the standing shocks. The sun stood directly overhead. Syl had been right. The Saints had accomplished much in a short time. It would have taken several days if only he and Milton were doing the work.

They trudged to the Wheeling cabin for dinner. The other men waved sweaty hands in farewell and left to return to their own families. They were indeed a strange lot.

"We'll do barley tomorrow," Elijah said. "And then corn."

Evan's throat ached when he thought what his own corn and wheat would have brought if they had just had time to harvest. He felt the rub of his boot on his blister and sniffed the strong smell of his own sweat. Judgment of God or not, he was not done for yet. They would make it somehow.

It was Milton's idea.

"Why don't we file on Congress land and live as neighbors?"

It was a gamble. But all of life was a gamble. His only alternative was to head west and seek work on a stage line. That meant his family would grow up without him. Or he would drag them along out west. Something Inga would hate. Months on the trail. Uncivilized country still troubled by the Red Men. No way for his boys to grow up. Maybe the hoppers would be gone by the time Ragna married and was old enough to care for the farm herself. Maybe it would never recover.

He would have to forget about Ragna and think instead of his family.

"Lying Jack pays five dollars for a fox, three or four for a mink, and two and half dollars for a wolf pelt. Hell, he pays ten to twelve cents a piece for muskrats." Milton paused to spit a perfect stream of tobacco at the end of the row and looked back to make sure no Mormon had heard him swear. "We could trap a hundred muskrats easy. We'd make money moving up here."

"But I know nothing about hunting or preparing hides."

"You don't have to know anything. Gunnar's old enough to run a trap line, and Knut can help him."

Evan's back ached by the time the last sheaf of wheat was tossed up on the wagon. The dust stuck to his sweaty face and arms, causing an irritating itch that would not go away.

"How about a quick jump in the lake?" Milton said. "I'd rather cool off than eat."

Elijah Wheeling joined them as Evan and Milton jogged toward the lake, peeling off their clothes as they went, diving into the cool water.

"Blood suckers on this end," Elijah said. "It's mud bottom."

"Have you been on the other side?" Evan said after he came to the surface and spewed out a stream of water from pursed lips. He thought to look around at available Congress Land before returning home.

"Yes, we have a sugar camp every spring on the other side of Battle Lake. Last spring we got sixty barrels of sap."

"Good land?" Evan floated, letting his arms drift in the water and the cool water drip off his face.

"More prairie, not so many hills. And richer soil than here. I'm thinking of staking a claim myself."

"Why would you leave your father's farm?" Milton said as he pulled a bloodsucker off his chest and threw it toward the shore.

"A man likes to have his own place," Elijah said gravely.

"A girl!" Milton said. "You're getting married!"

"Nothing's settled yet."

"Was she with you at the courting swing last night?" Milton said. "I'm thinking of visiting the swing myself."

The Saints called the swing in the middle of the village the courting swing because of the many romances nurtured there. In the evenings, after supper, the older children gathered for fellowship as witnessed their first night in town.

"Perhaps we'll be neighbors," Milton said.

Evan felt a twinge of guilt for considering such a bold move without consulting Inga. Nevertheless, times were desperate, and he wanted her settled before her next laying-in. It would be rough going the first year or two. They would have to live in a dugout—not easy with six children and a new baby on the way. Inga said it was time to get their own place. Here was his chance.

13

H.E. Gerry, of Garden City, Reports that the Grasshoppers are Very Thick.

St. Paul Dispatch, *August 30, 1873*

Please," Gunnar said. His pleading eyes were hard to resist. "Let me go to the store."

Nothing would have made Ragna happier than to leave the house and its desolation and run to the store. Maybe Mr. Van Dyke had new yard goods in stock. There might be the chance to glimpse the sewing machine Auntie Inga wanted. She sighed, picked Sigurd up from the floor, and wiped his face with the corner of her apron. Gunnar had chores to do, chores that someone else would have to do if she let him go.

Maybe there would be a letter from Uncle Evan. He could not stay away forever. Her eyes scanned the empty skies. Perfect harvesting weather. Maybe Uncle would send a few dollars home. They were out of flour.

"All right, then." She watched Gunnar's face crack into a big grin. "But wash your face and comb your hair."

"You're worse than Mor."

"And take Knut with you," Ragna said. Knut would love going to the store with Gunnar, although she knew Gunnar would never think to ask him along.

Ragna busied herself with the washing and ironing as the boys whooped and hollered down the path. She hoped with all her might that there would be a letter from Uncle Evan. Maybe good news would make Auntie feel better, cheer her up a little.

Auntie Inga stayed mostly in bed since the baby. She had given over the outdoor chores completely to Anders without a single directive. She did not tell Ragna what to cook or when to put the little ones to bed. Ragna feared she would never smile again.

The boys returned from the store later that morning with nothing but second-hand news and local gossip. Auntie was finally out of bed and sitting by the kitchen table. Ragna had fixed her a boiled egg and a piece of bread.

"General Custer says he'll tame the Sioux," Knut said.

Ragna noticed a smear of black licorice around the corners of their mouths. Sometimes Mr. Van Dyke treated children to free candy.

"Custer isn't scared a bit," Gunnar said.

"He's a fool then." Auntie's voice was flat and cold. She stirred the coffee in her cup with a spoon, going round and round in the murky liquid. Lately the brew was mostly ground hazelnuts. "Look what they did to us."

"Tell us," Gunnar said. It was not exactly a forbidden topic but one never encouraged by either Auntie or Uncle.

"That's enough," Auntie Inga said. Her face looked as if she had dipped it in the flour barrel. "You boys finish your chores."

They trailed out the door, and Ragna heard Knut whisper, "You'll be Custer and I'll be Red Cloud. We'll have our own battle."

Auntie Inga clicked her tongue in disgust. "Why is it always about shooting and killing?" Thin fingers smoothed back hair streaked with white. Ragna wondered when Auntie's hair had started to gray. Sigurd whined and Auntie picked him up. He fussed and pulled on her dress to nurse.

"All gone," Auntie said. "You're a big boy now."

Ragna fetched the milk and Auntie Inga took the cup and worked with Sigurd to drink. He drooled most of it across his clean dress.

"Auntie." Ragna hesitated about speaking her thoughts. "I don't want to go back to Norway. I'm an American now."

"You will do as your family wants," Auntie said in a flat voice. She wiped Sigurd's face and lifted the cup again to his lips. The edge of the metal clinked on his little teeth. "You'll find work and save money for a ticket."

"But why?"

Auntie looked at her as if she had never seen her before and set Sigurd on the floor. Appraising eyes swept over Ragna from top to bottom. Finally she said, "I was alone in this country. No woman should be in such a position."

"When were you alone?"

Auntie looked at Ragna a long moment before she spoke. Sigurd played at their feet but the boys were all outside, out of hearing. Auntie Inga picked up an empty spool that Sigurd had been playing with and turned it over in her hands, smoothing the wood with her thumb. She looked off into the distance.

"My man died on the ship coming over." Auntie's voice sounded weak and distant. "I was too young for common sense." She handed the spool to Sigurd. "Left alone, without money or language."

"How did he die?" Ragna's voice intruded into the empty room. "An accident?"

"*Nei*," Auntie said. "He took a fever." She reached down and wiped Sigurd's nose with the corner of her apron. "People die all the time."

"Is that when you met Uncle Evan?"

"They wouldn't let me enter America unless I was married or employed." She looked out the single window where the twins climbed the apple tree. "So I married a man on the boat."

"A stranger?" A stranger would be worse than marrying a man chosen by your family. Worse than being alone.

"*Ja*," Auntie said. "I wouldn't wish it on anyone." Sigurd tugged at her skirt, and she picked him up and placed him in her lap. "Mr. Ericcson was an evil man, a man of ambition and greed." Sigurd fumbled with her dress, seeking to nurse. "Quit!" She slapped his fingers, and he burst into a sad wail. Ragna took the crying baby from Auntie and tried the cup again. Sigurd gulped noisily.

"America is no place for a girl alone."

"I'm not alone," Ragna said. "I have you and Uncle Evan."

"But life is uncertain." Auntie rubbed her dry face with rough hands. "Anything can happen."

Ragna summoned all her courage and asked the question still unanswered. "How did you meet Uncle Evan?"

"Mr. Ericcson was . . ." she said and the hiss of name made Ragna picture a snake. "He worked me . . . and used me."

Ragna stood helpless in the power of Auntie's adult words, in the strength of her gaze so terrifying.

"I was his brood mare."

"Is he Gunnar's *far*?" Ragna whispered.

"*Nei*, thanks be to God." Auntie busied herself with stacking dirty dishes.

"But when did you meet Uncle Evan."

The only sound was the splash of water in the basin and the scouring of a kettle.

"Auntie . . ."

"Hush now," Auntie said. "I've said too much."

RAGNA LUGGED A BASKET OF WET SOAKERS and blankets out to the clothesline. Auntie Inga had two husbands before Uncle Evan. Ragna knew of several girls in the community already engaged or wed but felt herself too young, too naïve, not knowing anything about love or romance.

She liked the feel of wet clothes slapping her face and arms as she pinned them to the line. Auntie always mixed balsam needles in her soap pot so that it smelled of pine. Someday when she married, she would do the same. It would be like taking a little of Auntie Inga with her.

Ragna tried to ignore the bleak surroundings, concentrating on memories of greener summers when the smells of pines and clover inundated her senses. How different this year. She slapped a whirring grasshopper out of her hair.

"Let me help," Anders said beside her. "My *mor* hated when clean blankets dragged in the dirt."

She handed him two corners of a wet blanket and took the opposite corners. She noticed how his ring finger was shorter, thought again how he had lost that small tip, how it had pained him. She had a sudden impulse to touch the spot but looked away instead. Together they stretched gray homespun across the line and clipped it with wooden pins.

"That ought to hold it," Anders said.

"*Mange takk.*" Ragna felt tongue-tied in his presence, as she always did. He was nice and good-looking—and seemed in no hurry to leave. She reached for a wet towel and positioned it on the line. A breeze slapped it into her face, and she batted it away before reaching for another. She ignored the embarrassing bloodstained rags at the bottom of the basket, hoping Anders wouldn't notice.

"Ragna," he said. "Do you remember the uprising?"

"Of course," Ragna said, startled. She did remember it, just not a lot of details.

"You couldn't have been very old."

"Only six."

"Where were you when it happened?"

"Right here," she said. "Where else would I have been?"

"But you're alive." His face wore a confused look. "Your parents and little brother . . ."

"My sister and I were taken." Ragna's dry mouth croaked out the words, so often thought but rarely spoken. "Afterwards, Uncle Evan found me."

"Your sister?"

Ragna just shook her head.

"Is she alive?"

"She's not dead," Ragna said. "Just missing."

She finished hanging the towels, careful to pin the menstrual cloths out of sight while Anders was not looking, and picked up the basket.

"What are the twins doing?" She blew a strand of hair away from her face then wedged the basket on her hip and freed a hand to tuck the stray hair behind her ears. "Getting into trouble?"

"Trouble and boys go together," Anders said and laughed a throaty chuckle. "My *mor* always said *naar katten er borte danser musene pa bordet,* when the cat is away the mice will play."

He went whistling away to check on the boys but stopped halfway across the yard and turned around and called out, "I forgot to ask your sister's name." Blond hair blew around his face and strong muscles showed beneath the rolled up sleeves of his chambray shirt.

"Birdie." Ragna looked around to see if Auntie Inga was close enough to hear and disapprove. "My sister's name is Birdie."

The breeze carried the name across the field, beyond Anders, to the edge of her world. Ragna felt a thrill to speak her name. It was a name she carried deep within her every thought and every dream—but rarely voiced. She would like to stand on a hill and call Birdie's name until her sister heard and returned to her, as their mother once called them for supper. She reached up, fingered the button around her neck, and became lost in a daydream.

"Ragna!" Auntie's voice sounded angry. "How long does it take to hang up one basket of clothes?"

If only Uncle Evan would come home soon.

THE FOLLOWING SATURDAY, Anders hiked to the store with a bucket of eggs to trade for flour. When he returned, he handed a letter to Auntie Inga who was ironing shirts on the kitchen table. Her expression never changed, but Ragna saw the way her knuckles whitened as she set the flatirons back on the stovetop, grasped the missive in her chapped hands and sank into a chair.

"It's from your man," Anders said.

Auntie Inga had been droopy since the baby's death. Ragna sometimes had to remind herself that it had really happened, that a fresh mound in the graveyard held the little girl. Auntie never spoke of it, but once Ragna thought she heard weeping in the night.

Auntie opened the seal and read silently and then aloud. "They've found work with Mormons living north of here." Her words hung in the kitchen. "He's looking at Congress land."

Mormons! The papers talked about their many wives and strange beliefs. The smell of hot irons on wrinkled cotton lingered in the room, the clank of the irons placed back on the stove to heat. Anders excused himself for chores.

"Can I read it?" Ragna said.

Auntie Inga only nodded and Ragna scooped the letter from the table and read it by the light of the window.

> Dear Inga and children,
>
> Thanks to the Good Lord, we have found work in Otter Tail County at a Mormon settlement. The people are clean and pleasant. We expect the harvest to last another week and then we will return home. We hope to look at Congress Land while we are here. Tell the children to behave themselves until we get back. Anders should cut wood in his spare time. Perhaps we can trade it for meal at the mill.
>
> Yours truly,
>
> Evan

Ragna hoped Uncle earned enough money to get them through the winter—but not too much, she told herself. Her stomach tightened, and she busied herself slicing potatoes into the cast iron pan for supper. Not enough to send her back to Norway.

Auntie laid her head on the table and groaned.

"Are you sick?"

"Tired," Auntie said. "Can't get my strength back."

Ragna's heart raced. Women sometimes died after childbed. Auntie's white face and unkempt appearance proved she was still sick even though it had been several weeks since the birth.

"How can I help?" Ragna said. "Is there something I can do?"

The boys argued outside, and Sigurd wailed at Auntie's feet, pulling on her dress, wanting to nurse. Ragna scooped the baby into her arms and handed him a bread crust, jostling him back and forth to soothe him.

Auntie's silence filled the room, louder than the crying baby and the sounds of the boys outside the window.

"Tomorrow is Sunday," Auntie finally said. "I'd like a day of peace." She lifted her head from the table and stared out the window with a quivering lip. "A day to myself with no one around."

14

Investigation of the Canada Pacific Railway Scandal Commenced
St. Paul Dispatch, *August 31, 1873*

THE NEXT MORNING DAWNED clear and sunny. The boys hurried through their chores without prodding. Anders chopped extra kitchen wood. Auntie Inga drooped over the table, making no effort to help or give directions. Sigurd crawled under Knut's feet as he poured milk through the strainer into the milk pans. Ragna packed a hamper with corn bread and a crock of baked beans. The twins argued on the front stoop over who would swim the farthest and fastest.

Ragna remembered wistfully last year's Sunday School picnic with its fried chicken and fruit pies. They would make do with what they had. Knut filled a pail with well water and tied an old barrel lid across the top as best he could. Ragna gathered clean soakers for the baby and folded a quilt to bring along for his nap.

"Gunnar, fetch milk for the baby," Auntie Inga said. "Use the jug and cool it in the lake when you get there."

"Mor," he panted with a red face as he ran in with the jug. "There's a crock of pickles left. Can we have them for our picnic?"

Auntie looked up and nodded absently. Gunnar whooped and raced back to the root cellar dug into the floor of the *stabbuhr*. It would not be fancy, but they would have a picnic, and Auntie Inga would have her wish for a day of peace.

Anders hitched Old Doll to the traces and pitched straw into the corners of the wagon to make the ride a little smoother for the children. The twins jumped up and down in the wagon bed, and Anders reminded them not to scare Old Doll. Knut bragged how he would swim and Lewis begged to learn. Gunnar raced back into the house for a towel. Ragna held Sigurd securely in her lap.

"Mor says to watch that the little boys don't drown," Gunnar said when he returned to the wagon and leapt up into the box. "Says not to let them go deeper than their belly buttons."

A wail of protest went up from the wagon box, but Anders flicked the reins and clucked his tongue. "Don't fuss, boys. You'll learn to swim." Old Doll strained, swishing her tail against flies, and pulled the creaky wagon.

They drove away from the farm, away from the devastation of the grasshoppers and into a normal world. Sumac and devil's paint brush bloomed crimson along the trail beside yellow golden rod and blue stem grasses. Mexican robins sang from their perches on nearby ash trees. The fragrances of fall filled the air though it felt as warm as midsummer.

Sigurd dozed with the rocking of the wagon. Old Doll twitched her tail. Anders waved the whip to scare off the blue-tailed flies buzzing around Old Doll. He cast a glance at her then clucked the reins and whistled a tuneless melody.

Ragna smoothed her dress and pulled her bonnet over her face. She had never felt so grown up.

LAKE AGNES BOASTED A SANDY SHORE and cold, clean water. No bloodsuckers lurked, no muddy bottoms. The air smelled of lake and fish, not dead hoppers like at home. The fishing hole nestled behind oak trees and crimson sumac, hidden from the trail's view. Though the summer waned, the day grew hot and sultry.

The boys stripped down to their drawers. Knut and Gunnar jumped into the cold water while the twins stuck tentative toes into the lapping waves. Anders pulled a fishing pole from behind the wagon seat and set a grasshopper on the hook. Ragna was glad he had not removed his clothing to swim. The thought unnerved her, and she reminded herself to keep her head.

Mosquitoes swarmed around Ragna's face and neck where she sat with the baby on the shore but at least no grasshoppers whirled in their faces. Ragna gathered a small cedar branch and waved it over Sigurd's sleeping form. *Stakkers liten*, he was often lost in the commotion of their busy family. Ragna leaned over and kissed the sweaty blond curls lying across his forehead.

The water looked cool and inviting. Lewis and Sverre splashed and sputtered in the shallow water, squealing when the cold water drenched them, when the water went up their noses or into their eyes. She removed her shoes and stockings and stretched out on the blanket beside Sigurd.

It had been a long time since she had been swimming with the family. When she was six or seven, she had stripped down with Gunnar and Knut, splashed, and played as she wished. A few years back, during a scorching heat wave, Auntie had allowed her to swim with the younger boys, wearing her dress and petticoats. She remembered the feeling of cool water over her back and shoulders, the freedom of floating. Maybe she remembered splashing with Birdie long ago in the muddy lake next to their cabin.

She fingered the button around her neck, imagining Birdie rescued by the Sisters of Mercy and becoming a nun. Birdie, clothed in her long white habit, looked at her and was about to speak . . .

"Not too deep, Gunnar!" Anders called. Ragna snapped back to attention.

"Don't worry," Gunnar called back, "I can swim."

Ragna left the sleeping baby and went to the shore. "You mind, Gunnar," she called with both hands cupped around her mouth. Gunnar was at least twenty feet away from the shore—far past the safety of his belly button. "Or we'll go home right now."

Gunnar dog paddled back toward the shore, pouting and splashing. When he came close to Sverre, he reached over and pushed his younger brother's head under the water while Lewis howled in protest.

Ragna lifted her skirts and charged into the water. Gunnar saw her coming and let go of Sverre, who popped out of the water coughing, choking, and crying. Anders reached them before she did and pulled Sverre into his arms and patted him on the back.

"He's only scared," Anders said and looked at Gunnar with sharp eyes. "Only a bully picks on the little ones."

"Don't ruin it," Ragna said and placed a hand on Gunnar's arm. He stood level with her eyes. "This is supposed to be a fun day."

"I'm tired of playing with little kids," Gunnar's face relaxed from the scowl. "Come in swimming. No one will see."

"Please, Ragna!" Knut said. "You were always the best swimmer."

The water, luxurious after the sand and mosquitoes, swirled around her ankles and already wet the bottom half of her skirt. What would Auntie Inga say? She looked around. A stand of oak trees shielded them from view by anyone on the trail. She dragged her fingers through the water. She was already wet. Sigurd slept on the shore.

"Come on." Anders' smile revealed his chipped tooth. "I will if you will."

Ragna dove underwater and came up gasping from the cold water.

15

South Carolina Crops do not Promise as Good a Yield as Last Year. There is a scarcity of Negro labor.

St. Paul Dispatch, *September 16, 1873*

AFTER EVAN AND MILTON STAKED claims, Milton headed back to Tordenskjold to start working on his dugout. Evan turned toward home. Milton promised to help Evan when he came back with the family. It had been a long, lonely journey and his boots were in tatters.

He expected a hero's welcome, but when he walked up the dusty path towards the house, he could sense that something was wrong.

Inga turned her face away from him and stared off into space. "It's over," she said.

Evan saw her lip tremble and the upward thrust of her chin. It meant she would speak of it no further.

Their baby dead. A surge of guilt flowed through him for all his negative thoughts. Always before Inga carried and birthed their little ones with little or no problems. She might complain of being tired, especially if one of the other children took sick and she was up during the night. Sometimes she was downright grouchy in the last weeks. However, never before had he seen Inga stone cold and quiet.

Inga had pestered him all these years about owning land. It should be good news, the news she had wanted. But she acted so strangely that he hesitated to tell her. She had not smiled when he walked in the door or kissed him. After a whole month, she had not asked about his job, how much money he had made, nothing.

Evan reached for a cup of coffee from the kettle on the stove, weak and bitter, the grounds used over and over until there was little left except brown-tinted water. Maybe they should stay at the farm until spring. It would be easier for Inga. Then they must travel in the spring. Spring weather was uncooperative and unpredictable. He needed every day to break ground or there would be no crop next year. They must leave right away and make the best of it.

"Where are the boys?"

"I sent them to Van Dyke's Store to check the mail." She looked at him accusingly. "We've had one letter and you've been gone more than a month."

"I'm sorry," Evan swallowed a hard lump in his throat. "I should have written more." If only he had thought to explain his delay in the letter.

She picked up Sigurd from the floor and thrust him into Evan's arms. Then Inga turned towards the stove and poked the fire with an iron poker. She pulled out a frying pan and rubbed it with a heel of pork rind, then sliced potatoes and onions into the sputtering grease.

"How long before it's ready?"

"It's not like you warned me you were coming." Inga's voice was flat and her eyes dull. "I'm working as fast as I can."

"I have news." It is what she had wanted after all. "I filed on Congress Land in Tordenskjold Township."

She paused only an instant, then continued stirring the potatoes in the pan.

"It's about time."

Not a question about where it was or how they would manage. Just a reprimand for his years of poor judgment. He told himself she did not mean it, that once settled on the new place she would turn back into the Inga he knew and loved. The one who had stolen his heart that summer of the uprising while still married to another man.

Almost in a dream, Evan walked to the cemetery plot, carrying Sigurd on his shoulder. He usually avoided the place with its memories and reminders. He stood inside the rough fence, searching the ground for the new grave. A cross of woven sticks marked the grave and the dirt sank deeper than the surrounding ground. Mourning doves cooed and he sniffed the smell of fresh dirt and dried grass.

"I named her Ann Elin," Ragna said from the oak tree at the edge of the plot.

Her voice startled him and he looked up and saw her sitting on an extended limb. If grasshoppers had not eaten every leaf, he might not have seen her. Evan thought how young she was, still a little girl, climbing trees and riding branches like horses.

"It was a girl?" Evan said.

"*Ja.*"

Evan heard the grinding jaws of grasshoppers, the whispery sound they made when they flew. He had always thought to name his first daughter after his sister gone so many years now. Norwegian tradition demanded they name their first daughter after his mother, but he had planned to deviate from the practice. Instead, he would name their first daughter Christina. He had always imagined that his daughter would resemble his sister with yellow curls and gentle demeanor.

He swallowed hard. Evan could not fault Ragna for naming the little one. It deserved a name. *She* deserved a name. To think Inga had gone through this alone with no one but Ragna for comfort and assistance. It swelled his throat. He had failed again. How she must have felt to deliver a tiny baby to this place of loss.

"Come down," he said. "Let's find the boys."

How he had missed them while he was gone. It was not right for a *far* to be gone from the family as he had been the past month. It reminded him why he had quit his stagecoach job.

Grasshoppers crunched beneath his boots and Evan winced. His farm was dead. Not exactly his farm, he corrected himself, but almost his farm. Maybe it was the *Book of Revelation*, as Knut said. A plague, like the Mormons believed.

"Uncle." Ragna's voice carried a cautious tone. "Auntie wouldn't . . ."

She paused and picked up an agate from the ground. Evan watched her examine the rings in the stone and place it in her apron pocket. Sigurd giggled and twirled his fingers in Evan's beard. "She wouldn't look at the baby."

Evan felt the words as blows. "Not even once?"

"*Nei*," Ragna said. "She didn't ask if it were a boy or girl or shed a single tear."

It was worse than he thought.

"Uncle," Ragna roused him from his thoughts. "What will we do?"

She was crying. Evan knew that back at the house, Inga cried as well, only on the inside. He pulled Ragna into his left arm as they walked along the path. He heard himself telling Ragna about the move to Tordenskjold. He knew he was babbling and making little sense, his voice too cheerful and forced.

"And so you see we have to make a new start." He leaned down, pulled a lone blade of grass from beside a stone along the trail, and chewed on the sweet stem. "This land will yield nothing for a while longer."

"It's so hard to think of leaving . . . the graves . . ." He watched her wipe her nose on the back of her hand and gulp back a sob. "What if Birdie comes back while I'm gone?"

He let out a sigh. "I need your help until Inga is well again."

"But to move so far away," Ragna said.

"We leave a grave as well," Evan said. "Any word from your *bestemor*?"

Ragna shook her head and pulled away from him. She was not a child any longer.

"You must save money for a ticket."

"I won't go back."

"You will."

THE TWINS RAN SQUEALING TOWARD him as they neared the house and Evan scooped them up, one on each shoulder, and jigged around the yard, then carried them to the barn. Gunnar and Knut grinned while Ragna carried

Sigurd back into the house. Anders shouldered the ax and headed toward the woodpile. The boys answered their father's questions about chores and behavior while Evan pulled the stool closer to the heifer, washed her udders with a wet rag and stripped her teats. The pinging sound of fresh milk hitting the bucket filled the barn and the cat meowed for a taste. Evan squirted a stream at the cat and laughed as it licked its paws and cleaned its whiskers.

"We had licorice, Far," Lewis lisped through missing front teeth. "It's hard to chew without teeth."

"You'll have two big teeth before winter gets here."

"Anders tied a string around the loose teeth and jerked them out when Lewis looked away," Sverre said with a worried look, putting a thumb to his mouth and touching his front teeth as if to be sure his were still in place.

"It didn't even hurt," Lewis said.

"Then why did you cry like a baby?" Gunnar elbowed Knut, and they both giggled.

"That's enough," Evan said and leaned his cheek against the heifer's warm flank. It was so good to be home again. He sent up a silent prayer of thanks for his healthy boys. "I've news to tell. We are moving to Tordenskjold."

"By Uncle Ole?" Knut said.

"Closer to Ole." Evan dodged a swinging cow tail. "We'll have our own farm and grow everything we need, even our own sugar."

"Are there *skraelings*?" Sverre said with round eyes and popped his thumb in his mouth.

"They won't hurt you." Evan flicked a fly off his face before resuming the milking. "The bad ones are gone."

Evan told the boys about the sugar camp where the Ojibwa made sugar and syrup from maple sap. Of course, they had tasted maple syrup before but their farm did not have sugar maples.

"We'll live near a Mormon village," Evan said. "The Branch of Zion."

"What's a Mormon?" Knut said.

"A religion," Evan said. "Different from Lutherans."

"Like Catholics?" Gunnar said.

"We'll talk later." Evan pushed back from the cow and handed the bucket to Knut. He stood up and stretched, looking around the yard. "Anders, I need you to build a sturdy crate for the chickens. Gunnar, pack the tools into the barrel. Knut, help your *mor* in the house."

Knut groaned but Evan ignored him. He wondered how Inga would manage. "Twins, help your mother with Sigurd. Don't let him out of your sight."

Evan steeled himself to face Inga.

"When are we leaving?" Knut said.

"Tomorrow," Evan said and cast an anxious glance toward the sky. Not a cloud anywhere. "Or as soon as we can get packed up again. The sooner we go, the sooner we get there."

"Can Old Doll pull the wagon alone?" Gunnar said.

Evan stopped in midstride and weighed the question. It was true that Old Doll was no longer young. The epizootic nearly finished her. Most people thought it better to use a team of oxen for a long pull. Better for breaking new ground as well.

Long ago, he and his sister had dreamed of owning their own land and horses in America. It pained him to admit that owning a horse was a prideful thing. He had cried real tears when Steel Gray died in the plague. It would be the final admission of his failures if he were to give up on horses altogether.

"We'll trust the Good Lord to help Old Doll get us there," Evan said at last. "It will be a great adventure—like the Vikings going out to sea. Only we'll go out in this wagon.

The boys celebrated this plan with great cheering and hurrahing.

"Does Mor know about it?" Gunnar said. He looked at Evan with those accusative dark eyes.

It seemed he and his oldest son saw eye to eye on nothing.

16

The Wall Street Conspiracy to Advance the Price of Gold
St. Paul Dispatch, *September 17, 1873*

IT WAS TOO HOT TO SLEEP. Loons called from the lake. Mosquitoes whined around their beds, hovering for a chance to suck their blood. Behind it all, the grinding sound of grasshopper jaws. The loft felt smothery and close. Ragna pulled the curtain back from her corner, the sheet that gave her privacy from the boys. Just that simple act allowed a little air to circulate over her.

Sverre and Lewis tossed, restless, in their corner. A strong smell of urine wafted from Lewis's bed again. Knut snored softly with one arm hanging down over the loft edge, as if to catch a cool breeze if one passed by.

Auntie and Uncle spoke in murmured voices, their words just loud enough for Ragna to hear.

"Nothing from Norway?"

"*Nei,*" Auntie said. "You can hardly expect them to come through for us." One of the twins coughed, and Ragna strained her ears to hear. "We should have asked for help years ago."

"But the farm—you know they think we're rich."

"Then someone should tell them the truth. Our back is against the wall."

"You're making too much out of this."

"America is too hard for a single woman—I ought to know."

The voices settled to a hum. Lewis cried out in his sleep and rolled over closer to Sverre. A feeble breeze stirred the curtain on the single windowpane.

Ragna would not do it. Even if Uncle Evan found the money for her to go back to Norway, she would not go. She would run away first. Run away

99

and find Birdie. The newspaper said Clara Barton identified all those dead soldiers at Andersonville prison in Georgia. Surely someone could help her find her sister. It was much easier to find someone still alive. She fingered the button around her neck.

"Hush now." Uncle's voice pulled Ragna away from a wonderful daydream about her sister, how Ragna had put an ad in the newspaper and Birdie came knocking at the door after reading it. Ragna wiped sweat off her forehead with the corner of a sheet and slapped a thirsty mosquito on her cheek.

"You're not thinking clearly," Uncle said.

"I'm clear as a bell."

Sounds of tears and the rustling of cornhusks in the mattress.

It smelled like rain. Ragna wished it would storm down a great deluge, big enough to wash all the grasshopper eggs out of the soil and heal the farm.

However, common sense prevailed. They faced a long journey to Otter Tail County and did not need mud slowing them down.

"Maybe you should write another letter and explain how it is."

"One letter is enough." More rustling of the corn shuck mattress. "I won't beg."

Ragna breathed a sigh of relief. Thank God, she had switched the letters when she'd had the chance.

"And what about Anders?"

"What about him?"

The rustle of corn shucks, the creak of the bed frame.

"He could care for the house while we're gone, until we sell."

"*Nei*," Uncle said. "He'll go with us as far as Tordenskjold and then head northeast to the pineries."

"It's dangerous work."

"He's a fisherman, for Christ's sake, a grown man."

Ragna struggled to hear the following statement, suddenly hoping that Anders would go with them. It would be a comfort to know someone else, someone closer to her own age, a friend.

"Milton says he's got a sweetheart in Norway." Ragna held her breath and her heart pounded in her ears. "He'll work in the pineries for money to send for her."

Hot tears burned her eyes. She had not thought of Anders as a suitor but he had been so kind during the baby's funeral, with the baptism and all. She suddenly felt very alone.

"Ragna," Gunnar whispered from the darkness, his words startled Ragna. "Will Mor be happy now?"

"Maybe."

"What will we do if she doesn't get better?"

"She'll get better." She hoped she spoke the truth and that Auntie would improve now that Uncle Evan was home again. Uncle had earned enough money to get through the winter and make a new start in Tordenskjold.

"I'm scared," Gunnar said.

"I know," Ragna said.

She mentally started the novena. *"Holy Mary, Mother of God, help Auntie Inga to get better and make the grasshoppers go away. And show me how to find Birdie."*

Ragna's heart heaved and thumped in her chest. She was alone in the world without parents, sister, or brother. Uncle Evan and Auntie Inga had their own family. She was no more than a hired girl.

Not exactly a hired girl, she corrected herself. Uncle and Auntie loved her, the boys loved her, and the farm belonged to her so she was not a cotter.

The novena had been useless. Of course, it was a homemade novena, maybe missing important words. If only Auntie Inga would have let her learn the whole prayer from Mrs. Brorson. A real mother would have let her find out, not whooshed her out of the room before she could ask.

She reached for the button around her neck and closed her eyes as tight as she could. An owl hooted outside the cabin and whooshed down in a flurry of wings to catch a mouse scurrying in the grass.

Holy Mary, Mother of God, help me find my sister.

17

A Sauk Center Mill Swallows a St. Cloud Bank

St. Paul Dispatch, *September 20, 1873*

THEY LEFT ALEXANDRIA ON St. Matthew's Day, September 21. If they were lucky, they would be in Tordenskjold by Michaelmas, September 29. But anything could happen on the trail. Evan cast an anxious glance at the overloaded wagon. It was a heavy burden for Old Doll.

Evan had made his choice and now must live with it.

Their only hope was to make the plunge. Evan secured the ropes that bound the last barrel to the sides of the wagon box. A man never got anywhere without taking risks. He had left Norway with little more than the shirt on his back and the optimism of youth. He had never regretted it.

It was harder with a wife and family.

"Gunnar!" It was almost daylight. "Get the twins and hurry up about it. Crate the chickens."

You would think a boy almost eleven years old could see what needed to be done without being told. Why by that age, Evan had worked their Norwegian farm while his *far* and older brothers hired out to the nobleman in the village. His *far* had not hounded him about every little thing. Of course, his brothers loved giving orders.

Now his brother, Ole, mourned for his son. The thought brought a quick catch to Evan's breath. His brother and family might all be dead for all he knew. The thought made Evan's sad heart even heavier. He had never set eyes on his only nephew. Maybe it was too late to see any of them again.

Evan reached down and gathered Sigurd in his arms. Sigurd did not yet speak, barely walked, and carried dull eyes that hinted of feeble mindedness.

At this age, the other boys had been active and curious. It seemed Sigurd had no interest in anything but being held. The thought stabbed him in the chest. Surely, God would not add that burden.

Inga lumbered up on the wagon and plopped down in the driver's seat. Evan worried she might be too hard on Old Doll, maybe too rough with the bit or impatient in steep areas. He sighed. Inga must ride and so must take the reins. That was all there was to it. He would not burden Old Doll with his weight as well.

Besides, someone had to push the handcart holding the little ones. One could hardly expect their short legs to carry them to Tordenskjold. Thank God for Anders. He proved dependable and willing, and seemed content to travel with their little caravan.

Inga held the reins with a listless hand and did not glance back on the house that had been their home for almost ten years. She took the cat from Gunnar's outstretched hands and placed it on her lap, stroking its gray head.

"Far!" Gunnar called from the barn. "I can't find them."

"Look again," Evan said and unleashed his frustration on Gunnar. "For God's sake, can't you do even one simple thing?"

Sigurd wailed at the sound of his angry voice, and Evan felt his cheeks flush. He tried to hush the howling baby, embarrassed about blowing up over nothing.

"I'll go." Knut jumped down from the wagon wheel where he had been scanning the fields. "They might be in the cemetery."

"What are they doing there?"

"They followed Ragna," Inga said. "To say goodbye to the graves."

His anger melted when he thought how hard it was for Ragna to leave. He wondered if Inga thought about the grave of their little daughter.

He hoped he was not making a mistake. At least it was a short trip. The papers brimmed with stories of folks traipsing all the way to California or Oregon. They would be there in less than a week if all went well and would be snug in their new place by All Saints Day. He would start the fall plowing. Next spring he would be ready to plant. They would make it.

Though the children finally gathered at the wagon, Ragna still dawdled around the cabin door.

"Hurry up, now!"

She stood staring off into space, rubbing her fingers across the button around her neck as if she did not hear a word he said. Evan strode over to where she stood.

"Ragna!"

She looked at him with a face so pitiful that his anger changed to annoyance. Ragna held a penciled letter to her sister on a piece of brown wrapping paper: *Dear Birdie, we have moved to Tordenskjold Township in Otter Tail County. You can find me there. Love Always from Your sister, Ragna Larson.*

"I have to do this," Ragna said and the look in her eyes melted his resolve. "I won't rest unless I leave word."

In the end, Evan took the stone from the porch, the one used as a door stop, and drove in the tack that held the letter to the door.

"We've got to be going."

The sun shone over the eastern horizon when they placed the crate of chickens on top of the heaped wagon and tied it down with rope. The twins climbed into the handcart, and Evan placed Sigurd between them. Evan looked at the *stabbuhr* Lars had built so long ago. He looked at the cabin he and Inga had built, the walls sturdy and straight, and the wood shed and chicken barn. He looked at the trees stripped bare by the hoppers and the desolate fields. He could not bear the pain in his heart, the sadness that tasted like failure.

"Hey, boys," Evan said in a jolly voice. He would not let the family know his dark mood. "Did I ever tell you about my sea journey from Norway?"

"On the boat?" Sverre said and popped his thumb into his mouth.

Evan did not have the heart to reprimand him for the thumb. They needed all the comfort they could muster.

"*Ja,* on the boat." He cleared his voice and patted Old Doll on the rump. She stumbled against the heavy load, found her footing and moved forward, straining at the squeaking harness. Inga tightened her grip on the reins and looked back as if to make sure all the boys were there. Evan lifted the two handles of the handcart and pushed forward, the load in front like a wheelbarrow. The three boys were heavier than one might think. Anders boosted Sigurd onto his shoulders.

"It was on the *White Dove*, a sturdy ship with a sail as white as Ragna's petticoat."

"Uncle Evan!" Ragna said with eyes red from crying. "Don't talk about under things!"

"It was! I tell the truth," he said. "Why, on the *White Dove* I told my first lie."

"You told a lie?" Knut's eyes rounded in surprise.

"I'm sorry to say I did." Evan thought back to the lonely feeling that had chilled him to his very core, the fear of being alone in a strange land without knowing the language. "Your *bestemor* made me promise to keep the commandments, and I was barely out of her sight when I broke the ninth one."

"What was your lie?" Sverre took his thumb out of his mouth long enough to speak and then popped it back in.

"My family." Evan looked at his brood of boys and cast a worried eye toward Inga on the wagon seat ahead of them. She snapped the reins and hurried Old Doll with a clucking sound not unlike a brooding hen. A lump in his throat slowed his response but he continued with the jolly tone. "Another boy bragged about how he had an aunt and uncle waiting for him in Chicago. He bragged that they worked for a bakery and he would have all the bread he could hold and then some."

Their steps pulled them farther away from their yard. Evan hoped to keep the children occupied until they were out of sight of the home place.

"Not to be outdone, I made up a story about relatives waiting for me in Minnesota."

Anders lifted Sigurd onto Gunnar's back and draped the little one's legs around Gunnar's shoulders. Then he lifted Sverre out of the cart and put him on his own back in the same fashion. Evan smiled a grateful smile towards Anders and moved a little faster with the pushcart. It was one way to spare Old Doll and get the little ones to Otter Tail County.

"Tell us more, Far." Lewis' voice held a lisp that reminded Evan of his brother, Martin, who had died of the bloody flux when he was only six. "Tell us about the family you said you had."

"I said that I had an uncle in Minnesota who had a farm waiting for me."

His arms ached almost as much as his heart. "I wished that it were true. I wished with all my might. But *som man reder saa ligger man*, as we make our bed, so we must lie."

"What do you mean?" Ragna said.

"When we got to Chicago, his aunt and uncle would have invited me home with them and helped me get a start, but my friend told them I had family waiting for me in Minnesota and I couldn't spare the time."

"Did you want to go with them?" Knut said.

"More than anything. I was so homesick. I couldn't understand a word of American. I could hardly keep from crying."

"Grown men don't cry," Gunnar said with a snort.

"*Nei,*" Evan said. "Tears dwell in every person's heart. Your *bestefar* wept when my brothers died, and he was a descendent of a Viking chieftain."

The children digested this thought with sober faces. The cart pulled heavy and he thought how long the journey, how many miles they must travel over rough trails and steep hills.

"But what I didn't know was that although I thought I was lying, I spoke the truth." Evan shifted the weight and picked up his pace.

"The truth?" Gunnar said. "How can a lie become the truth?"

"Can you figure it out?" Evan laughed almost loud enough to forget about the stand of apple trees ruined by the grasshoppers after years of tending. "It's a riddle."

"A miracle," Knut said. "A miracle turned your lie into truth, just like Jesus turned the water into wine at the wedding in Canaan."

"You really did have an uncle in America when you got here," said Sverre. "Your Uncle Ole."

"Ole is our uncle, not Far's," Gunnar said. "Ole is Far's brother and came to America later."

Sverre put his thumb back in his mouth with a puzzled look on his face.

"Leave him alone," Lewis said. "He can guess if he wants."

"Boys, boys." Evan hated the way every conversation turned into an argument. "I'll tell you the riddle."

They were over the hill and the farm out of sight. Maybe they had gone a mile. Only thirty-nine left to go.

"Uncle Sam had a farm waiting for me here in America."

"Uncle Sam!" Knut said. "Congress land!"

"What's Congress land?" Sverre said. "Who is Uncle Sam?"

"Uncle Sam is another way of saying United States," Ragna said with a smile. "And Congress Land is free land given to settlers if they will build a farm and last five years without giving up."

"We won't give up, will we Far?" Sverre said.

"*Nei*, Son, we will never give up."

"And what about your family?" Knut said. "Did you find your family here?"

"The Good Lord had a family waiting for me here in America after all," Evan said. "Didn't He, Mother?"

For the first time Inga smiled a weak smile at Evan. "*Ja*, that He did."

Evan's heart settled in his chest. Inga smiled. They would start over, have their own place, and grow old together. Maybe Inga would yet have their daughter, Christina, named after his sister who died so long ago and whose hair graced the watch fob in his pocket.

Staghorn sumac furred crimson along the trail once they passed the desolation caused by grasshoppers. The color jolted Evan after the brown fields of the farm. He had not realized how much he needed color. Maybe it was the normalcy of the situation more than the color itself. Maybe it was Inga's first smile since he returned from the Saints. Whatever the reason, he felt his muscles relax and his anxiety decrease. He had always loved being on the trail. Back in the days when he drove the stage, he reveled in the solitude, the horses, and the people he met along the way.

Dried leaves whispered under the wooden wheels of the loaded wagon and swirled beneath their feet with every puff of wind.

"Will grasshoppers be there?" Lewis said soberly. "I don't want the hoppers to come to Tordenskjold."

"Not a grasshopper in Otter Tail County!" Evan said. "In fact, grasshoppers are forbidden by court order to cross into Otter Tail County."

"Really?" Knut said.

"That's what I've read in the paper." Evan thought of how easy it would be for a horde of hoppers to cross this dry land and descend anywhere they wished. It seemed impossible that only a few miles back their farm lay destroyed while here there was only lush abundant color and farmers working in their fields. "Decreed by law."

The older boys chuckled, and Evan hummed the opening bars of the Norwegian anthem about the famous admiral, Tordenskjold:

> Dette landet Harald berget, med som kjemperad, dette landet
> Haakon verget medens Oyvind kvad;

As comforting as the old words were to his heart, Evan realized they must look forward to an American future. There was nothing gained by singing about Norway's youngest admiral. It was time to be Americans. "Did I ever teach you the song from the War of Rebellion?"

"*The Union forever, hurrah, boys, hurrah!*" The boys stumbled over the English words, but the song kept them busy until the noonday sun grew hot and they stopped for a quick meal in the shade of an ironwood tree.

"Uncle," Ragna said in a soft voice. "Will there really be no grasshoppers in Tordenskjold?"

"I pray to God it will be so." Evan looked at his boys gathering wood for a small fire to cook a kettle of coffee. Lewis and Sverre carried one knotted branch between them big enough to heat an entire house on a winter night. "Just small wood. Just a small fire."

He could not fail again.

18

NEW PARTY MOVEMENT! Grangers in Council at Brownville
St. Paul Dispatch, *September 21, 1873*

ONCE ON THE TRAIL, UNCLE EVAN proceeded with more foolishness and storytelling than Ragna had ever known. He sang and jigged, told stories of Old Country trolls, exploits of ancient Vikings, and riddles. The boys loved it. She loved it, too, but noticed the sadness in his eyes.

It was as if Uncle Evan did not dare stop. Love for Uncle welled in her throat. He was the kindest and best. It was not that Auntie was mean—far from it. Uncle Evan was softer hearted than Auntie. They were different. She wished that Auntie were nicer to Uncle Evan. Auntie Inga looked straight ahead and did not laugh at his stories. Auntie could try harder. It was not his fault.

She fingered the button hanging around her neck and imagined Birdie coming over the hill toward them.

"Ragna!" Auntie said. "Are you listening? Take Sigurd and give Gunnar a rest."

Sigurd's soakers dripped wet and stinking. Ragna changed him and draped the wet diaper across the plow handles sticking up from the wagon. His dress would dry although she hated the touch of urine-soaked cloth against her clean apron. She would smell as badly as the baby. She cast an anxious eye towards Anders who had taken over pushing the handcart for Uncle Evan.

They straggled behind the lurching wagon. Old Doll struggled up every incline. Sigurd whined. The twins argued. Gunnar teased Knut until he swore. Auntie Inga threatened *chiliwinks*.

"We're almost there, boys," Uncle Evan said. "Watch for smoke from Mr. Carlson's fire."

By the time they stopped for the night south of Millerville, they felt as if they had been traveling all their lives.

"You're welcome to camp by the well," Mr. Carlson said. "I've a pot of rutabagas cooking."

"Do you see?" Anders said quietly as he unfastened Lady from the back of the wagon and led her to a shady spot for milking. Bobcat bawled for his mother's milk, but Anders left him tied until he could finish. "Not a grasshopper." He positioned the bucket and began the steady stripping that released the dull thrum of milk into the wooden pail. "We've left our troubles behind."

Ragna busied herself making camp. As she unpacked the blankets and canvas tarp, her mind wandered to Birdie.

"Ragna!" Auntie's angry voice interrupted her thoughts. She wiped a tired hand across her forehead and slapped at a deerfly buzzing around her hair. "Fetch the baking kettle from under the seat and start frying potatoes."

Ragna dropped the last blanket onto the ground and stared dumbly at Auntie Inga. It was as if her mind refused to return to the present.

"Don't you hear me?" Auntie's mouth crimped into a thin line.

"Here it is." Anders reached over, pulled the kettle from the wagon, and handed her the gunnysack of potatoes. "I'll strain the milk."

She took the potatoes from Anders's hands but did not look into his eyes. He saved to bring his sweetheart from the Old Country. Uncle's words swirled through her memory as fat sizzled in the cast iron pan warming on the fire. As she sliced potatoes, she thought again of Birdie and her hand reached up to finger the button.

It is my wedding day. Bestemor and Uncle Ivar arrange for me to marry a rich landowner in Norway. Birdie stands as my bridesmaid. I wear Bestemor's bunad and feel the adoring eyes of the groom at my side. The church bells ring, and I steal a glance toward the stranger I will marry.

It is Anders Vollen! I blush red to the roots of my hair. I thought it would be someone old and ugly, but it is clearly Anders, with his dear chipped tooth and missing fingertip.

"Ragna," Anders said. "Need more wood?"

"*Nei,*" Ragna said and stirred the potatoes with the edge of the butcher knife. She could not look at him, could not risk him knowing what she had been thinking. "I have enough."

She snagged a blade of grass from the foamy bucket of milk before pouring it into tin cups for the little boys. The smell of fresh milk mingled with that of the campfire. The twins chased the cat across the meadow where Mr. Carlson's young stock grazed in turkey-foot grass, tall enough to hide the cat completely. Patches of waving goldenrod dipped and twisted as the twins played in the tall weeds. Lady chomped on grass beside the wagon and Bobcat sucked his mother's teats in search of remaining milk.

"You boys mind the cat!" Auntie Inga said. "We'll need him to keep the mice out of our new granary."

No sign of grasshoppers. A normal September day.

Funny how it took the grasshoppers to teach her the beauty of normal. She had always thought of normal as before the uprising, before the deaths of her family and before being stolen by the Red Men.

Maybe she had been wrong all the time.

19

*Dr. Miller's Celebrated Indian Root Bitters: a Sure Remedy for
Dyspepsia, Fever and Ague, Colic, Cramps to Stomach, Heart-
burn, Diarrhea, Dysentery, Nervousness, Impurities to the Blood,
Loss of Appetite, Etc. Etc.*

St. Paul Dispatch, *September 21, 1873*

EVAN STRAINED LADY'S MORNING MILK into a can, tied a strong wire around the lid, hung it under the wagon, and cast an anxious look towards a rim of dark clouds to the west. Rain would make their journey even more miserable.

"What are you doing?" Sverre said.

"I've a surprise," Evan said. "By supper time we'll have fresh buttermilk."

"But where's the churn?" Lewis said.

"The trail is our churn." The wire looked strong enough to hold. "You'll see." Inga's scream interrupted their conversation. "Snake!"

A snake curled in a kettle under the wagon. Knut scooped it out and cradled it in his arms. "Can I keep it, Far?"

"A fine blow snake," Evan said calmly. "See how he puffs and struts, try-ing to scare us with his posturing?" Evan knelt down and pointed out the snake for the twins. They crowded close to examine the reptile. "There's not a poisonous snake to be found in these parts," Evan said. "Maybe a rattler or two down in the bluff country, but nothing here."

"Thank God for small favors," Inga was calmer now. "I'm as jumpy as the cat. And no, Knut, there will be no snake traveling along on this journey."

"You can find all the pet snakes you want in Tordenskjold Township."

"Are we almost there?" Sverre said. "I'm tired."

"You heard your *far*," Anders said. "We'll be there before you know it."

Inga poured bacon grease leftover from breakfast into a gourd and wedged it behind the seat. "Be careful of this grease," she said to no one in particular.

Lewis and Sigurd poked sticks in the ground and disturbed a family of angry yellow jackets. They stung Lewis on the hand and swarmed over Sigurd's face, stinging him around his mouth and eyes. Evan and Inga ran to the shrieking children and dabbed mud on the welts. His screams subsided to gasping sobs before he fell asleep in Inga's arms.

"Will he be all right?" Evan's heart thumped wildly in his chest. Once yellow jackets stung his father. His face had swelled and then his throat closed so tightly that his tongue stuck out of his mouth. The terror of it remained with Evan after all these years.

While Sigurd slept, Inga carefully inspected his welts. "He's all right." Her voice sounded weak with relief. "No more horseplay."

"I'm sorry," Knut said. "I didn't mean anything."

"Then be careful!" Inga said and pursed her lips as she picked up the reins. A hilly place about five miles out of Millerville proved too steep for Old Doll. The horse stopped in its traces and refused to budge. "You drive!" Inga handed the reins to Evan in disgust. "I'm sick of this old hay burner."

Anders took over the handcart and Ragna carried Sigurd asleep on her shoulder. Evan untied the cow and handed the rope to Gunnar. Losing the animals meant starvation.

After they finally inched over the hill, the brake gave out in a hideous squeal that reminded Evan of hog butchering time. The wagon pressed too close to Old Doll's heels. In spite of Evan's strong pull on the reins, Old Doll stumbled and swerved too close to the edge of the trail. A wheel slipped into a rut and the wagon tipped over entirely.

"Sweet Jesus!" Evan leapt from the wagon and barely avoided the falling load. The wire slipped off the can and milk spilled everywhere. The crate of chickens burst open and they squawked and flapped clumsy wings.

My God, Inga could have been driving. Evan rubbed his ankle and took a tentative step.

"Are you all right?" Inga said.

"Fine." Evan put his full weight on his ankle and walked with only minimal pain. "Nothing broken. Anyone hurt?"

After a quick head count, Evan's thoughts turned to his horse. "What about Old Doll?"

"She seems all right," Anders said as he unhitched her from the twisted traces. "We'll right the wagon."

"Look, the grease spilled over the canvas." Inga's lip quivered. "All lost."

"Not all," Evan forced himself to be cheerfully optimistic. "Nothing better than melted tallow to waterproof a canvas. We'll be thankful if it rains."

It turned out the loss was limited to milk and bacon fat. They pounded the chicken crate back together and the boys chased them down and got them back in the cage.

The accident set them back almost a whole day. By the time they had unloaded the wagon, righted it and repacked it, the sun dipped into the late afternoon sky.

"We'll camp here," Evan said. "And get a fresh start tomorrow."

"This is harder than I expected." Inga's eyes brimmed with tears. "Sigurd is running a fever, the boys are fighting, and just when we need her the most it's as if Ragna is a million miles away."

"It will be better tomorrow"

Evan wished Syl Wheeling would drive by with an empty wagon and rescue them. Of course, no one knew of his coming. They could expect no help except from Almighty God.

"Boys!" He pointed to a small lake in the distance. "Let's go fishing."

The Good Lord provided. Though the fish did not bite, Anders chunked a stone and killed a fat muskrat.

"Muskrat is good meat," Evan said. "Especially when there's nothing better."

"What does it taste like?" Gunnar said.

"Like beaver," Evan said. "Or maybe raccoon."

"Have you eaten those animals?" Knut eyed the rodent with suspicion.

"When I was new to this country." Evan employed his most cheerful voice and attitude. Crooked Lightning's stewpot often contained muskrat and other small animals as well. Many Beavers cooked anything available and it usually tasted just fine. Evan shook his thoughts back to the present. Even thinking about his old friend was enough to summon the nightmares. "And on the way to the Mormon settlement."

"What will Mor say?" Gunnar said.

"She'll thank the Good Lord for his bounty," Evan said. "Your Mor is a wise woman who knows an answer to prayer when she sees it." He looked at his boys, skinny and ragged, and hoped it was true. "We'll sell the pelt to Lying Jack."

THEY STRETCHED THE WAGON COVER over saplings to make a crude shelter for the night. Ragna slept next to Inga with Sigurd curled between them while the twins snuggled at their feet. Anders and the older boys wrapped up by the campfire, and Evan crawled in beside Inga on her other side. His body ached from the journey. Exhaustion forced his eyelids closed. It seemed he had just fallen asleep when Inga poked his ribs.

"Evan," she hissed.

"Go back to sleep."

"There's something on the tarp."

Evan heard small scratching noises all around him. He reached out a hand and felt moving fur and sharp feet. Cursing, he stumbled to the dying embers of the fire and added a little kindling. He knelt down and blew across the coals until the flames licked the dried grass and small sticks. As the fire lit the surrounding area, hundreds of mice swarmed over the tarp and sleeping boys.

Never had he seen mice so thick. They must have smelled the bacon grease on the tarp. He took a stick and poked the wagon cover a good quick hoist that sent the mice flying. Although they scurried away in every direction, they crept back as soon as the tarp stilled again. Even the cat did not scare them away. Inga placed the cat next to Sigurd in hopes the baby would be able to sleep.

There was nothing to do but sit up all night and chase the mice away as best he could. Anders heard the commotion and joined him by the fire.

"It's the bacon grease," Evan said.

"Let's hope it doesn't draw bears."

Evan looked out into the darkness. Loons laughed across the lake and whippoorwills sang in the trees. An owl hooted and a wolf howled somewhere in the distance. A cold dampness settled over them, and they huddled closer, feeding sticks into the fire.

The season was changing. Darkness came earlier and stayed longer. At least it was better than the Old Country where winter meant almost total darkness. In America, they enjoyed the luxury of daylight every day of the year.

"Muskrat is good," Anders said. "Tastes like reindeer meat."

"You're right." Evan remembered the tangy taste of reindeer at family feasts and felt a sudden longing for Norway. He pushed it back. There was no time to be sentimental.

"What were the Red Men like?" Anders said. "I've heard nothing good about them but in his book, James Fennimore Cooper describes them as honest and trustworthy."

"I once agreed with that philosophy," Evan said. He rolled the words around in his mind before speaking. "I trusted Crooked Lightning and yet in the end he turned against me."

"Who was Crooked Lightning?"

Evan hoisted the stick against the tarp and scattered mice in all directions. Their small eyes reflected the fire and glowed like fireflies in the darkness. One landed in the fire and squealed before dying in the flames. An acrid stench filled the air. An owl flew over the shelter, swooped down, and grasped a mouse with strong claws.

"Crooked Lightning was my friend and took part in the raids. He was hanged at Mankato."

"*Nei!*" Anders's face held a look of horror. "You knew someone hanged!"

"I did." Evan's voice was flat and even. He reached toward his pocket before he remembered it held no tobacco. "An Indian I named friend."

Evan thought of the way Crooked Lightning looked at him when he and Bishop Whipple visited him in the stockade before the hanging. His flesh crawled.

"And Ragna's family?"

"Killed."

"But her sister . . ."

"Dead, most likely."

Evan jerked the stick against the tarp again and sent more mice flying. They landed with small thuds all around the sleeping bodies. "The War of Rebellion, the Uprising, the Bank Panic, and now the grasshoppers."

"But look around you," Anders said. "No sign of hoppers and the best soil a man could ever find. Where else can a man own a farm for so little?"

Anders's words brought a great longing into Evan's heart, a wish to be young and naïve again, to believe that America held the secret to a golden future. They conversed in low tones about Congress Land still available.

"I'm thinking of forgoing the pineries and filing for a homestead instead. Mr. Van Dyke says the logging camps are nothing but bedbug camps. Says the work is dangerous. He knows more than one man crippled or killed by falling trees."

"There's a nice piece of land adjoining my claim, with a small lake and a perfect hill for a dugout."

"I'll look into it," Anders said. "We could trade work back and forth and live as neighbors."

Sigurd cried out in his sleep, and Inga squelched a small scream as she brushed a mouse away from his face. She sat up and pushed her hair back from her face with both hands. The twins stirred and the horizon purpled in the east.

"We may as well get started," Evan said. "We need to make up time if we'll get any plowing done before winter."

"I'll file on a claim," Anders said. "But I'd like to look around first. I'll be living there a long time and don't want to choose foolishly."

"That's a good idea," Evan said. The young man had a level head on his shoulders. With a start, Evan realized that when he was Anders' age, he had taken on the responsibility of an orphan and a widow with child. Far said war made a man old before his time. Though the Indian war had happened eleven years ago, it had changed Evan.

It seemed he had been an old man all his life.

20

Mark Twain Abroad! He describes the Snobbish Insanity Developed by the Visit of the Shah to England

St. Paul Dispatch, *September 22, 1873*

THE DAYS ON THE TRAIL MELTED into a slogging forward motion. A heavy wind slowed them down and then a rainy night kept them damp and awake. Evan had known Leaf Mountain was too steep for Old Doll to climb with a loaded wagon and had planned all along to veer south and west of the tallest hills. Rain made the already slippery trail even more treacherous. Evan toyed with the idea of stopping by Clitherall and introducing his family to the Saints, but it was more practical to head cross-country towards his claim.

That night he was too exhausted to sleep. A cold wind made it feel colder than it was, and Evan checked on each child, pulling blankets up over their shoulders, making sure they were safe and warm. He reached a hand across Inga and touched Sigurd's downy hair before lying down on his side of the blanket. Food, shelter, and clothing. Could he provide even these basic needs for his family?

Evan imagined what it would be like to drive his wagon into Clitherall and feel the welcoming hands of the Saints. It was tempting. Evan knew that if he would only commit to their strange religion, he and his family would never lack again. They could build another cabin along the lakeshore, and Ragna could meet a young man at the courting swing. Their larder would be filled with the crops he had helped harvest. Mrs. Wheeling would befriend his Inga and make her life easier.

However, as much as it appealed to him for those reasons, he had made a promise to his mother. She urged him to remember the commandments. Although there was not a specific commandment against the sect, he would not betray the true faith of Martin Luther just to keep his family fed.

Evan sighed and settled into a more comfortable position. If only he could speak to his old friend, Bishop Whipple. Not just about the Saints, but also about his recurring nightmares about the Indian war. Once settled, he might write a letter to the good man and ask his advice. The last he knew about Bishop Whipple, was that he was heading to Cuba to make peace with Spain. If anyone could speak peace into a situation, it was Bishop Whipple.

Ragna must find a job where she could earn her ticket home to Norway. He had promised Lars he would watch over his children and he'd done the best he could. Once Ragna was home, that responsibility would be finished.

"Can't sleep?" Inga's voice startled him at his side.

"Just thinking."

"About the Saints?"

"How do you know?"

"We've been married so long I can read your mind."

"If you can read my mind," Evan pulled back his hand from Sigurd's hair and cupped it around the curve of her hip. "Why do you ask?"

"Maybe I like the sound of your voice."

They talked about the Saints and newspaper articles they had read about their strange ways. "You'll like them," Evan said. "Hard workers and honest as the day is long."

"Do they have many wives?" Inga said. "Paper says they practice polygamy in Utah."

"*Nei*, and neither horns nor fishhook noses." Evan patted her hip and snuggled his face in her hair. Inga smelled of wood smoke and cooking grease. They were almost home but it was not quite home, yet. Just a stand of hardwoods and a splash of open prairie, a perfect site for building, a glimmer of potential in a land unspoiled by grasshoppers and free for the taking. She moved closer and spooned into his body. Sleep fell like a heavy blanket.

THE NEXT DAY THEY PULLED AWAY from the hill country and entered a more moderate terrain. Ribbons of burnished oaks lined pristine lakes and streams. Hilly stretches of fertile prairie intermingled with thick woods. Deer wandered in the forest and geese flew overhead in perfect vees, their calls like blowing trumpets over the prairies. Sverre stirred a pair of grouse dusting themselves on the trail. Surely, God had led them to this place of bounty.

Scattered farms dotted the area, visible by isolated plumes of chimney smoke. Evan's pulse quickened. His dream. Only a landowner could hope to leave anything to his children.

An axe sounded through the forest.

"Boys, listen!" Evan pulled the reins to bring Old Doll to a complete stop on the bumpy trail through the woods. "We're almost there. I think it's Milton's axe."

Old Doll pulled the jostling wagon through the last leg of their journey with Anders at the reins. The cow, still tied to the back of the wagon, lowed anxiously. Inga straggled behind, holding the hands of Sverre and Lewis. Ragna carried Sigurd, and Evan pushed the wheelbarrow, heaped with the barrel of heavy tools to lighten Old Doll's load. Gunnar and Knut ran ahead, following the sound of the axe. Gunnar carried the cat draped across his shoulder.

"I see him," Gunnar called back. "I can see Milton."

Ahead stood a small shelter in a nearby clearing. Evan felt Inga's eyes staring at the crude dwelling. Driven stakes supported poles stretched across the top. The roof consisted of strips of bark laid across the poles topped with pine boughs.

"*Velkommen.*" Milton's bearded face dripped sweat. He wiped his brow with the back of his arm and buried the axe in a stump.

The boys stared round-eyed at the rough clearing, the raw stumps, and the hut.

"Rest yourselves," Milton said. "I'll boil coffee."

"I'll cook the coffee," Inga said with a gentle laugh, more like her old self. "If you start the fire."

"You're a brave woman," Milton said. "I've set your shelter on fire three times with my carelessness." He pointed to the charred stakes on the west side of his shelter. "Not that it did much damage."

The men drifted into talk of game and soil, building sites and land still available. They paced out measurements for a dugout in the hillside and then paced off another dugout for a barn. After slurping scalding brew out of tin cups, Milton and Anders hiked towards the west to scout the parcel of land still available. Evan cast a longing eye as they walked away, but turned back to his tasks. He was a married man with a family. First things first.

"It's so small," Inga said as she looked at the stakes marking out the boundaries for the dugout. "How will we fit?"

"It's bigger than it looks," Evan said. "A dugout can't be so wide that the roof caves in—we'll dig deeper into the hill."

"Like gophers."

"Only for one winter," he said.

Inga called to the twins and busied herself with Sigurd. He wondered if she wished her first man had lived or if she would rather have been the wife of the rich Swede, Ingvald Ericcson.

His sister, Christina, would have hated living in a dugout. He remembered how she yearned for the long summer days of midnight sun that final winter of her life. "Just think, Evan," she had said though her eyes burned bright with fever and every cough spurted blood into her handkerchief. "In America there is sun every day of the year, not just in summer." He swallowed a lump in his throat.

Someday Inga would bear another daughter, this one named for his sister. They were still young and had their strength and health.

Evan and the boys began the tedious task of unloading the wagon. They needed the heavy tools stored underneat the furniture. He found himself praying with every box lifted from the wagon bed. *Dear Jesus, by all holy, please keep the grasshoppers away.* He stacked the barrels alongside the outside perimeter of the shelter. At least it offered a little privacy. He scanned the skies. Only blue sky and the whitest clouds.

After all these years in America, Evan was finally a landowner. He remembered Crooked Lightning's words, "The white man will not rest until he owns the whole world." Evan pushed the thought away and focused instead on the many tasks at hand.

"You boys drag these deadfalls over to the barn and build an outside pen for the animals." He straightened his back and wiped the back of his sleeve across his forehead. A flock of ducks flew overhead. "Maybe I'll shoot a duck for supper."

"And when you're done with the fence," Evan called out to the boys who were dragging their feet towards the scattered trees downed by Milton's neighborly axe. "We'll go fishing."

The boys ran to their work, squealing with delight over the promise of fishing. They were good boys. He needed to remember they were still young.

Anders and Milton joined Evan and his family for breakfast. The cold morning air made them hunker close to the fire and coddle their porridge bowls with both hands.

"No frost," Evan said. "But you feel the change coming."

"Back in the uprising," Inga said, "we saw our first frost in early September." She picked up the coffee pot and poured Milton another cup. "Remember, Evan?" She filled his cup as well. "The soldiers were able to see the Indians hiding around Fort Abercrombie after frost killed off the brush."

Evan felt his mind roiling. The grass had been heavy with white frost the morning he had gone out to the perimeter to relieve Jonas Wilson standing watch. His head tilted at a strange angle and when Evan touched him, he could feel the coldness of his body through his shirtsleeve.

Evan's heart pounded, and he burned his tongue on a gulp of hot coffee. Their talk shifted to available claims, other folks moving in, and the many tasks of getting started in the wilderness. Milton advised Anders to file sooner rather than later, lest he miss the chance for land next to them.

"I'd let you take Old Doll," Evan said. "But she's not up to it. You'll have to ride shank's mare."

"A young man like you can walk the sixty-five miles to Sauk Center in no time." Milton reached over and pinched another corner of cornbread.

"I'll work today and walk tomorrow. Be back in a week." Anders stood and stretched. "Do you need anything from the store?"

After a lengthy debate and count of coins, they decided that Anders should purchase a cowbell and a sack of flour. "We have enough flour until the new year if we're careful," Evan said. "But not enough to last the winter."

"Can you carry it such a long ways?" Inga said. "You might take the handcart."

Evan knew she worried about not having bread for the children. "Growing children need fresh milk and all the bread they can eat," was her oft-quoted philosophy.

"*Nei*," Anders said. "The cart would slow me down. After following the wagon this far, it will be a relief to be able to set my own pace. It won't be the first time I hoisted a burden that far."

Evan noticed Anders's eyes flit towards Ragna where she sorted beans for the soup pot. Maybe Ragna was the reason Anders planned a homestead next to theirs. Evan heaved a deep sigh. Everything always turned out so complicated. Anders already had a sweetheart, and Ragna must return to Norway.

Bite I det sure eple. Take a bite of the sour apple.

21

A Petition is Being Circulated in Brown County to the General Government for Relief of Homestead Settlers who are Obliged To Leave Their Claims to Get a Living Because their Crops are Destroyed By Grasshoppers

St. Paul Dispatch, *October 5, 1873*

Holy Mary, Mother of God. Ragna plunged the dasher up and down. She loved the Red Wing churn, just the size to hold in one arm and work the dasher with the other. *Pray for us sinners now and in the hour of our death.* Not that Ragna felt it was her hour of death, but the grasshoppers, *Bestemor's* sudden demand, and leaving home left her unsettled. The feeling would not leave.

Ragna watched Sigurd playing with Fisk and the twins while Auntie Inga washed Sigurd's soakers and spread them across bushes to dry. The men had been digging since daybreak and were as dirty as coalminers. They burrowed into the hill with picks and shovels, carefully setting aside layers of sod to use as thatching on the roof, and prying a huge flat rock out of the dirt that would make a perfect hearthstone.

"See, Inga," Uncle Evan said when they came to the cook shack. "The Good Lord provides. We'll place the stone under the stove to heat during the day and keep its warmth overnight when the fire dies down. We'll be warm as toast."

"Now you're thinking!" Anders said with a look of admiration on his dirty face as he took the dipper from Uncle Evan. "Is that how they do it in Norway?"

The men discussed the ancient Scandinavian method of heating rocks in huge fires until they cracked and split for use as roof tiles, walls, or foundations. Ragna noticed Anders looking at her while they talked, but she kept churning without comment as the men returned to their work.

Ragna's arm ached from the constant motion of the dasher. Dolly's milk was richer with the better pasture, and Ragna hoped her supply would increase enough to make more butter and cheese for trade. She pushed the dasher repeatedly.

It is only a bad dream. Mor and Far decide to stay in Norway instead of leaving for America. "I wish I had good black dirt of Minnesota," Far *says.* "But I couldn't risk the skraelings."

"Oh, Ragna," *Birdie says and her eyes shine blue as the fjords,* "what would our life have been if Far and Mor had gone to Minnesota when they had the chance?"

"How long until the butter turns?" Auntie Inga's voice interrupted her thoughts.

Ragna shook herself back to reality. "It's ready now, Auntie."

"Well get on with it," Auntie said. "There's supper to make."

Ragna worked the butter, her favorite task. Exactly the right amount of cold water to remove the bitterness and a precise measurement of salt worked into the butter across Auntie's wooden bowl with the paddle. Pressing it against the sides until it finally formed into a perfect lump of sweet butter. She filled the crock, secured the lid with a wire brace, and lowered it into a bucket of cool water. She placed the bucket in the shade. Her mouth watered at the thought of sweet butter on fresh bread.

Ragna picked up the butcher knife and peeled potatoes for dinner, carefully rinsing each naked spud in a pail of clean water before plopping it into the soup kettle filled with salted water. "Knut," she called. "More water from the spring."

"I just hauled two buckets!" Knut said.

"Hurry!" Auntie's voice squelched all argument. Knut snagged the empty bucket and dragged his feet towards the lake as the men dug holes straight into the hill on both sides of the dugout opening. Jammed logs stabilized the inside walls and provided a framework to fasten more logs across the front for a stout outside wall. Gunnar cut swamp grass with the hay knife to scatter across the dirt floor. Auntie said scattered grass would keep the dust down and make it feel more like home.

"Hay of any kind is needed for fodder," Uncle said with a frown. "We've a long winter ahead of us."

Auntie set her jaw, and Ragna noticed that Gunnar continued with the hay knife without another word said. Usually Auntie had her way.

The men dragged the iron cook stove into the dugout before starting the log front.

"We might as well save ourselves aggravation later," Milton said. "Anything else heavy to go in before we close it up?"

The men carried the last of the barrels into the dugout to be unpacked later. The dwelling was smaller than the kitchen back home. Ragna wondered where they would all sleep.

"You'll stay nice and warm." Milton stretched his back after the heavy lifting. "But there's a danger of fire with the thatch."

"Ja," Evan said. "Back home my father layered slate under the birch bark. But we're pressed for time."

"At least solid walls on three sides." Anders said. "No drafts will bother."

After dinner, Ragna washed the dishes in a pan of water heated over the fire and set on the end of the wagon. They were short of soap, something unheard of in better times. "Auntie," she approached the subject cautiously. "The soap is almost gone."

"Be careful with it," Auntie answered. "We'll trade with the Saints."

The casual way she mentioned the Mormons made Ragna look up from the dishpan. For some reason she had thought Auntie Inga would want them to stay away from the sect, as she wanted Uncle Evan to keep them away from the Catholic Brorson family.

"You'll go along to Clitherall," Auntie said. "I'm hoping to barter your midwifery for your ticket home."

"But I don't know enough," Ragna said. "Couldn't we do it together?"

Ragna thought of the lonely trail to Leaf Mountain and the winding road to Clitherall. She tried to imagine what it would be like to travel the road—most babies were born at night. She scrubbed the dirty plates and rinsed them with hot water from the teakettle. Just the thought of walking alone at night made her think of Birdie. She reached up to the button around her neck, but a voice interrupted her daydream.

"Anybody home?"

Three men rode in to the clearing straddled on workhorses without saddles, their long legs hanging down the sides of the giant horses. They spoke only American and had dark hair and eyes, faces burned by the sun though they were clearly white people.

"*Welkommen!*" Uncle Evan reached up to shake one of the rider's hands. "Syl, you are a welcome sight."

Auntie Inga sent Knut to the spring for another bucket of water and hurried to gather bread and butter. Uncle Evan and Milton dragged a downed elm into a shady spot and the men sat on its trunk.

"We'll water your horses." Anders and Gunnar led the animals to the lake.

"What brings you way over here?" Milton said.

"Elijah married," Mr. Wheeling said with a grin. "Filed a claim north of here." He removed his hat and wiped his face with a red bandanna handkerchief. "We've spent a couple days raising their cabin."

The men conversed of building methods, wood supplies, and fall work to be done while Auntie put water on for coffee.

"Sod is warmer," Mr. Wheeling said, "and keeps out the cold." He eyed the stack of logs nearby. "But a log front on the barn allows light and fresh air for the animals. Skimp a little on the chinking and you'll have light without window glass."

The twins chased the cat through the clearing, squealing and laughing. Auntie Inga frowned and motioned for Ragna to tend to them. Ragna placed a small dish of milk on the ground and called to the cat. It came running, leading the twins back to the clearing.

Ragna handed Sverre, Lewis, and Sigurd each a bread crust and dipped cups of water from the bucket as she listened to the men's conversation. "Keep quiet now," she whispered. "We've company."

"We thought to lend a hand." Syl broke a twig and picked his teeth. "Being we're in this neck of the woods."

"How kind of you," Uncle Evan said, and Ragna noticed his stumble over the American words.

"Looks like you've made a good start."

The men examined the dugouts and discussed how a longer stovepipe would draw smoke over the top of the hill, and ways to cope, living in such a shelter over the long winter.

"Ma'am," Syl said to Auntie as she poured water into the coffee pot. "We are not coffee drinkers. We'd just as soon drink the water plain."

Auntie looked confused but acquiesced, pouring water into tin cups and passing them around with the bread and butter.

"Let's get to work," Syl said around mouthfuls of bread. "One of us can help setting the logs. It goes better with four men, and two of us can start either on the barn or the plowing. What do you prefer?"

"The Good Book says to first tend your fields and then work on your house," Uncle Evan said. "I'll follow that advice."

"You are right, Brother!" Syl said with a booming laugh. "Spoken like a true Saint! John, hitch Blackie to the plow. Otto, gather stones and debris off the field. Maybe the boys could help."

He spoke like a general commanding his army. It was a comforting feeling. Heretics or not, the Saints and their help were most welcome. Uncle Evan attacked the project with new vigor and Auntie Inga wore a smile.

"Ragna," Auntie said. "Stir up a batch of biscuits." She scurried around with great industry, unpacking barrels of household goods and arranging them in an old wooden box pushed into the dugout wall as a cupboard.

"I'll be glad to use my stove again." Auntie paused to wipe her face with the hem of her apron. "It's hard cooking over an open fire."

Ragna knew firsthand how tricky it was to cook in a bake pan covered with glowing embers. It was cooking by guess and by golly. Too little and the biscuits were doughy, too long and they burnt to a crisp.

"We might be cooking over an open fire longer than we think." Auntie Inga pursed her lips and jutted her chin toward the dugout. "We can't light the stove until we can afford the new pipe."

By twilight, they had cleared and half plowed a large garden patch. The men marveled at the blackness of the soil, the exposure to sunshine and protection from the wind, the standing timber ready for next summer's cabin.

The new dugout nestled in the hillside with its log front, earthen sides, and thatched roof. A small window rested next to the door with the glass pane carried safely from Alexandria. The barn dugout squatted next to a makeshift pen for the animals.

Auntie was right. The swamp grass brightened the interior and made it a little lighter. Everything in place except for the stovepipe.

The twins gathered hazelnuts into a lard bucket near the place where Lady and Bob had been tethered in the grass. Sigurd napped in the wagon bed. Gunnar and Knut picked rocks thrown up by David's plowing. Ragna milked the cow and looked over her shoulders into the woods only a few times during the task. She would ask the Saints about Indians when she had a chance.

When the men gathered round the campfire after their work, Ragna poured cups of fresh, warm milk while Auntie ladled soup and passed the biscuits and fresh butter.

"We have need of so many things," Uncle Evan said as he blew on a spoonful of hot soup. "Perhaps we could negotiate a trade. Inga is good at midwifery and bone setting. I've a knack with horses. You know my work."

Syl listened with a thoughtful look. He lifted a callused hand and rubbed the side of his bearded jaw. "We have a situation."

Ragna did not know she was holding her breath until she let it out in a slow sigh. So much depended on his answer.

"Gjert Sevald is ill," Mr. Wheeling said. "His wife is not young and cannot bear the burden alone."

Perhaps they wanted Auntie Inga to stop and tend him from time to time. She would gladly care for the little boys while Auntie was gone. They needed a stovepipe. They needed seed for spring planting. Soap. The twins showed skin through holes in their britches. All of them needed shoes.

"Perhaps your daughter could stay with the Sevalds until he passes." Mr. Wheeling looked at Ragna and she felt her heart drop. "Through the winter."

She must not have heard correctly.

"I've never tended the dying," Ragna said in a quivery voice. Immediately she recognized the lie. She had tended Baby Ann Elin. It was as if she could feel the baby's cold skin. She gulped hard. She had never tended an old man. She did not know if she could.

"Of course she'll help out." Uncle Evan's eyes lit up, and Ragna remembered they were without money. One less person to feed would help the family. And wages.

She had never slept away from home. A shudder went through her. *Holy Mary Mother of God, pray for us now and in the hour of our death.*

"It's the least we can do for our neighbors." Auntie Inga set her jaw.

Uncle Evan and Mr. Wheeling discussed wages and barter.

Almost in a fog, Ragna entered the dugout and searched an open barrel in the corner. She gathered her extra dress and good apron, fresh rags, and clean underwear. She pulled her shawl, mittens, and catechism. As she bundled them together, her mind went to Birdie and she fingered the button around her neck.

"Hold my hand!" Birdie's legs are too short to keep up. She trips and cries out when a sharp stick pierces her chubby hands. "Birdie, hang on tight!"

"Quiet!" the Red Man says. "Don't look back!"

Somewhere I hear Mor's screams, smell burning wood, and see dark plumes of smoke rise above the trees. Maybe I hear Far's voice calling my name . . . I can't be sure.

The terror of the painted face and hissing voice turns my legs to water. He scoops Birdie into his arms and grabs my hand, drags me through thick woods away from our home, running as if he were afraid, too.

After a long time, maybe hours, maybe days, I drink cool water and feel a kind hand. Then sleep. That's all I remember. Except Birdie's face as she is dragged away. I stretch my hands toward her but cannot reach her. Then the slap that knocks me into darkness. Then swirling mist.

"Ragna," Auntie Inga said at the door. "What's taking you so long?"

"I'm afraid," Ragna said. "The nightmares . . ."

"The Lord will protect you."

"I won't know what to do."

"You'll know." Auntie pulled Ragna into her arms and squeezed her tight. She smelled of smoke, sweat, and cooking. "I've been alone before with no one but the Lord. He's kept me through many dark valleys."

"I don't want to go."

"I know."

WHEN THE SAINTS LEARNED OF ANDERS'S intent to file on a homestead, they insisted he travel with them as far as Clitherall and start out in the morning for Sauk Center.

"Blackie has a strong back and room for another rider," David said. "Ride behind me."

"*Mange takk.*" Anders looked toward Ragna, and she looked away. "I'd appreciate the ride."

"We pass the Sevald cabin on the way home," Syl said. "See how the Good Lord works out our path when we trust Him?"

"Can I come with you?" Sverre grasped the corner of Ragna's apron. "I don't want you to go."

Lewis popped his thumb in his mouth and pressed so close to her legs that Ragna feared she might trip over him if she tried to move.

"Come away, boys," Uncle Evan said firmly. "You'll see Ragna soon."

Auntie Inga pressed a bundle into Ragna's arms. "Maybe you'll get a chance for mending."

"I'll try, Auntie." How would Auntie ever get the work done without her?

"Be a good girl," Uncle said and his Adam's apple bobbed in his throat. "I'll stop by in a few weeks and see how you're doing."

Ragna's voice choked. She kissed the boys, even Gunnar who wiped his face with his sleeve. When Uncle Evan rescued her after Camp Release, he became her stability. She remembered that feeling of relief, like she never wanted to leave his side again. She had hated when he had to leave to drive the stage. Only when Uncle Evan was home did she feel safe.

Now she was leaving. *Ja*, it was only down the road, but still leaving his home and his table. She hugged Uncle Evan and was surprised that his cheeks were wet as well. Surely he would not cry for her leaving—though he had said tears dwelled in all men. His beard scratched her forehead.

"*Mange tussen takk,*" he whispered in her ear. "Many thousand thanks."

"Don't forget what I've taught you." Auntie bent to pick up Sigurd playing with wood chips on the earthen floor of the new dugout.

Ragna leaned forward and buried her face in Sigurd's neck, breathing in the sweetness of his baby skin, the sour smell of urine on his dress. She kissed his wet mouth and twirled a blond curl around her finger. "I'll miss you, *lille guten.*"

"We need to get going," Syl said from the door. "A full moon tonight but it'll be late by the time we reach the Branch of Zion."

"You're welcome to stay the night," Auntie Inga said. "Get an early start in the morning."

"Thank you," Syl tipped his hat. "But we've Meeting tomorrow and must get home."

Ragna dragged her feet to the men and horses. Anders hoisted his pack onto Otto's lap. Thank God, she would not travel alone with strange men.

"It will be all right." Anders helped her up on the horse behind John. She had no choice but to ride astride and hang on with all her might. John was as old as Uncle Evan was, but it still felt strange to hold onto his waist—and in such an unladylike position. "You'll have an adventure to tell your grandchildren." Anders spoke in Norwegian and the familiar language warmed her. The words almost intimate, like a hedge against the rest of the world.

Ragna tried to resist but could not help herself. She looked down into those bluest of eyes and felt her heart flip-flop.

22

Cranberries are Beginning to Ripen and the Indians are Commencing to Devote their Leisure Moments to Gathering Them.
St. Paul Dispatch, *October 5, 1873*

RAGNA DID NOT KNOW HOW SHE could stand it.

Anders entertained them during the miles to the Sevald cabin. He shared stories about fishing from the Loften Islands and his journey to America, how he learned to read and write English in Minneapolis before coming to the frontier.

"I'm a great reader myself." Mr. Wheeling said.

"My favorite book is by Cooper," Anders said.

"*The Deerslayer?*"

"*Nei,* that one I've not seen." Anders said. "*The Last of the Mohicans.*"

"It was from Mr. Cooper I first learned that Indians can be trusted," Mr. Wheeling said. "That was before I met the Prophet who said the same. We've found it true in the wilderness."

"Do Red Men live around here?" Anders said.

Ragna held her breath and looked back over her shoulders into the shadows. Indians could hide in a hundred places. She clutched John's jacket a little tighter.

"Of course," Syl said. "Every spring they return to Otter Tail Lake for spring sugaring and stay until after the fall rice harvest."

"We see them during the summer," Otto said. "In the winter they travel west."

Ragna felt the hair on her neck bristle. What if the *skraelings* came to the Sevald cabin and stole her away? She breathed in slowly.

"What is the best way to deal with them?" Anders said. "Say if one came to my cabin."

"Usually they ask for . . ."

"Well water or bread." The words came from Ragna's lips as if from a deep vault of memory.

"Exactly," Mr. Wheeling said. "How do you know?"

"We had Indian neighbors before the uprising." The words tingled on Ragna's lips. She had been allowed to talk of it so seldom that the words tasted foreign. "They came begging."

"Evan didn't mention it," Mr. Wheeling said.

"Not Uncle Evan," Ragna said. "My real parents, killed in the uprising."

A silence hung over the little band on the moonlit trail. Brush slapped their legs, and John pushed branches away from his face, holding them back until Ragna was safely past as well. Owls hooted and a wolf howled in the direction of Leaf Mountain. Ragna shivered with cold. The night air smelled of fresh turned soil and rotting leaves.

"You've suffered," Mr. Wheeling said at last. "Others in our community as well." He reined his horse and turned towards Ragna. "I pray the Lord brings you comfort."

The kindness of his words brought a lump to her throat.

Anders reached over in the darkness and touched her arm. The warmth of his touch burned on her sleeve long after a light shone through the trees. "There it is."

"Marta!" Mr. Wheeling called. "Are you home?"

He waited for an answer. When none came, he opened the door and walked in, motioning Ragna to follow.

Her resolve weakened. The log cabin reeked of urine and the smell of something old and rotting. Her stomach roiled and her heart pounded in her ears. A small lamp glowed on the table before a single window and a smoky flame smoldered in the fireplace at the far side of the cabin. It was hardly larger than the dugout and cluttered with dirty dishes, firewood, piles of soiled clothing, and papers.

Mrs. Sevald hovered over a man sprawled on the bed. Her face wrinkled into a hundred grooves, and she wore a dark-colored dress and a calico apron. Mrs. Sevald wiped her husband's whiskers with her apron as if the others were not there. She rinsed the apron corner in a bucket and wiped again.

"Marta," Mr. Wheeling said after clearing his throat several times. "I've brought a hired girl to help with Gjert."

She did not look up from her duties, only bent again to wipe Mr. Sevald's face. His eyes never opened.

"Marta," he repeated. "I've brought Ragna Jacobson to help you."

"Larson," Ragna said quietly. "Ragna Larson."

"Of course," Mr. Wheeling said. "Larson."

"I can stand it." Mrs. Sevald finally straightened up and turned her leathery face in their direction. It seemed she had trouble focusing her faded gray eyes and she squinted against the light. "I don't mind."

"Just for a while, Marta," Mr. Wheeling said. He seemed half-afraid of the older woman and spoke timidly, almost apologetically. "The Elders decided."

"I got no money for a hired girl."

"The Elders will take care of it," Mr. Wheeling said.

"I said I don't need nobody." Her voice rose to a higher pitch and she gripped her hands together in front of her. "I'm doing all right."

"It's only practical—you can't expect others to watch out for you during winter when you're out here all alone."

"I can stand it."

"Be reasonable." His voice lowered. "It would help Ragna's family," Mr. Wheeling looked back at Ragna in an apologetic manner. "They're having a hard time—lost everything to grasshoppers and are making do in a dugout with five other children." He shifted his feet. "You'd be helping them and getting a little relief yourself."

Ragna felt her cheeks crimson. The Saints gave her a job out of pity. Silence filled the cabin as everyone waited for Marta's reply. Ragna prayed a desperate prayer that she would refuse and then prayed she would accept her help so her family could make it through the winter with the needed stovepipe.

"All right, then," Mrs. Sevald muttered but she did not look at Ragna.

Mr. Wheeling excused himself and headed for the door.

Ragna followed him to the outside step.

"If you need anything," Mr. Wheeling said, "my son and his bride are your nearest neighbors. Just down this trail a couple miles."

"What's his name?" Ragna pushed down a feeling of panic.

"Elijah," Mr. Wheeling said. "I'll have him stop by and check on you."

"Ragna," Anders tipped his hat and handed her the bundles. "Don't forget your things."

"*Tussen takk.*" She gathered them close to her, sniffing the familiar scent of home.

"I'll be back in no time," Anders said. "And I'll stop by, too, to see how you're doing."

"*Nei,*" Ragna felt her strength melting away in relief. "It's too much trouble."

"Nonsense!" He pulled a book from an inside pocket of his jacket. "Read this when you're homesick."

It was too dark to read the title. He leaned over and kissed her forehead. It was a kiss like the one she might give to a younger brother. Even so, happiness surged through her and gave her the strength to face Mrs. Sevald.

Mrs. Sevald was a short, slight woman, with a thin white braid wrapped around her head and fastened with a wooden pin that stuck out from her head like a needle in a pincushion. Her face was all bones, sinew, and jutting chin. She spoke only American. Ragna hoped that Mrs. Sevald had not understood her conversation with Anders. She pulled the memory closer to her like a private treasure.

Mrs. Sevald barely looked up. Instead, she gathered dry linen from a basket and jerked the wet blankets off her husband. The man lay as if in a deep sleep, his arms twisted at a funny angle with the palms of his hands turned away from his body.

"Well," Mrs. Sevald said at last. "Are you going to help or stand there gawking?"

Together they bathed Mr. Sevald, changed his clothes, straightened his limp limbs and settled him for the night. Her cheeks burned with the shock of tending a naked man. What would Auntie say? Ragna's back ached from bending over the low bed. Mr. Sevald was not a big man, but tall, and his body was dead weight.

After they finished, Mrs. Sevald turned her back to Ragna and changed into a white flannel nightgown, bed socks, and nightcap. Then she blew out the lamp and crawled into bed beside her husband without a word.

Ragna stood in the darkness with only the flickering light from the fire and a moonbeam through the window. Looking out the window, she spied the outside toilet. A quilt draped across a chair by the table. Ragna sniffed it cautiously. Urine. Using all the strength she could muster, Ragna wrapped the stinky quilt around her shoulders and left the house. At least a full moon lighted the path.

Once inside the outhouse, Ragna was afraid to close the door. There might be snakes, spiders or bears—but she was desperate. She lifted her skirts and did her business as quickly as possible, praying her novena aloud in the darkness. Shadows hid a hundred *skraelings* waiting to pounce on her. A wolf prowled the night, his eyes on her. An escaped prisoner from St. Peter Insane Asylum lurked behind the woodpile waiting to chop her head off with an axe. However, there was no window in the outhouse to frame the face of a wild Indian. *Thank God for that.*

She ran back to the cabin with a sudden fear that perhaps Mrs. Sevald had locked her out to freeze in the darkness. Ragna pushed open the door, stepped into the house and quickly closed and barred the door. She walked firmly to the window and pulled the shutter. Darkness overwhelmed the room. Ragna quietly moved a pile of dirty clothes from before the fireplace and nudged a wooden crate away with her foot until she cleared a space to lie down on the floor. Mice scurried in the corners. The quilt stank of sickness. *Holy Mary, Mother of God.* She positioned her bundle as a pillow and then remembered the sewing. Thank God, Auntie had sent a torn sheet for mending. Ragna pulled out the home-smelling linen and laid it carefully over the quilt before pulling her shawl over herself as a blanket. It would have to do. Tomorrow she would find herself a bed if she must build it herself.

She pictured her family in the dugout. Sigurd asleep between Auntie and Uncle in the rope bed. Knut and Sverre sharing one bunk, Gunnar, and Lewis the other. She imagined the boys fighting for space, arguing until Auntie called their names. Then the settling sounds of night. Uncle's snoring. Sverre's heavy breathing. What if an elk or a stray buffalo wandered over the hill and collapsed through the roof? What if a Red Man peeked down the chimney hole or crept in to kill them in their beds?

She fingered the book from Anders. In the firelight, she saw it was the book by James Fennimore Cooper. It was too dark to read but she pulled it closer to her chest.

"So you're a papist." Mrs. Sevald's voice surprised her in the darkness.

"Excuse me?" Surely, Ragna had misunderstood the American words.

"Catholic." Mrs. Sevald's said. "You said it wrong. It's *Hail Mary, full of grace, the Lord is with thee; blessed art thou among women, and blessed is the fruit of thy womb, Jesus. Holy Mary, Mother of God, pray for us sinners, now and at the hour of our death, Amen.*"

"I'm confirmed Lutheran," Ragna said after a long pause. "But I like to pray to Mary—I lost my mother when I was little." She surprised herself with the words. She had never before connected the prayers to her loneliness for a mother. The statement burst out of her as if it had always been there.

A mouse ran across the floor in front of the fire. Ragna squelched a scream.

"I'll teach you the prayers," Mrs. Sevald said. "I was raised Roman and know all of them." She turned in bed and the ropes squeaked beneath her movement.

Flickering flames in the fireplace cast dancing shadows around the room. Ragna doubted she would sleep at all, but exhaustion heavied her eyelids in spite of her fears.

"You're leaving out Jesus, the most important part." Mrs. Sevald's voice quavered in the night. "If you're going to say them at all, you might as well say them right."

Ragna's thoughts scattered in a million directions, like sparks from the burning logs shooting up the chimney. She had started out the day as herself and ended up as someone else by nighttime. Was it possible to grow up in a single day? She had a job nursing a dying man, Anders had kissed her goodbye, and she would learn the prayers to bring Birdie home. Auntie would disapprove, but in spite of the homesickness that refused to leave, Ragna was satisfied.

She would not leave Jesus out again.

What a difference a single day could make. The day of the uprising. The day of the grasshoppers. The first day of a paying job. The day a young man kisses your forehead. She reached for the button around her neck and slipped into a beautiful dream.

Birdie meets me behind the woodpile, breathless with eyes glowing.

"Ragna!" Birdie wears an Indian dress decorated with tufts of partridge feathers, gray and brown like a bird's nest. She looks at me with blue eyes and smiles Mor's smile, the same smile I see in the mirror.

"I won't go back to Bestemor," I say. "I'm American now."

"I know," Birdie says. "But you have to."

"I think Anders Vollen likes me," I say. "But he has a sweetheart back home."

Birdie's face shines as bright as moon on snow, as clear as rays of sun on a midsummer day.

"If you were here instead of me," I say, "you would know what to say to him."

"He likes you," Birdie says. "He kissed you, after all."

"No more than I might kiss Sigurd." I remember the way he touched my arm in the darkness. His voice is very near, he stands close beside me . . .

"Girl!" Mrs. Sevald's voice startled her awake.

Embers glowed in the fireplace and Ragna's nose felt cold. Mrs. Sevald tugged at her man's nightshirt, struggling to put dry clothing on him. His eyes remain closed and Regna sniffed strong urine and that strange dead smell she had noticed before. Mrs. Sevald had lit the lamp. Ragna lurched to her feet still holding the book, still wearing her dress and shoes.

"Stoke the fire," Mrs. Sevald's voice sounded tired but not unkind. "Then help me change the sheets."

23

Prints 9 cents a yard; 9 pairs of hose for $1.00; 15 pounds of Dried Apples for $1.00; 8 ½ pounds of "A" Sugar for $1.00 and Everything Else in Proportion. Remember the Place—MOCK-ENHAUPTIS

St. Paul Dispatch, *October 5, 1873*

EVAN'S OLD NIGHTMARE RETURNED their first night in the dugout. He woke up with Inga's arms around him and her soothing voice in his ear.

"It's just a dream," Inga said. "Go back to sleep."

Evan swallowed hard and forced himself back to reality. The dugout was pitch black without even a shadow before his eyes. He sat up, reached over and pulled back the curtain over the window and cracked open the door. Cold air slapped his face and cleared his head while moonlight lit the room with a milky slit.

"You dreamed about Lewis . . ."

Evan nodded. Somehow, she always knew.

His friend, Lewis, murdered during the uprising. Evan remembered the startled look on his face, the slack skin beneath his scalped head. How he buried him in the garden patch, the touch of his cold skin, the blood and flies, the stench.

"It was long ago," Inga said.

Crooked Lightning had dug up his body and mutilated him even more. How could he have named the Sioux brave as friend?

Evan smoothed his beard with both hands and wiped his face on the hem of his nightshirt. "Sleeping in this grave reminded me."

"Shhhh." Inga patted his hand and pulled his head to her breast. "It's over. Forget it now."

Evan thought how hard it was to remember some things, like the age of his children or the names of people, and yet other things—like the smells of blood and death—remained impossible to forget though he tried with all his might.

Sigurd stirred. Fisk purred in the darkness. The comforting night sounds of his family surrounded him. Poor Ragna, alone with strangers in a place with windows. She hated windows.

The dugout smelled of fresh logs and damp earth. How strange to travel across the ocean to find a better living and end up living like gophers, no farther ahead, no progress made.

Evan swung his legs over the edge of the bed and slipped on his boots. It was cold without a fire. *Dear God in heaven let the Mormons bring the stovepipe soon so they would not freeze to death. Nei,* they would not freeze, he corrected himself. At least not for a while. If worse came to worse he would build a chimney as his far had once taught him, using mud and stones. However, a chimney would take time needed to ready his fields for spring planting, time he could ill afford. The Mormons were honest folk and could be trusted to keep their end of the deal.

Sverre coughed from his bunk against the opposite wall, so close that Evan could almost see him in the shadowy moonlight. He stepped over and pulled the covers over the sleeping boys. How beautiful, his boys, as they slept.

He rarely went back to sleep after one of his nightmares. Evan draped his old buffalo coat around his shoulders and leaned against the doorframe looking out through the slightly open door. The wagon perched like an ancient skeleton. They had used the wagon cover to reinforce the dugout roof to prevent leaks in the thatch. Trees on the west side of the clearing stood naked, their dropped leaves a thick covering on the forest floor.

He would have the boys gather acorns in the grove of oak trees next to the lake. They made decent cattle feed. Hogs loved acorns best of all, but his had been lost in the hog epidemic a few years back and he had no money to replace them. He would buy a shoat as soon as he could. Maybe a bred sow. A farmer had to keep all his options open. If the hog cholera came, he would have cattle to fall back on. If the epizootic plague went through again, he would have hogs and chickens.

Evan had eaten acorn meal at Crooked Lightning's fire. In a pinch, it would do for them as well. Inga roasted and ground them into a passable coffee. Another reason to gather acorns. The boys could fill the pushcart.

He needed every advantage to keep the wolf from their door.

Ahead lay the half-plowed field. Early potatoes would help them squeak by. It'd be close. They must fish every day and once the barn was up, he would take time for hunting. Extra meat was always welcome, and feathers from geese and ducks provided extra covering against the cold weather, surely on its way.

Syl said that Lying Jack bought hides, even muskrats. Every cent would help. There was a shoemaker at the Branch of Zion. He might trade hides for new shoes. Sverre's toes poked through holes. On the other hand, he might carve shoes from basswood in the stand behind the hill. His *far* had whittled many a wooden shoe for them when they were growing up.

And firewood. How much would they need to survive? Maybe the dugout would heat easier than a drafty cabin. He did not know.

Evan searched for a pencil stub in his jacket pocket and tallied his resources on a sheet of paper fished from the trunk: fresh cow and calf; horse; 11 hens and 1 rooster; 1 cat adept at catching mice and rats; 1 wagon, harness, and wagon cover; pushcart, plow, harrow, cradle, hay knife, flail, drag, and hasp; axe, 3 hatchets, 3 butcher knives, 2 hammers, anvil, crosscut saw, handsaw, shovel, pitchfork, spade, and 3 hoes; 14 linen sheets, 12 wool blankets, 8 feather pillows, 4 mattress tickings , 2 quilts, and a horse hide blanket made when Steel Gray died in the epizootic plague; cook stove, table, bench, 4 chairs, towels and rags to manage, butter churn, bowls and cutlery, cast iron skillet and bake pan with cover, teakettle, 4 crocks, jug, and 4 wooden buckets; a Town's Fourth reader, Webster's blue speller, Sander's Arithmetic, and the family Bible. He'd brought fifty pounds of potatoes from home— only fifty pounds from his entire crop. Their clothes were worn and of little value. The tally came to a rough estimate of $380.

On the profit side, Evan counted four Jerseys sold to Mr. Van Dyke for $96, a bargain for the man and enough for Evan to move the family to Tordenskjold. He and Milton each earned $28 cash during the harvest. Evan had a gold eagle tucked away for a rainy day. He tallied $144 cash money.

The expenditures made a longer cipher. At the start of their journey, they had purchased provisions: 100# flour; 50# dried beans; 25 # dried peas; 10# sugar; 10 # prunes; 10# dried apples; 2# saleratus; 50# corn meal; 25# oatmeal; 5# salt; 20# coffee; 10# bacon; 3# tea; 5# honey; 5# molasses; 1# corn starch; 1 bottle castor oil; 1 bottle cod liver oil; 1 box matches; 5 # candles; and 1# peppermint candies tucked away for Christmas. The total cost was $62.83. Nails and metal hinges for the door cost $4.02, new rope $4, the wagon cover $15, ammunition for the old Danzig shotgun $6, 5 skeins of yarn $2.10, 1 bolt of yard goods for shirts and trousers $3.50. He dared not tally the waste of seed and lost crop from the grasshoppers. And there was no measure of his foolishness in dealing with Ragna's property and neglecting to get his own place.

Som man reder sa ligger man. As we make our bed, so we must lie.

Total expenditures equaled $81.85. Anders would buy a cowbell for Lady and another 100# sack of flour. For this, Evan had sent $11.

This left $42.15 between him and starvation. He needed seed for next year's crops, the stud fee to breed Lady when the time was right, shoes for the children, fodder for the animals, and enough wood to heat the dugout. Thank God, Ragna traded labor for the stovepipe.

There was no measure for the loss of their baby daughter.

Just the thought of their daughter brought a lump to his throat. They were starting from the bottom rung of the ladder. They had so little to offer. Maybe it was for the best that God had taken her away.

Then, Ragna's passage to Norway.

Evan determined to be a stronger person, a kinder man. He would be a more understanding husband, a better father. He would quit swearing and keep rein on his temper. God had spared him during the uprising when better were taken—there must be a reason.

Gunnar was a constant source of irritation, always curious, seldom obedient. *Eplet faller ikke langt fra stammen.* The apple does not fall far from the tree. Inga's first man must have been the same.

Knut was more like Evan, compliant and dutiful. Moreover, where Knut had red hair, the color of Evan's beard, Gunnar was dark-haired with matching dark eyes. Of course, Inga had brown eyes. Sometimes when Evan looked at Gunnar, he saw Inga's first man.

What was that verse from the Holy Book? "Ye shall know the truth and it will set you free." Maybe it was time to talk to Gunnar about his real father.

He would wait until better situated. They still had time.

24

Mr. and Mrs. Burdick lost their Eight Month Old Son Last night. A Bright Child who Showed Great Promise

St. Paul Dispatch, *October 30, 1873*

IN THE DAYS THAT FOLLOWED, Ragna discovered a certain satisfaction in tending the sick man. It came natural to her, like midwifery. Ragna thought to rub goose grease on Mr. Sevald's cracked lips. Ragna convinced Mrs. Sevald to put a pallet on the floor by her man's bed so she could sleep without interruption. Ragna folded old rags into padding to protect the straw tick from accidents. When Mr. Sevald developed a rash, Ragna knew to brown flour in a dry skillet to make a soothing powder.

Ragna had milked the cow, churned butter, made milk toast for supper and made broth from a venison haunch brought by Elijah Wheeling. She cleaned the cabin, scrubbed the floors, and kept up with the extra washing from the sick man. The days took on a pattern. Almost normal.

Uncle Evan had not come for his promised visit.

Worry wrapped around her until she felt like she might explode. What if Sigurd caught the croup or Knut cut himself on a slipped axe. What if Auntie fell behind in her work? So many things needed to be done before winter.

One thing kept Ragna from dying of homesickness. Although Mrs. Sevald avoided conversation, she kept her promise. She pulled an old rosary from her locked trunk and taught Ragna the prayers.

"You'll have to make do without beads," she said. "This was my mother's and I'll not part with it."

Ragna fingered the carved beads while Mrs. Sevald turned a tintype of a severe looking man towards the wall.

"Don't mind Joseph Smith," she said. "The Prophet will look the other way while we say our prayers."

Mrs. Sevald taught Ragna how to make the Sign of the Cross. Together they prayed the Apostles Creed which Ragna knew from Confirmation—except for the use of Holy Catholic Church instead of Holy Christian Church. Then Mrs. Sevald prayed the Our Father, Hail Mary, and the Glory Be, speaking a phrase and waiting for Ragna to repeat it before moving on. She ended with Hail, Holy Queen and the Sign of the Cross.

"After you learn the rosary," Mrs. Sevald said, "we'll start on the Mysteries."

Ragna suspected the ancient words comforted Mrs. Sevald as much as they did her, though the woman had converted to Mormonism. Mrs. Sevald did not discuss Mormonism with her, and Ragna kept her questions to herself.

After the mysteries, Ragna determined to ask about the novena that would bring her sister home.

One cloudy day Mrs. Sevald peeked through the window and spied Mr. Wheeling coming up the road. She hurried to turn Joseph Smith's face back towards the kitchen. Mr. Wheeling carried a gunnysack of provisions and news from the settlement. He stomped his feet and walked directly to the fireplace where he held out cold hands to the flames.

"It's cold." Frost dusted the scarf around his neck, sprinkled white on the brim of his fur hat. "Feels like snow moving in."

Mrs. Sevald did not answer. Instead, she walked to her husband's bedside and straightened the covers without saying a word before heading to the cupboard.

Mr. Wheeling looked at Ragna, "I hope things are going well."

"Mr. Sevald is the same."

"You've been busy." Mr. Wheeling cast an approving eye around the cabin. "You'll make a fine wife for some lucky man."

Ragna felt her cheeks flame and looked frantically for something to do, anything to escape his probing eyes.

Mrs. Sevald rummaged in the cupboard for bread and jam to serve the guest. "We need water."

With great relief, Ragna grabbed her shawl and mittens along with the bucket hanging from its rope handle. "I'll be right back."

The full bucket banged against her leg as she lugged it back towards the house. *Holy Mary, Mother of God.* Mr. Wheeling would send her a Mormon husband if she did not watch out. He had a way of telling people what to do.

She sloshed ice-cold water with every step. The water froze the hems of her dress and apron. She would not do it. An arranged marriage waited for her in Norway, and she refused that, too.

Ragna pushed through the cabin door where Mr. Wheeling sat eating a bowl of applesauce covered with thick cream. As her eyes adjusted to the dimness, she noticed bread, butter, and a dish of wild plum jelly on the table. Ragna wiped tears off her face and blamed it on the cold wind more than homesickness.

She could not help but overhear their conversation.

"No, I couldn't spare her."

"We were just talking about you," Mr. Wheeling said, turning to look at her as she set the water bucket by the dry sink. "One of our women is near confinement."

Marta leapt to her feet and threw an oak log into the fireplace, her face twisted into a scowl. Ragna cast an anxious glance toward her.

"Mrs. Cornelia Ludwig," he said. "My daughter-in-law's older sister. Lives about ten miles northwest."

"I told you no," Mrs. Sevald said with a sharp voice. "There might be a storm and she wouldn't get back."

Mr. Wheeling's mouth turned into a small circle and he tapped the table-top with the tip of his spoon. "I'm thinking Mrs. Ludwig could spend a few weeks with Elijah and Bertha. She'd be close enough to send for Ragna when her sickness comes upon her."

The set of his jaw told Ragna the matter already settled. A vague irritation flitted across her mind. He had not asked if she wanted the work. Of course, she would have agreed, knowing the needs of her family. She should be grateful. However, a nagging suspicion made her reluctant. Uncle Evan was determined she would earn passage to Norway. Hiring out with the Sevald's paid for the stovepipe. Anything more would go toward passage.

"You'll get along for a few days without Ragna," Mr. Wheeling said.

Mrs. Sevald's eyes flashed and she turned to her husband's bed and yanked off the wet blankets. "We've work to do."

Mr. Wheeling drained his glass of buttermilk. Ragna gathered her courage. "Have you news of my family?"

"One of our men delivered the length of stovepipe shortly after you left." He scraped the last of the applesauce from the dish, licked the spoon and stood to his feet. "They were well."

A physical pain pressed against her windpipe until she could not speak. They had the stovepipe—it was worth being a hired girl to know the little ones would keep warm this winter.

"And your friend, Anders Vollen, winters at the Branch of Zion."

Ragna's chin jerked up in surprise.

"He earns money for start-up."

Ragna felt a rush of adrenaline. "What kind of work?"

"Teaching school."

"Didn't know he was a teacher," Marta said, "being a foreigner."

"He's had education in Norway and Minneapolis." Mr. Wheeling buttoned his coat and wrapped a knitted muffler around his neck and beard. "He's a bright young man, and our scholars need a teacher."

If only her family lived close enough for the boys to attend. The longing for the boys' schooling brought an ache to her chest.

"He'll teach until almost-Christmas and then again from mid-January until spring planting."

Ragna's mind swirled in a million directions. Anders would not build his dugout, would not clear his fields for spring planting, or get any improvements done this winter. Then another realization halted her scattered thoughts.

He would not be stopping by.

Mr. Wheeling rode away, and Ragna stood by the window fingering the button around her neck, deep in thought.

Mrs. Sevald turned the tintype of Joseph Smith back to the wall, sat down at the table and sipped a glass of buttermilk. "What we need is a nice cup of tea," she said at last, interrupting Ragna's daydream.

Mrs. Sevald rummaged through her old trunk and brought out a small wooden box, carved with hearts and swirling rings. Ragna moved closer to examine the delicate carving covering the dark mahogany. Mrs. Sevald pulled a key ring from her apron pocket and carefully unlocked the box.

"Put the kettle on, Ragna dear," she said with a gleeful smile. "It's tea time."

25

The Hard Times, Here and Elsewhere

St. Paul Dispatch, November 13, 1873

"MRS. SEVALD, DO YOU HAVE NUTMEG?" Ragna said. She scraped a patch of frost off the window and peered outside. "Auntie Inga gives a pinch of nutmeg for the flux."

Ragna lost count of the number of times they had changed Mr. Sevald's bedding during the night. His bowels groaned with each watery mess. Mrs. Sevald's eyes drooped and showed dark smudges under them.

"No," Mrs. Sevald said. "I used the last in the pumpkin pudding." She folded her red and cracked hands, rubbing them as if she were still washing them. "And for God's sake," she said. "Call me Marta. I've had about all I can take of being called Mrs."

"Marta." The name rolled strange on her tongue, and she knew Auntie Inga would disapprove its use. "Sometimes black tea helps." Ragna hoped she had not overstepped. Since Mr. Wheeling's visit, she and Mrs. Sevald—Marta, she corrected herself—had enjoyed tea every day after praying the rosary. Though forbidden by the Saints, the hot brew encouraged them and gave them extra strength.

Marta looked over at Mr. Sevald. "He would never approve," she said. Marta slowly shook her head and frowned. "He believed every word of Joseph Smith's wisdom."

Ragna was surprised but at the same time, not surprised. Marta had shown a certain disregard for Mr. Wheeling, leader of the Saints. Not that Marta ever said a word against him, but she did not speak to him as to other people. Almost disrespectful, but not openly. Besides, Marta drank tea and prayed the rosary.

"We're low on wood," Marta said. "We'll freeze to death in another day or two and be done with this world." She seemed to think it a perfectly natural solution to the problems at hand.

When Ragna offered to visit Elijah Wheeling and request a load of wood, Marta was quick to reply.

"It's too cold to be out and about."

"I'll dress warm." Ragna kicked herself for not noticing the low wood supply earlier. If a storm came up, they would be in trouble. No way around it, she must go today. With Mr. Sevald so poorly, he needed the fire roaring day and night.

In fact, the walk might do her good. Ragna felt closed in and ready for something different. Maybe Cornelia Ludwig had arrived to spend a little time with her sister before her confinement.

How wonderful to visit a blood relative, a real sister.

"Then wear this." Marta wound a musty-smelling gray shawl around Ragna's head and shoulders, and knotted it in front of her mouth. It draped to her knees and Ragna felt like a small girl dressed up in her mother's finery.

"Do you have mittens?" Marta demanded. "You're not leaving this house without mittens."

"Ja." Ragna pulled stout gray mittens over her fingers. "It's my feet I worry about."

Ragna pulled on Mr. Sevald's heavy wooden clogs at Marta's urging. Lined with felt, they were large enough for two pair of woolen socks.

"I'll be all right now," Ragna said. "Keep giving him the salty broth . . . it's all I know to do without nutmeg."

"Take these hot stones for your apron pockets," Marta said. "I've had them heating for Gjert's bed, but I've plenty more on the hearth."

"Mange takk!" Ragna teared at her kindness. "I'll return before dark."

"Hurry then," Marta said. "Tell Elijah I'll pay cash money." She looked out the frosted window, breathed on a patch of frost and scraped it away with her fingernails, then looked again. "It's clear—you should get there without a storm creeping up on you."

A low groan emanated from the bed, and Marta hurried to her husband's side.

"If the weather changes," she said fiercely as she spooned broth into his gaping mouth. "Don't be so foolish as to take chances. This old woman has weathered many a storm and one more won't kill me."

Ragna lifted the latch and squinted into the blinding sunshine. She tried not to think about Auntie in the dark dugout although thoughts of her family were ever with her, taunting her with homesickness, causing her chest to ache with unshed tears. Frigid air burned the inside of her nostrils and stiffened her eyelashes.

She scanned the bushes lining the trail for signs of Red Men. Surely, even the *skraelings* had more sense than to venture out on such a day. The clogs slipped on the icy path as Ragna hurried north on the faded track. It was only a little more than a mile but seemed much farther with the icy cold freezing her every breath. Ragna pulled the corner of Marta's shawl in front of her face, and her hand grasped the button hanging from the string around her neck.

> *Birdie's face chases all thoughts of loneliness and cold out of my mind. I forget the Red Men, forget the grasshoppers, and forget Mr. Sevald dying. Birdie looks at me with the eyes of love, the kind of love only genuine family members have for each other.*
>
> *"Don't slip and fall," Birdie says. "A broken bone means certain death in this cold."*
>
> *"But these shoes are clumsy," I say. "I can scarcely feel my feet. And my hands are stiff and burning."*
>
> *Birdie takes my arm and guides me over an icy spot in the trail. "Don't worry, I'll never leave you again."*

Smoke spiraled straight up from Elijah Wheeling's chimney. Overhead sundogs coddled the sun. It seemed odd that the sun, in all its brightness, offered no heat. She knocked on the door, her mittens muffling the sound, as sharp pains went up her hands and arms.

"Come in, come in." Elijah Wheeling opened the latch. His lower face sprouted a sparse red beard with pimples interspersed in the patchy hair. His mouth turned up into a welcoming smile. "I never thought for company on such a day."

The inside of the cabin felt warm and moist after the freezing desert of the outside where dryness was almost as vexing as the cold. Her nose dripped, and the delicious smell of roasting meat and onions filled the small cabin.

"Bertha, it's the Sevald's girl."

Ragna stomped her feet and unwound the shawls from her upper body. She needed Uncle Evan's buffalo robe on such a day.

"Come near the fire," his wife said.

The missus was about her age, maybe even younger. Her yellow hair twisted into into thick braids wound tight at the back of her neck. Tiny tendrils escaped and curled around blue eyes and freckled nose. She wore a gray dress and apron, homespun and plain. Even so, next to her, Ragna felt large footed and out of place.

"Sit down," the missus said with a worried frown. "I don't like the look of your face."

Ragna looked up in surprise and Elijah laughed aloud.

"Is that any way to treat company, Wife?" His eyes fastened on Mrs. Wheeling with such looks of affection that Ragna turned away.

"I mean," Mrs. Wheeling said as her face bloomed crimson from the neck up. "I think your cheek is frost bitten."

A thorough examination proved only a false alarm. Ragna removed the cooled stones from her pocket and placed them by the fireplace to reheat. Mrs. Wheeling fetched a blanket and wrapped Ragna in its scratchy folds. It smelled of cedar and made her sneeze.

"What brings you out?" Elijah said. "It's not Mr. Sevald?"

"*Nei,*" Ragna said and took a sip of hot broth from a tin cup the missus pushed into her hands. "Wood. We use more with the sick man, and we're almost out."

Elijah bundled on his clothes and hurried to load the sledge. It seemed the energy left the cabin with him. Funny, how a man filled a room. She had noticed it with Uncle Evan. Maybe even Mr. Sevald in his own way. Certainly Mr. Wheeling walked into a room with the thunder of God, at least the thunder of his God.

"How is Mr. Sevald?" Mrs. Wheeling said as she sat down at the table and picked up her knitting.

"He has the flux." The English words felt as clumsy in her mouth as Ragna felt in the presence of the American wife.

"How terrible!" Mrs. Wheeling deftly turned the row and began a furious purling of stitches across the wooden needle. "They're good people."

"Could we borrow some nutmeg?"

Mrs. Wheeling looked up with a curious expression.

"Nutmeg helps the flux," Ragna said. "My Auntie thinks so, anyway."

"I'm sorry but I haven't any," Mrs. Wheeling said. "My mother used to have a remedy but I don't remember what it was."

There was nothing else to say. Ragna wondered how to address the young Mrs. Wheeling. Perhaps it was ill mannered to call a married woman by her Christian name. She had always thought of Elijah Wheeling as Elijah, but maybe that was rude as well.

"I'm sorry to cause such trouble to Mr. Wheeling," Ragna said at last. "It's a cold day to ask for favors."

A quick laugh filled the room, almost like the ringing of a bell. "Call him Elijah," she said. "And please call me Bertha. Mrs. Wheeling makes me sound as old as my mother-in-law."

"Bertha," Ragna smiled. "Have you been married long?"

"Only a month," Bertha said and blushed again.

Outside wood clattered into the sled box. The broth was salty and hot. Ragna's feet burned and ached after being half frozen. She wiggled her toes to keep the circulation going.

"Have you seen Mrs. Sevald's fancy work?"

"*Nei*," Ragna said. "What kind of fancy work?"

"The most wonderful crocheting and embroidery I've ever seen." Bertha pointed to a dresser scarf draped over the trunk by the bed. "She gave this wedding gift."

Ragna fingered the French knots and delicate lace, remembering another like it draped over the top of her *mor's* dresser. The memory needled her mind but remained unclear.

"She promised she'd teach me . . . but then her man took sick."

"Maybe afterwards . . ." The words hung in the air.

"Of course," Bertha said. "Afterwards."

After an awkward silence, their conversation turned to weather, recipes and plans for spring vegetable gardens.

"I thought your sister might be here."

"Next week." Bertha blushed again. "She thinks the baby due in another week."

"It's hard to tell with first babies." Ragna did not yet know how to figure when babies were to be expected. She would have to ask Auntie Inga next time she saw her.

"It's hard without our mother," Bertha said in a quiet voice. "She died last spring when the pox went through." Bertha traced her finger over the top of her knitting needle, counting stitches. "She nursed the LaFond family just west of here when they took sick."

"I'm sorry," Ragna said. At least Bertha had known her mother through childhood, through the hardest years. It would be a loss at any time.

"She was the midwife for the Branch of Zion." Bertha studied the hem of her apron. "That's why we're so short of help."

"Did you ever go along to births?"

Bertha shook her head. "She wanted to wait until we were married."

"Auntie felt the same at first but decided I needed to learn. I'm still learning," Ragna said. "*Nod larer naken kvinne a spinne.*" The Norwegian words popped out before Ragna thought to bite them back. *Necessity is the mother of invention.*

"What did you say?" Bertha's eyes rounded with interest.

Ragna could have kicked herself for being so ignorant as to speak Norwegian. Bertha would think her uneducated and stupid. But the proverb was the first thing that entered her head. She fumbled for the translation.

"Your sister needs a midwife, and I need the work. So together we work it out," Ragna said.

"Say it again, please." Bertha's face broke into a smile. "I like the sound of it, almost like music."

How strange that old words bridged the gap between an American wife and a hired girl, a jeweled gift of friendship.

Ragna repeated the saying. "It's a favorite of my Auntie's. She has one for every occasion."

"Who is your auntie?" Bertha's eyes shone blue as the clear December sky.

"My parents are dead." Ragna thought to add something about the uprising but hesitated. "I was raised by godparents."

"Maybe you could teach me the Norwegian sayings," she said. "I'd like to learn them."

"I will," Ragna said. "And you can help me with my American."

"Your English is fine," Bertha said and turned the needle to start another row. "You don't need my help."

"My reading is slow," Ragna admitted. "We could help each other."

Elijah stepped in the door. "The sledge is loaded. You can ride back with me." He wiped a runny nose with the back of his mitten. His face was chapped red from the north wind. "I'd like to get going so I can be home by milking."

Ragna saw his eyes go to his wife again. Ragna wondered at the thread that tied a man and wife together. She had learned in Confirmation what God had joined, no man was to put asunder. It was a mystery.

"Come again soon," Bertha took her hand and looked earnestly into her face. "I need a friend."

Ragna's heart thumped in her chest. "I'll be here for your sister's lying in." A friend. An equal. "And I know Mrs. Sevald would love company any time."

"Maybe we both can learn her fancy work."

As she rode behind the clomping horse on the wood filled sledge, Ragna fingered the hot stones in her pocket and snuggled behind a buffalo robe thrown across her lap. It was only a little more than a mile. A friend.

She needed one.

26

The Village of Worthington has Passed an Ordinance Prohibiting Billiard Playing

St. Paul Dispatch, *November 23, 1873*

O N SAINT CLEMENT'S DAY, November 23rd, a dark-skinned man dressed in a buffalo coat rode up to the dugout on a gray mule. His breath hung like clouds of vapor before his wide nose, and thick pink lips. Frost coated the ends of his kinky gray beard and hair. He was far from young. Maybe the age of Syl Wheeling. Two pack mules followed close behind.

"You be Mr. Jacobson." The man slid off his mule, removed a leather mitt and shook Evan's hand. "I's the trader man, Jack Wilson."

Evan's breath quickened. They needed so many things. "*Velkommen*, Mr. Wilson." Years ago, Evan had known a black soldier at Fort Snelling with the same stretchy lilt to his voice.

"They calls me Lying Jack." The man flashed a jovial smile with teeth whiter than any Evan had ever seen. "At least my friends."

Evan looked at him in confusion. Syl Wheeling had referred to the trader as Lying Jack, but it seemed impossible any man would introduce himself by such a title, let alone a trader.

"Don't believes every handle," Jack said. "This man don't lie much—and only then if good reason."

"My *far* used to say that *Kjaart barn har mange navn*." Evan said. "A pet child has many names."

Jack slapped him on the back and his laugh boomed across the yard. "I likes you already, Mr. Jacobson."

"Call me Evan." The boys peeked around the corner of the barn door, Sverre with a thumb in his mouth, gaping at the strange sight of a black man in their yard. "Gunnar! Knut! Care for Mr. Wilson's mules."

The older boys bounded forward and reached for the reins. One of the mules nipped at Gunnar's coat sleeve, its teeth snapping like a turtle.

"Watch out for Nellie," Lying Jack said. "Him's cold as a witch's tit and bites when he feel like it."

The boys giggled. Such language! Evan hoped they would not repeat the phrase in front of their mother. Lying Jack's color, accent, and openness were as foreign as if he were a Red Man or a circus curiosity.

"Come in and we'll see if the missus has any coffee."

"Been liking you more and more, Evan Jacobson!" His laugh rolled across the yard and Evan noticed how his eyes swept the rough dwellings, the wagon, and the scarred earth where the plow had cut sod. "Coffee and a warm fire am just what this white man needs." He laughed loud and long. "Did you know that in this country I'm a white man? Compared to an Injun this black man am white."

The twins followed the men into the shelter, and Lying Jack scooped Sigurd up in his arms and tickled his tummy. Inga's face carried a worried expression. "It's all right," Evan said in Norwegian. "He's the trader."

"So I gather," Inga said and jutted her chin.

Then, still holding Sigurd in one arm, Lying Jack dug into his pocket and pulled out a small package wrapped in brown paper. "Here's a little present for you, missus, and them childings." He handed the package to Inga with a smile that could have melted butter. Inga eyed the package and sat on the stump chair. The twins gathered close around her.

The man was a troll if he could sweet talk Inga that easily.

"Open it!" Lewis said.

Sverre popped his thumb into his mouth while Inga carefully unknotted the string and placed it in her apron pocket. Then she unfolded the brown paper. "Maple sugar lumps!" Her eyes shone. "*Mange tussen takk!*"

Sverre reached a hand towards the treat.

"Wait," Inga said. "We'll have it with coffee."

"Sit down." Evan gestured to the rough benches lining the long table. Inga fed a chunk of dried oak into the firebox and poked it down with a stick. It was cool in the dugout, especially on the floor, but without drafts. The longer stovepipe made an almost smoke-free fire.

"Syl Wheeling says you were hit by them hoppers," Jack said as the fragrance of coffee filled the dugout. "They're bad in some places."

"Far says it's against the law for grasshoppers to come into Otter Tail County," Sverre said with a lisp. "The judge signed a court order."

"Yer father is right!" Lying Jack placed Sigurd on his knee and bounced him up and down. "The sheriff'll stop 'em at the county line."

Gunnar and Knut burst into the dugout with runny noses and eager looks and spied the sugar on the table.

"Did Nellie behave?"

"*Nei*, she nipped but Gunnar slapped her nose," Knut said.

Evan scowled. Gunnar should know better than to misuse a guest's mule.

"Oh, that Nellie is a cold one," Lying Jack said. "As cold as . . ." He looked at Inga pouring coffee into tin cups and then flashed a grin at the boys. "As cold as well water in January."

The boys burst into spasms of laughter, and Inga turned her head. "Shush!" she said. "That's enough, boys."

"But he said outside that Nellie was as cold as . . ." Gunnar said.

"Enough!" Evan said. "Or you'll have no sugar."

The boys had seen no one except Milton for over a month and had never seen a black-skinned man. They were behind in their schooling, had no regular church service although there was talk of a new church starting west of them. Gunnar should be starting confirmation. They were turning into heathen.

"How many cows have'n you?" Lying Jack blew over his scalding brew. His mouth showed a strange mixture of red and dark when he pursed his lips. "Any blackleg among them?"

"One healthy cow and bull calf," Evan said. "My horse still suffering from the epizootic."

Inga gave each boy a sugar lump about the size of a nickel while the men conversed about various diseases and conditions affecting farm animals. One by one, each boy dipped his lump into Evan's coffee cup, watching the brown coffee saturate the lump and then carefully popped it into his mouth lest he lose a single grain. Evan had done the same with his *far*. He could almost taste the delicious sweetness and remember the smell of the Norwegian cabin, its cooking fires and boiling fish.

"The peoples want oxen," Lying Jack said. "They're strongest for plowin'new ground."

"That may be true, but I've only Old Doll."

"But you have'n a wagon," Lying Jack said. "And no travelin' plans."

"That's right." Evan wondered where the conversation was going. "I've five years left to prove up the claim."

"I'd trade fer 'em," Lying Jack said. "And maybe the bull calf. There's always somebody looking for a good wagon."

Old Doll was family, purchased from Bror Brorson when Evan was still driving the stage and earning regular money. My God, had it come to this? To lose both Old Doll and the wagon. How low would they slip in such hard times?

Inga flashed him a warning look. "*Tomme tonner ramler mest*," she said in Norwegian. Empty barrels are the noisiest.

"Let me show yous boys my packs," Lying Jack stood and pulled on his fur hat and leather mitts. "Who'll help me carry in the goods?"

The boys clamored into coats and mittens and scrambled out the door. Sigurd howled when the trader set him on the floor. Evan scooped him up into his arms. "It's all right, *Lille Guten*," Evan said. "You shall have sugar, too."

He dunked a lump into the swallow of coffee left in his cup and placed it into Sigurd's mouth. The baby licked his lips in surprise. *Stakkers liten*, he had not tasted enough sugar in his short life to know what it was. "Next year when the wheat is harvested, you will have all the sugar you want."

"Watch out for that man," Inga said as she cleared dirty cups off the table and stacked them into the dishpan warming on the stove. "There's something about him."

"Syl said he's honest," Evan said. "Besides, what choice do we have? Like it or not, he's our only source for supplies outside of the settlements."

Lying Jack returned to the dugout with a sack over his back. Behind him trooped the boys, each with a small bundle. "Up on de table, boys," he said.

Out of the sack came dried figs, a bottle of Lindsey's Liniment, ammunition, a cast iron kettle, tin cups, raisins, navy beans, maple sugar, wild rice, parched corn, wheat berries, cornmeal, buckwheat, molasses, and salt.

"You have a regular store." Inga seemed to have lost her distrust for the man. "Do you have silk thread?"

"We sent money with Anders Vollen for flour," Evan said as Inga looked over the spools in Lying Jack's bag. "We expected him by now."

"I met him," Lying Jack said. "He sends your flour with me—and a cow bell. I'll fetch it in before I leave."

"Where's Anders?"

"The Saints sent him to Pig's Eye. Convinced him to help everybody by taking their rig and oxen to fetch a full load." Lying Jack scratched his curly beard. "Nary a pound of flour this side of Sauk Rapids."

"It would have been a long walk," Inga said.

"And hard to carry a sack of flour all the way back," Evan said and shook his head. He wondered that Anders would so easily change his mind.

"The Saints have ways of convincing peoples." It was as if Lying Jack had read his mind. Evan flushed.

"It's their'n way," Lying Jack said. "Honest as the daylight but not above asking favors."

"How much flour did he bring back?"

"Four barrels and plowshares." Lying Jack reached over, picked up Sigurd and laughed when the baby plunged both hands into his curly beard. "And a new iron kittle for sugaring."

Lying Jack sat down on the bench again. "Let me tell what happened to their old sugaring kittle." He laughed loud and long. "The Indians asked to borry it."

Sverre popped his thumb into his mouth and sidled closer to his father.

"Dem Saints," Lying Jack said and paused for a long moment while the boys leaned forward to catch every word. "Always trying to please and so they lent the kittle. A good one that cost twenty dollar." He took a small parcel of peppermint drops from his pocket and handed one to each boy. Knut's hands shook as he accepted the candy and Evan flushed with the shame of it. Someday they would be back on their feet, able to give candy to the boys.

"Do you have more of that coffee, Missus?"

"*Ja*," Inga said flustered by her lack of manners. "I'll get it for you."

"Boys," Evan said. "Thank the good man for your candy."

"*Mange takk*," the boys said in unison with mouths stuffed full of candy.

"Sit down so you don't choke," Inga said. "And keep quiet."

"When they didn't bring the kittle back," Lying Jack said. "The Elders took a little sashay over to der camp and found it." He sipped his coffee.

"What happened?" Gunnar begged. Evan shot him a warning glare.

"It was full," Lying Jack said. "Full of something the Saints hadn't membered to wurry about."

"What did they forget to worry about?" Sverre said after taking the peppermint out of his mouth.

"Polecats." Lying Jack laughed until the tears ran down his face and into his beard. "The Indians left skunks soaking in the kittle and then went off and forgets about 'em."

"Real skunks?" Lewis said.

"Real as your pretty mammy," Lying Jack said. "They leaved such a stink in the cast iron that it was ruined for sugaring."

Evan wondered if the man told a story.

"Are you sure?" Gunnar said.

"Sure as shootin'," Lying Jack said. "I've got the proof with me." He pulled out a furry black and white hat, long tail hanging down behind. "I traded."

"Aren't you ascared of the Red Men?" Knut said.

"Scared?" Lying Jack said. "Not unless I'm late fer supper." He looked up as if he were tallying figures. "You see, I'm married to an Indian woman."

The conversation was going in the wrong direction. Inga had no regard for Red Men and would not approve of the boys hearing about an Indian wife. Evan picked up a small dried nutmeg. "Don't you need nutmeg, Inga?"

"Do you travel by the Sevald homestead on your way home?" Inga said. "Would you be so kind as to deliver a letter to Ragna Larson, their hired girl?"

Evan had hoped to visit Ragna himself but could not spare the time. It was too far to walk back and forth in a single day. Old Doll was needed for plowing and pulling logs out of the grove for firewood. Thank God, Inga had thought of a letter.

"Yes, ma'am," Lying Jack said. "Just give it to me, and I'll drop it off'n next times I rides by."

In Norwegian, Inga told Evan what goods she wanted and what prices were reasonable. Then she left him to bargain while she pulled a sheet of paper from the wooden box under her bed and penned a letter to Ragna.

By the time Lying Jack was ready to leave, Evan had traded three muskrat skins and a silver dollar for nutmeg, a sack of navy beans, a spool of thread, and a sack of parched corn. The sack of flour lay safely on the table alongside the cowbell. Ragna's letter rested inside the trader's pocket.

Evan also agreed to trade the wagon, wagon cover, Old Doll with harness, and Bobcat for a pair of oxen in the spring.

"I'll fetch 'em before plow time," Lying Jack said as they reloaded the pack animals. "You can build another wagon by then, a small one for traipsin' to the settlements, and whittle yourself a yoke."

"The deal's off if I'm not satisfied."

"Carve yer yoke." Lying Jack cinched the packs onto Nellie who promptly reached out and nipped his sleeve. He slapped its nose, pulled his hat closer over his ears and then tucked his beard into the front of his coat. "You'll not be disquieted any."

"We wondered about Anders," Evan said. "Worried he ran into trouble."

"No trouble, but the Saints pay him for schoolteaching their childs," Lying Jack said. "Sends word he won't be back until Christmas time."

He was a bright young man, that was easy to see, but Evan wondered when Anders had the chance for an education.

If only his boys could attend school. Gunnar and Knut were getting older and needed schooling now if it would take. There was talk of a church to the west of them, but Milton heard they had services in Danish.

"*Mange takk*, Mr. Wilson," Evan said. "Come again."

"I'm askin' you straight out," Lying Jack said as he mounted his mule. "You've welcomed this Negro man to your table but would you welcome my woman?"

Evan hesitated only a moment. "We'd be proud to have you both any time." He did not know what Inga would say to this.

"Then I'll come," he said, "but only if you call me Lying Jack like my friends do."

"Yack," Evan said and blushed at his poor pronunciation. "I will try my best but your name is impossible for a Norwegian."

Lying Jack's booming laugh followed him across the clearing and down the trail.

27

President Grant's Fifth Annual Message was Read to Congress on Tuesday

St. Paul Dispatch, *November 4, 1873*

ON A GLOOMY NOVEMBER afternoon when not a ray of sunshine forced its way through the clouds, someone hailed the Sevald cabin. "Anyone to home?"

"Land sakes." Marta peeked through the window and pushed strands of loose hair behind her ears. "It's the trader." She reached for the latch on the door. "He always comes at the worst possible time."

Ragna cast an anxious glance toward Mr. Sevald. His flesh had fallen away until every bone showed on this face. Each breath brought a tight grimace to his mouth. Marta sat up most nights with him.

"Welcome, Mr. Wilson," Marta said as she opened the door to the huge black man bundled in his buffalo coat. "Come in out of the cold."

"My mules, Ma'am," he said. "Can I put 'em up in your barn?"

"I suppose," Marta said. "There's hay."

Ragna could not keep her eyes off the giant of a man with the black face and hands. She had seen a black man once before when she was very young. An image of a skinny black man wearing a soldier's uniform popped into her mind, maybe during the uprising. Ragna wondered if Mr. Wilson was black all over—and then blushed at the thought. What would Auntie say?

Marta hung his heavy coat by the fire and urged him to sit at the table.

"Nothing like a cup of tea on a cold day," Lying Jack said in appreciation as Marta poured a steaming cup. "It warms de bones."

167

"It's a soothing drink," Marta said. "I could use a little more if you have it." Her face clouded for a moment. "Just between us."

Lying Jack's laugh boomed through the cabin and Ragna looked towards Mr. Sevald, hoping he had not awakened the sick man. "Your secret is safe wid me," he said. "You're not the first of de Saints to sneak a few tea leaves."

"My man is the Saint among us," Marta said. "I'm just a tag-a-long."

Ragna wondered what she meant.

"Miss Larson," Lying Jack said. "I bring mail."

Ragna's heart pounded. Uncle Evan had not visited though it had been over two months. Maybe *Bestemor* sent a ticket. Maybe bad news from home. Sickness. Accidents.

Lying Jack pulled two letters from his inside pocket and handed them to Ragna. "You are de popular young lady." His eyes melted brown with his smile. "Words from home and from your young man."

"*Mange takk.*" Ragna's hand shook as she took the letters from his black hand. Auntie's perfect penmanship spelled out her name on a folded sheet of paper. The other addressed to Miss Ragna Larson, Tordenskjold, Minnesota. Neither were stamped. First she breathed a prayer of thanks. At least nothing from *Bestemor.*

Then she blushed to the roots of her hair. Anders. He had written to her. Of course, it meant nothing. It might be an announcement of his marriage, for all she knew. Her fingers refused to move and she sat staring at the letters in her hands.

"Girlie," Lying Jack said at last. "If you don't read them letters, you'll bust right out of yer skin." He sipped his tea. "Missus, would you please let her from de table to read the mail while we conduct a little trade?"

"Of course," Marta said. "You're excused, Ragna."

Ragna settled on a wooden stool before the fire facing away from the table. She wished she had a room to flee to, a room of her own with a door that closed.

"You can see Gjert is dying," Marta told Lying Jack as Ragna opened the letter from Auntie Inga. "There's nothing to do but keep him comfortable."

Marta spoke calmly. Ragna wondered how she could stay so calm. If it were someone in Ragna's family, she would be distraught. If it were Birdie . . . she opened the letter and tears gathered in her eyes at sight of the familiar Norwegian script.

Dear Ragna, we hope you are well and remembering to be a good girl. It must be hard for Mrs. Sevald to lose her man to such an awful illness. Help her as much as you can.

We are all well and settled. The dugout is warm except for the floors. The longer stovepipe is most effective—there's hardly a day when the house smokes up. Mange takk for your part. We say a prayer of thanks to the Good Lord daily for warm shelter and food on the table. The boys are busy with firewood and fishing. We store extra fish in a wooden box hanging from an oak tree by the barn. It's cold enough to keep the fish frozen and out of reach of animals. If nothing else, we will have fish soup through the winter months. The lake is active with fish—it should be enough.

Last night Evan brought in a basswood log. He will carve shoes for the twins and hopes to finish by Christmas. Of course, they won't be a surprise since there's no place to work away from curious eyes. Shoes will be a welcome gift as theirs are bursting open on their grow-ing feet.

Uncle Evan hoped to visit but Old Doll isn't as young as she once was and is worn down after breaking sod. The men are logging off the piece of land directly east of the dugout and Old Doll must drag the logs to the building site. On Sundays, she needs her rest for the coming week. Uncle Evan has arranged to trade her for a pair of oxen from Lying Jack who takes this letter to you.

We all miss you. The boys ask about you every day. Milton visits often—otherwise we have seen only the Saints and now the trader. Maybe you could send a letter with Lying Jack as he comes through every so often. Don't forget your prayers or Catechism.

With Love, Auntie Inga

Ragna's throat closed and choked. Tears spilled down her face and splattered the page, making the ink run. They were fine. They missed her. They loved her. As she loved them. Funny how *Bestemor* thought she was Ragna's only remaining family. Ragna had family in America. More real than those in the Old Country.

She could not bring herself to open the second letter with Marta and Lying Jack so close. She tucked it into her apron pocket for later and gathered a scrap of brown wrapping paper she had tucked into her bundle. She plucked a lead pencil from Marta's knitting basket and wrote a note to the family.

> *Dear Ones, it was so good to hear from you and to know that all is well. What do the boys do to keep out of your way, Auntie? How are you managing to keep up with all the work?*
>
> *I do not know how much longer I will be needed. I plan to attend one of the Mormon women at her lying-in. I'm glad for the stovepipe. I miss you all and pray for you every day. Kiss Sigurd and the twins for me. And Knut and Gunnar.*
>
> *I must keep this short as Lying Jack waits for my letter before leaving. Now that I know there is a way to send mail, I will write again soon.*
>
> *Love Always,*
>
> *Ragna Larson*

Ragna folded the letter into the shape of an envelope, dabbing a glob of melted candle wax and sealed it. She carefully wrote *Mr. and Mrs. Evan Jacobson, Tordenskjold, Minnesota,* across its back. Then she handed it to Lying Jack.

"Only one?" Lying Jack said. "I expected two."

Ragna blushed and stuttered for the right English words. Marta came to her rescue. "She'll likely have another next time you stop."

"My, oh me!" Lying Jack slapped his thigh and laughed loud and long. "I 'most forget somethin' important." He dug in his coat pocket and pulled out a small package wrapped in brown paper, about the size and weight of a chicken feather when he placed it in Ragna's hand. "It's a little somethin' from yer young man," he said, "from the settlements."

Marta pulled on her shawl and mittens. "I'll walk with you to the barn and fetch the tea from your pack. What was the price again?"

Ragna held the package in her hand after Marta and Lying Jack left the cabin. A gift. Something just for her and sent by a real friend. She carefully untied the small string around the brown paper, thanking God and the Virgin Mary that she could be alone while she opened it. Inside was a licorice whip. Her thoughts flitted back to when she had first bumped into Anders at Van Dyke's Store so long ago. He had been reading the Mohican book and eating a licorice whip. Her face burned.

Then she carefully opened the other letter and smoothed it out on the table. Mr. Sevald moaned in his sleep.

> *Dear Ragna,*
>
> *You know I planned to file on my claim in Sauk Rapids and buy flour for your family. When the Saints heard this plan, they insisted I drive a yoke of oxen all the way to St. Paul and buy four barrels of flour and a few other items needed by the community. I would file my claim on the way. It seemed like a good idea as the prices are much better in the larger cities and in one trip I could bring enough for many families. But it was harder than I thought and took two whole weeks. Oxen are the slowest animals ever created. The team wouldn't hurry no matter how much I yelled or prodded. I could have been back and forth twice in the same time if on foot.*
>
> *The Mormons are decent people—they provided plenty of food for my journey and the free use of their oxen in return for buying their supplies. They also promised help with my cabin next summer. As I have more time than money, I took them up on their offer. It wasn't until I was on my way that I realized the responsibility of carrying other people's money. I hardly slept worrying about robbers or other trouble. As it happened, on the way home I ran into an ice storm and needed the oxen shoed be-*

fore I could return home. Luckily, the Saints had sent extra money for emergency use only. I found a blacksmith in Sauk Rapids who shoed them although it took my last penny—he charged $1.25 per hoof! Can you imagine such prices? We traveled surefooted the rest of the way—even up Leaf Mountain.

The best news is that I have a paying job throughout the winter teaching school at Clitherall. There are 23 scholars and I will teach until mid-December and then again from late January until spring planting. They are paying $23 a month plus room and board, a whole dollar for every pupil. It is almost too good to be true. The money will allow me to get started on my homestead in the spring. I have arranged for Milton to put up a lean-to on my homestead and to keep a presence about the property in case of claim jumpers.

Once I have a crop in and a cabin built, I will be freer to live and speak as I wish.

Mr. Wheeling has agreed to loan me the use of a mule to return to Tordenskjold over Christmas. I will give you a ride home. If you cannot stay the entire month, I am willing to take you back to the Sevald's at New Year's. Think about it and discuss it with Mrs. Sevald. I will stop by in December and find your answer.

Are you reading The Last of the Mohicans? As teacher, I will surely quiz you on it when I see you.

Yours truly,

Anders Vollen

The letter quickened her heart and lit a flicker of hope. Perhaps he had given up on his Norwegian sweetheart. Surely, she must be mistaken. He was a friend, a kind friend who encouraged her out of respect for Uncle Evan.

She had underestimated him. To think he was educated enough to teach American scholars.

Ragna was in the middle of a perfect daydream about Anders when the door slammed. Marta placed the bundle on the table and warmed her hands before touching her husband's forehead.

"Marta," Ragna said and weighed her words before speaking. "What will you do after Mr. Sevald . . . after he . . . when . . . ?"

"You mean when he dies." Marta's eyes snapped, and she jerked the blankets up over his shoulders. He slept, mouth hanging open, a strange gurgling sound in the back of his throat. "Just speak it out, girl," she snapped. "It's not like I don't know he's dying."

"I worry about you," Ragna said. "That's all."

An awkward silence stretched out, and Ragna had almost decided that Marta would not answer. Obviously, she had offended her. She should have kept quiet.

"One thing the Saints do well is care for their own," Marta said. "You needn't worry. I'll be well cared for."

"Will you stay here alone?" Ragna had been thinking about Marta's situation. Living in the country all alone was out of the question, but Marta would never be able to stand living in the settlement with all eyes on her every movement.

"I've a son," Marta said in a strangled voice. "Back in Illinois."

Ragna held her breath.

"I'm thinking of going back to live with him afterwards—even though it means quitting the Saints and going back to the Catholic Church."

Ragna let out her breath in a heavy sigh. Good. She could breathe again.

"Just think, it's been over thirty years since my last confession." Marta's voice trailed off. The kettle bubbled on the stove. A burning log settled in the fireplace. Mr. Sevald's breathing stopped for a long moment and then resumed with a snort.

Marta sighed and gathered the dishes off the table. "Time for chores," Marta said.

Ragna trudged to the barn, pulling her shawl tightly around her head and shoulders, and plunked down on the milking stool beside the brindle heifer. Homesickness pressed in again. She leaned her right cheek against the cow's warm flank a long minute before stripping the slow ping-ping of milk into the bucket

She could not swallow the lump in her throat. It was almost a month to Christmas. The weeks stretched before her like years.

And if Mr. Sevald lingered? Must she refuse Anders's kind offer for a ride home in order to fulfill her commitment to Marta? What if Mrs. Ludwig's childbed delayed?

"Ragna!" Marta's voice called from the barn door. "Elijah Wheeling is here. It's time for that new baby."

28

Catarrh—Its Treatment and Cure

St. Paul Dispatch, December 4, 1873

EVAN TRUDGED THROUGH DEEP SNOW back to the dugout after a long afternoon of logging. Gunnar and Knut ran ahead, churning the snow into a messy path. Gray clouds crowded the horizon. The setting sun glowed gold through the gloom. Freezing sweat chilled him, and he rubbed his hands together and stomped his feet, ax propped over one shoulder. Working with an ax jolted every part of a body, and he ached all over. He quickened his pace, his growling belly reminding him of suppertime. Inga would have hot soup ready.

He calculated the number of work days needed to harvest logs for a cabin. He figured the walls required forty-eight logs, twenty more for the gables, and seven for the roof. That made seventy-five logs. A lot of chopping. It was heavy and dangerous work. Felling trees made widows, but Inga would not spend another year in the dugout if he could help it.

Evan imagined a stout log cabin nestled in the side of the hill across from the barn, not a bachelor shack like Milton planned. One that would shelter his family for many years to come.

They had a system. He and Milton chopped down the trees and Old Doll dragged them to the building site where Gunnar, away from the danger of falling trees, trimmed branches from the logs. Knut gathered smaller branches into a slash pile. Evan pushed his thoughts away from the dangers of handling an ax, gashed legs, or missing fingers. A man earned his bread by the sweat of his brow, and the sooner the boys learned that lesson, the better. They would be careful. He would teach them.

Syl promised a work team from the Branch of Zion to help raise the cabin when the time came, and Evan knew he was good for his word. They would make a day of it, fix a good meal and celebrate a new beginning.

A memory of Crooked Lightning intruded into his thoughts. "The white men will never stop until they own the whole world," he had said with sad eyes, as if a great change was coming and he was powerless to avoid it.

"I can't help it." Evan said aloud. "You cared for your people, and now I care for mine."

The sound of a clanking cowbell greeted Evan as he stepped into the clearing. The boys played around the woodpile. Sverre held Fisk, the gray cat descended from Solveig and Rasmuss's original wedding gift. Everything bore the mark of raw beginnings: the rough wooden door, the primitive fence where Old Doll chewed hay, the log outhouse with its uneven ends, the snowcovered-thatched roof with smoking stovepipe sticking out the middle, stumps scattered ragged across the clearing. A crooked snowman with a corncob smile and stone eyes stood beside the path.

"Look, Far!" Knut said. "We've built Uncle Ole."

The name brought a lump in his throat. What grief Ole must feel at the loss of his son. Evan's other brothers had not lived past childhood. What a logging crew they would have been! He reached toward his empty tobacco pocket, his thoughts in Norway as he stomped numb feet and stepped into the dugout.

Inga greeted him in an absent-minded way as she stirred something on the stove. She wore her apron inside out and dirty dishes simmered in the dishpan on the back burner.

"It's Sigurd." Inga's voice pitched and strangled. "I thought it was the croup but maybe it's something worse."

Evan walked the few steps to the bed where Sigurd lay swathed in blankets. Evan called his name, but the boy's eyes did not open. Evan's heart raced and he remembered Ole's family. "Not smallpox?"

"No spots." Inga's face stretched over her bones and her eyes glowed like coals of fire from sunken sockets. "But his throat is tight."

A chill settled into his very bones. When his *far* had built his brother's coffin so long ago, each pounding nail reminded Evan of the Roman soldier pounding nails into the Savior—each blow a stab of grief. Martin had been healthy one morning and dead the next. "Maybe it's nothing." He laid his hand on Sigurd's face and pulled away when he felt how hot it burned.

"Fever," Inga whispered as if she had no strength to speak aloud.

"What about the boys?"

"They seem fine," Inga said, and Evan strained to hear. "I sent them out to play. They shouldn't be around . . . in case . . ."

Common custom was to send children away from home when someone sickened. Evan racked his brain. Milton was their only neighbor, but his dugout was even smaller than theirs was. The Saints were ten miles away. "Maybe the twins could visit Milton's for a few days."

"And the big boys?"

"I'll rig up a bunk in the barn and keep them out of the house until . . ." The unspoken words louder than those unsaid. They would stay away until Sigurd recovered or died.

"It's these cold floors." Inga's face tightened with anguish. "I should have kept him off the floor."

It was not Inga's fault. It was his decision to move his family to such a desolate place. His poor judgment had long been a curse. The way he had trusted Crooked Lightning when common sense dictated otherwise. The way he had hesitated to buy his own place and lost his savings in the panic. The way he had poured his best years into building up Ragna's farm. Now this.

"I'll tell the boys to stay out." Evan leaned over and kissed Sigurd's flushed cheek as he slept.

"I'll pack the twins' bundle," Inga said, "and send the last baking in case Milton is short."

"Dear God." Inga's lips quivered and tears formed in the corners of her eyes, her face colorless except for burning eyes that glowed like a candle from somewhere deep within her, a place Evan did not know. Evan looked away from her eyes. They were too bright, too fierce. "I can't bear to lose another one."

He put his arm around her rigid form, tried to draw her close, laid his face against her hair that smelled of stale smoke and grease.

"Where would we bury him?" Inga's voice shrilled with anxiety. "And where would we find a minister to preach the service?" She pushed away and did not lean into him, clenching her chapped hands into tight fists. "You must have a coffin ready in case . . ."

"He'll be all right in a day or two," Evan said, pushing down the rising fear in his chest. "We'll be careful with the others, just in case."

Evan pulled his muffler tighter around his neck as he hurried towards the barn. My God, anything could happen. As always, in times of great stress his thoughts pulled backward to the uprising. He tried to push the memories away but his mind riveted back to Camp Release as his pulse quickened and breathing came in ragged gasps. Ragna's small face would be branded forever in his brain. So pathetic and helpless in the mob of children, not understanding their language, and all alone. Her dirty face and bruised cheek. How she clung to his leg and refused to let go.

It could happen to his children, too. A quick death by accident or sickness and Inga would be alone with the children. Of course, Milton would step in. He was a friend to stand by in hard times. Ragna was certain to be dependable. Even his old friend, Bror Brorson, might help in a pinch, though Inga disapproved of their Catholicism. Better to have them turn to the Estvolds at Pomme de Terre or the Rognaldsons at Foxhome. If worse came to worse, the Saints would take them in. He must tell Inga to think of the Saints if he died and no one else would help her. He would tell Gunnar and Ragna so they would know what to do if both he and Inga were taken.

The thought of his boys raised Mormons went against him. They were good people but Evan did not want his boys raised in the sect. Martin Luther was good enough for his family.

As he neared the barn, his breathing slowed and reasoning returned. Surely, the Good Lord would care for them. God had brought them this far and would not abandon them now. He was allowing fear to paint a darker picture than it actually was. It was probably nothing. Sigurd would be better in a day or two.

"Why can't we go, too?" Knut stuck out his lower lip.

"They get all the fun," Gunnar said. "All we do is work."

"Your mor needs you." Evan said to Gunnar as he lifted Sverre up onto Old Doll's broad back. "Sigurd is sick and the twins will be in the way." He patted Sverre on the leg and hoisted Lewis up beside him.

"You big boys will camp out with Old Doll and the cows. It will be a real adventure."

"Like the Mohicans?"

"What are you talking about?" Evan pulled an old horsehide blanket around the little boys and tucked it under their legs. The sun was already a glimmering lip on the western horizon. Soon it would be pitch black.

"Mr. Cooper wrote adventures about the *skraelings*," Knut said. "Anders told us."

"You shall have adventures," Evan said. "Only with pretend Red Men. Stay away from the house for now. We don't want you catching anything."

"Far," Sverre said. "Will the Red Men come to Uncle Milton's?"

"*Nei*," Evan chuckled. "The Indians will stay inside the pages of Mr. Cooper's book of adventures."

Evan led Old Doll and adjusted his buffalo coat. He must walk into the wind the short half-mile to Milton's cabin and ignore his growling belly. He must travel while there was light.

"I want an adventure, too." The wind almost stole Lewis's small voice away. "I'd rather stay with my brothers."

"You must be very brave." Evan's lungs ached from the cold. He pulled his scarf over his mouth.

"Tell us a story," Sverre said. "About the *skraelings*."

Evan felt the old anxiety rise in his chest. Would it never leave him? "Boys, I'll tell you something even more exciting than the Red Men." He glanced back at the dugout, and then stretched his steps to cover as much ground as possible, then pulled down his scarf to speak above the wind. "Let me tell you about the time I drove the stage right into a cyclone."

MILTON CRACKED THE DOOR to his little shelter. A ratty fur hat covered unkempt hair and a full beard sprouted over his lower face. He wore his old army jacket and holey mittens. Dull eyes suggested he had been sleeping, but he brightened when he recognized Evan.

"Come in, come in." He flung the door open. The wind swirled in with them, flickering the thin light of the lantern. Milton's dugout was nothing to brag about, smaller than Evan's by half, with a thatched roof, dirt floor, and a single pane of glass braced into a cutout place in the south wall of sod, beside the door. Stumps served as chairs and a board propped between the blocks of sod with stumps underneath the opposite was his table.

The twins held onto Evan's legs, hiding their faces in his trousers. "It's Sigurd," Evan said by way of explanation as he patted the boys with mittened hands. "He's sick and we thought it safer to keep the little ones away."

"Smallpox?"

"*Nei,*" Evan said. "No spots . . . fever."

"It's always something." Milton shook his head.

"Do you have medicine?"

"A pint of peppermint schnapps for emergencies." Milton scratched his head. "You're welcome to it if you think it might help."

"Could you keep the boys a few days?"

Milton gripped Evan's hand with his own. "I'm stir-crazy and the winter barely started. I'd appreciate the company." He pulled off his hat and ran his fingers through greasy hair leaving it standing straight up like a wild man. "I've already read the entire Old Testament and am starting on the New."

"We have a few books," Evan said. "I'll bring one next time I come."

The wind moaned around the thatched roof and a few grains of sand scattered onto the table. The kerosene lantern sputtered on the table, making a small circle of flickering light. Sverre clutched Evan's leg as if he would never let go.

"Look at this blackboard!" Milton touched a finger to the window and scraped letters into the heavy frost. "You will leave smarter than you came."

Sverre popped his thumb into his mouth and pulled it out only when Evan frowned at him. "I can write my name."

"So can I," said Lewis. "We don't know numbers."

"Then numbers you shall learn," Milton said. "It won't be the first time a boy learned his numbers on a frosty windowpane."

"You boys mind Uncle Milton and don't be any trouble."

"Yes, Far."

"I'll be back tomorrow to check on you."

Sverre snuffled and Lewis threw a protective arm around his shoulders. They were close. Evan wondered what it might feel like to have a brother who loved you so openly. He and Christina had shared a special bond between them. A sudden pang of loss reminded him again of her death and the new worry over Sigurd. "Be good, boys."

Milton and Evan left the boys scraping their names in the frosty window and walked out to where Old Doll stood waiting. Evan handed Milton the cloth-wrapped loaf of bread and the small bundle of clothing along with the horsehide blanket. Milton pressed the bottle of schnapps into Evan's hands.

"*Mange takk*," Evan said. "We didn't know where else to turn."

"I'm your neighbor," Milton said with a choked voice. "Of course you come to me."

Old Doll stomped and snorted. Evan wiped frost from her nose and eyes. The weather was turning colder and the days were short.

"Say a prayer for our least one," Evan said. "Such fever."

"I'll do that. Thank Inga for the bread."

Snow creaked under Old Doll's hooves, and Evan pulled his scarf over his nose as he rode away from the dugout. At least the wind was at his back for the trip home. It was cold. Colder than a witch's tit. He smiled to think how shocked Inga would be at such language. Then he sobered. Perhaps peppermint schnapps would help Sigurd's fever. Inga would know.

He searched his mind for remedies his parents had used in the Old Country. Hot tea with honey for colds. Balsam tea for congestion. Salt water gargles for sore throats. Rubbing a chest with goose grease for pneumonia. Fried-onion poultices for coughs. Burnt flour for rashes. Blowing tobacco smoke into aching ears. He thought of the graves left in the churchyard of Tolga. Too many graves.

Above, Orion shown clear and true. He searched for the Big and Little Dipper and the comforting North Star. A squiggle of green light shifted in the northern sky, the same northern lights he had known in his homeland. Evan fixed his eyes on the colors as Old Doll carried him home.

"Dear God," Evan said aloud, his voice lost in the wide expanse of sky, "take care of little Sigurd and I'll be a better person." He searched his mind and easily found a list of faults. "I'll be a better husband and father, and go to church when I can."

He listened but heard nothing but the moaning wind at his back.

29

Hard Times will Probably Stop Work on the Stillwater City Hall
St. Paul Dispatch, *December 4, 1873*

R EMEMBER MY COUSIN?" Elijah shielded his eyes from the sun's glare with a mittened hand, driving the horse and sleigh back to his cabin.

His cheeks were cherry red, and his beard was no thicker than last time she had seen him, barely a whisper of scraggly hairs across his chin.

Overhead sundogs, bright patches of light on each side of the sun, shone through a milkly sky. Words swirled away in the wind. It was as if they were snatched from her lips.

"*Nei,*" Ragna said and hid behind the layers of scarves swathing her head and neck. She reviewed what she knew about childbed. If only Auntie could be with her. She reached for her Catechism tucked in her bag, patting it for reassurance.

"Otto," Elijah shouted again. "A little older. Was at your place with my father. Whoa, there!" He pulled back on the reins. "Has a nice piece of land just east of Clitherall Lake."

Ragna smelled wood smoke as the cabin came in sight. It was closer than she remembered. She would visit Bertha again if Mr. Sevald lived.

One never knew about death. It came either too early or too late. Ann Elin's death was too early. Mr. Sevald's too late. She leaned forward for a better look at the cabin hidden behind a clump of aspen. It was like all frontier dwellings, rough but serviceable and holding great potential. Smoke spiraled from the chimney.

"Otto seeks a wife."

He probably would meet one at the courting swing in Clitherall, Ragna thought. Uncle Evan told how eligible young people in town gathered at the swing in the evening. It seemed like such a grand thing to do, almost exotic. Ragna often wished for other young people in her life.

"He wants to come courting at the Sevald's."

"What?" Ragna suddenly realized what Elijah meant and turned crimson beneath her twice-wrapped scarf.

"He could deliver the next firewood."

Her feet were blocks of ice, her throat scratchy, and her tongue refused to work even if she had a reply. A marriage meant security—*Bestemor* would have no further say over her life. And it would mean the farm would be hers. Actually his. She would have to answer to a husband, obey him.

"I think you'd like him."

The horse stopped in a soft drift of snow before the cabin. Ragna jumped down without a word and hurried into the house holding her small bundle. She had no interest at all for a Mormon suitor.

Mrs. Cornelia Ludwig met her at the door, holding a hand to her lower back. She dipped her head in a quick bow. Mrs. Ludwig stood skinny as a stork with a rounded belly hidden beneath her many shawls and a long neck that jutted forward like a goose. She walked in long steps, leading forward with her neck and hurrying as if she were behind schedule and trying to catch up.

She looked nothing like her calm, blue-eyed sister.

"Hello, Mrs. Ludwig," Ragna said.

"Please call me Cornelia."

When Cornelia spoke, American words tumbled so fast that Ragna had to pay close attention in order to catch what she was saying. Cornelia fairly groveled, wringing her hands with a simpering smile, eyes darting in all directions and hurrying to her next chore in the middle of a sentence. Her hair was as mousey as Ragna's, nothing pretty or curly about it. It took Ragna a long moment to figure out what was unusual about Cornelia's face.

Cornelia had one brown eye and one green.

"Cornelia had a sharp pain this morning and we thought for sure her time had come," Bertha said with a nervous laugh. "I hope we didn't bring you out in this cold for nothing."

Elijah changed into his barn coat and excused himself for chores. He hurried out of the kitchen with his coat unbuttoned and threw a kiss back towards his pretty bride. He seemed glad to get out of the house before the conversation turned embarrassing, something female.

Ragna glanced around the cozy cabin. The windowpane steamed from a pot of soup cooking on a small iron stove. A new rag rug curled flat before the door, really too pretty to step on. The stovepipe glowed red from a roaring fire hidden in the stove's iron belly. The oven door propped open to allow extra heat into the room.

Cornelia stretched her legs across the small cabin floor in two steps, gathered a sack of dried beans from a nail by the door and hurried back to her seat by the stove, shelling beans as if the house were afire, as if her very life depended on shelling as fast as she could.

"Don't go," Bertha whispered. "I wouldn't know what to do if the baby came before we could fetch you again."

Ragna unbuttoned her coat and unwound the long muffler from around her neck and hair. She stretched chilled hands toward the hot stove. At least she could stay awhile and make sure it was a false alarm.

If only they served hot coffee—her mouth salivated at the thought. Another reason to avoid Mormon suitors. She would serve coffee in her home someday. The pot would warm on her stove all day, just as her parents had enjoyed. Even if ground acorns or parched corn stretched the coffee beans. Hot coffee added comfort to an ordinary day.

"Warm yourself." Bertha took Ragna's wraps, hung them on a nail in the corner and directed her to a chair by the stove. "You must be frozen." She wore such an expression of admiration that Ragna flushed under her gaze

"It's cold," Ragna said. "A good day for a new baby."

Cornelia blushed and giggled, covering her mouth with her hand and looking down into her lap. At least it seemed that Ragna knew more about childbirth than these two young women did.

"Any spotting?"

"A little." Cornelia bent her face lower over the pods in her lap and shelled until the beans scattered across her lap and skittered across the floor. Ragna noticed the red spreading to the tips of her ears as she bent to retrieve the beans.

"Bloody?"

Cornelia's nod energized Ragna. "It's labor. It starts with a bloody show or broken water."

Cornelia looked up in surprise and laid a hand on her stomach. "Another one."

"You're in labor."

"You've seen for yourself that Cornelia always does things in a hurry," Bertha laughed. "Let's hope this baby comes soon."

However, the baby took its time.

The day passed, broken only by intermittent pangs that seemed to accomplish nothing. Ragna glanced out the window, seeing the early darkness of winter, watching the moon climb the sky. There was nothing more to say. They had shared all the polite conversation stored in them.

Bertha mixed a batch of bread dough. Ragna pulled the Catechism from her pocket and read the page listing the order of service for emergency baptism. She would be prepared this time. Cornelia hung onto the bedpost during the pangs and hiked across the floor between them. It seemed to Ragna they were irregular. If only she had a timepiece to measure them.

Elijah readied to fetch Cornelia's husband and seemed glad to get away from the women and their mysterious mutterings.

"How long does it take?" Elijah's voice was as quiet as the water bubbling on the stove.

"A while yet." Auntie Inga always said that most babies were born in the wee hours of the morning. "Probably not until dawning."

Elijah grabbed a slice of bread and cup of soup before bundling up and heading out. It would be a grueling ten-mile ride there and back again. Bertha cast a worried glance at her man, urged him to bring another pair of mittens, pulled baked potatoes from the oven and, using potholders, pushed them into his coat pockets to warm his hands during the journey and provide lunch along the way.

"Here's the heated stones for under your feet," she said. "Don't catch cold."

Ragna turned her face away from their goodbye, thinking how it must feel to have a man, to mourn the separation of even ten miles.

"Keep walking," Ragna told Cornelia firmly. "Walk and keep walking."

"She's tired," Bertha said. "She needs to rest a little."

"Walking hurries things up," Ragna said. "Helps the waters break."

Cornelia fairly ran across the little cabin, back and forth into the night. Ragna urged her to slow down, to pace herself, but it was as if Cornelia had only one speed—fast. She hiked the few steps across the floor, turned on the ball of her thin foot and hiked back, stretching her legs, always leading with her chin.

She reminded Ragna of a goose her parents had kept. The thought astonished her, a clear memory of something before the uprising. The way she and Birdie ran away from the goose with its stretched neck and nipping beak.

Cornelia dripped sweat and changed to the color of oatmeal. "Something's wrong." She turned her mismatched eyes upon Ragna. "I can't do this."

"You're exhausted," Bertha said and turned to look at Ragna with an accusatory expression on her face. "Can't she rest?

"I know you're tired, but it's better to keep moving." The pains should be closer together and harder. Not stopping. Auntie said that sometimes the waters refused to break. She said to push a crochet hook into the birth canal and snag the sack holding the water if necessary. Ragna's face burned red to think of it.

Bertha hooked her arm around Cornelia's back and tried to keep up as Cornelia dragged her across the floor, back and forth, never slowing down though tired almost to tears.

Cornelia paused and held onto the bedpost. "I can't do this."

"You will do it." Ragna hoped she was right. "You have to."

"I'll die like my mother."

"Bertha said your mother died of smallpox." Ragna wanted to keep Cornelia talking, walking, and her mind on other things. The worst lay ahead and she needed to be calm and focused.

"She means her real mother," Bertha said. "She died when Cornelia was born."

Ragna's heart pounded until she thought her chest would explode. Her words sounded as from a great distance. "But she's your sister."

"Adopted. Our families were killed in the massacre."

"The Saints took us in." Cornelia's face drooped chalky white. "After Camp Release."

At that moment, a flood of water gushed down the front of Cornelia's nightgown and onto the puncheon floor at her feet. Bertha reached for a towel as Cornelia cried out and doubled over in pain.

"Thank God." Ragna had dreaded the thought of breaking her water.

"Help me!" Cornelia gasped in pain. "It hurts!" Ragna had to look away from the different colored eyes and their agony. "I can't stand it."

30

Many of the Settlers in the Vicinity of Lake Shetek are Said to be Destitute and Suffering

St. Paul Dispatch, *December 7, 1873*

EVAN POKED ANOTHER CHUNK of firewood into the stove box as puffs of choking smoke watered his eyes. He tended the roaring fire all night, waking up whenever the temperature dropped, trying to help. Each time he roused to fire the stove, Inga was up with the baby.

She never slept. She spooned boiled milk between Sigurd's clenched teeth, mopped his face with a wet rag, wrapped and rewrapped the blankets. Inga worked like a shadow, silent and ghostly, rarely speaking, hardly taking her eyes off the fretful child.

Evan scraped a clear space in the window and eyed the eastern lip of purple morning. Another bitter day. St. Clement's Day had come and gone without notice—funny they had forgotten the feast day. In Norway, there would have been *rommegrot* and *fattigmand*. In Tordenskjold, they ate muskrat and parched corn soup, struggling to stay warm, all hardship and want.

Evan scraped again and looked towards Milton's place, but trees blocked the view. He hoped the twins had slept well. Were still healthy.

"Evan!" Inga's voice turned his attention back toward the sick child.

As the feeble light of morning brightened the dugout, they saw the spots. Sigurd wore a covering of fine rash on every inch of skin. Spots on his belly, on the bottoms of his feet, even the insides of his mouth and tongue. The familiar childhood illness everyone experienced at one time or another. Spots all over. Not the pustules of small pox or chicken pox. Not the swollen neck of mumps. Just spots.

"Measles." Tears dripped into Evan's tangled beard. "Thank God!"

Most children survived measles. Gunnar, Ragna, and Knut had them the year blackleg disease threatened his herd. He and Christina were sick over St. John's Day during midsummer so long ago. Mor had draped reindeer hides over the windows to keep out the midnight sun that might blind eyes weakened by fever.

No worry about too much sun in the dugout on this December day.

It could be worse. Sigurd could have smallpox or the choking death of diphtheria, a killing typhus or deadly lung fever that snatched many children away forever.

Though Sigurd was not out of the woods yet, he would live. Gunnar and Knut could safely return to the dugout. It would be safe for the twins to come home in a few days.

Thank God.

Inga tucked blankets over Sigurd and lowered herself to the cornhusk mattress. Evan did not realize she was weeping until he saw her shoulders heave. Awkwardly he sat beside her, placed an arm around her shoulders, tried to pull her closer. "It's all right, Inga. Don't cry."

Her sobs grew to keening wails, frightening in their intensity, like the sounds of the Red Men during the uprising.

"It's only measles," Evan said. "He'll be all right, you'll see."

Inga's wails grew louder, hoarse cries that made the hair on his neck stand up, and woke the dozing baby.

"I never looked at her." Sobs muffled her words. "I feared God was punishing me."

"Shhh." So that was it. "Shush now."

"You don't understand," Inga said. "I asked God to get rid of it, told Him I couldn't bring another baby into the world after the grasshoppers."

"It will be all right." Evan pushed his face into her smoky hair. "Shhh now."

"Will God forgive me?"

"Of course, He forgives you," Evan said. "And it was His will that she was taken, it had nothing to do with you."

Sigurd's piercing cry interrupted and Evan leapt to his feet with a great feeling of relief. Inga reached to tend the baby.

"*Nei*, you've been up all night," Evan said. "I'll care for the little man."

"Boiled milk," Inga said. "Keep him covered." He had never known her voice to sound so weary.

Evan watched her slump into the lumpy bed, roll towards the earthen wall, and fall asleep as soon as her head hit the pillow.

As he spooned drops of milk between Sigurd's chapped lips, Evan wondered about her first man. Surely, Gunnar Thormondson would have built a decent house by now. Maybe he would have known how to keep the grasshoppers away. He wondered if Inga yearned for her first love, wished he had lived.

He sighed and pulled Sigurd closer to him, drawing the coverlet around them and humming a Norwegian song.

Sigurd was slower than his brothers. Slower to walk. Slower to talk. Why, Gunnar had spoken complete sentences at Sigurd's age. Bright, that one. Like his *far*, no doubt. Looking down at Sigurd, Evan hoped he was not to blame for Sigurd's lack. Surely, the strong Viking blood in his veins passed to his children. He pulled Sigurd closer, hummed louder, and rocked him back and forth in his arms. It seemed to comfort the whimpering boy lying against his chest.

A fierce protectiveness boiled up within him. He would protect his family the best he could. He would build this farm if it killed him. Evan figured he had another twenty years of work in him, maybe thirty if God gave him the strength. He could do it.

"Evan." Inga's words startled him from his thoughts. "I've been thinking."

"What is it?"

"About telling Gunnar."

"What?"

"I might have died losing the baby," she said. "Or taken with fever. I could die and he'd never know the truth."

"You're talking foolish now," Evan said. "You're not going to die."

"That's not what I mean." The earthen walls absorbed her weary words. "I'm the only one to tell Gunnar about his real *far*."

So that was the way of it. The old jealousy burst into his chest. Evan leapt from the chair and laid Sigurd on the bed beside Inga. He pulled the teakettle to the hottest part of the stove, shaking it to make sure it contained water.

Inga had been thinking about her first man, just as he thought. He slammed the stove lid with enough force to rattle the stovepipe and allow small puffs of smoke to filter out into the room when he thrust a small piece of oak into the firebox.

"Don't be mad," Inga said.

"I'm not mad."

"It's my duty to answer questions about his *far*," Inga said. "Tell him about his grandparents."

The ancient anger filled him, the berserker rage that gave him the strength of a Viking warrior.

The tilt of Inga's chin visible in the dim light told him that she would not back down.

"I'm telling him today," she said.

"It's not a good time." Evan pushed the anger down, forced himself to speak calmly though his hands trembled and strange lights danced before his eyes. He could imagine how Gunnar would look at him, scorn him, and wish for his real father. As Inga did.

"I've made up my mind."

"Then tell him, God damn it." Evan slapped on his hat and wrapped his scarf around his face and neck, pulling on his jacket and buttoning it so that the edges did not match in front and allowed the neck to gape open.

He stormed out of the dugout into air so cold that it burned his lungs and made him gasp. He looked around for something to throw, something to punch with his fist.

With bare hands, Evan picked up a slab of hewn maple, one he hoped to work into a new yoke for the coming oxen, and heaved it as far across the yard as it could go. The end thumped against a tree trunk, sounding like a booming drum in the frigid temperature. He kicked a frozen drift and stubbed a toe against a hidden chunk of ice. He hobbled to the barn, cursing and feeling like a total fool, pulling a ragged splinter from his finger.

By God, a woman could drive a man crazy.

By the time he stumbled to the barn, the anger had almost drained out of him.

It would be a disaster if Inga told Gunnar. He saw it clearly. The cleansing wave of anger caused him to see things as they were. Gunnar needed to hear the truth from him. Gunnar was almost a man, as his *far*, he needed to tell him. Inga was wrong. It was *his* duty to tell Gunnar the truth.

He would tell Gunnar how much he had loved him from the very start, how he had always been glad he had spared Gunnar the misery of bearing the name of Inga's second husband. If he told Gunnar first, there was a chance he might salvage their relationship. *God help him say the right thing.* Before he had married, Evan had thought Inga carried the son of that miserable Swede. Everyone knew that a son took after his father. Blood was thicker than water, after all.

When Inga told him how Gunnar's real *far* died on the ship coming from Norway, Evan had thought their troubles were over. He thought they were free of the past and could go forward unencumbered. He had been wrong.

"Hurry," Gunnar said when Evan opened the barn door. "It's freezing."

The boys huddled with blankets in a stack of hay as Bobcat and Lady chewed their cuds. Lady's bell clanked as she reached for another nibble of hay. The barn smelled of manure and the moist heat from the animals made it much warmer than the outside air.

Knut peeked out from behind Gunnar's blanketed form. "How's Sigurd?"

"Peppered with measles," He should be thanking the Good Lord as he had promised the night before. "Remember when you had the measles?"

"I remember," Knut said. "Mor made pudding for our sore throats."

"We're cold," Gunnar said. "And starving."

"Then run to the house," Evan said. "You can't catch the spots again."

Knut let out a yell and ran out into the frigid morning. Gunnar started to follow but Evan placed an arm on his sleeve. "Wait," he said. "I want to talk to you."

"I've done nothing wrong!" Gunnar's eyes widened. "I did my chores like you said."

"You're not in trouble," Evan heaved a sigh. Hens scratched in the corners and Lady stomped her hind hoof and clanged the bell again. Bobcat lifted a dripping nose from the water trough and mooed softly. The normal smells of barnyard animals, the normal sounds. "Sit down a little."

Gunnar perched on the edge of the trough farthest away from Evan, ready to bolt if the conversation soured.

"Sometimes we don't see eye to eye on things." The old turmoil swirled in his gut, the same feelings that always surfaced when things went wrong. This was going badly already.

"There's no easy way to say this." Evan unbuttoned his jacket and pulled the buttons through the correct holes. "So I'll just say it right out. Your *mor* was a widow when we wed."

"What?"

"During the uprising . . . times were bad. Many died." Evan plunged his hand into his coat pocket and fingered a handkerchief. "We married on the day you were born."

"You're not my real *far*?" Gunnar's face turned white as the snowy drifts.

"If being your *far* means that I've cared for you since the day you were born," Evan struggled to suck air into his lungs. "If it means that I've fed you and clothed you and tried to teach you everything you need to know . . ." Evan's voice broke. "And if it means I love you as my own," he said, surprised at tears filling his eyes, "then I am your *far*."

"What's my real name?"

"Gunnar Jacobson. You were born after the wedding—legally you are my son."

"But you're no more my *far* than you are Ragna's."

"In the eyes of the law you are my son. The same as adoption."

"Why didn't you tell me?"

"We waited until you were old enough."

"But who . . . ?"

"Your *mor* will answer your questions." It had gone as Evan suspected it would. Gunnar looked at him with the expression Evan had always dreaded. Evan could see in Gunnar's eyes that he wished for his real father.

"You've always picked on me."

"That's enough."

"I hate you." Gunnar's eyes flashed. "Whip me all you want, but it won't change a thing."

Gunnar bolted out of the barn, leaving the door wide open, and raced towards the dugout. Evan watched Gunnar's legs churn like a paddlewheel. The boy clutched the blanket around his shoulders while the ends flapped in the wind like the wings of a wild bird.

Evan picked up the pitchfork, glad for a reason to avoid returning to the dugout. As he shoveled manure, he remembered how he and Inga had met. As first, Evan had thought Inga was the man's servant. Ingvald Ericcson had sauntered into the fort and left his young wife to unload the heavy trunks. Inga had struggled with the baggage, just a slip of a girl.

He brought her a dipper of cold water and she had looked up at him with those brown eyes. "*Mange tussen takk*," she had said and the sound of her voice speaking the Norwegian language felt like a warm hug from his homeland. He fell in love with her at that moment—and found out later that she was Ericcon's wife.

All that summer Evan made excuses to stop the stage at their place by Pomme de Terre. Ericcson had grand ideas of running for office and spent most of his time away from the farm, leaving Inga alone with the heavy work. It had been easy for Evan to pretend he had a chance.

When Evan realized she was expecting, his dreams crashed around him. Evan poked the pitchfork into the top of the manure pile and reached for the broom to finish sweeping the barn floor. It was bad enough to covet another man's wife, but worse when there was a child.

During the siege of Abercrombie, it was once in Evan's power to kill the son-of-a-bitch. Evan stood night watch when Ericcson crawled into the fort. Evan could have gotten away with it. He could have said he thought Ericcson was a skulking Indian.

Evan could not commit murder even if it meant he and Inga would be free to marry. Evan could not go against the teaching of his mother and Martin Luther.

Even if the bastard deserved killing.

Evan swept dust and chaff into the manure pile and put the broom back in the corner where it belonged. Inga would be surprised the cat was out of the bag. Let her be surprised. She wanted Gunnar told and by God, he had told him. Now she could deal with the consequences.

But love for Inga softened his anger. He did not wish trouble upon her. She had been through enough.

Nei, , Evan had known all along . . .especially when he was angry.

Gunnar was not to blame for his father's fever. Just as Ragna was not the reason for the death of her parents. Many tragedies and sorrows happen in this life. In Confirmation, he had memorized the verse from Job, "man is born to trouble as sure as sparks fly upward."

They had reasons to be thankful. Ragna had found work with the Saints and provided the stovepipe that made their winter bearable. Sigurd lived. He and Inga had married though it had seemed impossible from the beginning. Ragna would earn money for her passage home. *Nei,* things had turned out for the best. In spite of grasshoppers, Indians, and questions too hard to answer, they would make it.

After all, truth sets people free. He had learned that in Confirmation as well. He gathered the milk buckets for chores.

Som man reder sa ligger man. As we make our bed, so we must lie.

31

Scarlet Fever is Raging in Meeker County

　　　　　　　　　　St. Paul Disptatch, *December 7, 1873*

AUNTIE INGA WAS RIGHT ABOUT babies being born in early morning. The baby burst forth as purple rays first colored the eastern horizon. Ragna worried she felt something pull while she guided the baby's head out of the birth canal.

"It's a girl!" Bertha said. "Cornelia, you have a daughter."

Cornelia collapsed back on the bed as white as the muslin sheets, stretching her arms towards the baby. "She's beautiful."

The girl baby had a few dark hairs across her scalp, thick lips, and a flattened nose. Her dusky face was as purple as Ann Elin's had been in death. Ragna shook her gently until reassured by hearty crying. She was alive, at least, though not beautiful. She looked nothing like Ragna's little brother born so long ago. The memory came sharp as the odor of childbed. She choked back a sob.

Ragna laid the infant on Cornelia's chest. Auntie would have guessed the weight, but Ragna had not yet mastered the talent. Of course, there were no scales in the wilderness and the size of the child mattered little as long as it was healthy. Auntie said smaller babies were sometimes heartier than larger babies were. It was a mistake to judge merely on size.

Ragna tied the cord in two places with clean strings. Then she took a deep breath and cut the cord between the two knots with a sharp knife. This was always the scariest part for her. With the cord cut, there was no going back. If she had tied loose knots, if she forgot something, the baby might die.

Everything looked fine. Only a few drops of dark red blood dripped from the severed yellow cord. "I have to rub your womb." Ragna pressed deep into Cornelia's lower abdomen with the heel of her hand.

"Ouch!" Cornelia said. "You're hurting me!"

"You'll bleed if I don't." A hemorrhage could snatch a mother away in minutes. "Put the baby to breast."

Auntie Inga said the most important thing to do was to get the baby nursing. The sucking brought the afterbirth and halted the bleeding, along with pressing into the new mother's belly and rubbing the flabby organs.

"Why won't she nurse?" The baby squirmed against Cornelia's breast, twisting her head away. "Something's wrong."

Ragna turned her attention to the baby, picked her up and wrapped swaddling blankets around her. She looked healthy. The cord was tied tight, no danger there. Her pink skin still covered with thick cream from Cornelia's body. No sign of a birthmark. Ragna laid her again on Cornelia's chest.

"Bertha," Ragna said as the afterbirth slipped into a basin, all in one piece and looking normal. "Prop the baby so it can reach the nipple."

The baby let out a thin cry, and Cornelia burst into tears.

"I can't do it," she wailed. "Something's wrong."

"Don't cry." Bertha's cheeks flushed bright red, and her braids fell down in straggling strands. "Everything's fine."

The new baby found her fist and sucked a strong suck. "She's hungry," Cornelia said. "I don't have any milk."

"The milk doesn't come in for a few days." Ragna racked her brain for remedies Auntie Inga had known. "Rest now." Ragna hoped she said the right thing. "We'll try again later."

Ragna checked the rags under Cornelia's hips. Only a small amount of blood. She gathered the soiled linens, the scattered blankets, and the pan holding the afterbirth. Almost without thinking, she straightened the little cabin, put a kettle of water on the stove, and fixed Cornelia an egg. New mothers needed nourishment. A distant memory flickered across her mind of Mrs. Spitsberg bringing sweet soup after her brother's birth.

Mor had called out to Saint Olaf during her sickness and afterwards Far boosted the newborn high with strong farmer hands and bragged he would grow up to be president. Each memory caused an avalanche more. She tried to hold on to them, to remember them for later when she could savor them. Their voices. The taste of raisins and currants in the sweet soup. Smells of blood and new milk.

Cornelia cried herself to sleep with the baby on her chest. Ragna poured herself a cup of hot water—what she would give for a strong cup of Auntie Inga's good coffee. Or Marta's hidden tea. She sighed and sipped. Hot water was better than nothing.

"You need sleep," Bertha said. "You've been up all night."

"So should you." Ragna felt too wound up to sleep.

"I couldn't sleep if I tried," Bertha said as the baby let out a thin cry.

"Have you any honey?"

"No honey," Bertha said. "But maple syrup."

Ragna rubbed Cornelia's nipple with a bit of syrup and set the baby to nurse.

The baby latched onto the nipple so firmly that Cornelia woke up with a yowl. "Ouch! That hurts."

"Try to relax. The colostrum is good for the baby."

"It hurts too much."

"What will you name your baby?" Ragna searched for something that would focus Cornelia's mind on something else. She was as nervous as a new colt.

"Josephine Bethelda," she said and her eyes sparkled with tears. "After my mothers."

"Your real mother?" Ragna said.

"They were both real—Josephine my birth mother," Cornelia said, "and Bethelda, my adopted mother."

"It's a lovely name." Someday Ragna would name a daughter Ann Elin Inga after her mothers. Cornelia was right—both mothers were real.

Cornelia nodded and drifted off to sleep with the baby still attached to the nipple. Ragna checked the rags padding the bed. A small trickle of blood.

She thought to rub her abdomen again but decided to wait a while. Let her sleep. She had been through enough.

Exhaustion swept over Ragna. Her eyelids drooped and pains pricked behind her eyes.

"Rest yourself," Bertha said and pulled a low rocking chair closer to the stove and opened the oven door.

Ragna slumped into the chair, enjoying the gentle rocking motion as Bertha pulled out her knitting and sat in a chair on the other side of the stove. Outside the window, trees bent low before the rising wind. It looked like a storm coming up. She hoped with all her might that the men would make it home first.

The baby was born, and she needed to get back to Marta.

Ragna rested her eyes for a long moment then watched Bertha purl a steady row of gray wool. Ragna imagined the feel of warm wool passing through her fingers, the warmth of the garment lying across her lap. Maybe Uncle would trade for a ewe—how wonderful to have wool again. Her hands itched for knitting as well.

"I hope her milk comes in soon." Bertha's needles clicked as she spoke. "You worry about someone so nervous. Mother told of a friend who never gave a drop of milk. Had to boil cow's milk and feed the baby from a soaked rag until it was old enough to drink from a cup."

"What do you know of Cornelia's real mother?" Ragna hoped she was not intruding

"Cornelia's mother died in childbed before the uprising." Bertha said. "We know that much because her older brother was taken with her."

"You're not blood-related?" They looked nothing alike.

She shook her head. Bertha's lower lip quivered and she bent her head over her knitting. After a long pause she looked up with tears on her face. "I don't know a thing about my family." She wiped her eyes on her sleeve. "Just shadows of memories."

"Brothers or sisters?"

"It's hard to remember. I was little, maybe two or three when they found me, and I didn't speak English."

"What language did you speak?" Ragna could hardly hear her voice above the beating of her heart. Coincidences happened all the time and Bertha had curly blond hair and lovely blue eyes.

"German . . . they think I was from Milford. That's where Cornelia's family lived, and they found us together."

Bertha's needles clicked in a steady chatter as Ragna's heart sank. It was most unlikely but she had to ask.

"Have you heard of stork bites?" Ragna said. "A birthmark on a shoulder as if the stork had left a mark?"

"No," Bertha said. "Why do you ask?"

"No reason." It was a foolish thought. Of course, Bertha was someone else's sister, not hers. "I lost my family in the uprising, too."

"Do you remember them?"

"A little. Remembered this morning how a neighbor brought sweet soup for my mother after my brother's birth."

"Did you have a sister?"

Ragna nodded.

"Maybe we are lost sisters," Bertha said and her face lit up like the fireflies Ragna once caught with Birdie. "Maybe we were meant to rediscover each other."

Ragna was tempted. It would be such a comfort to find a sister. But the birthmark. It would not be fair to Birdie if she quit looking.

"My sister had a stork bite on her shoulder."

"Oh." Bertha looked disappointed.

It was time to check on the new mother, rub her belly and reposition the baby to the other breast. Cornelia would have sore nipples unless Ragna did her job. The padding must be changed and the soiled rags washed.

"Bertha!" Cornelia's shriek raised the hair on the back of Ragna's neck, reminded her of the skraelings during the uprising. "I'm bleeding."

32

A Little Child of Mr. Mosier was Burned to Death by a Kerosene Explosion

St. Paul Dispatch, *December 8, 1873*

WHEN RAGNA PULLED BACK THE quilts and saw the red stain creeping across the bed and saw how the blood dripped onto the floor, she knew Cornelia was dying. Ragna gasped, panic stricken, unsure what to do. Although Auntie talked about women bleeding out after childbed, Ragna had never seen it before.

"I'm scared!" Cornelia said, her voice weak, her cries almost a whisper. "Tell Manly I'm sorry—so sorry to leave him."

"Don't talk that way." Ragna rubbed deep into Cornelia's belly, not minding the pain she caused, tears falling in gulping sobs. Maybe there was still a chance.

"Bertha, promise you'll take the baby." Cornelia's face had a fierce look, an expression so desperate that Ragna was glad to turn away, to keep busy. Ragna raised Cornelia's feet on pillows, pushed a spoon of water between her lips, shook the baby awake and forced it to latch on to the breast again, rubbed deep into her abdomen and then did it all again.

Bertha knelt beside the bed, clutching Cornelia's hand, praying for a miracle, asking God to stop the bleeding, to spare her sister's life.

Ragna prayed a desperate prayer as well as she worked. *Now and in the hour of our death.*

Cornelia's face lost all color as she bled away into the cornhusk mattress beneath her. "Promise me, Bertha." Her voice barely a whisper.

At first Ragna thought Cornelia slept, but too much blood spilled across the bed. The ragged breathing ceased. Ragna lifted the sucking baby from Cornelia's breast and the baby howled. Bertha burst into wild sobs.

"Oh, God," Bertha said. "What will we do? There's no milk for the baby."

Ragna led the weeping aunt to the rocking chair and placed the squalling infant into her arms. Ragna cleaned up the worst of the blood and pulled the blankets over Cornelia's face.

"Do something!" Bertha's voice shrilled higher than the baby's howling. "What will we do?"

Ragna boiled cow's milk, watered it down and sweetened it with maple syrup. Ragna soaked a clean rag and put it into the baby's mouth after dipping it into the warm liquid.

Ragna knew what it meant to grow up without a mother. She longed to fix it, make it better. There was no way to fix it. The baby would die as well if she did not take nourishment. They were still trying to get the baby to suck from the rag when the men returned.

Manly Ludwig, still wearing his overcoat and mittens, dropped to his knees beside his wife's body. Ragna rued the bloody bedding with its raw odor. It was bad enough that he saw his wife cold and silent.

A gangly man with a face scarred from smallpox, Manley Ludwig pulled off his cap and showed wild hair, thin and balding. His teeth were bad but he wept genuine tears over his dead wife, and Ragna knew him for a good man. He had lost his wife and maybe his daughter—he could never care for her alone.

It was her fault.

Ragna bundled in her shawl and scarves and escaped to the icy outhouse in the backyard. Sleet filled the air, stung her eyes and slammed into her cheeks. The northwest wind howled across the yard and clouds, the color of Bertha's wool, blocked a thin sun. Ragna did not know if her tears were from the ice or from her heart. She slammed the door shut behind her. Pale light filtered in through the moon-shaped slit in the upper wall and the acrid smell of human waste sickened her.

She clasped the button with all her strength.

Someone calls at the door.

"Sister," she pleads. "Let me in."

It's Birdie. I throw the door open as wide as it will go and fall into her arms. "Oh, Birdie, I've done a terrible thing."

"It's not your fault." *Birdie shushes me as Mor once quieted me, her voice gentle.* "You did your best."

"But I'm a murderer," *I say.* "I'm no better than the skraelings *that killed our parents. I was too busy to pay attention.*"

"You were tired."

"Don't leave." *My heart pounds until my ribs will burst apart.* "I can't live without you."

"You could have told Bertha she might be your sister."

"I couldn't abandon you."

"As I cannot rest until we're together again."

"Don't leave me, Sister."

"Shh . . ." *She kisses my cheek.* "Don't be foolish now. You know I'll never leave you."

Someone rapped hard on the door. "Ragna!" Bertha said. "Are you all right?"

There was no denying it. Ragna's neglect had robbed Bertha of a sister, someone she loved and cherished. From now on Bertha would be like her, without family, without a sister.

At least Bertha had a husband. There was no denying Elijah.

"It's cold," Bertha said. "Come in by the fire."

"I'll be right there." Ragna wiped her face on the back of her hand, straightened her collar, and removed her bloody apron. Blood spattered her dress and the tops of her shoes. Like a butcher, she thought. Like a killer.

A fleeting image of blood spattering across Birdie's face flickered through her mind. She shook her head. She was imagining things.

She cracked opened the squeaky door, and Bertha fell into her arms. "Oh, Ragna!" Her tears wet Ragna's neck. "It's too terrible."

A gust of wind sent them scurrying to the cabin. Manley sat silently in the corner holding his daughter in stiff arms. Baby Josephine wailed, and Bertha hurried to pick her up.

"Maybe more milk," Ragna said.

The baby turned her face away from the rag, screamed and drew up her knees in protest. "She doesn't want it," Bertha said. "What will we do?"

"Maybe someone at the settlements . . ." Ragna said.

Elijah pulled on his coat and dropped hot stones from the stove into his pockets. "I'll find a wet nurse."

Bertha clung to the wailing infant, weeping. "I promised Cornelia I'd take care of her."

Manley struggled to his feet and looked around in confusion. "I'll go with you," he said to Elijah.

"Stay here and take care of the chores." Elijah's voice startled Ragna. Like his *far*, he took charge without hesitation.

Manley nodded, buttoned his coat and left for the barn without taking his mittens.

"Will he be all right?" Bertha's forehead creased with concern.

"The Good Lord will help him," Elijah said firmly. "Just hold on until I get back."

"Will you take the baby with you?" Bertha said.

"*Nei*," Ragna said. "It's too cold."

"I'll bring a woman," Elijah said. "Ella Tuttle has a new baby."

"And Dorcas Romney," Bertha said. "She was Cornelia's good friend." Speaking her sister's name brought a flood of tears to Bertha's eyes again. She pulled the baby to her cheeks and held it close. "There, there." She snugged the blanket around the wailing infant. "It will be all right, you'll see."

Ragna dreaded touching Cornelia's cold body.

Just an hour ago Cornelia was filled with life—all the doubts and fears, loving concern. All taken away in a heartbeat. *Holy Mary, Mother of God, be with us now and in the hour of our death.*

As she forced herself to bring a basin of warm water, her thoughts went to Birdie. "I miss my sister," she said.

"Tell me about her." Bertha walked the floor holding the fussing baby.

"We played hide-the-thimble and kick-the-can." Keeping her mind on Birdie made it easier to uncover the body, remove the drying blood. Anything to keep her mind off what she was doing. "In the summertime we caught fireflies."

The words rushed out like Cornelia's blood had flooded the mattress. "We were both taken during the uprising but only I returned." She choked a little and forced herself to remove Cornelia's bloody gown. "I've always wondered where she is, if she lives."

"What do you think?"

"She's alive," Ragna said. "I imagine a million ways how she'll come home." Ragna pulled a clean gown over Cornelia's stiffening limbs. "I think of her every day."

"You're lucky." Bertha's voice sounded as far away as the settlements. "I wish I could remember something."

It was true. To remember anything was a gift. *Thank you, God. Thank you for every clear memory.*

"Uncle Evan says she's dead and that I should reconcile myself to it." Ragna rolled Cornelia away from her, folded back the soiled linen under her body and rolled her towards herself as she pulled the sheets free. "I suppose he's right."

"We're in the same boat," Bertha said. "Your sister is missing and mine is gone." Tears choked her voice and she buried her face in the baby's blanket for a brief moment before looking up again. "We can pretend." She sniffed and paced across the floor again. "You'll be my sister, and I'll be yours. We won't be alone anymore."

"*Mange takk,*" Ragna said and strong emotion welled up in her chest making speech difficult. "We'll pretend."

33

BANKRUPT SALE! A Rare Chance for a Lady or a Business Man
St. Paul Dispatch, *December 15, 1873*

W E SHOULDN'T HAVE TOLD HIM." Evan stood on the table and carefully positioned flat pieces of wood among the lattice of branches in the thatched roof overhead. An annoying leak had dripped on their bed during the night when a warm wind blew in from the southwest. My, God, a man at least deserved a dry bed.

"It was time," Inga said. "Should have done it long ago."

For the last few days, Gunnar had not spoken to Evan other than surly answers to direct questions. He seemed equally unhappy with his mother, avoiding her altogether. Evan sighed. *"Nar det regner pa presten sa drypper det pa klokkeren."*

"If it rains on the preacher it drips on the sexton." Inga laughed. How good to hear it. How long had it been? Before the grasshoppers, surely.

"Are you talking about the drip on your pillow or the overflow from Gunnar's storm?"

"Does it matter?"

Evan pushed the board into place and tucked wood shavings around the gaping ends. "Maybe this will stop the damn drip."

"Evan!"

"I know. But a man is sorely tried by a dripping roof."

He hoped to bring the twins home now that Sigurd was better, but Inga thought another day would be safer, in case Sigurd might be contagious. Jubilation about the moderating temperatures subdued when the roof started dripping drops of black mud. A hurry-up job never worked. Evan snugged the rough board a little tighter into the thatch and yowled when a sliver pushed under his thumbnail. "Damn it!"

"Quiet," Inga said. "Sigurd will hear."

Evan doubted Sigurd would hear.

Since the measles, something had happened to Sigurd's hearing. Evan first noticed when Gunnar dropped an armload of firewood beside the stove and a falling stick had upset the iron poker propped up against the stove. The poker crashed against the side of the stove and everyone jumped in surprise except Sigurd, who never batted an eye and kept playing as if nothing had happened. Since then, Evan had watched Sigurd nap in the midst of loud noises from his older brothers. Something was wrong.

He had not said anything to Inga. It seemed cruel to bring it up when there was nothing to change it. Why, Bjron Barsness from Tolga had been deaf as a stump after measles. Evan would wait a while longer to tell Inga. Wait until the weather warmed and the boys were home. Wait until they were no longer cooped up in this hole like so many gophers. He sighed and sucked on his bleeding thumb.

"Gunnar wants to carry the bread over to Milton and the boys."

Evan pulled his thumb out of his mouth. Gunnar knew the way, the trail was plain and the weather mild. If Gunnar went, Evan would have time to chop a new fishing hole in the ice and maybe catch a few muskrats. Lying Jack called muskrat pelts "Minnesota money" and said that anyone who would not eat a good muskrat deserved to go hungry.

Their stores were pitifully low. They would be glad for any meat on their table.

"Ja," Evan said. "Let his young legs carry the bread. Knut and I will go fishing."

34

*The Thief Who Stole the Horse and Buggy from Hall McKin-
ney has been Captured at Detroit Lakes*

St. Paul Dispatch, *December 15, 1873*

MR. WHEELING FIRST SUGGESTED the plan during a visit. Said
Manly Ludwig needed a wife to raise his daughter and keep
house for him.

Marta barely batted an eyelash, reached for the water dipper and refilled
Mr. Wheeling's glass. "I have need of Ragna." Her voice was as flat and hard
as the hearthstone in front of the fireplace. "She has no time for marrying."

Ragna held her breath. She felt like a Negro slave before emancipation,
as if she stood on the auction block.

"Manly Ludwig is a God-fearing man," Mr. Wheeling said. "Has a nice
piece of ground with improvements as the law demands. His daughter is healthy
and will be weaned off the breast and ready to return home within a year."

Ragna remember his tears at Cornelia's bedside, his bad teeth, and
pocked skin and thinning hair. A shudder swept through her. Maybe marrying him would atone for her sin and save the baby from being a motherless
child. Save him from being a widow man. Make a bad situation better. Prevent her from returning to Norway. She could take the place of Cornelia
and become Bertha's real sister, but thought of living away from her father's
farm came as a physical pain in her chest.

"I can't spare her." Marta pursed her lips in a hard line. "It's out of the
question."

Mr. Wheeling nodded to Ragna, stood to his feet and buttoned his
jacket. "Do you have need of anything?"

"No," Marta said. "Elijah sees to us."

"Good day, then." With his hand on the latch he turned as if he remembered something. "Anders sends word that he'll pick you up for Christmas."

Anders! A wave of emotion swept through Ragna, and she allowed herself the luxury of a few tears. Surely an entire lifetime had passed since she had last seen Anders or her family.

Mr. Wheeling left in a swirl of cold air. Marta swept his snowy tracks out the door with a willow broom, swept until the wet prints were gone, until she was out of breath and her face had returned to normal color.

"Girlie," she said and pointed a bony finger towards Ragna. "Don't be in too much of a hurry to wed."

Ragna busied herself with the wash, scrubbing Mr. Sevald's urine soaked bedding in a wooden tub of soapy water, trying to swallow the lump in her throat and the pain in her chest.

"When you marry, your freedom is over." She propped the broom into the corner behind the door. "Don't forget it."

Ragna nodded.

"And if you marry a Saint," Marta scowled her lips into a deep pout, "it's worse."

Ragna nodded, thinking of teatime and hot coffee. Thinking of the graves back in Alexandria, her father's dream of black dirt and prosperity.

"Every individual thought a sin, every idea scrutinized by the Elders." Marta slammed the broom into the corner and headed toward the stove. "Tithes and offerings, nothing of your own, not even your man. He answers to the Elders, too."

Ragna wrung out the soapy sheet until her hands were raw, and then dipped it in a tub of rinse water, pushing it into the clean water.

"You have your prayers and your own ideas." Marta filled the teakettle and added a stick of kindling. "Don't give them up too quick."

Ragna pulled the wet sheet from the rinse water and felt the cooling water drip down her arm to her elbow and onto the puncheon floor. She had been the cause of Cornelia's death. It was her duty to care for her daughter.

"Look at me," Marta said, "and learn."

Marta stomped over to the wall and again turned Joseph Smith's tintype to the wall. "Don't make a foolish mistake that you must live with the rest of your life."

Ragna thought about it while she wrung out the rinsed sheet and draped it over the rocking chair to dry by the fire. The thought stayed with her through the next week and lingered in her mind as she washed the eggs and mended an apron. The idea would not leave while she milked the brindle heifer and scattered feed to the hens. Maybe this is what God demanded of her. At least she would not have to go back to *Bestemor*.

"Ragna," a voice calls from the haymow. "Don't do it."

"Birdie!" Ragna leaps to her feet from the three-legged stool used for milking, careful to spare the partially filled bucket.

Birdie climbs down the hayloft ladder dressed in a blue gingham dress and matching ribbon. Her hair pulled into blond braids wraps around her head. Embroidery decorates a snow-white apron of real Hardanger lace.

"If you wanted to marry a stranger you could go back to the Old Country." Birdie's voice sounds worried, anxious. "And a Mormon! Mor and Far would never approve—nor Bestemor."

"Think of Auntie Inga," Birdie says as she pats her braids and struggles to push a stray curl behind her ear. "She married that stranger from the boat and has never been the same."

"But it's my fault," I say.

"What about me?" Birdie presses. "I'm your sister. You don't need another to take my place. Don't give up on me."

"Ragna!" Marta called from the doorway clutching a draped shawl over her head. "Your young man is here."

35

Bold Robbing of Railroad Train in Iowa

St. Paul Dispatch, *December 15, 1873*

I'M SKUNKED." EVAN PULLED HOOK and line from the frigid water. Knut's lone pike, pitiful and tiny, flopped on the gray ice. "Your *mor* will cook soup on that one." Wind gusted from the west, and low clouds hovered over the horizon, dark and menacing. "I hope your brother returns before the storm."

"Far," Knut's voice cracked. "Gunnar says you're not his real *far*."

"That's right." Evan took a deep breath and tried to push down the anxiety that choked his throat. A pileated woodpecker drummed on a nearby oak tree, its rhythm matching the beating of Evan's heart. "Your *mor* was married before, but her man died in the uprising."

"Did the *skraelings* kill him?"

"An accident." Ingvald's heels had gouged the horse's sides, cruel and selfish to the very end, and when its hoof stepped into the gopher hole Ingvald had gone flying into a stone pile. Killed before their eyes. Dark thoughts pushed into Evan's mind, memories of the dying. Those killed and butchered.

"Are you my real *far*?"

Waves of apprehension, thick and cloying. A young man did not consider how he must answer his children later on for the deeds of his youth. Impossible to explain how he had fallen in love with a married woman. Certainly sinful to tell a young boy that he had prayed that Ingvald Ericcson would fall into the hands of the Red Men so that he could marry his beautiful wife.

"You're too young to remember when we bought Old Doll from Bror Brorson."

"Old Doll?" Knut cocked his face to the side with a puzzled look.

"She came to us already bred. When she foaled, Steel Gray acted as the colt's father." Evan hoped with all his might that he was making sense. "And afterwards Steel Gray sired the rest of her colts."

"I remember Steel Gray," Knut said.

"That's what happened with us. Gunnar's father was gone before he was born. But he's always been a son to me and always will be."

Gunnar would never know how lucky he was that a gopher hole tripped Ericcson's horse and broke his neck.

They gathered their gear and Evan stabbed the fish through the eye with a sharp stick carried for that purpose. "You carry supper home to your mor."

Knut's glad eyes looked up at him from beneath his knitted cap. They showed not one drop of hostility.

"I'M WORRIED ABOUT THE LITTLE BOYS," Inga said over thin fish soup. "Milton isn't the most stable man I've known."

"He's better since the move." Milton seemed freer since the panic took the blood money from his bank account. "He'll be fine. It's just one more day."

Sigurd played with a tin cup and spoon. Banging and giggling. His spots were almost gone. Milton's dugout was little more than a hole in the ground. Not much room for the twins to run off excess steam.

The door flew open and Gunnar, red faced and puffing, pushed into the cabin. "Lewis is sick." He puffed to catch his breath. "Spots."

"My, God!" Inga pushed away from the table and pulled her shawl from the hook lodged in the dirt wall. "I'll go. Evan, you'll have to care for Sigurd." She wrapped a scarf around her head and neck. "We can't risk taking him out in such weather."

"Wait a minute! You can't stay with Milton," Evan said. "It wouldn't be proper."

Inga hesitated, like a deer looking at the hunter.

"Gunnar will mind Sigurd and Knut while we're gone." Evan considered the options. "We'll send Milton back to stay with the boys."

"But, Sigurd," Inga's voice rasped. "We both can't leave the baby."

"Sigurd is almost well." Evan reached for his coat and hat. "I won't let you go alone. You need someone to keep the fire going. We have no choice."

Gunnar removed his outer clothes and hung them on a peg in the wall. He headed toward the stove and scooped soup from the kettle.

"Gunnar is old enough to keep watch on Sigurd," Evan said.

Gunnar looked up in surprise.

"Besides, Knut will help . . . and Milton will soon be here," Evan said. "I'll come by every morning to check on them."

Inga gathered a crock of muskrat fat, half a loaf of bread wrapped in cloth, the sack of coffee beans and grinder, and a small package of dried beans.

"If only Ragna were here," she said. "We have need of her, and she's off tending strangers."

"We'll be fine," Evan said. "She'll soon be home for Christmas."

"Sigurd needs boiled milk every hour," Inga said. "And some of that frozen barley soup in the corner. Put it on the stovetop and use it as it melts."

"What else?" Gunnar said. "How will I know what to do?"

"Keep Sigurd warm," Inga said. "Make sure he's covered at night. Change his soakers." She kissed Sigurd's pale face and quickly hugged Knut and Gunnar.

"We're counting on you," she told Gunnar. "No monkey business, now."

"*Nei, Mor.*" Gunnar's face was serious. "I'll take care of everything."

"Keep a fire going," Evan said. "Don't fill the stove too full—there's always danger of fire." He buttoned the last button on his coat. "Keep a bucket of snow on the table to melt for water."

"I know, I know." Gunnar spooned the last of the soup into his bowl and set it on the table.

"And remember," Evan said and paused to form his thoughts, "Milton isn't used to children. You're in charge of your brothers."

"He'll regret the day he met us," Inga said as she tied her warmest shawl around her head.

"Don't worry, Mor." Knut picked up Sigurd and wiped his nose on an old rag hanging on the wall for that purpose.

"I don't like the look of the weather," Evan said. "Something's brewing to the west." Evan made a quick decision. "Knut, better do the milking now." It was better safe than sorry. "It's early but I don't want you out if the weather turns."

Knut grabbed the wooden bucket by the door and shuffled into his jacket.

"Gunnar, you stay by Sigurd," Inga said. "No matter what, you stay with him."

"I will, Mor." Gunnar's face was serious for once. "Don't worry. You can count on me."

They were half way to Milton's when Evan remembered the hens. "I hope they remember to gather the eggs," he said.

"How can you even think about hens when our boys are sick?" Inga quickened her step until she was almost running, her smooth shoes slippery on the snowy path.

Icy pellets of sleet started falling when they got over the rise, and by the time they reached Milton's door their eyelashes frosted with ice and their lips were blue.

"Come in," Milton said. "Good God, you look like icicles."

The smell of sickness slapped them in the face when they stepped into the dugout. "Mor! Far!" Sverre ran at them with such force that Evan almost toppled over. He burst into tears and hugged Evan's knees with all his strength. "Lewis is sick."

Inga was already at Lewis' bedside. "Why does he have his eyes bandaged?"

"It's all I knew about measles," Milton said. "I remembered that light can blind a person with measles, so I shut out the light."

"It's dark enough in here already," Inga said and untied the blue hand-kerchief around his eyes. "No need for blindfolds." Wailing sobs came from Lewis' mouth. He clung to his mother and refused to let go.

"There, there!" Inga said. "How long has he been sick?"

"Since last night," Milton said.

Evan placed the supplies on the table, and the milk bucket on the floor. The boys had looked well yesterday morning, but thinking back, Lewis had been quiet, not quite himself.

"I didn't dare leave him to come for help," Milton said. "And Sverre was too young to go alone."

"You did the right thing," Inga pushed back wild strands of hair behind her ears.

"Sorry to inconvenience you this way," Evan said. They were taking advantage of this good neighbor's kindness. "We already owe more than we can repay."

"It's nothing," Milton said. His beard framed his face in gray, pointing to a perfect vee down the front of his shirt where red drawers peeked out between missing buttons. "The least I can do."

"Bring a cup of milk," Inga said.

Evan took the cloth off the bucket and dipped a cup of thin milk. The cold weather was hard on the animals. The milk was watery, not as rich as it should be. *Dear Jesus, let it be enough.*

"We have another favor to ask," Evan said. "Would you trade places for a few days until Lewis is well again?" The dugout was little more than a hovel with a thatched roof. *My God, how did Milton stand it?*

Milton looked dazed, almost confused.

"Inga and I will stay here with the twins if you'll go back to our place and mind the others."

"I think you should try to get word to the trader to bring medicine," Milton said. "There must be something they can take to get better."

They discussed how they could work it out. How Milton would leave on Old Doll the next morning to try to find Lying Jack or at least find a way to get word to him. Evan would return to his dugout at least part of the time Milton was gone.

It was the only sensible solution. However, as Milton bundled up and headed out into the snow, Evan hoped they were not making a mistake.

36

The Epizooty is Raging in Mower and Olmstead Counties
                                   St. Paul Dispatch, December 20, 1873

ELLO, RAGNA," ANDERS SAID with hat in hand. His cheeks flamed
red. Flushing warmth crept up her cheeks, too.

"Anders." Ragna pushed down her excitement at seeing him, this
first connection with her people since autumn. She pushed back from the
cow and held the filled bucket away from its slapping tail.

Words escaped her. She was suddenly aware of her worn dress, her plain
face, and messy braids. Thoughts jumbled in her mouth. Nothing came out
at all. She studied the toes of her worn shoes and was horrified to see
smudges of Cornelia's blood.

"Are you ready to go home?"

"Oh, Anders." Tears prevented speech. He would think her a baby. Com-
pare her to his sweetheart in Norway.

"Young man," Marta said. "If you have any sense at all you'll kiss her."

Anders laughed and Ragna's heart fell. What was Marta thinking?

"Of course." Anders leaned over and kissed Ragna on the cheek. He
smelled of fresh air and wood smoke. A faint odor of horse clung to his
jacket. His lips felt chapped, slightly rough on her cheek.

"Hello, Ragna," he whispered. "It's time to go home."

Marta took the bucket of milk and returned to her house. Ragna
grabbed the pitchfork to finish the chores while Anders led the borrowed
mule inside for water and feed. She felt tongue-tied, afraid to say anything
lest she say the wrong thing.

"Let me help," Anders said after he removed the saddle from the mule
and wiped it down with wisps of hay.

He took the fork from her hand and pitched hay to the cows while Ragna searched for eggs in the hens' usual hiding places. She carried three brown eggs in her hand.

"That ought to do it," she said.

As they stepped into the cabin, Mr. Sevald moaned, and Marta hurried to the stove and pulled the teakettle over to the hottest burner.

"You'll have tea before you leave." It was not a question.

"A quick cup," Anders said as he glanced out the window. "We'd best be on our way if we hope to be home by dark."

Ragna pulled out her shawl and gathered her catechism and extra clothes. Then she took Anders' book from the basket by the table and wrapped it inside a clean apron.

"How did you like it?" Anders said with a grin.

"I'm not quite finished." She felt ashamed to admit that the English words were slower and more tedious than if they had been in Norwegian.

"Mrs. Sevald," Anders said. "I bring you a present from Mrs. Wheeling."

He pulled a brown, paper-wrapped package from his coat pocket and handed it to her. "Something from Lying Jack."

"What is it?" Marta held it carefully, untying the string and looping it around her fingers to form a small skein. She slipped the string into her apron pocket and then unwrapped the brown paper.

"Peppercorns!" Her voice sounded breathless. "How long has it been since we've had pepper in this house?"

"Mrs. Wheeling sends her regards. Says they're all praying for your man."

Marta carefully folded the paper around the precious orbs of flavor and tucked them into a teacup on the shelf.

"She's a good person."

"That she is, ma'am."

Ragna wondered if anyone would ever unwrap a present from her and call her a good person.

"You're wool gathering, Ragna!" Marta's voice cracked with authority. "I said get the teapot down, and let's have a cup."

Marta took down the sugar bowl—real white sugar, not just maple sugar—for the occasion. *She's acting funny,* Ragna thought. *As if she's trying to impress Anders.*

"Ragna has been a godsend." Marta passed the sugar bowl to Anders. Ragna looked up in surprise. Marta was not one to offer compliments. "She's a cheerful worker and a good companion."

Ragna looked down into her cup. What was Marta trying to do?

"When Syl Wheeling tried to talk me into letting her to marry that widower with the new baby, I told him that I couldn't do without her."

"Marta!" Ragna couldn't keep quiet. "Anders has no interest in such things."

"Hmmmph." Marta said and poured another cup of tea. "I just want to give you the credit you deserve."

Ragna sneaked a peek at Anders and was surprised to see a look of concern knitting his brow.

"Those Saints are always looking for women," Marta continued. "In Utah they're taking more than one wife, if you can believe the papers."

"We need to be going," Anders said. "I hope you can get along without Ragna until after Christmas."

"Of course," Marta said. "She deserves time with her friends and family."

Marta made no sense at all. One minute she could not get along without her and the next she did not need her.

A sharp rap interrupted their conversation. Marta peeked out the window, hurried back to the table to clear away any evidence of the tea. Then she straightened her spine and opened the door.

"It's Otto Nelson." He craned his neck to look into the house. "I've come with a load of wood."

"Come in and warm yourself," Marta said with a brusque voice and manner. Not at all like the friendly warmth she had shown Anders. "Anders, you and Ragna had best be leaving. It'll be dark by the time you get home."

Marta almost pushed them out the door past the startled-looking Otto Nelson, who stood with hat in hand. He nodded to Anders and Ragna but did not speak. Ragna noticed Anders glared at the man.

The mule, a little long in the tooth, rode sturdy and dependable. Anders sat astride the beast and pulled Ragna up behind him. She barely knew where to place her hands but held on tightly after the first jolt forward. Better to hang on than be tossed off. It seemed a long ways to the ground.

Mor had once said that she had been sick all the way across the ocean. "You were too seasick to enjoy the adventure." Ragna could almost smell the cooking fire clinging to her mother's apron as she remembered the words. Precious words.

"Are you all right?"

"*Ja,*" Ragna said and gripped Anders around the waist with both hands. She buried her face in the back of his jacket. It smelled like wood smoke and shaving soap. She pushed away thoughts about Manley Ludwig and Gjert Sevald. She refused to think about her parents sleeping in the small cemetery plot back at the farm. She turned away from memories about Birdie and thought instead how nice the journey.

Anders gripped the reins with one hand and placed a warm hand on hers.

"Are you warm enough?"

"*Ja,*" she answered. "And you?"

"You're like a heated brick at my back."

He talked then, of his trip to St. Paul with the oxen, of the classroom escapades of Mormon scholars. She laid her ear against his back and felt the words vibrate through his jacket as well as hearing them from his mouth. She felt as if she could stay there forever, feeling the warmth of his body, knowing they were alone and without scrutiny, not having to look into his face as he spoke or try to cover emotions that were better left unsaid. He was taken, after all, saving money for a Norwegian sweetheart.

"I'm making good money," Anders said. "It means a delay in my plans."

He had said this before. She listened but did not reply.

"A man cannot hope to marry until he has something to offer a girl."

Her heart sank. He was just a friend promised to someone else. She had always known that. In spite of the kisses. A kiss like the one she might give to her brothers, after all. She thought of Mr. Ludwig and his plight. If she did nothing, she must return to Norway.

She pulled her face away from his jacket. Tears coursed down her cheeks and she wiped them on her shawl.

"What's wrong?"

"Nothing," she said. "Just the wind."

"Tell me about the woman who died." His voice sounded gentle. "That must have been terrible for you."

Sobs overtook her, and she was unable to answer for a long minute. She hated crying in front of anyone. She was almost grown, surely too big to cry like a baby. Anders pulled the reins and twisted to look into her face.

"It wasn't your fault," he said fiercely. "Things happen. It was in the hands of God. Just like when Ann Elin died—it wasn't your aunt's fault. It just happened."

She sniffed and gulped another sob.

"What did Mrs. Sevald mean when she said that the Saints want you to marry the widow man?"

"He needs someone to care for the baby." She hiccupped an unladylike snort.

"Don't be ridiculous." His voice gentled again. "You deserve more than that, Ragna Larson. Not just to be a replacement wife—but the one first chosen and loved above all else."

With that he turned sharply, clucked to the mule and touched a heel to its flank. The animal lurched forward, and Ragna hung on with all her might lest she topple into the snow.

RAGNA FELT SOMETHING WRONG BEFORE they entered the dugout. Everything was too quiet, no boys playing outside, no one chopping at the wood-pile, and only a small plume of smoke from the pipe sticking up from the thatch. The path wiggled to the doorway, sloppy and uneven. It looked as if Knut had shoveled it, or one of the twins.

She studied the stovepipe. By rights it belonged to her. She had worked these many weeks for Marta and the sick man in exchange for it. It made her feel both proud and ashamed. Proud that she had contributed something valuable to Uncle and Auntie who had done so much for her, ashamed that she was worth so little—her weeks of tedium valued at only a metal pipe.

She slipped off the mule before Anders had a chance to help her down and hurried to the door. How dismal and primitive, like gophers living in the ground. So unlike her *far*'s house, her old home.

"Anyone here?" she called as she pushed open the door. Sigurd played on the bed facing the other way. He did not turn at her greeting.

"Sigurd," she said. When he did not respond, she tapped him on the back. He greeted her with squeals of delight. He was not the fat baby she had left, his face white against the earthen wall, all color gone from his lips. He drooped like a geranium in need of sunlight and felt almost weightless when she scooped him into her arms. She kissed his sour neck.

"He's been sick," Gunnar said from the corner where he was hanging wet soakers to dry. The stench of urine filled the dwelling. "Measles."

"Where is everyone?" Dirty dishes piled on the table, unmade beds, slop jar overflowing, wood chips lying on the floor. "Where's Auntie?"

"At Milton's," Gunnar gave her a squeeze. "Oh, Ragna." He burst into tears. "First Sigurd, then the twins."

"Where is Uncle Evan?"

"At Milton's with the little boys." Gunnar looked older, paler and thinner. "Sigurd took sick first, and Mor sent the twins to Milton to keep them from it but they got it anyway and are too sick to be moved."

Ragna's mind swirled like the cold air following Anders into the dugout. Milton and Knut followed on his heels. How embarrassing that Anders would see Auntie's house in such disarray. What he must think. She grabbed the snot rag from the peg on the wall and wiped Sigurd's green nose. He squirmed away and coughed a feeble cough. He felt feverish.

"Ragna!" Knut threw both arms around her waist until she almost dropped the baby.

"I've missed you so!"

Milton tipped his hat. "Are we glad to see you," he said. "We've been batching it here and making do."

In the flurry of explanations, excuses and greetings, she pulled the coffee pot over to the hottest burner and pushed a stick of kitchen wood into the firebox. She searched for the coffee beans.

"Mor took them with her," Gunnar said. "There's tea."

"Then tea it will be," Ragna sighed. It seemed the world conspired to keep her from the one thing she longed for.

"Ragna," Anders said. "I've talked to Milton. Since he cannot stay alone with you and there's no room at his dugout, I'll bunk in the barn with him."

"Have you had the spots?"

"*Ja,*" Anders nodded. "In Norway."

"But this will inconvenience you . . ."

"*Nei,*" he said with a cheerful smile. "I'll get busy splitting that pile of wood."

37

Representatives From the southwest Counties to Meet with the Governor to Counsel as to the Best Means of Rendering Aid to Destitute Settlers

St. Paul Dispatch, *December 20, 1873*

IT WAS NOT THAT THEY WERE ALONE—far from it. Evan and Inga crammed into Milton's dugout and the twins kept them busy day and night. Sverre came down with the spots the very day they arrived and was much sicker than either Lewis or Sigurd had been.

Evan did not dare to leave Inga alone while Sverre was so ill. It would kill Inga if he died. Evan had been absent for their daughter's death—he would not leave Inga again to face such tragedy. If Milton had a problem, he could send Gunnar for help.

Evan's stomach wrenched whenever he allowed himself to think about the boys left alone with Milton on their place. He had hoped to be gone only for a night or two, but Sverre's condition kept him longer. Evan did not exactly distrust Milton, but it would have been easier if Ragna were there instead. Ragna was a stouthearted girl and knew what to do. Evan lacked the same confidence in Milton.

Evan returned to their farm for a short time every morning to make sure things were going well. They were not going well, but the older boys and Milton were managing the best they could. So what if the house was a mess and Sigurd wore stinky soakers, dried and reused—not washed each time he wet himself, as Inga was so particular about.

Inga did not ask, and he did not tell her. Sigurd could stand a little stink and the boys would survive. Although Sigurd drooped pale and listless, he did not seem any worse.

How different it felt to have only the twins with them. When they first married, they had six-year-old Ragna and the new baby. The four other babies came in short order.

It almost seemed they were newlyweds again. Except back then, they had been hopeful that life, although it had taken a harsh turn, would straighten out for them again.

Now the boys. Measles, of all things. Sigurd's hearing. A sharp pain gripped Evan's throat with the thought of his sweet baby going through life deaf. Sigurd's words had already been slow in coming.

The walls of Milton's dugout pressed close on all sides. The barrel stove smoked, filling the hut with a choking haze. It left no room for much of anything except sleeping. Inga had her knitting and while she knitted, they talked, sprawled out on the small cot that served as Milton's bed, no space for a bench or chair of any kind. Next to this hovel, their dugout looked like a palace with its open space and fancy stovepipe. They were indeed lucky to have Milton for their neighbor. He had spent time making their lives better and let his own place lack.

Milton might have been a good man for Evan's sister, Christina, if only consumption had not taken her back in Norway. He and Christina had dreamed of living next to each other in America and owning good horses. *Oh, Christina, what would you think of this dark hole in the ground?*

"Tell me about your sister," Inga said.

"You troll!" he said. "How did you know I was thinking about her?"

"I was thinking about her, too," Inga said. "Thinking that we should have named our baby girl after her as we always planned."

Her serious tone stopped any teasing.

"We'll have another daughter," Evan said. "And this time she'll be healthy and fat."

"I'm a terrible person."

"Shh . . . don't say such a thing."

"For a baby to go unwanted and unmourned . . ." She jerked at her yarn until it snapped in two.

"You've mourned her every day." Evan pulled the quilt over Sverre's shoulder as he slept on the bench beside the cot. "As I have."

He reached for her and laid his hand across her hip.

"Christina was like a twin to me," Evan said. "I think of her when I watch our boys playing together. What one didn't think of, the other did."

"Your poor *mor.*"

"*Ja*, she suffered with our mischief, but she was too busy keeping the family together after Far died."

"You were spared." Inga pulled the yarn tighter around her needles. "Thank the good Lord for that."

"You would have liked Christina." Evan tried to think of a way to describe her. "She was tougher than other girls, maybe from having seven brothers, and blunt in her speaking."

"Blond and blue-eyed," Inga said. "Like Borghilde, Ragna's little sister."

"*Ja.*" The familiar sorrow pressed in. The screams and smoke. "Like Birdie."

"You were right in telling Ragna what you knew," Inga said stoutly. "And right in telling Gunnar."

"Maybe I'd hoped that if I didn't talk about it, the uprising never really happened."

"But like Milton's blood money from the war," Inga said, "it stewed into a bitter brew that nearly poisoned us."

"Milton needs a wife." Evan reached over and pinched the rag dipped in oil that served as their only light. Blackness filled the room except for the crack around the tiny door of the firebox that heated Milton's dugout. "That's why I was thinking of Christina. She would have been good for him."

Sverre coughed, and Inga reached over and patted his back, shushing him back to sleep.

"What if Ragna takes up with a Saint?"

"Someone else has his eye on Ragna if you haven't noticed," Inga said with a laugh. "There's no need to worry about her turning Mormon."

"Not Anders."

"Who else?"

"But you said he saved money for a sweetheart." Was he unaware of something between the two of them? A protective thought ran through his mind, and he hoped they were not using this unexpected time together to get too friendly. Ragna was naïve in many ways, sheltered. He had promised her father to care for her.

"I was mistaken," Inga said. "It's his cousin that needs money for a sweetheart's passage. Anders once thought to help him earn the money but changed his mind once he filed a claim."

"At least she'll be near us," Evan said with a sigh. "But her *bestemor* won't be happy."

"We're her family now."

The dugout smelled of damp earth, wood smoke, and the sour smell of unwashed bodies and sickness. Someday they would be in a house again with real floors and glass windows on every side. There would be room for any child God saw fit to send their way. They would make it.

"Remember the Abercrombie siege?" Inga said. "Such a time."

"When that woman died in childbed during the battle," Evan's voice cracked, "I almost went crazy, thinking it was you."

"Still too early for me, even though I had lied to Mr. Ericcson and let him believe the baby was his."

"What choice did you have?" Evan growled. "Sometimes when Gunnar's mad at me, I wish there were some way I could tell him how good he has it compared to having Ingvald Ericcson as a *far*."

"I hate myself for being so weak as to marry him."

"You were desperate," Evan said. "They wouldn't let you off the ship."

"I should have thought of something else," Inga said with a sigh. "Even gone back to the Old Country." Sverre's heavy breathing slowed to sleep. "It was as if I sold myself to that horrible man."

Evan's heart dropped. Maybe Inga wished for her first husband. Wished she had returned to the Old Country. "But then I wouldn't have met you or had our beautiful children."

"During the siege I asked God to free you." It was easier to confess truth under cover of darkness. "I prayed the Sioux would kill him—with a slow, agonizing death."

Inga laughed. "I prayed as well. There I was, big and pregnant. In a bad situation, carrying Gunnar's child, married to Mr. Ericcson and in love with you."

The boys stirred. The trouble with twins—if one cried, the other woke and cried as well. Evan hummed a little Norwegian tune to quiet them. Darkness covered them like a heavy quilt.

"I've thanked God many times that I didn't kill him," Evan said. "It was a test. There I was, standing night guard with my gun pointed at what I thought was an Indian sneaking into the fort."

"But you heard your *mor*'s voice."

"Telling me of the commandment. When I saw it was your man, I was sorely tempted to shoot anyway."

"You did the right thing, and God blessed you. Mr. Ericcson died from his own foolishness." Inga leaned over and kissed Evan's bristly cheek. "*Nur enden er god er alting godt.* All's well that ends well."

"I never thought it would be like this," Inga said. "I dreamed of life in America but never thought it would turn out like this."

Evan felt the cut of disappointment. He had done his best. In truth, they were no better than cotters in the Old Country.

"I never thought I'd be so blessed," Inga continued. "Just think, the two of us together, five healthy boys and a place of our own."

38

*The Mills of St. Cloud are Running on Short Time because
Wheat is so High that Milling is not Profitable*
                              St. Paul Dispatch, *December 20, 1873*

K NUT," RAGNA SAID, "EMPTY THE SLOP JAR. Gunnar, fetch wood."
They barely grumbled, and Ragna realized how desperate their situation was. Auntie must be wild with worry. She patted Sigurd on the back and felt a rising fear when she realized how small he was, how frail. He had lost weight. He was still sick.

She prodded him to drink a cup of broth, but he turned away. She passed him to Knut when he returned with the empty slop jar. "Sit with him while I do some work." Where should she begin? Ragna straightened the house, put a soup bone to boil, started a batch of bread dough and eyed the stinking soakers.

"We're low on wood." Gunnar said as he dropped an armful of kindling in the box. His cheeks flushed with cold, and Ragna was surprised how deep his voice had become. When had he grown so tall?

"Then busy your hatchet," Ragna said. She dipped floured hands into the sticky dough. "Auntie would have apoplexy if she saw this house."

"Can Knut do it?"

"Don't you feel well?" Ragna eyed the boy and placed a floury hand on his forehead to check for fever. Sigurd howled and reached out toward her.

"I'll go!" Knut handed the baby to Gunnar and pulled on his coat and cap as he left the house. Gunnar jiggled the baby first on one hip and then the other, standing close to Ragna where Sigurd could keep an eye on her.

"Everything is wrong." Gunnar's lip quivered and tears sprouted in his eyes. "Far told me," he said and choked back a sob, "Far isn't my real *far.*"

Ragna wiped her hands on her apron and stretched her arms around the two boys. She knew this day would come, had known since that first night when she realized that Gunnar's father had been someone else. She knew how it felt to be fatherless.

"Shush now." She rubbed Gunnar's back and kissed the top of Sigurd's blond head. Sigurd squealed and grabbed her around the neck. Ragna took him and held him close, releasing Gunnar.

"My real *far* died before I was born," he said.

"I know."

Gunnar's head jerked back in surprise. "How did you know?"

"I remember when you were born." She weighed her words. "They married the same day so you would never be without a *far*." She chose her words cautiously, anything to spare him hurt. "You were born with the caul over your face, and Uncle Evan knew to pull it away before you suffocated."

"They lied to me," he sniffed and pouted his lower lip. "All these years they've lied to me."

"Uncle Evan isn't my real uncle," Ragna said. "The best day in my life was when he found me and took me home with him." The sun slipped behind a cloud and the dugout grew dark enough to need the lamp. "I miss my parents and sister and brother, but I thank God for you boys and Auntie Inga and Uncle Evan." She laid the baby on the bed and covered him with a wool blanket. "Do you think he and Auntie Inga could be any better to me if we were flesh and blood relatives?" The truth of her words warmed her. How could she have doubted the blessing of their loving care? "Would you love me any more if I were your real sister?"

He shook his head and smiled a wry grin. "Mor says I'm lucky to have Far."

"We're all lucky to have him," Ragna said.

Anders pushed through the doorway, emptied water buckets into the copper boiler and headed back to the lake for more with Gunnar at his heels. He and Gunnar filled the boiler with water and buckets of snow, breaking up chunks of ice to fit and firing the stove until the metal pipe glowed red.

With a worried glance at Sigurd, Ragna covered the dough with a clean dishtowel and set it close enough to the fire so the yeast could work. It was risky baking bread in the wintertime because cold killed the yeast. She washed her hands and wiped them on her apron. Then she dipped a scoop of soft soap from a gourd on the windowsill.

Sigurd stirred from the bed. *Stakkers liten*, they were all sick and worn out. Knut and Gunnar had done more than usual with Auntie gone. Ragna turned to the tub of hot water. She had just started scrubbing the dirty clothes when Anders returned with another bucket of water.

"Let me do the scrubbing," he said and rolled up his sleeves after setting the filled bucket on the table.

"I'll do it." Ragna had never heard of a man doing laundry. Of course the men helped by hauling water from the lake, lugging used water out again after it was over. She had never known a man to dip his hands into the hot water and rub the clothes on the washboard.

"My *mor* taught me well," Anders said. "I'll take over so you can catch up with the others tasks that need doing."

With a quiet nod, Ragna turned over the washboard, swept out the old grass still on the floors from last fall and scattered dry sand from a pail kept near the stove in case of fire. It was at least cleaner than the worn hay. She scrubbed the table and took a scraper to the stovetop. She aired the linen and made the beds up fresh, careful not to disturb the baby.

"I like to watch you work," Anders said from the washtub. "You remind me of home. My *mor* attacked dirt like a Viking chieftain invading the Irish."

Ragna laughed in spite of herself and glanced over to Sigurd, still sleeping on the bed. Winters were hard on children. On everyone.

Afterwards, Anders hung the clean clothes out to dry. They instantly froze. Later they would take them inside and thaw them out enough to iron them. The dugout was as clean as it could be. Not that it would ever be clean, with its dirt walls and floor. However, it was at least orderly and sweeter smelling. A pleasant aroma wafted from the soup pot on the stove and Anders lugged out the dirty wash water.

"Leave the rinse water," Ragna said. "Sigurd could use a bath."

"In the winter?"

Ragna hesitated. Sigurd smelled sour and his bottom was red and blistered. His hair lay plastered to his head with dried sweat and grease. "I think I'll risk it," she said at last, wondering what Auntie would say. "I'll keep him close by the fire afterwards."

"I'll help you." Anders collected Sigurd from the bed and started to undress him. "Young man," he said as he pulled buttons out of their holes with fingers wrinkled from the washtub. "You're going to have a bath."

SIGURD CONTINUED PALE AND WEAK, fussy and fretful. A harsh cough settled in his chest, and Ragna counted every breath, worried the bath had set him back, afraid that little Sigurd would quit breathing altogether.

Auntie sent a litany of instructions telling Ragna how to care for Sigurd so that he did not relapse into pneumonia. Ragna fried onions for a poultice, spooned soup between his chapped lips, and rubbed muskrat grease between his thin shoulder blades.

Two days before Christmas, Ragna found the mending pile and positioned herself in front of the single windowpane with needle and thread. Sigurd slept, and the boys were fishing. Poor Auntie had fallen behind. If only she had a sewing machine. Ragna reached up to finger the button hanging around her neck.

> Sleigh bells ring outside and Birdie bursts through the door dressed in a red velvet cape and muff. Her cheeks bloom rosy as sumac leaves in autumn.
>
> "I'm finally here."
>
> It's as if my legs are frozen. I struggle to go to her, to hug Birdie after all this time. She laughs a laugh brighter than the sleigh bells, more beautiful than the sound of her voice.
>
> "What's wrong?" Birdie says. A fur hood frames her face, blue eyes dancing with excitement. "Is this all the welcome I get?"

"Where have you been?"

"I've been living with Bishop Whipple at Fort Snelling. But when he moved to Cuba, I came back to you." She turns and points to a wooden crate at her feet. *"I've brought a Christmas gift—a new sewing machine for Auntie."*

Words choke in my throat and I can't take my eyes away from her face, the face that looks so much like Mor, but with the eyes of Far.

"Did I tell you where I board at Clitherall?" Anders pushed open the door and his voice jolted her from her daydream.

Ragna looked up from her sewing. "I thought you were fishing."

"The others can freeze—I want to talk to you while I have the chance."

Ragna smiled, and Anders launched into a description of the bachelor's quarters at Clitherall where all the single men stayed. "Everyone is either looking for a bride or saving money to send for sweethearts."

"From the Old Country?"

"*Nei*, mostly from Illinois—that's where most of the Saints are from."

"But you'll need more money than them."

A puzzled look crossed his face, but Milton called through the open door before Anders could answer.

"The trader is here."

"Who?" Anders said.

"Lying Jack," Milton said. "We sent word for him to bring medicine. He's not alone."

"I'll put on the kettle," Ragna said. A muskrat simmered in the stewpot. They would have company for dinner. They were short on supplies, and she needed to bake again. Plenty of potatoes but little else.

Lying Jack roared into the cabin, all laugh and bluster, stomping his feet at the door, telling jokes and tall tales. Ragna looked over to where Sigurd slept, hoping the commotion would not awaken him. All day Sigurd had been as limp as a cat, mewling and fretful. Thank goodness, he slept. Knut and Gunnar followed close on his heels, carrying packs from Lying Jack's mules.

"Good afternoon, Missy."

"Good afternoon, Mr. Wilson."

"I brung my missus," he said. "Your father says were all right."

"Bring her in out of the cold." Ragna pushed her hair back, hoping her braids were tight. It was not often company came, and a woman at that. Thank God, she had readied the dugout. Auntie would die if she knew how bad it had been.

A small Indian woman wrapped in a striped blanket entered the room. Her eyes darted from Ragna to sleeping Sigurd to the stewpot on the stove.

"Come in," Ragna said after regaining her composure. The sight of an Indian usually caused her limbs to quiver, but this woman seemed harmless. Uncle Evan would not have allowed it had he thought her dangerous. Her eyes were gentle, like the eyes of the baby fawn Gunnar tamed for a pet a few years back.

"Sit down and rest yourself, Mrs. Wilson."

The woman carefully unwound the blanket around her and folded it into a neat pile in the corner. She shuffled towards the table and sat on the wooden bench. She said nothing. Just looked at Ragna, at the cup on the table, at the stovepipe stuck into the thatch. Her eyes settled on Sigurd as he lay sleeping in the bed. His chest rattled with every breath. Ragna noticed a frown crease Mrs. Jack's forehead.

"Miss Larson," Lying Jack boomed and his teeth glowed white beneath his black skin. "I've bringed trade goods—goods you'd be needing for Christmas."

Ragna had almost forgotten Christmas. The reason she had come home, she reminded herself. The reason Anders was not at Clitherall.

As Lying Jack spread out the goods on the table, she poured tea for his wife. Her silence unnerved Ragna. Made her uneasy. The way she looked at Sigurd made Ragna wonder if she was plotting to steal him away.

The little boys crowded around the packs. Ragna had no money and did not know if Uncle had need of goods—or money to pay for them. Milton carefully examined an adz, and Anders eyed the licorice whips.

As if reading her mind, Anders caught her eye and smiled. "I've never been able to pass up licorice."

Lying Jack bundled a handful of the black strings together and wrapped them in a piece of clean muslin. "You give them cloth to your lady friend—she'll embroidery your initials on it and make you a fine hanky."

Lying Jack's laugh boomed through the dugout, filled the room, and somehow made the sun shine brighter than it did.

Gunnar and Knut fairly drooled over the candy.

"You boys have sumpin' to trade?"

Gunnar and Knut whispered and after a quick trip to the barn came back with eleven muskrat pelts, the results of many hours trapping and curing the hides.

"Aha!" Lying Jack said. "Muskrat skins—Minnesota money. These'll trade for a pound'm candy."

After more whispering between the two of them, Knut spoke up in a squeaky tenor. "We want something for our *mor.*"

Ragna swallowed a lump suddenly lodged in her throat. They were good boys. Such good boys. Kind like their father.

The boys pawed through the goods on the table, examined small mirrors and fine-toothed combs, and settled on a china hummingbird perched on a wooden branch.

"Your mammy'll smile" Lying Jack said. "'Course, birds come dear."

His twinkling eyes relieved Ragna's concerns. She knew he would sell the knick-knack for the eleven pelts spread out on the floor beside the table. She counted them in her mind and then over again. Eleven—the same number of years since Birdie had been taken, since her family had been killed. Ragna eyed each one, trying to remember. The first year Uncle Evan found her at St. Cloud, the second year they moved back to her farm, the third year Knut was born, but the rest blurred together in memory. Maybe she should count backwards instead—this year when the grasshoppers forced their move and Ann Elin was born. Last year Sigurd was born. The epizootic plague the year before.

Anders tucked the licorice into his pocket and inspected more goods outside the dugout. There was too much to buy, too many necessary items. Ragna supposed that all young men faced the same situation unless they inherited something already in place. Her farm would have been that leg up, as Uncle Evan called it. Now ruined.

She imagined for a quick moment what it would feel like to have a farm already under cultivation and a sturdy cabin waiting for her and her new husband. Her *far*'s dream echoed to her across the years, from before the uprising when he gloated about the good black Minnesota dirt calling to him across the ocean waters.

The grasshoppers had ruined the farm her *far* had worked so hard to build, the farm Uncle Evan had continued in his name. It would take a miracle for the land to recover. A million grasshoppers laid a million eggs and a million new grasshoppers hatched to repeat the cycle. A million times a million equaled what number? Disaster, that's what.

She turned back to the hagglers around the table and poured Mrs. Wilson another cup of tea. Mrs. Wilson said nothing. The boys whooped with exuberance when Lying Jack agreed to throw in a five-pound bag of popcorn and a half sack of peppermints along with the knick-knack for their mother. Ragna fetched muskrat soup and brought it to the table. Mrs. Jack ate without comment, bright eyes looking over the rim of her cup. Lying Jack slurped down his soup in one hurried swoop and started repacking his bags.

When Lying Jack packed his supplies to leave, she was surprised when he pressed a small bag of coffee beans into her hand. "Merry Christmas," he said in a quiet voice, most unusual for Lying Jack. "Thank you."

Ragna stared at the beans in surprise. She had done nothing but what good manners demanded but at the same time, knew his wife would be unwelcome in most homes. The memories of the uprising were still too raw, too fresh. Even if it had been eleven years, one year for each muskrat pelt traded to Lying Jack for Auntie Inga's present.

"Have you news of the Sevalds?" Ragna hoped Mr. Sevald would survive while she was gone, then hurriedly changed her mind and hoped that he would die—of course, peacefully in his sleep, so she needn't leave her family.

"I visit 'em tomorrow," Lying Jack said. "Or day after."

"Tell them hello," Ragna said, wishing she had something to send as a little gift. "And Merry Christmas."

"And I'll be see'n Elijah and him bride," he said.

"Greet them as well," Ragna said with a half-choked throat. She wanted to be home with her family, back with Marta, and visiting Bertha all at the same time. "Next time I'll have a letter ready," Ragna said. "Tell Marta I'm delayed because of measles."

Sigurd let out a hoarse cry. As Ragna picked him up and felt his forehead for fever. Mrs. Wilson spoke to her husband in her native tongue.

"Her asks what's wrong with the boy," Lying Jack said. He spoke almost apologetically, as if it were a burden to intrude with the question.

"It's the spots." Ragna pointed to the fading rash on his face and arms while bouncing him on her hip to calm him. Sigurd's face was shocking in its whiteness and his head drooped as if he was too weak to hold it upright. His gums bled and she wiped away a splash of blood dripped onto his chin.

With a jolt, she realized that Sigurd was worse—much worse. He pushed the cup away.

"They call it scurvy among the seaman," Anders said. "When the teeth bleed."

"We had it in Andersonville," Milton said. "From malnutrition."

Mrs. Wilson wrapped herself in her blanket and left the dugout. Ragna wondered if she had offended her, if she should have spoken up about the measles from the beginning. Uncle Evan said that measles was deadly to the Indians. Maybe Mrs. Wilson feared catching them.

Soon, the Indian woman returned with a small leather pouch. From it she poured a measured portion of dried berries, pine needles, and leaves into her empty cup and made motions for Ragna to pour hot water over the dried ingredients.

Medicine.

"*Mange takk!*" Ragna could have kissed her in relief. She had been so worried. Surely, something was terribly wrong. She handed the baby to Gunnar and poured the boiling water from the stove. A pungent steam filled the dugout fragrant with cedar and balsam.

Mrs. Jack motioned Gunnar to bring Sigurd over to her and then positioned Sigurd over the cup and draped a dishtowel to capture the steam. She fanned the fragrant mist towards his mouth and nose, holding his small hands to protect him from the hot liquid. She cupped her free hand and patted his small back firmly and without hesitation. Sigurd whimpered. She seemed too rough.

Then Sigurd coughed a violent cough and brought up a clot of dark-colored mucous. Mrs. Wilson murmured approval and kept patting his back while more dark phlegm came up. Then after it seemed he had finished coughing, Mrs. Wilson tenderly lifted the cup to his lips and helped him sip the cooled tea. Before long, Sigurd leaned his head against Mrs. Jack and fell sound asleep.

"Good." Mrs. Wilson's voice sounded low and musical. "Him sleep."

Ragna inspected the remaining tea left on the table. Juniper berries, some kind of dried pine needles, maybe dried blossoms of some kind, but she could not identify the remaining ingredients. "What is it?" she looked at Mrs. Wilson, but Lying Jack answered.

"There's Balm of Gilead, juniper berries, sumac, pine needles, and a pinch or two of Sioux mumbo-jumbo. Nothin' that will hurt him."

"*Tussen takk,*" Ragna felt tears welling in her eyes. "I didn't know what to do."

Mrs. Wilson spoke to Lying Jack and pulled out a tied bundle of dried sumac. Ragna recognized the fuzzy berries and red leaves.

"Her says him needs sumac tea." He reached up to scratch his thick hair and listened to another flow of Indian language from his wife. "Says you all drink it or them teeth will fall out. First them bleed, then fall out."

"Him teeth," Mrs. Wilson plucked berries off the dried bundle and poured boiling water over them. It brewed into a beautiful, pink solution. "Drink."

Ragna took a sip and pulled away at the sour taste. Lying Jack laughed hard and long. "It's good. Won't hurt nobody."

Mrs. Wilson pulled the drawstring on the leather pouch and gave it to Ragna with a nod. There was something about her eyes. Something gentle and good. Nothing to fear.

"Mr. Jack," Ragna said. "The little boys are sick at Milton's dugout." She knew what she must do. "Could I trade these coffee beans given to me for more medicine? The twins need it."

She held her breath as Lying Jack scratched his curly beard. He eyed his wife for a long minute and then nodded. "You drive a hard bargain, Missy." His laugh was loud and long, filling the dugout with goodwill. "I'll make the trade though me hate to rob yourn mornin' coffee."

"It would mean a lot to me, Mr. Jack," Ragna said. "I'll ask one of the men to take it over."

"No need," Lying Jack said, pocketing the package of coffee beans. "We pass by on our way." Mrs. Jack hoisted a pack up on her shoulder and followed her man out of the dugout without another word.

"I like him," Anders said after the door closed behind the traders. "It makes me wonder how people could ever think the blacks inhuman."

"And Indians," Milton said pulling off his heavy buffalo skin coat and sniffing the soup hungrily. "Lots of folks don't think they're human either."

"It's time for a change," Anders said as he rubbed the edge of his new adz with the back of his thumb. "Time to look beyond the color of skin."

"Were you scared?" Gunnar said in a near whisper. "Of the *skraeling*?"

"Shame, Gunnar!" Ragna said. "She brought medicine."

"But weren't you scared?" he pressed. "Like the face in the window."

Something loosed in her chest. Something let go and left her as sure as the phlegm coughed out of Sigurd's lungs. Anders was right. It was time for a change. She gathered the dishes from the table and stacked them. Then she poured water from the bucket into the metal dishpan and pulled it over onto the hottest part of the stovetop, opened a stove lid and poked a chunk of dry oak into the firebox. She scooped a handful of soft soap from the gourd on the shelf and swooshed it through the warming water with her hand.

There were a few bubbles, not many, as the soap was coarse, made from goose fat. Not the high quality soap Auntie usually made.

"Ragna . . ." Gunnar said.

"Stop."

Gunnar stared at her.

"I've been scared all my life, and I'm not going to be anymore." She put the cups into the water and scrubbed them with an old rag. The dishwater soothed her cold hands. Sigurd stirred in his bed. The earthen smell of the walls pressed against her nose. "Eleven years is a long time—long enough."

39

Important Action at the Legislature—What the Senators Say of the Indian Bureau—How the Vermillion Indians are Starving Because of Neglect and Dishonesty of Agents

St. Paul Dispatch, December 21, 1873

IT WOULD HAVE BEEN CRUEL TO LEAVE her standing in the cold. Lying Jack and his woman crowded against the small stove and single bunk. Evan could feel Inga's recoil as the Indian's blanket rubbed against the bed. Inga had strong convictions that all Indians were lousy. However, it was cold out, and Inga would have to make do.

"We heard telled about them sick boys." The earthen walls absorbed the sound of Lying Jack's voice until it sounded quiet, almost respectful.

Sverre barked a harsh cough.

"Measles," Evan said as Inga turned to the child.

The Indian woman stretched out a brown hand holding a leather pouch. She bobbed her head, indicating he should take it from her hand.

"What's this?"

"Medicine," Lying Jack said. "Injun herbs and such . . ."

"We couldn't possibly . . ." Inga's voice trailed off as Lewis' weak cough interrupted. "We were hoping for medicine from a doctor."

"We don't have nuthin' from no doctors," Lying Jack said. "Linament or castor oil. Whiskey."

"*Mange takk,*" Evan took the bag from her hand. It was lightweight, like picking up a parcel of feathers. "What do we owe you?"

"Already paid for." Lying Jack's chuckle lit up his face. "Them daughter of your'n traded back the Christmas present I'd gived her."

"Ragna?"

"Her's a good girl."

"She's not our daughter," Evan said. "But we've raised her since her parents died." He caught himself from mentioning the uprising. It would have been awkward bringing it up. What good could come from dredging old wounds?

Inga frowned at him, tilting her chin and saying without a single word that no Sioux medicine would pass through the lips of her children. Sverre barked and coughed until he gasped for breath. They would try anything, Evan decided.

"Thank you for the medicine. We're most appreciative."

Mrs. Jack motioned instructions, and Inga reached for a kettle of water from the stove. The room filled with the pungent fragrance. Then the woman picked up Sverre and after holding his face over the fragrant steam, began pounding his back with her cupped hand. The hollow sound reminded Evan of native drums from Crooked Lightning's camp so long ago. Sverre coughed up a stream of putrid phlegm. She gave him some sips from the cup.

Inga picked up Lewis and copied the regimen until Lewis also expelled green mucous and had some of the liquid.

The pounding continued until Mrs. Jack nodded and laid Sverre back on the bed. He fell asleep, and though his color was like dirty snow, he breathed easier. Lewis's long legs dangled down from Inga's arms, and she laid him beside the sleeping Sverre.

"*Mange takk,*" Inga said and tears dripped down her face. She sniffed and pushed back strands of wayward hair from her face.

Inga busied herself making coffee, and Evan cleared spots for their visitors to sit. No bigger than a teepee, Evan thought, as he balanced on a stack of firewood in the corner.

"Evan," Inga said. "Please hand me the cups."

The Indian woman scrutinized Evan's face as he passed the tin cups over to Inga. Her steady gaze embarrassed him, made him wonder what he had done wrong.

The woman said something in her tongue and Lying Jack looked at her in surprise. "Evan," he said, "Evan Jacobson."

Mrs. Jack spoke faster and louder in her native tongue. Evan worried he had done something to offend her, though he could not imagine what it might have been.

"Her wants to know about Badger," Lying Jack said in an apologetic voice. "Says you is the man-with-the-wooden-wheels, a life-and-death friend."

Evan's mouth dried to dust. She was older, her hair streaked with gray and her jowls drooped into deep lines around her mouth. It was the same woman, though, the woman from Crooked Lightning's teepee.

"Many Beavers."

She nodded, and her eyes glowed like two coals.

"What's she saying?" Inga said. "What are you talking about?"

"Inga," Evan said. "This is Many Beavers, Crooked Lightning's woman."

40

*A New Throat Disease Has Appeared Among the Children of
Albert Lea, which proves Fatal, and the Schools have been Closed
in Consequence.*

St. Paul Dispatch, *December 22, 1873*

RAGNA STEAMED SIGURD'S LUNGS again, pounding as Mrs. Jack had
shown her. She repeated the procedure twice after supper and decided to do it once more during the night. It was as if Sigurd im-
proved with each treatment. Certainly, his color was better.

Knut and Gunnar snored softly in their bunk as Ragna poked sticks into
the fire, breaking a branch to fit into the firebox, smelling the comforting
fragrance of burning pine. The stovepipe banged with the temperature
change.

Someone tapped on the door and opened it without waiting for an answer. Ragna turned in surprise, pushed stray hair back into her nightcap and
snugged the shawl around her shoulders.

"Anders," she said. "Do you need something? It's the middle of the night."

"To talk." His eyes were puffy, and his face wore a haggard look. She
hoped he was not ill. "We've got to talk."

"Then sit," Ragna said and motioned to the table. "I'll fix tea." What
would Auntie say? The sleeping boys were hardly chaperones, and Ragna was
not dressed. She knotted the shawl.

"We can't go on this way."

"What do you mean?" Ragna's heart beat in her chest. She reached for
the tea can, spooned a heaping teaspoon of leaves into the teapot and added
steaming water. She dropped a single sumac berry into the pot.

"I can't even sleep, worrying that you'll marry that widow man."

"What are you talking about?" Ragna laughed and set the teapot on the little table and covered it with a clean dishtowel to keep it hot.

"I can't take a wife until I get my claim going."

Ragna sat down across from him but could not look at him. Sigurd stirred, and she reached over and pulled the blanket over his shoulders.

"It will be another year or two before I have anything at all to offer but I've a perfect slope for building and the Saints promise to send a work team as part of my pay for teaching." He stood to his feet and paced back and forth before the door. "It will take time, but someday I'll have something. You'll see."

"But what about your sweetheart?"

"What?" his face blanched and he stopped pacing. "I don't have a sweetheart."

Ragna's voice dropped to a whisper. "I thought you did."

She held her breath, suddenly aware of her straggled hair and faded shawl. When she looked up, she looked past the chipped tooth and perfect smile into the bluest eyes she had ever seen. As blue as the fjords Mor used to tell about. As blue as Birdie's eyes.

"I have a girl picked out." He moved around the table to sit beside her on the bench and took her hand.

"Me?"

"Who else?"

"But you don't know me." She choked back a sob and was shocked to feel the unexpected flow of tears. They came from a deep place, a forgotten place. The place of her worst fears, the place of her deepest memories.

"Then I'll learn to know you." He rubbed a callused thumb across her finger and Ragna pulled her hand away. "We have our whole lives ahead to get to know each other."

She busied herself pouring tea. Wiped her nose.

"But you don't know what I've done."

The stove glowed red from the dry oak. Knut turned in bed and dropped his arm over the side of the bunk. Sigurd whimpered a fussy cry.

"Tell me," Anders said. "I want to know."

She felt as if her future balanced on the head of a pin. If she told him, he might change his mind. If she did not tell him, she would always feel guilty. *Holy Mary, Mother of God . . .*

"It's my fault Mrs. Ludwig died in childbed," she said at last. She waited for him to turn against her, push away. "I was tired and didn't pay attention like I should."

"Women die all the time." He reached over and turned her chin so she had to look at him. "She may have died in spite of anything you could have done."

"It was my fault."

He sat quietly for a long time. "So you would marry the widow man to atone for your sin?"

Ragna nodded, and fat tears dripped down her face.

"Would that bring her back?"

"*Nei*, of course not . . ." She felt the need to unburden herself, to confess everything. "And I like to pray," she struggled to explain, "to the Virgin Mary."

"What?" His face wore the look of incredulity. "But you're confirmed."

Ragna looked him full in the face and spoke her heart. "It's what kept me from losing my mind all these years without Birdie."

He did not reply, and she busied herself, pouring the tea. Anders sipped and replaced his cup on the table. He looked at her for a long moment. "Do you think a Saint would marry a woman who prays to the Virgin Mary?"

"Maybe not," her mind swirled in confusion. "I never thought of that."

"One thing I've learned at the Branch of Zion is how much they want their children raised in their faith." He reached for her hand, but she pulled it away and reached for her cup instead. "Bertha plans to take the baby after she weans. It's already settled."

A heavy burden left Ragna's chest. Of course, Anders was right. She had heard Bertha promise to take her niece.

"Besides," Anders added quietly and reached for her hand again. This time she did not pull away. "Even Catholics believe that Jesus alone atones for our sins."

"And I have to find my sister," Ragna surprised herself. "She's lost somewhere, and I have to find her." The tears flowed harder then. "I've waited all these years and she hasn't come home, so I have to go out and find her myself." She reached for a hanky and wiped her eyes. "I can't bear the thought of her all alone and needing me."

"I'll help you," Anders said. "We'll look for her together."

"But Uncle Evan says I have to return to Norway," Ragna said with a hiccough. Fisk rubbed against Ragna's legs and meowed for a dish of milk. "You can see that everything is a mess."

Sigurd stirred and coughed in his sleep. Ragna took a sip of tea. Anders seemed absorbed in looking at the bottom of his cup. Outside the rooster crowed. It must be almost morning.

"Don't you care for me, even a little?" Anders said.

Ragna thought a long moment and then nodded. "I do care for you," she said in a low voice.

"Then promise me you won't marry that widow man." Anders took her hand in his and leaned closer. "That's all I ask."

Ragna waited for him to kiss her but he pulled back.

"I'll talk to your Uncle as soon as I get a chance," he said. "I want to do this right."

41

*PANIC! The Prices of my Entire Stock of Dry Goods Has been
Reduced to Correspond with the Large Decline in the New York
Dry Goods Market. B.F. Zahn*

St. Paul Dispatch, *December 22, 1873*

VAN'S MIND JUMBLED AND TURNED. It was as if he could not grasp the words. "You say Crooked Lightning *rescued* the girls?"

Many Beavers nodded and spoke to Lying Jack in her language.

"Her says Crooked Lightning taked the white girls, Badger and Little Bird, to save them from Blue Bottle." Lying Jack crossed one leg over the other while sitting on a block of wood.

"Both girls?" Evan remembered how pathetic Ragna had looked in the crowd of children of Camp Release, so ragged and dirty. "I found only Ragna."

Many Beavers's voice slipped into a sing-song rhythm. She spoke a while and then looked at Lying Jack, nodding for him to translate as Evan gathered Sverre into his arms and held him tight. The sun was setting. Although the fire burned hot, a sudden chill fell over him.

"Blue Bottle killed them's mother and father," Lying Jack said, "and the little boy-baby."

Many Beavers spoke another long while.

"Then Blue Bottle set the house afire."

The old terror swept over Evan. He smelled the smoke again, felt sweat drip down his back as he ran toward the flames. Sverre squirmed, "Not so tight, Far."

"Crooked Lightning taked the girl children from the house and brought them to his nephew, Drumbeater, for safe keeping. That Blue Bottle was a mean skunk and had this crazy notion that Little Bird's white hair would charm him so he couldn't get killed," Lying Jack said. "He didn't care nuthin' for Ragna, the girl the Indians called Badger. She says that Badger has the heart of a mother bear protecting her cubs."

Many Beavers spoke again.

"Blue Bottle came looking for Little Bird so Drumbeater and Many Beavers taked the girls back to the soldiers. Drumbeater was honor bound to protect them because of his uncle's life-and-death friend, Evan Jacobson, the man-with-the-wooden-wheels."

Evan felt a lump grow in his throat and tears press against his eyes. Crooked Lightning's life-and-death-friend. Crooked Lightning had not betrayed him.

"Drumbeater handed the girl-children to the soldiers but Many Beavers climbed on the wagon with them." He listened a little longer to Many Beavers' words. "They hadn't traveled far when Blue Bottle jumped out of the bushes and dragged Little Bird off the wagon." Many Beavers spoke faster and her hands moved with her words. "Badger screamed and lunged after her sister."

Evan held his breath and leaned forward from his seat on the bed.

"Blue Bottle grabbed Little Bird, slit her throat and took her scalp before Many Beavers knew what was happening. Blue Bottle kicked Badger away and then the solders came."

Evan's heart sank. Dead. He had always known it.

Many Beavers wiped tears off her face and spoke another torrent of words. "She tried to explain to the soldiers but they didn't understand her language. Says they buried the girl alongside the trail."

"Badger quit talking after that," Lying Jack said. "Her wouldn't eat or drink or say anything. She mournful for her sister."

Many Beavers' voice lowered.

"She says they thought Little Bird's medicine was very big because of her yellow hair but they were wrong."

"Badger's medicine stronger than Little Bird," Many Beavers said in halting English. "Heart of a warrior. Will be a mother of chiefs."

Then the beautiful truth sunk in. The truth that sets men free. Crooked Lightning had saved Ragna and Borghilde from certain death. He had remained a true friend. Evan let out a long sigh.

He and Bishop Whipple had visited Crooked Lightning in the Mankato stockade where he awaited hanging. Evan would never forget the rancid odor of dirty hair and unwashed bodies and the clatter of chains. Crooked Lightning's eyes glittered like black stars.

"If my friend travels to the Mountains of the Turtle," Crooked Lightning had said, "remember the family of Crooked Lightning."

Had it been a message? Had Crooked Lightning not wanted to admit before the other warriors that he had saved the two small girls?

Crooked Lightning participated in the uprising, Evan was certain about that. But Crooked Lightning had saved the girls. He had risked his life to rescue Lars's family. He had failed Crooked Lightning by not believing in him. Not the other way around. A burden the size of a boulder fell from his chest.

He had been wrong about Crooked Lightning.

Evan must tell Ragna as soon as possible. She needed to know the truth.

THE NEXT MORNING, EVAN BLEW ON HIS cold hands and held them towards the stove. Ragna sat dreamy-eyed at her sewing, idly fiddling with the button she always wore around her neck. Sigurd played at her feet. Thanks to Many Beavers and her medicine, the boys were all better. Gunnar and Knut worked muskrat hides by the woodpile and Milton and Anders fished on the frozen lake.

There would never be a better time to tell Ragna, but Evan wished Inga were there to help him deal with whatever emotions erupted with the telling. Inga would know better how to deal with Ragna. She always knew best but he must face this alone.

"I've had news," he said and Ragna looked up, almost as if surprised to see him, though he had been inside a full minute. "About Birdie."

Ragna's mouth dropped open and she dropped the mending to the floor. "What?" She stood to her feet.

"It's not what you hoped for." Evan swallowed hard. Nothing would soften the telling. "The Indian woman who was here?"

"Mrs. Wilson."

"She was Crooked Lightning's wife." It was coming out all wrong. "Crooked Lightning was the face in the window."

Ragna reached out to the earthen wall for support. The stovepipe contracted with a thump and the boys argued outside the door.

"Sit down, Ragna." He loved her like a daughter, as much as he loved his own boys. It was not easy breaking her heart—but it had to be done.

42

At Summitville, N.Y. One Hundred Employees of the New York
and Oswego Railroad have Chained a Locomotive to The Track,
Spiked the Switches and Torn up the Track. They Declare they
will Allow no more Trains to Pass until the Company Pays their
Wages Already due.

St. Paul Dispatch, *December 23, 1873*

SHE'S THE ONE?" RAGNA'S MOUTH gaped, and she picked up Sigurd from the floor and clutched him tightly against her chest. She remembered gentle hands, fresh water, and safety. "Does she have Birdie?" Ragna held her breath and watched Uncle's face. She had to know.

"She's gone," he said with a hard swallow that bobbed his Adam's apple. "Killed after Camp Release."

"*Nei!*" Her heart pounded like a hammer inside her chest and she squeezed Sigurd until he squirmed. "You're mistaken."

A feeble sun shone through the dirty window and the earthen walls absorbed the light and sound of their voices. Bobcat bawled in the pen next to the house. Lady's bell clanked. The rooster crowed. Uncle's face crumpled and he worked his mouth and reached toward his empty pocket before he spoke.

"Many Beavers said that a Sioux brave named Blue Bottle had some crazy Indian notion that Birdie's scalp was a lucky charm." Uncle Evan swallowed again. "He sneaked up to the wagon and pulled Birdie away. You screamed and the soldiers came running." He took a step closer to Ragna, his eyes dripping with tears, and put his hand on her shoulder. "Blue Bottle killed her—scalped her—in front of you." He wiped the back of his free hand across his face. "You can't remember. It was too terrible."

In her dream, Birdie always pulled away, their eyes met and then it ended with the slap that sent her into darkness.

"She didn't suffer." Tears dripped down his face and into his beard. "It happened fast."

The dream, over and over, reaching hands, screams, and the slap. Maybe she had been knocked unconscious and did not see Birdie's murder. Maybe the shock caused her to blackout.

A memory of Birdie's bloody face skated through her mind. Birdie was dead. She would never come back. Sigurd squealed, and she set him gently on the floor.

"It's true then." The words wrenched from her, the bitter truth both crushing and freeing. It had been right in front of her all the time. Like pulling back a thin curtain and seeing Birdie through the windowpane, only inches away and in plain sight.

"He rescued you." Uncle Evan's voice sounded like before the grasshoppers, before the move to Tordenskjold, before Ann Elin's death. "My life-and-death friend, Crooked Lightning, was the face in your window." The words flowed without restraint. "He took you to save your lives. He hid you until Camp Release."

"The face in the window was the face of a friend?" How could she have been so wrong? The face in the window was good and the dream was bad. She walked to the window, scratched the frost with the back of her thumbnail and watched the boys stack another muskrat hide on top of the woodpile. Five others draped over the stacks of drying wood. Eleven plus six. One for each year of her life. Eleven for the years since the uprising. Six for the years before.

The memories rushed in from all sides: Mor's face as she pulled a loaf of bread from the oven, Birdie's skinned knee, the voice of Far singing in church, Baby Evan screaming to be nursed. Each memory bruised her mind, too thick to slide across her consciousness without plowing a furrow into her brain.

She felt the room spinning. Anders walked up the path towards the house. Darkness, swirling darkness, pushed everything from her mind. Birdie was dead. She had been dead eleven years and Ragna had not remembered.

Far away, the door creaked, and Anders called her name. Tears and sobs would not stop. Wails of grief startled Sigurd until he began to cry, too. She felt Anders's arms around her, and she laid her head against his shoulder. She could not stop the keening wails. She could only muffle them by pressing her face into his shirt.

The room was still spinning, but the wails ended, and she stepped back to see Uncle Evan, Milton, and the boys gathered around.

"Ragna," Anders said in a hoarse whisper, pulling her close again. "What's wrong?"

Uncle cleared his throat. "Ragna has bad news today."

Without looking at him, Ragna knew how his mouth would work, how he would bite his lower lip and pull at his beard. "She learned today that her sister, Birdie, is dead."

"Are you all right?" Anders' breath warmed her cheek and he smelled of fresh air and lake water. "Somebody fetch a glass of water."

Birdie was dead. The tears came again with the understanding. They gushed from her eyes, and it was if the earth shifted beneath her. Gulping sobs forced her to sit down lest she fall down. Uncle Evan told Knut to mind Sigurd and Anders pulled a chair closer to her and kept his arm around her. Gunnar stood with a cup of water.

Birdie would not be coming back.

Anders pulled her to his chest, his arms around her in front of everyone. "It's all right, Ragna," he whispered into her ear, and his tears fell down upon her hair. He kissed her cheek. "It will be all right."

Ragna finally pulled her face out of Anders' shirt. She blew her nose into his borrowed handkerchief and wiped her eyes. She took the cup of water from Gunnar and nodded when he smiled at her. Then she leaned back against Anders's strong arms. She cast an anxious glance at Uncle but he seemed not to notice. Even if Uncle had disapproved, there was nothing else to do but sit there and lean against Anders. Her world had stopped. It had come to a complete halt. She leaned her whole weight against him. His body a warmed brick to her back.

Her mind emptied. Everything she ever knew drained out with the tears. She could not remember what she should say next, could not think of a single word. Gunnar knelt on the floor at her other side and glared protectively at Anders.

Ragna pulled Gunnar's hand into her lap and held it with both of hers. He was like a brother to her, Gunnar was. All the boys were. She did not have a sister, but she had brothers. She loved them as much as Birdie. The tears flowed harder with the thought, and she wiped her eyes with her sleeve without dropping Gunnar's hand.

Uncle Evan cleared his throat. "It's time I told you," he said. "A story about all of us, our family."

"Tell us, Far," Knut said and sat on the bench.

Uncle reached toward his empty pocket. His mouth worked and his Adam's apple bobbed. It was as if Ragna felt the words before she heard them.

"A long time ago a young man came to America from far across the ocean."

"That was you," Knut said.

"I was lonely and afraid."

"You were never scared," Knut said.

"Shh . . . !" Gunnar said. "Listen."

"I had big dreams and bold ambitions, but didn't know a single word of American."

"Not one word?" Gunnar said.

"What words I knew, I didn't speak, for I thought maybe they were swearing words." Uncle lifted Sigurd onto Knut's lap, kissed the top of his head, and settled into a chair next to the table. They were crammed in the little dugout, the lamp sputtered on the table, smelling of smoky muskrat fat. "The language made it hard to find work." Uncle tugged at his beard, still red though his hair was starting to silver around his ears. "So when Bishop Whipple gave English lessons at the mission, I was quick to attend."

"At Fort Snelling?" Knut said.

Uncle Evan nodded. "And there I met my first real friend in America."

"Ragna's *far*?" Gunnar said.

"*Nei*, not Ragna's *far*." Uncle Evan looked at Ragna with a gentle look. "My first friend in America was Crooked Lightning, a Sioux Indian."

"A *skraeling*?" Gunnar said and pulled his hand away from Ragna and leaned forward towards his father.

"Nothing ugly or dirty about him," Uncle Evan said and his voice carried a reproving tone. "Crooked Lightning proved a better friend to me than I to him."

Ragna said nothing, just leaned back against Anders, feeling the warmth of his body against her back, listening to Uncle Evan talk about times of friendship at Crooked Lightning's camp. She had known that Uncle had a Sioux friend but had never heard his name, never heard him talk about their friendship in any detail. Other than the face in the window, Ragna had only fleeting memories of the man. Of his voice urging them to be quiet and hurry. Of the touch of his hand pulling her through the woods, away from her parents.

"Crooked Lightning warned me about the Indian unrest," Uncle said. "And during the uprising he went against his own people to rescue Ragna and her little sister." He looked at Ragna. She felt the love flowing from his eyes. The love warmed her as much as the feel of Anders' body against her back. "He rescued them because they were my friends, and he knew I loved Ragna's *far* as a brother. Crooked Lightning knew I was Godfather to Lars's baby son." His Adam's apple bobbed again. "Friendship means more to Indians than white folks."

"What happened to Birdie?" Gunnar said.

"In spite of all he did, Ragna's little sister was killed." Uncle's voice choked and he paused a moment. "But Ragna lives because of Crooked Lightning."

Outside the cattle lowed, reminding everyone that it was soon time for chores. A blue jay squawked at the woodpile, and the cat rubbed against Ragna's legs.

"Where is he?" Knut said. "Crooked Lightning, I mean."

"Hung after the uprising." Uncle looked into each face. "He did wrong and paid the price. But he rescued Ragna." His tears started then. Rolled down his face and stole the strength of his voice. "And that was something very good."

Birdie gone. Forever. The truth hung like a cold stone in her chest. She was gone, as sure as the graves in the family cemetery.

"And it was during the Indian war that Ingvald Ericcson, your *mor's* husband, was killed when his horse took a fall." Ragna pulled her attention back to Uncle Evan's story. "Ingvald was a bad man who mistreated her. She married him in desperation after her first husband, Gunnar's *far*, died of fever."

"Was Gunnar's real *far* a bad man?" Knut said.

"*Nei*, Gunnar Thormondson was a good man, a Norwegian, much loved." Evan looked at Gunnar. "And our Gunner will grow up to be a fine man like him."

Gunnar's eyes glowed, and Ragna squeezed his hand tightly. Uncle told how he and Auntie married the day Gunnar was born. "Do you remember, Ragna?"

Ragna nodded, breathed deeply and wiped her face with her sleeve. "Gunnar was born with the caul and that means good luck all his life."

Birdie, unlucky. Born with a stork bite instead of the caul.

"We married so that Gunnar would never be without a *far*," Uncle said and looked at Gunnar. "And so you would not go through life with the name of that evil man."

Gunnar turned his head and smiled at her. She and Gunnar shared the common sorrow of losing a father. Nevertheless, they had Uncle Evan. They were lucky.

"We need coffee," Uncle Evan said and pulled the sack of beans from his pocket. "Gunnar, fetch a pail of water and a load of kitchen wood. Knut, grind the beans."

Anders helped Ragna to her feet. Her legs tingled with weakness and memories pressed in from all sides. After Camp Release, Birdie had cried for a toilet while bouncing in the wagon, but the soldiers could not under-stand Norwegian. Ragna had felt the dampness of Birdie's dress when she wet herself, smelled the sharp odor of urine on her clothes. It was as if Ragna could smell Birdie's wet clothes again. She reached up and touched the button hanging around her neck.

Anders slipped an arm around her waist.

"After coffee, you and I will have a private discussion." Uncle spoke to Anders, and Ragna felt her cheeks flush as Anders pulled back his arm. "But first, we have coffee."

43

Six Pair of Twins were Born in Douglas County in 1873
St. Paul Dispatch, *January 3, 1874*

AFTER COFFEE, EVAN CHOPPED timber in the south forty when Anders sought him out. Evan hoped to down at least one more tree before heading back to gather Inga and the boys. It was time they were all home again.

"Sir," Anders said and his voice squeaked, stretching the word sound into two syllables. "You wanted to speak to me?"

Evan straightened his back and looked at the young man standing before him, wondering what Lars Larson would think of him. Ragna deserved the very best. He owed it to Lars to get to know him before this issue with Ragna went any farther.

Evan sunk the ax into a stump and motioned for Anders to take the other end of the two-man saw propped against a tree. Evan positioned the ragged blade against the bark of an oak tree and pulled the saw toward him, then motioned for Anders to pull the saw toward his side. Back and forth, they pulled until the blade bit into the bark.

"You seem to like our girl." Evan pulled the saw.

"I do." Anders' voice squeaked again as he pulled the saw in his direction. "I'd like your permission to come courting."

"What does she have to say about that?"

"She agrees." Anders pulled the saw again, puffing with the exertion of the cutting blade.

They pulled back and forth as Evan considered what to say. Ragna was supposed to return to Norway. There was the farm. Her future. Marriage to Anders meant she would live near neighbor to them, stay part of their lives.

"I made her promise that she wouldn't marry the widow-man," Anders straightened without pulling back the saw. "She has no business even considering such a union."

"Hmm." Evan motioned Anders to get back to sawing and waited until it was his turn to pull the saw. "The Mormon has a nice place, according to Ragna. What have you to offer?"

"Nothing," Anders said and pulled the saw so hard that the blade buckled. "Only my good name and devotion—and a strong back. And a claim without improvements."

"Her *bestemor* wants her to return to Norway." Evan pulled the saw, enjoying seeing the young man squirm. Overall, it was cheap entertainment. He would be sure to tell Inga about it.

"Why would she return to Norway?" Anders pulled back the saw. "It's a graveyard. There's nothing there."

"They hope to find her a good match." Evan pulled back the saw. "It might not be a bad situation for her. She'll have the proceeds of her farm someday."

"What do you mean?" Anders straightened up and dropped the saw handle. "What are you talking about?"

"Ragna's farm." Evan stood up, too, and walked toward Anders. "Her father's farm in Alexandria. Filled with grasshoppers."

"I didn't know it was her farm," Anders said slowly, his shoulders drooping. "That changes everything."

"Why does it change anything?" Evan reached toward his empty pocket and then instead leaned over and snapped a twig to use as a toothpick.

"I didn't know she was wealthy, a landowner with a farm under cultivation."

Evan's heart melted and all his reservations fell away. Anders had not known about Ragna's farm. He was a decent young man and would be a good match for his Ragna.

"Tell me about yourself," Evan said and propped the toothpick in the side of his jaw. "The boys say you were a seaman on the North Sea."

"There's not much to tell." Anders blushed red to the roots of his hair. "I was trying to make a good impression." He heaved a big sigh and said in a firm voice. "I lied about being a seaman."

Evan looked up in surprise.

"I lied just as you lied," Anders said. "You told us how you lied about having an uncle in Minnesota, to make it feel less scary." He swallowed hard. "I lied about being a seaman. It sounded much better to say that I had chipped my tooth and nipped the tip of my finger off on the North Sea than to admit it happened with a meat cleaver in a nobleman's kitchen."

Evan laughed. "You're fooling me, now." He picked up his end of the saw and motioned for Anders to return to his end. They began the tedious back and forth with the blade biting into the bark.

"*Nei*, it's the truth." Anders said and pulled the saw. "My *mor* was a widow woman who earned our keep by cooking and cleaning for our rich neighbor. I helped in the kitchen, chopping meat, peeling potatoes, hauling water and doing the wash."

"It was good of you to help her," Evan said and pulled the saw. "I helped my *mor* after my *far* died."

"I was ashamed to be seen in the kitchen," Anders said. "I hurried through my duties before the master's sons would see me. We were the same age."

"And how did you break your tooth?"

"Fighting with my cousin," Anders said with a laugh. "Nothing brave or romantic about that either."

"And your learning?" Evan said. "Where did you get your education?"

"The nobleman let me sit in with his sons during their lessons," Anders said. "I came out with schooling as well as shriveled hands from washing their drawers."

They sawed in earnest, chips flying in all directions, the tree leaning to one side. They pulled out the saw and pushed on the side of the gash, pushing until it toppled over with a great crash of falling branches.

"You may come courting if Ragna allows it." Evan wiped his brow and caught his breath. "But Inga won't allow any foolishness like I saw this morning."

Anders blushed crimson but smiled a big smile, showing the tooth.

"We love her like a daughter," Evan said. "You will treat her with the utmost respect."

IN MID-AFTERNOON, EVAN LED OLD DOLL to Milton's cabin, determined to bring his family home. It had been a long siege, but not as long as the six-week siege of Fort Abercrombie, he chuckled to himself, but long enough.

The sun warmed him enough so that he removed his mittens and loosened his muffler. A beautiful Minnesota day with a sky as blue as the jays fluttering through the woodlot. A cardinal chirped from an elm tree. The ground covered with fluffy white snow. Red, white, and blue like a Union flag.

The boys met him with a shout, eager to return home to their brothers.

"We want to see Ragna," Lewis lisped.

"She's home and waiting for her boys," Evan said.

He entertained Inga with a detailed account of his earlier conversation with Anders as she packed their few belongings and bundled the twins in blankets to make the trip home. Just as they were ready to leave, Evan spied Lying Jack and Many Beavers coming up the trail to Milton's dugout.

"What do they want?" Inga said. "They must have forgotten something."

"I'll see." Evan walked out into the yard to greet them.

Lying Jack waved, jumped off his horse and shook Evan's hand. "Nice to see you again, my friend."

Evan nodded toward Many Beavers. "*Welkommen!*"

"We's don't have time to stay, but my wife here wouldn't rest until she told you something," Lying Jack said. He shrugged apologetically, as if afraid of bothering him. "You know how a woman gets sometimes if she's got something in her craw." Lying Jack chuckled without smiling. "You knows how it is."

"What do you want to tell me?" Evan said and a cold fear settled inside of him. He felt the fear of it before he heard the words. It was something bad, he knew it, evidenced by the serious expression on her face and her determination to come back and tell him.

"I'll be by to pick up Old Doll and the cattle as soon as the snow goes out," Lying Jack said. "I'll bring the ox team when I come to pick up the trade goods"

"That will be fine," Evan said. They had covered this all before. He looked expectantly at Many Beavers who sat on her pony in silence.

Evan kept quiet. Just stood and waited while she made up her mind to speak.

"They come," Many Beavers said at last after a long silence. "Grasshoppers. They come."

With that, she reined her horse and headed down the trail. Lying Jack shook his head, waved, and then followed after.

Evan swallowed hard as the realization hit him. He remembered Gunnar's walk across the ridgepole and felt as wobbly and out of balance as the boy had been. The grasshoppers were coming here, too. The world seemed suddenly a more dangerous place, more precarious. He turned and put his arms around Old Doll, nuzzled his face in her mane, whispered into her ear the warning of Many Beavers.

"What is it?" Inga said as she carried Sverre out of the cabin completely swathed in blankets. "What did she want?"

Evan took Sverre from her arms and propped him up on Old Doll, then headed back into the cabin for Lewis.

"Nothing special," he said as he lifted Lewis behind his brother. They clung to each other tightly, complained about too many blankets covering their eyes so they could not see where they were going. "You boys will be home in no time."

Inga stepped beside him, holding the bundle of knitting and clothing. She put an arm through Evan's and held his hand with hers.

"It's time we head home," she said with a smile. "To our own place."

44

A Man by the Name of Williams, living in Meeker County, Claims the Palm, because he raised 70 Bushels of Corn to the Acre Last year.

St. Paul Dispatch, *January 4, 1864*

MEMORIES HURT SOMETIMES," Auntie said. She turned the dough in the kneading bowl, punching it with a closed fist. The yeasty smell filled the dark dugout. What a relief to have Auntie Inga and the twins home where they belonged. Nothing had been right without them.

Ragna nodded from her sewing. It was as if Auntie Inga could read her mind. She had been thinking of her parents, how they had scolded her for chasing the goose the morning of the Indian raid. The stitches across the torn sheet were like her steps chasing the mean old gander.

"It's as if you want to go back and do things differently so they won't turn out the same." Auntie slapped the dough and rolled it over the table again, pushed it back into a ball and pressed down on it with the heel of her hand. "Like one might rework a cuff or collar."

The twins napped in the big bed with Sigurd tucked between them. Still weak from their ordeal, they gained ground day by day. Lewis's gums still bled when he ate but not as badly.

"I felt that way when my first man died."

Ragna looked up in surprise. "How old were you?"

"Seventeen," Auntie said and turned the dough. "Your age. We were young and in love and thought nothing in the world could stop us." She kneaded again with the heel of her hand. "After he died, I kept trying to figure out what I had done wrong, how it might have been different." Auntie dipped her fingers into a bowl of rendered muskrat fat. "When I learned I couldn't leave the ship without a husband, I panicked. Married an older man just because he had money." She rubbed fat across the top of the dough. "Just thinking of him after all these years makes my skin crawl."

Ragna shuddered, tied off a knot and bit the thread with her teeth.

"You see, I felt it was the only way out. I was too young to realize that God has many doors to our problems." She pulled the dough bowl to a warm spot by the stove, touching to make sure it was the right temperature for the yeast to work.

"What do you mean?"

Auntie dipped her hands into the washbasin and scraped the dough from her fingers. "I thought I'd never love anyone except Gunnar . . . but then I met your uncle. He loved me in spite of the terrible mess I'd fallen into. I'm not saying it was right." Her chin jutted up, a sure sign that she would not change her opinion. "We were in love though I was married to another." She shook the water from her fingers and wiped her hands on her floury apron. "It was a miracle from the Hand of Almighty God that Mr. Ericcson's horse tripped in a gopher hole."

Sigurd whimpered in his sleep, and Sverre reached an arm around him.

"I was glad he died," Auntie said. "I hated him."

Ragna drew in a gasp.

"I was trapped by a terrible decision," Auntie said in a quieter voice. "But God made a way." She dipped more muskrat grease and rubbed the fat into her chapped hands. "I've married both for love and money and I recommend the former."

Ragna blushed deep red to the roots of her hair. Auntie was talking about Anders. Without saying a word or mentioning his name, she was giving advice.

"Auntie," Ragna said and glanced over at the sleeping boys to make sure they were still asleep. "I did wrong by Cornelia Ludwig." Tears filled her eyes. Crying was all she had done since learning about Birdie's death.

"You feel that way," Auntie said firmly and sat at the table. "There's nothing guaranteed in this world. I've learned that through my years." She took a needle from the pincushion and threaded it against the light. "She could have died a hundred ways. Sickness, or fire, or on the trail. Life and death are in the hands of the Lord." She pulled the thread through the needle and knotted the ends. "Marrying her man wouldn't make it right, even if he'd have you. You'd have to turn Mormon."

Outside Bobcat bawled. "And it wouldn't fix it for that baby girl either." She looked at Ragna and smiled the tender smile usually reserved for the youngest member of the family. "It's not easy mothering another woman's daughter."

It was not easy being a daughter to someone else's mother either.

"Anders wants to come courting." Ragna spoke the words with the same sweetness she used in saying the names of her parents . . . or Birdie.

"He's a fine young man." Auntie Inga pulled the needle through a shirt with such force that she snapped the thread in two. "But I'll tell you straight out that there will be no night courting allowed in this house."

Ragna's mouth gaped. "We never thought to ask such a thing." Her face burned to think of the old custom of allowing the courting couple to sleep together as long as they were sewn into bed sacks. She licked her lips and her voice came out near whisper. "Bundling is not the custom here."

"My parents were against night riding," Auntie Inga said. "Never allowed it in our family." She jerked the needle through Sigurd's worn baby dress and pursed her lips tight. "Too many girls end up in the family way in spite of the bed sacks."

They sewed quietly for several minutes with the distant sounds of axes, the lowing cattle and the thump of shifting logs in the stove. Ragna had not considered what courting might mean. Surely, Anders would not expect overnight visits. Waves of gratitude for Auntie's protective rules washed over her. Ragna would say that Auntie and Uncle would not allow it—if Anders brought it up at all.

"He can't take a wife until he gets started, maybe after the first harvest, if all goes well." Ragna surprised herself. She had not thought of it so plainly before.

"You've plenty of time." Auntie folded Sigurd's now mended dress and picked up Sverre's torn trousers. "No need to rush into anything."

"Milton says the hoppers won't last forever."

Auntie sewed silently for a minute, stitching as if her life depended on it though Ragna knew she despised sewing. Someday she would buy Auntie a sewing machine. She would do it. She had bought the stovepipe, after all. Nothing was impossible.

"The truth of the matter is that I'm not sure I want to live away from my parents' graves, grasshoppers or not." Ragna picked up Uncle Evan's trousers from the mending pile, the ones with a torn pocket. She pushed the needle through the worn fabric. "I'm homesick away from their graves." Even as she spoke, Ragna felt a stab of guilt. Something must be wrong with her to have such feelings.

"Ragna, dear," Auntie said and laid the shirt in her lap. "My Gunnar does not sleep in his watery grave, but in my heart forever." Her eyes filled with tears and she wiped them away with the back of her hand, leaving a slight glisten of muskrat fat across her cheeks. "Wherever you go, you carry your family with you as I do my sweet young husband."

45

PINCHING THE EAGLE. Foreigners Show their Patriotism and Americans Shirk.

St. Paul Dispatch, *January 4, 1864*

AFTER SUPPER, MILTON SAID GOODBYE and headed home. He and Anders would spend the next week working on Anders's claim, putting up logs for next summer's building.

"Walk with me, Ragna," Anders said. "Before I go to Milton's."

Ragna blushed and looked toward Uncle Evan, who nodded. She took her shawl from the peg on the wall, wrapped a scarf around her neck and tugged on mittens.

"Can I go along?" Gunnar said.

"*Nei,*" Uncle Evan said. "You must study your Catechism before bed."

Ragna followed Anders out the door. A full moon shone bright on the white snow, making it almost light.

"Look," Anders pointed toward the sky. "Northern lights."

They stood together, gazing at the pulsating purples and greens in the night sky, not saying a word. Anders put his arm around her shoulders and held her hand in his. His touch warmed her, sent electrical currents up her arms.

"I love the *nordlys,*" Anders said. "They remind me of home."

Ragna knew little about the northern lights. She was usually in bed by dark. She tried to remember if her parents had spoken of them. She would ask Uncle Evan.

"I've spoken with your Uncle, and he gives permission for courting," Anders said and chuckled. "Although he warned me to keep my hands to myself."

Next week Anders would return to the Branch of Zion School and Ragna to Marta and Gjert Sevald. Ragna both looked forward to and dreaded leaving the little dugout in Tordenskjold. The boys were almost back to normal and Auntie no longer needed her help.

"I'll send letters with Lying Jack," Anders said. "And maybe visit you at the Sevalds if Marta agrees."

Ragna licked her lips and pressed them together while taking a deep breath. She must tell Anders of her decision. He needed to know where she stood before he made improvements on his claim.

"Someday I will go home," Ragna said.

Puzzlement crept into his eyes and expression. "To your *bestemor* in Norway?"

"*Nei*, my father's farm," Ragna said and blushed. "Milton thinks the hoppers won't last forever."

Anders turned silent. "I hadn't realized the farm belonged to you until I spoke to your uncle." His words came out slowly and thoughtfully. "I didn't know you were wealthy—a landowner with fields under cultivation, a sturdy house and barns."

"The farm is all I have left of my family," Ragna said, knowing her decision might mean she would lose Anders. She gathered her courage though her lips trembled. "I could never live anywhere else."

They stood in silence, Ragna's heart thudding in her chest. Long ago, Gunnar had teased her that a suitor would marry her for her farm—even if she were plain and stupid. Auntie gave him a stern scolding and a *chiliwink* alongside his head for saying such a thing. Now it seemed the opposite. She knew she was not being fair. He had his plans. He had his dreams.

"I've written *Bestemor*, telling her about Birdie and my decision to stay in America." Ragna's words on the page had come no easier than her words to Anders. "I told her I won't give up my family's dream."

Anders squeezed her hand.

"I told *Bestemor* about Mrs. Jack and Birdie." Once written down, there was no turning back. Birdie was dead.

Out of the corner of my eye, I glimpse Birdie drawing away. She smiles and reaches an outstretched hand toward me.

Her ragged dress changes to dazzling white and a crown of gold rests on her perfect yellow curls. White feathery wings encircle Birdie and lift her higher.

"Anders, I have to tell you something," Ragna choked back a sob and jerked the button around her neck until the string broke. "I've carried this button since the uprising, telling myself and everyone else that it was from my sister's dress." She held out the button in the palm of her hand.

It was plain and ordinary, carved bone, nothing special at all. Anders reached out and covered it with his hand.

"But it wasn't from my sister's dress. I found it on the ground by the soldier's camp. I always knew it wasn't my sister's button at all."

"I've been thinking," Anders said. "I'm going to carve a grave marker for Birdie. I'll have time over these next few months while I'm stuck in the bachelor's quarters."

"Oh, Anders," Ragna said. Hot tears sprouted in her eyes, and she tried to swallow the sobs in her throat.

"We'll place it in the family cemetery next to Ann Elin and your family."

Ragna drew in her breath.

"You're crying!" Anders' face etched with concern. "Did I say something wrong?"

Ragna shook her head and wiped tears from her face. It was what she had always wanted—a marker to show that Birdie had lived. And died.

Once Birdie had a grave marker, she would be at rest.

Ragna looked at the small chip in his front tooth and then looked up into the bluest of eyes, those eyes as blue as the fjords of Norway, as blue as her sister's eyes.

"Tell me that you'll wait for me," Anders said. "I love you and want you to be my wife."

"But your claim," Ragna said.

"I can always teach, even in Alexandria," Anders said. "We'll make it work."

She answered with a kiss, not at all like the kiss she would give a little brother.

It was no easy thing to start out in the shadow of the grasshoppers. Sickness and trouble lurked everywhere. There were no guarantees in life. With the help of God, they would make it. They would farm her father's land, live in the house built by her loving uncle, and raise their children in the middle of family memories.

Someday they would have a daughter and name her Birdie. And maybe another named Inga Ann Elin. Anders needed many sons to help with the farm, and they would name their firstborn son Lars Evan. Their children would fulfill her father's dream.

Ragna turned her head and rested it against Anders' chest until she could hear the beating of his heart. Its steady rhythm beat as faithful as the friend Uncle Evan had been to her father in his promise to care for her. It was unending, like the friendship Crooked Lightning had shown to his life-and-death friend. The face in the window no longer a terror but a friend with an outstretched rescuing hand. Birdie laid to rest in peace with a stone to guard her memory.

For the first time in a long while, everything felt right.

THE END

Book Club Questions

1. Ragna believed that if her sister were found, everything would be better. How do you feel about this? Is this a common trait? Why or why not?

2. In BIRDIE, we see Inga change into a more negative person. Why or why not do you think this is realistic? Would making her happier have changed her character?

3. Marta, the elderly Mormon woman, turns back to her childhood religion. Do you think this is a common occurrence? What makes childhood religion more attractive to us as we get older?

4. Lying Jack was a real frontier personality in 19th century Minnesota and is quoted as saying that he was the first "white" man in these parts. Of course, he was describing himself as non-Indian. Did his self-description surprise you? Why or why not?

5. Posttraumatic stress syndrome became a diagnosis in the 20th century. Why or why not do you think Evan suffered from posttraumatic stress after the 1862 Uprising. How did his mental state affect his family? His decisions?

6. Evan and Inga raise a combined family. What makes a family? Was Gunnar less than a son to Evan because he was not blood-related? Did Ragna hold a place in the family though she was an orphan?

7. "Then you will know the truth, and the truth will set you free." John 8:32 NIV

Evan, Gunnar, Ragna and Anders learned new truths about themselves or others. Did learning the truth help or hinder them? Give examples.